Keeping!

MICHELLE CONDER
SUSANNA CARR
ROBYN DONALD

First Published in Great Britain 2016
By Mills & Boon, an imprint of HarperCollins*Publishers*
1 London Bridge Street, London, SE1 9GF

A SECRET WORTH KEEPING? © 2016 Harlequin Books S. A.

Living The Charade, Her Shameful Secret and *Island Of Secrets* were first published in Great Britain by Harlequin (UK) Limited.

Living The Charade © 2013 Michelle Conder.
Her Shameful Secret © 2013 Susanna Carr.
Island Of Secrets © 2013 Robyn Donald Kingston.

ISBN: 978-0-263-92055-0

05-0316

Printed and bound in Spain
by CPI, Barcelona

LIVING THE CHARADE

BY
MICHELLE CONDER

From as far back as she can remember **Michelle Conder** has dreamed of being a writer. She penned the first chapter of a romance novel just out of high school, but it took much study, many (varied) jobs, one ultra-understanding husband and three very patient children before she finally sat down to turn that dream into reality.

Michelle lives in Australia, and when she isn't busy plotting loves to read, ride horses, travel and practise yoga.

To my fabulous editor, Flo,
for encouraging me to try new things,
and to Paul, for his endless love.
You both make all the difference!

CHAPTER ONE

IF the world was a fair place the perfect solution to Miller Jacobs's unprecedented crisis would walk through the double-glazed doors of the hip Sydney watering hole she was in, wearing a nice suit and sporting an even nicer personality.

Unlike the self-important banker currently sitting at the small wooden table opposite her who probably should have stopped drinking at least two hours ago.

'So, sexy lady, what is this favour you need from me?'

Miller tried not to cringe at the man's inebriated state and turned to her close friend, Ruby Clarkson, with a smile that said, *How could you possibly think this loser would be in any way suitable as my fake boyfriend this coming weekend*?

Ruby arched a brow in apology and then did what only a truly beautiful woman could do—dazzled the banker with a megawatt smile and told him to take a hike. Not literally, of course. Chances were she'd have to work with him at some point in the future.

Miller breathed a sigh of relief as, without argument, he swaggered towards the packed, dimly lit bar and disappeared from view.

'Don't say it,' Ruby warned. 'On paper he seemed perfect.'

'On paper most men seem perfect,' Miller said glumly. 'It's only when you get to know them that the trouble starts.'

'That's morose. Even for you.'

Miller's eyebrows shot up. She had good reason to be feeling morose. She had just wasted an hour she didn't have, drinking white wine she wouldn't even cook with, and was no further towards solving her problem than she'd been yesterday. A problem that had started when she'd lied to her boss about having a boyfriend who would *love* to come away for a business weekend and keep a very important and very arrogant potential client in check.

TJ Lyons was overweight, overbearing and obnoxious, and had taken her 'not interested' signs as some sort of personal challenge. Apparently he had told Dexter, her boss, that he believed Miller's cool, professional image was hiding a hot-blooded woman just begging to be set free and he was determined to add her to his stable of 'fillies'.

Miller shuddered as she recalled overhearing him use that particular phrase.

The man was a chauvinistic bore and wore an Akubra hat as if he was Australia's answer to JR Ewing. But he had her rattled. And when TJ had challenged her to 'bring your hubbie' to his fiftieth birthday celebration, where she would also present her final business proposal, Miller had smiled sweetly and said that would be lovely.

Which meant she now needed a man by tomorrow afternoon. Perhaps she'd been a little hasty in giving Mr Inebriated the flick.

Ruby rested her chin in her hand. 'There's got to be someone else.'

'Why don't I just say he's sick?'

'Your boss is already suss on you. And even if he wasn't, if you give your *fake* boyfriend a *fake* illness, you still have to deal with your amorous client all weekend.'

Miller pulled a face. 'Don't mistake TJ's intentions as amorous. They're more licentious in nature.'

'Maybe so, but I'm sure Dexter's are amorous.'

Ruby was convinced Miller's boss was interested in her, but Miller didn't see it.

'Dexter's married.'

'Separated. And you know he's keen on you. That's one of the reasons you lied about having a boyfriend.'

Miller let her head fall back on her neck and made a tortured sound through her teeth.

'I was coming off the back of a week of sixteen-hour days and I was exhausted. I might have had an emotional reaction to the whole thing.'

'Emotional? You? Heaven forbid.' Ruby shivered dramatically.

It was a standing joke between them that Ruby wore her heart on her sleeve and Miller kept hers stashed in one of the many shoeboxes in her closet.

'I was after sympathy, not sarcasm,' Miller grumped.

'But Dexter did offer to go as your "protector", did he not?' Ruby probed.

Miller sighed. 'A little weird, I grant you, but we knew each other at uni. I think he was just being nice, given TJ's drunken pronouncements to him the week before.'

Ruby did her famous eye roll. 'Regardless, you faked having a boyfriend and now you have to produce one.'

'I'll give him pneumonia.'

'Miller, TJ Lyons is a business powerhouse with a shocking reputation and Dexter is an alpha male wannabe. And you've worked too hard to let either one of them decide your future. If you go away this weekend and TJ makes a move on you his wife will have a fit and you'll be reading the unemployment pages for the next twelve months. I've seen it happen before. Men of TJ Lyons's ilk are never pinned for sexual harassment the way they should be.'

Ruby took a breath and Miller thanked God that she needed air. She was one of the best discrimination lawyers in the country and when she ranted Miller took note. She had a point.

Miller had put in six hard years at the Oracle Consulting Group, which had become like a second home to her. Or maybe it *was* her home, given how much time she spent there! If she won TJ's multi-million-dollar account she'd be sure to be made partner in the next sweep—the realisation of a long-held dream and one her mother had encouraged for a long time.

'TJ hasn't actually harassed me, Rubes,' she reminded her friend.

'At your last meeting he said he'd hire Oracle in a flash if you "played nice".'

Miller blew out a breath. 'Okay, okay. I have a plan.'

Ruby raised her eyebrows. 'Let's hear it.'

'I'll hire an escort. Look at this.' The idea had come to her while Ruby had been ranting and she turned her smartphone so Ruby could see the screen. 'Madame Chloe. She says she offers discreet, professional, *sensitive* gentlemen to meet the needs of the modern-day heterosexual woman.'

'Let me see that.' Ruby took the phone. 'Oh, my God. That guy would seriously have sex with you.'

Miller looked over Ruby's shoulder at the incredibly buffed male on the screen.

'And they cater to fantasies!' Ruby continued.

'I don't *want* him to have sex with me,' Miller yelped, slightly exasperated. The last thing she needed was sex, or her hormones, to derail her from her goal at the eleventh hour. Her mother had let that happen and look where it had got her— broke and unhappy.

'You can have a policeman, a pilot, an accountant—*urgh*, seen enough of them. Oh, and this one.' Ruby giggled and lowered her voice. 'Rough but clean tradesman. Or, wait—a sports jock.'

Miller shuddered. What intelligent woman would ever fantasise over a sports jock?

'Ruby!' Miller laughed as she took the phone back. 'Be serious. This is my future we're talking about. I need a decent guy who is polite and can follow my lead. Someone who blends in.'

'Hmmm…' Ruby grinned at one of the profile photos. 'He looks like he would blend in at an all-night gay bar.'

Miller scowled. 'Not helping.' She clicked on a few more. 'They all look the same,' she said despairingly.

'Tanned, buff and hot-to-trot,' Ruby agreed. 'Where *do* they get these guys?'

Miller shook her head at Ruby's obvious enjoyment. Then she saw the price tag associated with one of the men. 'Good God, I hope that's for a month.'

'Forget the escort,' Ruby instructed. 'Most of these guys probably can't string a sentence together beyond "Is that it?" and "How hard do you want it?"' Not exactly convincing boyfriend material for an up-and-coming partner in the fastest growing management consultancy firm in Australia.'

'Then I'm cooked.'

Ruby's eyes scanned the meagre post-work crowd, and Miller thought about the sales report she still had to get through before bed that night; she was still unable to completely fathom the predicament she was in.

'Bird flu?' she suggested, smoothing her eyebrows into place as she racked her brain for a solution.

'No one will believe he has bird flu.'

'I meant me.' She sighed.

'Wait. What about him?'

'Who?' Miller glanced at her phone and saw only a blank screen.

'Cute guy at the bar. Three o'clock.'

Miller rolled her eyes. 'Five years of university, six years in a professional career and we're still using hushed military terms when stalking guys.'

Ruby laughed. 'It's been ages since we stalked a guy.'

'And, please God, let it be ages again,' Miller pleaded, glancing ever so casually in the direction Ruby indicated.

She got an impression of a tall man leaning against the edge of the curved wooden bar, one foot raised on the polished foot pole, his knee protruding from the hole in his torn jeans. Her eyes travelled upwards over long, lean legs and an even leaner waist to a broad chest covered by a worn T-shirt with a provocative slogan plastered on the front in red block letters. Her lips curled in distaste at its message and she moved on to wide shoulders, a jaw that looked as if it could have used a shave three days ago, a strong blade of a nose, mussed over long chocolate-brown hair and—oh, Lord—deep-set light-coloured eyes that were staring right back at her.

His gaze was sleepy, almost indolent, and Miller's heart took off. Her breath stalled in her lungs and her face felt bitingly hot. Flustered by her physical reaction, she instantly dropped her eyes as if she was a small child who had just been caught stealing a cookie. Her senses felt muddled and off-centre—and she'd only been looking at the man for five seconds. Maybe ten.

Ignoring the fact that she felt as if he was still watching her, she turned to Ruby. 'He's got holes in his jeans and a T-shirt that says "My pace or yours?" How many glasses of this crap wine have you had?'

Ruby paused, glancing briefly back at the bar. 'Not him—although he does fill that T-shirt out like a god. I'm talking about the suit he's talking to.'

Miller turned her gaze to the suit she hadn't noticed. Similar-coloured hair, square, clean-shaven jaw, nice nose, *great* suit. Yes, thankfully he did look more her type.

'Oh, I think I know him!' Ruby exclaimed.

'You *know* Ripped Jeans?'

'No.' Ruby shook her head, openly smiling in the direction Miller dared not turn back to. 'The hotshot in the suit beside him. Sam someone. I'm pretty sure he's a lawyer out of our L.A. office. And he's just the type you need.'

Miller glanced back and noticed that tall, dark and dishevelled was no longer watching her, but still some inner instinct told her to run. *Fast.*

'No!' She dismissed the idea outright. 'I draw the line at picking up a stranger in a bar—even if you do think you know him. Let me just go to the bathroom and then we can share a taxi home. And stop looking at those guys. They'll think we want to be picked up.'

'We do!'

Miller scowled. 'Believe me, by the look of the one who

needs to become reacquainted with a razor all it would take is a look and he'd have you horizontal in seconds.'

Ruby eyed her curiously. 'That's exactly what makes him so delicious.'

'Not to me.' Miller headed for the bathroom, feeling slightly better now that she had decided to call it a night. Her problem still hovered over her like a dark cloud, but she was too tired to give it any more brainpower tonight.

'Would you stop looking at those women? We are not here to pick up,' Tino Ventura growled at his brother.

'Seems to me it might solve your problem about what to do with yourself this weekend.'

Tino snorted. 'The day I need my baby brother to sort entertainment for me is the day you can put me in a body bag.'

Sam didn't laugh, and Tino silently berated his choice of words.

'So how's the car shaping up?' Sam asked.

Tino grunted. 'The chassis still needs work and the balancing sucks.'

'Will it be ready by Sunday?'

The concern in his brother's voice set Tino's teeth on edge. He was so *over* everyone worrying about this next race as if it was to be his last—and okay, there were a couple of nasty coincidences that made for entertaining journalism, but they weren't *signs*, for God's sake.

'It'll be ready.'

'And the knee?'

Coming off the back of a long day studying engine data and time trials in his new car, Tino was too tired to humour his brother with shop-talk.

'This catch-up drink was going a lot better before you started peppering me with work questions.'

He could do without the reminder of how his stellar racing year had started to fall apart lately. All he needed was to win this next race and he'd have the naysayers who politely suggested that he would never be as good as his father off his back.

Not that he dwelt on their opinion.

He didn't.

But he'd still be happy to prove them wrong once and for all, and equalling his father's number of championship titles in the very race that had taken his life seventeen years earlier ought to do just that.

'If it were me I'd be nervous, that's all,' Sam persisted.

Maybe Tino would be too, if he stopped to think about how he felt. But emotions got you killed in his business, and he'd locked his away a long time ago. 'Which is why you're a cottonwool lawyer in a four-thousand-dollar suit.'

'Five.'

Tino tilted his beer bottle to his lips. 'You need to get your money back, junior.'

Sam snorted. 'You ought to talk. I think you bought that T-shirt in high school.'

'Hey, don't knock the lucky shirt.' Tino chuckled, much happier to be sparring with his little brother than dissecting his current career issues.

He knew his younger brother was spooked about all the problems he'd been having that so eerily echoed his father's lead-up to a date with eternity. Everyone in his family was. Which was why he was staying the hell away from Melbourne until Monday, when the countdown towards race day began.

'Excuse me, but do I know you?'

Tino glanced at the blonde who had been eyeballing them for the last ten minutes, pleasantly surprised to find her focus on his little brother instead of himself.

Well, hell, that was a first. He knew Sam would get mileage out of it for the next decade if he could.

He turned to see where her cute friend was but she seemed to have disappeared.

'Not that I know of,' Sam replied to the stunner beside him, barely managing to keep his tongue in his mouth. 'I'm Sam Ventura and this is my brother Valentino.'

Tino stared at his brother. No one called him Valentino except their mother.

Switch your brain on, Samuel.

'I do know you!' she declared confidently. 'You're at Clayton Smythe—corporate litigation, L.A. office. Am I right?'

'You are at that.' Sam smiled.

'Ruby Clarkson—discrimination law, Sydney office.' She held out her hand. 'Please tell me you're in town this weekend and as free as a bird.'

Tino willed Sam not to blow his cool. The blonde had a sensational smile and a nice rack, but she was a little too bold for his tastes. His brother, however, he could see was already halfway to her bedroom.

Some sixth sense made him turn, and his eyes alighted on the friend in the black suit with the provocative red trim at the hem. She glanced at her empty table and her mouth fell open when she scanned the room and located her friend.

Then her eyes cut to his and her mouth snapped closed with frosty precision. Tino saw her spine straighten and grinned when she glanced at the door as if she was about to bolt through it. His eyes drifted over her again. If she'd bothered to smile, and he hadn't just ended a short liaison with a woman who had lied about understanding the term 'casual sex', she was exactly his type. Polished, poised and pert—all over. Pert nose, pert breasts and a pert ass. And he liked the way she moved too. Graceful. Purposeful.

As she approached, he took in the ruler-straight chestnut-coloured hair that shone under the bar lights, and skin that was perhaps the creamiest he had ever seen. His eyes travelled over a heart-shaped mouth designed with recreational activities in mind and the bluest wide-spaced eyes he'd ever seen.

'Ruby, I'm back. Let's go.'

And a voice that could stop a bushfire in its tracks.

Tino felt amused at the dichotomy; she should be leaning

in and whispering sweet nothings in his ear, not cutting her friend to the quick.

'Hey, relax. Why don't I get you a drink?' he found himself offering.

'I'm perfectly relaxed.' Her eyes could have shredded concrete as she turned them on him, but still he felt the effect of that magnificent aquamarine gaze like a punch in the gut. 'And if I wanted a drink I'd order one.'

Well, excuse the hell out of me.

'Miller!' Her friend instantly jumped in to try and ease the lash of her words. 'This is Sam and his brother Valentino. And—good news—Sam is free for the weekend.'

The woman Miller didn't move, but the skin at the outside of her mouth pulled tight. She seemed about to set her friend on fire, but then collected herself at the last minute.

'Hello, Sam. Valentino.'

He noticed he barely rated a nod.

'I'm very pleased to meet you. But unfortunately Ruby and I have to go.'

'Miller,' her friend chided. 'This is a perfect solution for you.'

This last was said almost under her breath, and Tino directed an enquiring eyebrow at Sam.

'It seems Miller needs a partner for the weekend,' Sam provided.

Tino eased back onto the barstool. *And what? They were recruiting Sam?*

He cocked his head. 'Come again?'

'No need,' the little ray of sunshine fumed politely. 'We're sorry to disturb you and now we have to go.'

'It's fine.' Sam raised his hand in a placating gesture Tino had seen him use in court. 'I'm more than pleased to offer my services.'

Services? Did he mean sexual?

Tino felt the hairs on the back of his neck stand on end. 'Would somebody like to fill me in here?' He sounded abrupt, but clearly someone had to protect his little brother from these weird females.

'Miller has to go away on a work weekend and she needs a partner to keep a nuisance client at bay,' her friend Ruby explained helpfully.

Tino eyed Miller's stiff countenance. 'Tried telling him you're not interested?' he drawled.

She snapped her startling eyes to his and once again he found himself mesmerised by their colour and the way they kicked up slightly at the corners. 'Now, why didn't I think of that?'

'Sometimes the things right in front of us are the hardest to see,' he offered.

'I was *joking*.' She looked aghast that he might have taken her sarcastic quip seriously and it made him want to laugh. It wasn't too difficult to see why she was in need of a *fake* partner, and he revised his earlier assessment of her.

She might be pert and blessed with an angel's face, but she was also waspish, uptight and controlling. Definitely not his type after all.

'Aren't you taking a client out on Dante's yacht this weekend?' He reminded his brother of the expedition both he and Dante, their older brother, had been trying to drag him along to.

Sam groaned as if he'd just been told he needed a root canal. 'Damn, I forgot.'

'Oh, really?' Ruby sounded as if she'd been given the same news.

'Okay—well, time to go,' Miller interjected baldly.

Tino wondered if she was truly thick, or just didn't want to see what was clearly going on between her friend and his brother.

'You do it.'

Tino's eyes snapped to Sam's.

'You said you were looking for something different to do this weekend. It's a great solution all round.'

Tino looked at his brother as if he had rocks in his head. His manager and the team owner had told him to take time out this weekend and do something that would get his mind off the coming race, but he was pretty sure posing as some uptight woman's fake partner was not what they'd had in mind.

'I don't think so,' Little Miss Sunshine scoffed, as if the very idea was ludicrous.

Which it was.

But her snooty dismissal of him rankled. 'Have I done something to upset you?' His gaze narrowed on her face and he almost reached out to grip her chin and hold her elusive eyes on his.

'Not at all.' But her tone was curt and her nose wrinkled slightly when her eyes dropped to his T-shirt.

'Ah.' He exhaled. 'It's just that I'm not good enough for you. Is that it, Sunshine?'

Her eyes flashed and he knew he'd hit the nail on the head. He wanted to laugh. Not only had this chit of a woman not recognised him—which, okay, wasn't that strange in Australia, given that the sport he competed in was Europe based—but she was dismissing him out of hand because he looked a bit scruffy. That had never happened before, and the first real smile in months crossed his face.

'It's not that, I'm just not that desperate.'

She briefly closed her eyes when she realised her faux pas and Tino's smile grew wider. He knew full well that if she had recognised him she'd be pouting that sweet mouth and slipping him her phone number instead of looking at him as if he was about to give her a fatal disease.

'Yes, you are,' her friend chimed in.

Tino casually sipped his beer while Miller glowered.

'Ruby, *please*.'

'I can vouch for my brother,' Sam cut in. 'He looks like he belongs on the bottom of a pond but he scrubs up all right.'

Now it was Tino's turn to scowl. He was about to say no way in hell would he help her out when he caught her unwavering gaze and realised that was just what she expected—was actually *hoping*—he would say, and for some reason that stopped him. He wouldn't do it, of course. Why enter into a fake relationship when he had zero interest in the real deal? But something about her uppity attitude rattled his chain.

Before he could respond Sam continued. 'Go on, Valentino. Imagine Dee facing the same problem. Wouldn't you like some decent guy to help her out?'

Tino's glare deepened. Now, that was just underhand, reminding him of their baby sister all alone in New York City.

'It's fine,' the fire-eater said. 'This was a terrible idea. We'll be on our way and you can forget this conversation ever happened.' Her voice was authoritative. Calm. *Decisive*.

He took another swig of his beer and noticed how her eyes watched his throat as he swallowed. When they caught his again they were more indigo than aquamarine. Interesting. Or it was until he felt his own body stir in response.

'You don't think we'd make a cute couple?' He caught the wild flash of her eyes and his voice deepened. 'I do.'

Her tipsy friend was practically clapping with glee.

Miller held her gaze steady on his, almost in warning. 'No, I don't.'

'So what will you do if I don't help you out?' Tino prodded. 'Let the client have another crack at you?'

He ignored his brother's curious gaze and focused on Miller's pained expression at his crude terminology. Man, but she was wound tighter than his Ferrari at full speed, and damn if he didn't have the strangest desire to unravel her.

He tried to figure out his unexpected reaction, but then decided not to waste time thinking about it.

Why bother? He was about to send her packing with four easy words.

He threw her his trademark smile as he anticipated her horrified response. 'Okay, I'll do it.'

Miller sucked in a deep breath and gave the man in front of her a scathing once-over. He was boorish, uncouth and *dirty*—and he had the most amazing bone structure she had ever seen. He also had the most amazing grey-blue eyes surrounded by thick ebony lashes, and sensual lips that seemed to be permanently tilted into a knowing smirk. A *sexually* knowing smirk.

But clearly he was crazy.

She might need someone to pose as her current boyfriend, but she'd rather pay an escort the equivalent of her annual salary than accept *his* help. His brother would have been a different story, but no way in the world could she pretend to be interested in this man. He looked as if all he had to do was crook his index finger and a woman would come running. If she didn't swoon first.

Swoon?

Miller pulled in the ridiculous thought. The man had holes in his jeans and needed a shower, but all that aside he was far too big for her tastes. Too male.

The loud clink of a rack of freshly washed glasses brought her out of her headspace and Miller felt a flush creep up her neck as she realised she'd been staring at his mouth, and that both Ruby and Sam were waiting for her to respond.

Her eyes dropped to the man's tasteless T-shirt. Ruby must have be more affected by alcohol than Miller had realised if she seriously thought Miller would go along with this.

'Well, Sunshine? What's it to be?'

She hated his deep, *smug* tone.

About to blow him out of the water, she was choosing her rejection carefully when it struck her that he *wanted* her to say no. That he was *counting* on it.

Miller exhaled slowly, her mind spinning. The sarcastic sod had never intended to help her at all this weekend. That momentary soft-eyed look he'd got when his brother had mentioned their sister was just a ruse. The man was a charlatan and clearly needed to be brought down a peg or two. And she was in the mood to do it.

Pausing for effect, Miller steeled herself to let her eyes run over him. She was so going to enjoy watching him squirm out of this one. 'Do you happen to own a suit?' she asked sweetly.

CHAPTER TWO

TAPPING her foot on the hot pavement outside her Neutral Bay apartment building, Miller again checked to see if she had any missed calls on her phone. She still couldn't believe that rather than squirm out of her phony acceptance of his help last night that thug of a man had collapsed into a full belly laugh and said he'd be delighted to help.

Delighted, my foot.

It wouldn't surprise her one bit if Valentino Ventura did a no-show on her today. He seemed the type.

Something about the way his full name rolled through her mind pinged a distant memory, but she couldn't bring it up. Maybe it was just the way it sounded. Both decadent and dangerous. Or maybe it was just the sweltering afternoon sun soaking into her black long-sleeved T-shirt combined with a sense of trepidation about this situation she had inadvertently created for herself.

She'd spent years curbing the more impetuous side of her nature after her parents had divorced and her safe world had fallen apart, but it seemed she'd have to try harder. Especially if she wanted to create a life for herself that didn't feel as precarious as the house of cards she'd grown up in.

Miller sighed. She was just tired. She'd averaged four hours' sleep a night this week and woken this morning feeling as if she hadn't slept at all.

A pair of slate-coloured eyes in a hard, impossibly handsome face had completely put her off her breakfast. As had the dream she'd woken up remembering. It had been about a man who looked horribly like the one she was waiting for, trapping her on her bed with his hands either side of her face. He'd looked at her as if she was everything he'd ever wanted in a woman and licked his beautifully carved lips before lowering his face to hers, his eyes on her mouth the whole time...

Miller's lips suddenly felt fuller, dryer, and she shivered in the afternoon heat and scanned the street for some sign of him. It must have been all those images of escorts that had set off the erotic dream, because no way could it have been about someone as reckless as she felt this man could be.

Okay. Miller gave herself a mental shakedown. She wasn't waiting around any longer for Mr Ripped Jeans to turn up. He'd had no intention of helping her out—perfectly understandable, given they were strangers and would likely never see each other again—but she couldn't fathom the tiny prick of disappointment that settled in her chest at his no-show.

Feeling silly, she shook off the sensation, frowning when a growling silver sports car shot towards the kerb in front of her and nearly rear-ended her black sedan.

About to give the owner a piece of her mind for dangerous driving, she was shocked to see her nemesis peel himself out of the driver's side of the car. She crossed her arms over her chest and puffed out a breath. He sauntered towards her, a slow grin lighting his face.

The man oozed sex and confidence, and moved with a loose limbed grace that said he owned the world. Exactly the type of man she detested.

Even though she was five foot seven, Miller wished she'd worn heels—because Valentino was nearly a foot taller and those broad shoulders just seemed to add another foot.

After her dream she had been determined to find him unattractive, but that was proving impossible; in a white pressed T-shirt and low-riding denims, he was so beautifully male it was almost painful to look at him.

And by the shape of his biceps the man clearly spent a serious amount of time in a gym.

Fighting an urge to push back the thick sable hair that had a tendency to fall forward over his forehead in staged disarray, Miller rallied her scrambled brain and tried to conjure up a polite greeting that would set the weekend off on the right foot. Polite, appreciative and unshakably professional.

Before she could come up with something he spoke first. 'The suit's in the back. Promise.'

His deep, mocking tone had her eyes snapping back to his and she forgot all about being polite or professional.

'You're late.'

His lips curved into an easy smile as if her snarky comment hadn't even registered. 'Sorry. Traffic's a bitch at this time on a Friday.'

'You'll have to watch your language this weekend. I would never go out with a man who swore.'

His eyes sparkled in the sunlight. 'That wasn't in your little dossier.'

He was referring to the pre-prepared personal profile Ruby had insisted she hand over last night before she'd hightailed it out of the bar at the speed of light.

'I didn't think writing down that I had a preference for good manners would be necessary.'

'Seems like we'll have some things to iron out on the drive down.'

Miller bit her tongue.

Seems like?

Was he being deliberately thick-headed? His brother was a lawyer—a good one, according to Ruby—but perhaps nature had bestowed Valentino with extreme beauty and compensated by making him slow on the uptake.

'Did you fill out the questionnaire attached to my personal profile?' she asked, wishing she had checked what he did for a living.

'I wouldn't dare not.'

His humorous reply grated, and she flicked a glance at the shiny phallic symbol he was leaning against. Was it even his? 'I want to be on the Princes Highway before every other weekender heading out of the city, so if you'd like to fetch your bag we'll get going.'

'Ever heard of the word *please*?'

The muscles in Miller's neck tightened at his casual taunt. Of course she had, and she had no idea why this man made her lose her usual cool so completely. 'Please.' She forced a smile to her lips that grew rigid as he continued to regard her without moving.

'Are you always this bossy?'

Yes, probably she was. 'I prefer the term *decisive*.'

'I'm sure you do.' He pushed off the car and towered over her. 'But here's a newsflash for you, Sunshine. I'm driving.'

Miller stared at him, hating the fact that he made her feel so small and…out of her depth. 'Is that a rental?'

'Actually, yes.' He seemed annoyingly amused by her question.

Closing her eyes briefly, Miller wondered how she had become stuck with the fake boyfriend from hell and how she was ever going to make this work.

'We're taking my car,' she said, some instinct warning her that if she gave him an inch he'd take the proverbial country mile.

He crossed his arms over his chest and his biceps bulged beneath the short sleeves of his T-shirt. Alarmingly, a tingly sensation tightened Miller's pelvic muscles, the unexpectedness of it making her feel light-headed.

'Is this our first official argument as a couple?' he asked innocently.

Okay, enough with the amusement already. 'Look, Mr Ventura, this is a serious situation and I'd appreciate it if you could treat it as such.' She could feel her heart thumping wildly in her chest and knew her face was heating up from all the animosity she couldn't contain.

Valentino cocked an eyebrow and stepped back to open the passenger side door. 'No problem, *Miss Jacobs*. Hop in.'

Miller didn't move.

'It would flay my masculinity to let a woman drive.'

Miller hated him. That was all there was to it.

Not wanting to play to his supersized ego, and feeling entirely out of her element as he regarded her through sleepy eyes, Miller made a quick decision. 'Well, I'd hate to be accused of insulting your masculinity, Mr Ventura, so by all means take the wheel.'

His slow smile told her that he'd heard her silent *shove it* and found it amusing. Found *her* amusing. And it made her blood boil.

Hating that he thought he'd won that round, she kept her voice courteous. 'As it turns out I don't mind if you drive. It will give me a chance to work on the way down.'

'But you're not impressed?'

'Not particularly.'

'What *does* impress you?'

He folded his arms across his torso and Miller's brain zeroed in on the shifting muscles and tendons under tanned skin. What had he just asked?

She cleared her throat. 'The usual. Manners. Intellect. A sense of humour—'

'You like your cars well-mannered and funny, Miss Jacobs? Interesting.'

Miller knew she must be bright red by now, and hate turned to loathing. 'This isn't funny.' She caught and held his amused gaze. 'Are you intending to sabotage my weekend?'

It gave her some satisfaction to see an annoyed look flash across his divine face.

'Sunshine, if I was going to do that I wouldn't have shown up.'

'I don't like you calling me Sunshine.'

'All couples have nicknames. I'm sure you've thought up a few for me.'

More than a few, she mused silently, and none that could be repeated in polite company.

Desperate to break the tension between them, Miller moved to the back of her car and pulled out her overnight bag. Valentino met her halfway and stowed it in the sports car before holding the passenger door wide for her.

Miller raised an eyebrow and gripped the doorframe, steeling herself to stare into his eyes. This close, the colour was amazing: streaks of silver over blue, with a darker band of grey encircling each iris.

She sucked in a deep breath and ignored his earthy male scent. 'You need to understand that I'm in charge this weekend.' Her voice wasn't very convincing even to her own ears but she continued on regardless. 'On the drive down we'll establish some ground rules, but basically all I need you to do is to follow my lead. Do you think you can do that?'

He smiled. That all-knowing grin that crinkled the outer edges of his amazing eyes. 'I'll give it my best shot. How does that sound?'

Terrible. It sounded terrible.

He leaned closer and Miller found herself sitting on butter-soft leather before she'd meant to. Her brain once again flashing a warning to run. Taking a deep breath, she ignored it and scanned the sleek interior of the car: dark and somehow predatory—like Valentino himself. It must have cost a fortune to rent, and again she wondered what he did for a living.

She couldn't look away from the way his jeans hugged his muscular thighs as she watched as he slid into the driver's seat. 'You're not a lawyer like your brother, are you?' she asked hopefully.

'Good God, no! Do I look like a lawyer?'

Not really. 'No.' She tried not to be too disappointed. 'Do you have the questionnaire I gave you?'

'No one could fault your excitement about wanting to get to know me.'

He reached into the back, his body leaning way too close to hers, and handed her the questionnaire.

Then he started the car, and Miller's senses were on such high alert that the husky growl of the engine made her want to squirm in her seat.

'You'll notice I added to it as well,' he informed her, merging into the building inner city traffic.

She glanced up, feeling completely discombobulated, and decided not to distract him by asking what he'd added. She concentrated on the questionnaire.

His favourite colour was blue, favourite food was Thai. He'd grown up in Melbourne. Hobbies: swimming, running and surfing—no wonder he looked so fit! No sign of any cerebral pursuits—no surprise there. Family: two sisters and two brothers.

'You have a big family.'

He grunted something that sounded like yes.

'Are you close?' The impetuous question was too personal, and unnecessary, but as she'd spent much of her youth longing for siblings her curiosity got the better of her.

He glanced at her briefly. 'Not particularly.'

That was a shame. Miller had always dreamed that large families were full of happy, supportive siblings who would do anything for each other.

'What does "Lives: everywhere" mean?' she asked, glancing at the questionnaire.

'I travel a lot.'

'Backpacking?'

That got a hoot of laughter. 'Sunshine, I'm thirty-three—a bit old to be a backpacker.'

He threw her a smile and Miller found her eyes riveted to his beautiful even white teeth.

'I travel for work.'

She blinked back the disturbing effect he had on her and once again scanned the questionnaire. 'Driving?' She couldn't keep the scepticism out of her voice as she read out the answer under 'Occupation'. 'Driving what?'

He threw her a quick look. 'Cars. What else?'

'I don't know. Buses? Trains?' She tried not to let her annoyance show. 'Trucks?' God, don't let him be a taxi driver; Dexter would never let her hear the end of it.

'Don't tell me you're one of those stuck-up females who only go for rich guys with white collar jobs.'

Miller sniffed. She'd been so busy working and establishing her career the last time she'd gone for any man was back at university. Not that she would be telling him that. 'Of course not.'

But she did like a man in a suit.

He snorted as if he didn't believe her, but he didn't elaborate on his answer.

Sensing he might be embarrassed about his job, she decided to let it drop for now. Maybe he wouldn't mind pretending to be an introverted actuary for the weekend. No one really knew what they did except that it involved mathematics, and not even Dexter was likely to try and engage him in that topic of conversation.

She flipped the page in front of her and found her eyes drawn to his commanding scrawl near the bottom.

Her nose wrinkled. 'I don't need to know what type of underwear you wear.' And she didn't want to imagine him in sexy boxer briefs.

'According to your little summary we've been dating for two months. I think you'd know what type of underwear I wear, wouldn't you?'

'Of course I would. But it's not relevant because I'll never need to use that information.'

He glanced at her again. 'You don't know that.'

'I could have just made something up had the need arisen.'

'Are you always this dishonest?'

Miller exhaled noisily. She was never dishonest. 'No. I loathe dishonesty. And I hate this situation. And what's more I'm sick of having men think that just because I'm single I'm available.'

'It's not just because of that?'

'No,' she agreed, thinking of TJ. 'My client isn't really attracted to me at all. He's attracted to the word *no*.'

'You think?'

'I know. It's what has made him his fortune. He's bullish, arrogant and pompous.'

'Not having met the man, I'll have to trust your judgement. But if you want my opinion your client is probably more turned on by your glossy hair, killer mouth and hourglass figure than your negative response.'

'Wha—? Hey!' Miller braced her hands on the dashboard as the car swerved around a bus like a bullet, nearly fainting before Valentino swung back into the left-hand lane two seconds before hitting a mini-van.

'Relax. I do this for a living.'

'Kill your passengers?' she said weakly.

He laughed. 'Drive.'

Miller forgot all about the near miss with an oncoming vehicle as his comments about her looks replayed in her head.

Did he really think she had a killer mouth? And why was her heart beating like a tiny trapped bird?

'I don't think we can say we met at yoga,' he said.

'Why not?' She didn't believe for a minute that he could be interested in her, but if he thought he would be getting easy sex this weekend he had another thing coming.

His amused eyes connected with hers. 'Because I don't do yoga.'

Miller felt her lips pinch together as she realised he was toying with her. 'You're enjoying this, aren't you?'

'More than I thought I would,' he agreed.

Miller released a frustrated breath. No one was going to believe she was serious about this guy. Her mother had always warned her not to lie, and she mostly lived by that creed. Yesterday, she'd let blind ambition get in the way of sound judgement.

Okay, maybe not blind ambition. Possibly she was a little peeved that she'd felt so professionally hamstrung in telling TJ Lyons what she thought of his lack of business ethics.

'Maybe we just shouldn't talk,' she muttered, half to herself. 'I know enough.' And she was afraid if he said any more she'd ask him to pull over so she could get out and run away as fast as she could.

'I don't.'

She looked at him warily. 'Everything you need to know is in my dossier. Presuming you read it?'

'Oh, it was riveting. You enjoy running, Mexican cuisine, strawberry ice cream, and *cross-stitching*. Tell me, is that anything like cross-dressing?'

Miller willed herself not to blow up at him. 'No.'

'That's a relief. You also like reading and visiting art galleries. No mention of what type of underwear you prefer, though.'

Miller channelled the monks of *wherever*. 'Because it's irrelevant.'

'You know mine.'

'Not by choice.' And she was trying very hard not to think about those sexy boxers under his snug-fitting jeans.

'So what *do* you prefer?'

'Sorry?'

'Are you a plain cotton or more of a lace girl?'

Miller stifled a cough. 'That's none of your business.'

'Believe me, it is. I'm not getting caught up in a conversation with your client not knowing my G-strings from my boy-legs.'

'*Potential* client. And I thought all men talked about was sport?'

'We've been known to deviate on occasion.' He threw her a mischievous grin. 'Since you won't tell me, I'll have to use my imagination.'

'Imagine away,' she said blithely, and then wished she hadn't when his eyes settled on her breasts.

'Now, there's an invitation a man doesn't get every day.'

Miller shot him a fulminating glare, alarmed to feel her nipples tightening inside her lace bra.

Striving to steady her nerves, she made the mistake of reading out the next item he'd added to the questionnaire. '"Favourite sexual position."'

'I haven't finished imagining your lingerie,' he complained. 'Though I'm heading towards sheer little lacy numbers over cotton. Am I right?'

Miller faked a yawn, wondering how on earth he had guessed her little secret and determined that he wouldn't know that he was getting to her. 'You've written down "all".'

He threw her a wolfish grin. 'I might have exaggerated slightly. It was getting late when I wrote that. Probably if I had to name one... Nope. I pretty much like them all equally.'

'I wasn't asking.'

'Although on top is always fun,' he continued as if she hadn't spoken. 'And there's something wicked about taking a woman from behind.'

His voice had dropped and the throaty purr slid over Miller's skin like a silken caress.

'Don't you think?'

Miller released a pent-up breath. She'd had one sexual partner so far and it hadn't been nearly exciting enough for them to try variations on the missionary theme. She hated that now all she could visualise was her on top of the sublime male next to her and how it would feel to have him behind her. *Inside her.*

Her heart thudded heavily in her chest and she suddenly found her attention riveted by the way his long fingers flexed around the steering wheel. Imagining them on her body.

'What I think is that you should concentrate on driving this beast of a car so we don't run into one of those semis you're so determined to fly past.'

'Nervous, Miller?'

He said her name as if he was tasting it and Miller's stomach clenched. Oh, this man was a master at sexual repartee, and she'd do well to remember that.

Miller shook her head. 'Are you ever serious about anything?'

He threw her a bemused look. 'Plenty. Are you ever *not* serious about anything?'

'Plenty.' Which was so blatantly untrue she half expected her nose to start growing.

He passed another car and Miller absently noted that after her earlier panicked response he was driving *marginally* less like a racing car driver. That thought triggered something in her mind and her brow furrowed.

Determined to ignore him for the rest of the trip, she pulled her laptop out of her computer bag.

'What happened to the getting-to-know-you part of our trip?'

He threw her a sexy smile that shot the hazy memory she'd been trying to grab on to out of her head and replaced it with an image of the way he had insolently leant against the bar last night.

'I know you run, swim, work out, and that you take your coffee black. Your favourite colour is blue and you have four siblings—'

'I also don't mind a cuddle after sex.'

'And you don't have a serious bone in your body. I, on the other hand, take my life very seriously and I am not interested in whether you like sex straight up or hanging from a chandelier. It's not relevant. What I'm looking for this weekend is someone to melt into the background and say very little. Starting right now.'

Tino smiled as he revved the engine and manoeuvred the Aston Martin around a tourist bus. He hadn't enjoyed himself this much in…he couldn't remember.

He was in a hot car, driving down a wide country highway on a warm spring afternoon, completely free from having to answer questions about his recent spate of accidents, his car or the coming race. The experience was almost blissful.

With any luck his anonymity would hold and he'd forget the pressure of being the world's number one racing driver on an unlucky streak. Because, as he'd told Sam, it was all media hoopla and coincidence anyway, and he'd prove it Sunday week.

He glanced at the stiff woman beside him and involuntarily adjusted his jeans. He hadn't expected her to give him a hard-on but she had. Which was surprising, given that her black linen trousers and matching shirt were about as provocative as a nun's habit.

His eyes drifted over the blade-straight hair that curtained her delicate profile from his view down over her elegant neck to the gentle swell of her breasts. Was she wearing lace underneath? By the blush that had crept into her face before he'd guess yes. The thought made him smile, and his gaze lingered on her hands as they poised over her computer keys.

She had an effortless sensuality that drew him, and whenever she glared at him hot sparks of sexual arousal threatened to burn him up.

They'd be good together. He knew it. It was just a pity he had no intention of using the weekend to test his theory.

He wasn't looking for a relationship right now, sexual or otherwise, and he had very strict guidelines about how women fitted into his life. The last thing he wanted was a woman getting into his headspace and worrying about whether or not he was going to buy it on the track every time he raced. He'd seen it too many times before, and no way would anyone land him with that kind of guilty pressure.

He still remembered the day he had watched his father clip the rear wheel of another car, flip over and slam into a concrete barrier. It had been one of those races that had reinvigorated race safety procedures and it had changed Tino's life for ever. He'd still known that he would follow in his father's footsteps, but after feeling helpless in the face of his beloved mother's grief, and fighting his own pain at losing his father, he'd locked his emotions away so tight he wasn't sure he'd recognise them any more.

Which was a bonus in a sport where emotions were considered dangerous, and his cool, roguish demeanour scared the hell out of most of his rivals.

His approach was so different from his father's attitude to the sport he'd loved. His father had tried to have it all, but what he should have done was choose family or racing. Emotional attachments and their job didn't mix. Any fool knew that.

CHAPTER THREE

'THIS it?' Valentino pulled the car onto the shoulder of the road and Miller glanced up from following the GPS navigator on her smartphone.

'Yes.' Miller read the plaque on the massive brick pillar that housed a set of enormous iron gates: 'Sunset Boulevard.' *So* typical of TJ's delusions of grandeur, Miller thought tetchily.

Valentino announced them through the security speakers, and the sports car crunched over loose gravel as he pulled around the circular driveway and stopped between an imposing front portico and a burbling fountain filled with frolicking cherubs holding gilded bows and arrows.

'Who's your client?'

Miller didn't answer. She was too busy staring at the enormous pink-tinged stone mansion that looked as if it had been airlifted directly from the Amalfi Coast in Italy and set down in the middle of this arid Australian beach scrub—lime-green lawns and all.

Her car door opened and she automatically accepted Valentino's extended hand. And regretted it. A sensation not unlike an electric shock bolted up her arm and shot sparks all the way down her legs.

Her eyes flew to his in surprise, but his expression was so blank she felt slightly stupid. At least that answered her earlier unasked question. No, he *didn't* find her attractive; he'd just been enjoying himself at her expense.

She registered the opening of a high white front door in her peripheral vision and felt her world right itself when Valentino dropped her hand.

'Miller. You made good time.'

She glanced towards her boss.

'And I can see why.' Dexter stared at Valentino and then cast his appreciative eyes over the silver bullet they'd driven down in.

A bulky figure followed Dexter down the stone steps and she pasted a confident smile on her face when TJ Lyons ambled forward like a cattle tycoon straight off the station.

'Well, now, isn't this a surprise?' he boomed.

Suddenly conscious of Valentino behind her, Miller nearly jumped out of her skin when she felt his large hand settle on her hip. Both men looked at him, eyes agog, as if he was the Dalai Lama come to pay homage.

'Dexter, TJ—this is—'

'We *know* who he is, Miller.' Dexter almost blustered, sticking his hand out towards Valentino. 'Tino Ventura. It's a pleasure. Dexter Caruthers—partner at OCG. Oracle Consultancy Group.'

Valentino took his hand in a firm handshake and a cog shifted in Miller's brain.

Tino?

'Maverick,' TJ said, addressing Valentino.

Maverick?

Had TJ and Dexter mistaken Valentino for someone they knew?

Valentino smiled and accepted their greetings like an old friend.

No! He couldn't *possibly* know her client!

'Miller, you dark horse,' TJ guffawed, slapping Valentino on the back. 'You certainly play your cards close to your chest. I'm impressed.'

Impressed? Miller looked up at Valentino, and just as her boss started asking him about the injury he'd incurred in a motor race in Germany last August his name slotted into place inside Miller's head.

Tino Ventura—international racing car legend.

She would have stumbled if Valentino hadn't tightened his hand on her hip to steady her.

She swore under her breath. Valentino must have heard it because he immediately took charge. 'It's been a long drive, gents. We'll save this conversation for dinner.'

Miller smiled through clenched teeth as he took their bags from the car and handed them to a waiting butler.

'Roger, please show our esteemed guests to their room,' TJ said, turning to the formally dressed man.

'Certainly. Sir? Madam?'

Miller refused to meet Dexter's eyes even though he was burning a hole right through her with his open curiosity.

She deliberately moved out of Valentino's reach as he went to place his hand at the small of her back. Her skin was still tingling from his earlier unexpected hold on her.

Ignoring his piercing gaze, Miller concentrated on keeping her legs steady as she preceded him up the stone steps.

Tino Ventura!

How had she not put two and two together? It was true that she didn't follow sport in any capacity, but as the only Australian driver in the most prestigious motor race in the world she should have recognised him. It was being introduced to him as Valentino that had thrown her, but even then, she conceded with an audible sigh, she'd been so stressed and distracted she might not have made the connection.

None of that, however, changed the fact that he should have told her who he was. That thought fired her temper all the way up the ornate rosewood staircase, ruining any appreciation she might have had of the priceless artworks lining the vast hallways of TJ's house.

Not that she cared about TJ's house. Right now she didn't care about anything but giving Valentino Ventura a piece of her mind for deceiving her.

'Stop thinking, Miller.'

Valentino's deep voice behind her sent a shiver skittering down her spine.

'You're starting to hurt *my* head.'

'This is your room, madam. Sir.'

The butler pushed open a door and Miller followed him inside. The room was spacious, and a tasteful combination of modern and old-world. At the far end was a large bay window with sweeping ocean views encompassing paper-white sand and an ocean that shifted from the brightest turquoise to a deep navy.

'Mr Lyons and his guests are about to adjourn to the rear terrace for cocktails. Dinner is to be served in half an hour.'

'Thank you.' Valentino closed the door after the departing butler. 'Okay, out with it,' he prompted, mimicking her wide-legged stance with his arms folded across his chest.

Miller stared at him for a minute but said nothing, her mind suddenly taken up by the size of the four-poster bed that dominated the large room. She glanced around for a sofa and found an antique settee, an armchair and a curved wooden bench seat inlaid into the bay window.

She heard Valentino move and her eyes followed his easy gait as he perched on the edge of the bed, testing the mattress. 'Comfy.'

He smiled, and she fumed even more because she knew he was laughing at her discomfort. 'I'm not sleeping with you in that,' she informed him shortly.

'Oh, come on, Miller. It's big enough for six people.'

Six people *her* size, maybe... Why hadn't she thought of the sleeping arrangements before now?

Probably because her mind had been too concerned with finishing her proposal and she hadn't wanted to dwell on the fact she was even in this predicament. But she *was* in it, and it was time to face it and work out how she was going to make this farce work with her fake and *very* famous boyfriend.

'It would have been nice if you had thought to let me know who you are,' she said waspishly.

'I did tell you my name. And my job.'

Miller pressed her lips together as she took in his cavalier tone and relaxed demeanour. That was true—up to a point. 'You must have known that I didn't recognise you.' She paced away from him, unable to stand still under his disturbing grey-blue gaze.

Valentino shrugged. 'If I'd thought it was going to be an issue I would have mentioned it.'

'How could you think it *wouldn't* be?' she fumed, stopping mid-pace to stare at him. 'Everyone in the country knows who you are.'

'You didn't.'

'That's because I don't follow sport, but… Oh, never mind. I need to use the bathroom and think.'

After splashing cold water on her face Miller glanced at her pale reflection and thought about what she knew about her fake boyfriend other than the garbage he'd thrown at her in the car. Taxi driver… How he would laugh if he knew she had entertained that thought for a while.

Okay, no need to rehash *that* embarrassing notion. It was time to think. Strategise.

She knew he was a world-class athlete and a world-class womaniser with a penchant for blonde model-types—although she couldn't recall where she'd read that, or how long ago. Regardless, it still made it highly improbable that they would be seeing each other. And she knew everyone who saw them together would be thinking the same thing—including Dexter, who would not be backward in asking the question.

Of course she'd refuse to answer it—she never mixed business with her personal life—but Dexter was shrewd. And he'd be too curious about her "relationship" to take it lying down. Anyone who knew her would. Serious, ambitious Miller Jacobs and international playboy Valentino Ventura a *couple*?

God, what a mess. They had as much in common as a grass-hopper with an elephant.

'You planning to hide out in there for the rest of the week-end?'

His amused voice brought her head around to stare at the closed door. Wrenching it open, she found herself momentarily breathless when she found him filling the space, one arm raised to rest across the top of the doorjamb, making him seem im-possibly tall.

She pushed past him and tried to ignore the skitters of sen-sation that raced through her as her body brushed his. Anger. It was only anger firing her blood.

Taking a couple of calming breaths, she turned to face him. 'No one is going to believe we're a couple.'

'Why not?'

Miller rolled her eyes. 'For one, I don't exactly mix in your circles. And for two, I'm not your type and you're not mine.'

'You're a woman. I'm a man. We share a mutual attraction we can't ignore. Happens all the time.'

To him, maybe.

Miller smoothed her brows, her mind filled with an endless list of problems. 'You're right. We can't say we met at yoga…'

'Listen, you're blowing this out of proportion. Let's keep it as close to the truth as we can. We met at a bar. Liked each other. End of story. That way you'll feel more comfortable and it's highly probable—not to mention true.'

Except for the liking part. Right now Miller couldn't recall liking anyone *less*.

Valentino opened his bag on the bed.

'Why are you here?' she asked softly.

His eyes met hers. Held. 'You know why I'm here,' he said, just as softly. 'You challenged me to be here.'

Miller arched an eyebrow. 'I thought you said you were thirty-three, not thirteen.'

A crooked grin kicked up the corners of his mouth and he

pulled his shirt up over his rippling chest. Lord, did men really look that good unairbrushed?

Last night's dream flashed before her eyes and she was relieved when he turned his back on her. Only then she got to view his impressive back, and her eyes automatically followed the line of his spine indented between lean, hard muscle. 'What exactly are you doing?'

He dropped his T-shirt on the bed and turned to face her. 'Changing my shirt for dinner. I don't want to embarrass you by coming across too casual to meet your friends.'

Ha! Now that she knew who he was she knew he'd impress everyone downstairs even in a clown suit.

Tino shrugged into his shirt and tiny pinpricks of heat glanced across his back as he felt Miller's eyes on him. A powerful surge of lust and the desire to press her up against the nearest wall and explore the attraction simmering between them completely astounded him. He'd been trying to keep things light and breezy between them—his usual *modus operandi*—but his libido was insistently arguing the toss.

'Next time I'd prefer you to use the bathroom,' she said stiffly. 'And these people aren't my friends. They're business colleagues—although as to that I doubt I'll know many of the other people in attendance.'

'How many are staying here?'

'I think six others tonight. Tomorrow night at TJ's fiftieth party I have no idea.'

'I thought this was a business weekend?'

'TJ likes to multi-task.'

Tino rolled his silk shirt sleeves and noticed her frowning at his forearms. 'Problem?'

His question galvanised her into action and she crossed to her small suitcase and started rifling through it.

'I'll be ten minutes.'

Five minutes later she reappeared in the doorway and padded over to the wardrobe. She barely looked different from the way she had when she'd gone in. Black tailored pants, a black beaded top, and a thin pink belt bissecting the two. She perched on the armchair and secured a fancy pair of stilettos on her dainty feet. The silence between them was deafening.

'Am I getting the silent treatment?'

She exhaled slowly and he noticed the way the beads on her top swayed from side to side. 'I hope you're not currently in a relationship.'

'Would I be here with you if I was?'

'I don't know. Would you?'

Her chin had come up and he was surprised he had to control irritation at her deliberate slur. She didn't know him, and he supposed, given his reputation—which wasn't half as extensive as the press made out—it was a valid question.

'Okay, I'm going to humour that question with an answer—because we don't know each other and I understand you feel compromised by the fact that I'm a known personality. I don't date more than one woman at a time and I never cheat.'

'Fine. I just…' Her hand fluttered between them. 'If we really were going out you'd know I hate surprises.'

'Why is that?'

She glanced away. 'I just do.'

Her answer was clipped and he knew there was a story behind her flat tone.

'I don't suppose there's any chance you can just fade into the background and not draw attention to yourself, is there?'

Tino nearly laughed. So much for coming on to him once she found out who he was. He shook his head at his own arrogance. But, hell, most women he met simpered and preened and asked stupid questions about how many cars he owned and how fast he drove. This gorgeous female was still treating him like a disease. And she *was* gorgeous. She'd dusted her sexy mouth with a peach-coloured gloss that made him want to lick it right off.

'We need to go downstairs.' She sounded as if she was about to face a firing squad.

She grabbed a black wrap from the back of the cream chair

and stopped suddenly, nearly colliding with him. He felt a shaft of heat spear south as he touched her elbow to steady her, and knew she felt the same buzz by the way she pulled back and went all wide-eyed with shock, just as she had by the car.

A shock he himself still felt. He hadn't anticipated being this physically attracted to her. He reminded himself of his iron-clad rule of not getting involved with a woman this close to the end of the season—particularly *this* season, which had started going pear-shaped three months ago.

So why couldn't he stop imagining how she would taste if he kissed her?

He stepped back from her, out of the danger zone. 'You might want to think about not jumping six feet in the air every time I touch you.' He sounded annoyed because he was.

'And *you* might want to think about not touching me.'

Large aquamarine eyes, alight with slivers of the purest gold, stared up at him, and the ability to think flew out of his head. Her eyes reminded him of a rare jewel.

Then she blinked, breaking the spell.

Get a grip, Ventura. Since when did you start comparing eyes to jewels?

'You really have the most extraordinary eyes,' he found himself saying appreciatively. 'A little glacial right now, but extraordinary nonetheless.'

'I don't care what you think of my eyes. This isn't real so I don't need your empty compliments.'

How about the back of my hand across your tidy tush? The thought brought a low hum of pleasure winging through his body. He did his best to ignore it. 'Are you usually this rude or do I just bring out the best in you?'

Her shoulders slumped and she stepped back to put more space between them. 'I'm sorry. I'm...uncomfortable. This weekend is important to me. I wish I'd just given you chicken pox and handled everything myself. I let Ruby convince me this would be a good idea.'

Tino felt contrite at her obvious distress. 'Everything will be fine. Just think of us as two people going away for a weekend to have some fun. You've done that in the past, surely.'

'Of course,' she said, her reply a little too quick and a little too defensive. 'It's just that I would never choose to come away for a weekend with a man like you.'

He stiffened even though he knew by her tone that she was being honest rather than deliberately insulting, but, hell, he had his limits. 'What exactly is it about me that you don't like, Sunshine?' he queried, as if her answer didn't matter. Which, in the scheme of things, it didn't.

Her lips pursed at the mocking moniker, but he didn't care.

'We really need to go down.'

Tino crossed his arms. 'I'm waiting.'

'Look, I didn't mean to offend you. But I'm hardly your type either.'

'You're female, aren't you?' He couldn't help the comment. The desire to get under her skin was riding him.

'That's all it takes?'

Her incredulous tone drew a tight smile to his lips. 'What else is there?'

She shook her head. 'See, that's why you're not my type. I like someone a little more discerning, a little more...' She stopped as if she'd realised she was about to insult him.

'Don't stop now. It's just getting interesting.'

'Okay—fine. You're arrogant, condescending, and you treat everything like it's a joke.'

Tino deliberately kept his chuckle light. 'For a minute there I thought you were going to list my faults.'

She threw up her hands and stalked away from him. 'You're impossible to talk to!'

'True, but I make up for it where it counts.'

Her sexy mouth flattened and he just managed not to laugh. 'Sunshine, you are *so* easy to rile.'

She huffed out a breath and eyed him with utter disdain. 'Please remember that we are playing by my rules this weekend, not yours. When we're in company just...' She smoothed her brows. 'Just follow my lead.'

She pinned a frozen smile on her face and sailed through the door, leaving a faint trace of summertime in her wake.

Tino breathed deep. He didn't understand how a woman so intent on behaving like a man could smell so sweet. Then he wondered if she had sex like a man as well: enjoyed herself and moved on easily.

The unexpected thought made him snort as he followed her down the hall.

He might not know the answer to that, but he was damn sure they were bound to have another argument when she learned he played by no one else's rules but his own.

And as for following her lead...

CHAPTER FOUR

'So, HOW did you two meet?'

Miller swallowed the piece of succulent fish she'd been chewing for five minutes on a rush and felt it stick in her throat. It was the question of the night, it seemed, as TJ's guests tried to work out how an uptight management consultant could possibly ensnare the infamous Tino Ventura.

She grabbed her water glass and stiffened as she felt Valentino's strong fingers grip the back of her chair. He'd done that constantly throughout the meal, sometimes playing with the beads on her top, and she'd felt the heat of his touch sear through her clothing and all the way into her bones. The man was like a furnace.

Fortunately he took control of the conversation, having already warned her to say very little, but she could see he was as tired of the interest as she was.

Tuning out, she wondered if she shouldn't stage a massive fight right here and end the charade before they slipped up. Or before *she* slipped up—because he seemed to be doing just fine. And maybe she would feel better if Dexter didn't keep throwing her curious glances that told her in more than words that he didn't buy the whole international-racing-driver-boyfriend thing one bit.

When they had arrived for dinner men had immediately enclosed Valentino in a circle as if he were an old friend, and the women had raked their eyes appreciatively over his muscular frame. Most of them had looked at him as if they wouldn't say no to being another notch on his well-scarred bedpost. Something that didn't interest Miller in the slightest.

Oh, she found him just as sexy as they did, but she had a ten-year plan that she had nearly accomplished, and she wasn't about to get involved with a man and let him distract her. Especially a man who treated women like sex bunnies.

Pushing back her chair, Miller politely extricated herself to the powder room. After locking the bathroom door she leant against it, closed her eyes and felt her heartbeat start to normalise now that she was out from under Valentino's mesmeric spell.

It didn't help that he kept touching her, and she really needed to talk to him about his ability to follow her lead. He hadn't taken *any* of her subtle hints all night. And every time he touched her—whether it was a fleeting brush of his fingers across the back of her hand at the dinner table or a more encompassing arm around her waist while sipping champagne—it made her feel as if she'd been branded.

When she had envisaged having a fake boyfriend she'd imagined someone dutifully trailing in her wake and playing a low-key, almost invisible role. But there was nothing invisible about Valentino Ventura, and it annoyed her that her own eyes were constantly drawn to him, as if he really was some god who had deigned to grace them with his presence.

Deciding she couldn't hide out in the powder room any longer, Miller exited to find Dexter lounging against the opposite wall, waiting for her.

She didn't want to think about Ruby's suspicions that Dexter was interested in her as more than just a work colleague, but there was no doubt he was behaving differently towards her all of a sudden.

'So…' Dexter drawled, a beer bottle swinging back and forth between his fingers. 'Tino Ventura?'

Miller smiled enigmatically in answer.

'You *do* know he's got a reputation for being the biggest playboy in Europe?'

She knew he *had* a reputation—but the *biggest* playboy? 'You shouldn't believe everything you read,' she said, though by the way he'd charmed everyone at dinner she could well believe it. Women were always falling for bad boy types they hoped to reform, and even clean-shaven he looked like a fallen angel.

'I don't see it, you know,' Dexter added snidely.

Miller narrowed her eyes. He might be her direct superior, but he wasn't behaving like it right now. 'My personal life is none of your business, Dexter. Was there something you wanted?'

'Your part of the presentation we're supposed to give to TJ tomorrow.'

'I e-mailed it just before I left to come down here.'

'Cutting it a bit fine?'

About to ask him what his problem was, she nearly screamed when she felt a warm male hand settle on the small of her back. She tried to quell the instant leap of her heart but it was already galloping away at a mile a minute.

She knew her reaction hadn't done anything to alleviate Dexter's scepticism about her relationship, but frankly this internal sense of excitement when Valentino came close was too unfamiliar and disconcerting to deal with head-on. She would have given anything to do what she'd done as a child in uncomfortable situations: run away to her room and lose herself in her drawings.

'Hey, Sunshine, I wondered where you'd got to.' Valentino's warm breath stirred the hair at her temple, and his gaze lingered on her mouth before lifting to hers.

He was terribly good at this, Miller thought, swallowing heavily. It was just a pity that *she* wasn't.

'Just discussing work. Nothing important,' she said breathlessly.

'In that case, you won't mind if I join you?'

'Of course not.' She smiled at Dexter, as if her world couldn't be more perfect. Anything was better than gazing up into Valentino's sleepy grey gaze.

'So, by my reckoning,' Dexter said, looking from one to the other, 'you will have met around the time of Tino's near fatality earlier in the year. In Germany. Funny, I don't recall okaying any trip to Europe in—what?—August, was it? In fact, I can't recall your last holiday at *all*, Miller.'

Near fatality?

Miller's eyes flew to Valentino's calm face and too late she realised she would of *course* know about this if they really were going out. Collecting herself, she attempted fascination with the conversation.

'Miller wasn't on holiday when we met,' Valentino answered smoothly. 'It was while I was recuperating in Australia.'

Dexter frowned theatrically. 'I thought you convalesced in Paris? Your second home town?'

'Monaco is my second home town.'

Miller noticed he hadn't directly answered Dexter's question. Clever.

'So, what do you make of your run of bad luck since your recovery?'

'It's nice to know you're such a fan, Caruthers.' Valentino's voice was smooth, but Miller felt sweat break out under her armpits.

She tried to keep her expression bland, but mild sparks of panic were shooting off in her brain. She had a vague recollection of Dexter talking sport during various meetings, but she'd had no idea he was such a motor racing fan either.

'I follow real sports.' The beer bottle swung a little too vigorously in his loose hold. 'Football, rugby, boxing,' Dexter opined.

Valentino smiled in a way that made Dexter's comment seem as childish as it was.

Undeterred, her boss tilted his head. 'And you know, of course, that Miller doesn't follow *any* type of sport.'

'Something I'm hoping to change once she sees me race in Melbourne next weekend.'

Miller felt like an extra in a bad theatre production, and

wondered why they were talking over her head as if she was some sort of possession.

'Ah, the race of the decade.' Dexter's remark was as subtle as a cattle prod.

Again, Miller had no idea what he was talking about and snuck a glance up at Valentino—to find his easy smile still in place.

'So they say.'

She could feel the tension coming off him in waves, and knew he wasn't as relaxed as he wanted them to believe. She couldn't blame him. It couldn't be easy, having Dexter grill him this way.

'You'll have to wear earplugs, Miller. It gets loud at the track,' Dexter said, valiantly trying to regain a foothold in the conversation.

'I'll take care of Miller,' Valentino drawled. 'And you'd do well not to believe everything you read on the internet, Caruthers. My private life is exactly that. Private.'

There was no mistaking the warning behind his words and Miller stared up at Valentino, slightly shocked at the ruthless edge in his tone. Gone was the dishevelled rogue who had baited her so mercilessly in the car on the drive down, and in his place was a lean, dangerous male you'd have to be stupid to take on.

And what was Dexter doing, talking about her as if they had a more personal relationship than they did?

Miller was about to take him aside and ask him but TJ chose that moment to intrude.

'There's the guest of honour!' he announced, his eyes fixed on Valentino.

Guest of honour? Since when?

Miller was starting to feel like Alice down the rabbit hole, but at least she could tell that TJ had backed off in his openly male interest in her; his awe of Valentino clearly overrode his lustful advances.

Almost ignoring her completely, TJ launched into a spiel

about his newest car on order and Miller was glad of the reprieve.

Eyes gritty with tiredness, she wished herself a hundred miles away from this scene.

Then she noticed the men looking at her and realised she'd been unwittingly drawn into a conversation she hadn't been following. Turning blindly to Valentino for assistance, she immediately became lost in his heated gaze.

Her breath stalled and she had to remind herself that this was just pretend. But, *wow*, the man could go into acting when his racing career ended and win a truckload of awards.

Hearing her phone blast Ruby's unique ringtone in her evening purse, Miller latched onto the excuse like a lifeline, not quite meeting Valentino's eyes as she slipped away from the group.

Heading straight for the softly lit Japanese garden she'd glimpsed from the dinner table, she let the subtle scent of gardenias and some other richly perfumed flower wash over her as she walked.

Tino watched Miller wander down the steps and along a rocky pathway towards the infinity pool that glowed as cobalt-blue as her eyes.

Dexter laughed at something TJ had said and Tino glanced back to find that his eyes were also on Miller. As they had been most of the night. Even a blind man could tell that they had history together. And the way her boss had tried to stamp his ownership all over her had Tino wondering if Miller hadn't needed an escort this weekend for more than just a deterrent for her avaricious client. Perhaps she needed cover for an office affair as well.

He was sure he'd heard talk about Dexter being married, and as a third generation Italian from a solid family background if there was one thing Tino didn't condone it was extramarital affairs.

His brows drew together as he considered the possibility

that Miller and Dexter were lovers, and he didn't like the feeling that settled in his gut.

Was that why she flinched every time he got within spitting distance of her? She didn't want her "real" boyfriend to get jealous? If so, she'd soon learn that he wouldn't play *that* particular game. Not for another second.

Tossing back the last of his red wine, Tino placed the glass on a nearby table before heading down the steps to the garden.

Obviously hearing his quiet footfalls on the loose pebbles, Miller turned, her face half in shadow under the warm light given off by the raised lanterns that edged the narrow path.

Tino stopped just inside the wide perimeter he'd come to recognise as her personal space and her eyes turned wary. As well they might.

'I came down here to be alone,' she said, her dainty chin sticking out at him.

Tino widened his stance. 'Are you having an affair with Caruthers?'

'*What?*'

She seemed genuinely appalled by the question, but she needed to know this was a boundary he wouldn't cross. 'Because if you are this little ruse is over.'

Her gorgeous eyes narrowed at his blunt comment.

'Of *course* I'm not having an affair with Dexter. But even if I was it would be none of your business.'

'Wrong, Sunshine. You made it my business this weekend.'

Miller shook her head. 'That's rubbish. You were the one who *offered* to come, and I can tell you I'm not very happy with the job you're doing so far.'

Tino felt a surge of annoyance that was as much because of his attraction to her as because of her snotty attitude. 'Want to explain that?'

She leaned in towards him and he got a whiff of her sexy scent. Unconsciously, he breathed deep. 'You agreed that you would follow my lead, but despite your silver-tongued sophistication you've failed to pick up on any of my signals.'

'Silver-ton…? Sunshine, you are deluded.'

'Excuse me?'

She mirrored his incredulous tone and Valentino didn't know whether to put her over his knee or just kiss her. The woman was driving him crazy. Or her scent was. He'd never smelt anything so subtly feminine before, and on a woman who seemed determined to hide her femininity it didn't bear thinking about. Like his unusually possessive exchange with her deadbeat boss inside.

'I never promised to follow your lead. That was an assumption you made before you so imperiously waltzed out the door. And if there's nothing going on between you and Caruthers, why is he behaving like a jealous boyfriend?'

'Why are *you*?'

'Because it's my job. Apparently. Now, answer the question.'

Her gaze turned wary again. 'I don't know what's up with Dexter except that he doesn't believe you and I are a couple.'

Tino rocked back on his heels and regarded her. 'I'm not surprised.'

She flashed him an annoyed look. 'And why is that? Because I'm not your usual type?'

Since when was a ballbreaker any man's usual type?

'Because you act like a startled mouse every time I touch you.'

'I do not,' she blustered. 'But if I do it's because I don't *want* you touching me.'

'I'm your *boyfriend*. I'm supposed to touch you.'

'Not at a business function.' She frowned.

He felt completely exasperated with her. 'Anywhere.' His voice had dropped an octave because he realised just how much he had enjoyed touching her all night. How much he wanted to touch her now.

Incredible.

'That's not me,' she said on a rush.

Her tongue snaked out to moisten her heart-shaped mouth; that succulent bottom lip was now glistening invitingly.

Valentino thrust his hands into the back pockets of his jeans and locked his eyes with hers. 'If you want people to believe we're a couple you're going to have to let me take the lead, because you clearly know diddly squat about relationships.'

She looked at him as if he'd just told her the world was about to end. '*Now* who's making assumptions? For your information, if we were in a real relationship something else you would know is that I'm not the demonstrative type.'

She had thrust her chin out in that annoyingly superior way again, and Valentino couldn't resist loading her up. 'Well, that's too bad, Miller, because if we were a real couple you'd know that I *am*.'

Which wasn't strictly true. Yes, he liked to touch, but he didn't usually feel the need to grab hold of his dates and stamp his possession all over them in public—or in private come to that. The only reason he had with Miller was because she had avoided eye contact with him most of the evening, and with all the interest in their relationship he'd had to do something to make it appear genuine.

In fact she should be *thanking* him for taking his role so seriously instead of busting his balls over it.

'Listen, lady—'

'No, *you* listen.' She stabbed a finger at him as his mother used to do when he was naughty. 'I am in charge here, and your inability to read my signals is putting this whole farce in jeopardy.'

Tino thrust a hand through his hair and glanced over his shoulder as the lilting murmur of chattering guests wafted on the slight breeze. 'Is that so?' he said softly.

'Yes.' She folded her arms. 'Trust me—I know what I'm doing.'

'Good, because right now anyone watching you spit at me like an angry cat will think we're having a humdinger of an argument.'

'That's fine with me.' She gave him a cool smile that he knew was meant to put him in his place. 'It will make our relationship seem more authentic than anything else that's gone on tonight.'

Valentino saw red at her self-righteous challenge.

He stepped farther into her personal space and gripped her elbows, gratified when her eyes widened to the size of dinner plates.

'What are you doing?' she demanded in a furious whisper.

Yeah, what are *you doing, Ventura?*

Tino stared down at her, watching the pulse-point in her neck pick up speed. His body hummed with sexual need and he wondered what it was about her he found just so damned tempting.

She was more librarian than seductress, and yet she couldn't have had more effect on his body if she'd been standing in front of him naked. It was a thought that was a little disconcerting and one he instantly pushed aside.

He wasn't *that* attracted to her. But he *was* that annoyed with her, and while he might not have ever felt the need to put a woman in her place before he did now. And he'd enjoy it.

'Why, Miller, I'm just doing what you asked. I'm going to make this farce of a relationship look more authentic.'

Before she could unload on him he took full advantage of her open mouth and planted his own firmly over the top of hers in a kiss that was more about punishment than pleasure.

Or at least it was meant to be. Until she stupidly tried to wriggle away from him and he had to clamp one hand at the back of her head and the other over her butt to hold her still.

She fell into him, her soft breasts nuzzling against his chest, her nipples already diamond-hard. They both stilled; heat and uncertainty a driving force between them. Her silky hair grazed the back of his knuckles and his fingers flexed. Her eyes slid closed, her soft whimper of surrender sending a powerful surge of lust through his whole body.

Her silky hair slid over his knuckles and made his fingers flex, and then she made a tiny sound that turned him harder than stone.

Tino couldn't have stopped his tongue from plunging in and

out of the moist sweetness of her mouth if he'd had a gun to his head. All day he'd wondered if she'd taste as good as her summery scent promised, and now he had his answer.

Better.

So much better.

He was powerless to pull back, his brain as stalled as the Mercedes he'd accidentally flooded in the second race of his professional career.

He gave a deep groan of pleasure as her arms wound around his neck, and he gripped her hips to pull her pelvis in tightly against his own.

His arousal jerked as it came into contact with her soft belly, and it was all he could do not to grind himself against her.

So much for not being that *attracted to her.*

He urged her lips to open even wider and she didn't resist when he possessed her mouth in a carnal imitation of the way his body wanted to possess hers. An instantaneous fire beat flames through his body, and her low, keening moans of pleasure were making him hotter still.

He had to have her.

Here.

Now.

His hand slid to her bottom, the outside of her thighs, drawing her in and up so that he could settle more fully in the tempting vee of her body. He felt her fingers move into his hair, her feminine curves pressing closer as she rubbed against him. Tino couldn't hold back another groan—and nearly exploded when he heard someone clearing their throat behind him.

Bloody hell. He drew his mouth back and took a moment before reaching up to unwind Miller's arms from around his neck. She made a moue of protest and slowly opened passion-drugged eyes. He knew when her senses returned from the same planet where his had gone that she'd be more than pissed.

'Sunshine, we have company,' he whispered gruffly, his unsteady breath ruffling the top of her hair.

He gave her time to compose herself before turning to face

the person behind them. He was certain it was Caruthers. He also gave himself time to get his raging hard-on under control. Not that it seemed to be responding with any speed.

Miller looked up at Valentino and was aghast to realise that she had become so completely lost in his kiss that she had quite forgotten they were in a public place.

Never before had she been kissed like that, and heat filled her cheeks at the realisation that she wouldn't have stopped if Dexter hadn't turned up. That she would have had sex with Valentino in the middle of a garden like some dumb groupie.

Not wanting to dwell on how that made her feel, Miller shoved the thought away before lurching backwards.

'Dexter…' she began, trying to organise her thoughts on the hop. She was almost glad when Valentino took over.

'You wanted something, Caruthers?'

Miller closed her eyes at Valentino's rough question and wished the ground would open up and swallow her whole.

'I came to let Miller know that TJ has opened champagne in the music room. As we're here in a professional capacity to win the man's business, it might be prudent for her to join us.'

Miller smoothed her eyebrows and stepped out from behind Valentino, determined that Dexter wouldn't see how mortified she felt right now. 'Of course.' She forced herself not to defend her actions, even though she desperately wanted to.

'Good. I'll leave you to pull yourself together,' Dexter said stiffly.

He was clearly upset with her, and he had good reason to be, Miller thought. She *was* here in a professional capacity, and even if she and Valentino really were lovers it didn't excuse her poor behaviour.

Although they *had been* secluded from the other guests, Dexter had found them—which meant anyone else could have.

A small voice informed her that Valentino had probably achieved his goal and put paid to Dexter's suspicions about the genuineness of their relationship, but Miller wasn't listening.

She wouldn't have chosen to do it that way, and she was furious that Valentino hadn't given her a choice. Furious that he had used his superior height and strength to hold her against him to prove a point. A point he had clearly enjoyed.

As did you. The snide voice popped up again, reminding her of how she had wrapped her tongue around his and tried to climb his body to assuage the ache that was still beating heavily between her thighs.

God, what a mess.

Valentino moved his arm in a gesture for her to precede him up the path and Miller determinedly made the same gesture back to him. He cocked an eyebrow at her, his eyes lingering on her mouth; his trademark sexy grin was more a warning than an indication of pleasantness.

Miller narrowed her eyes and thought about stomping on his foot as she strode past, but she decided not to give him the satisfaction of letting him know he had succeeded in rattling her again.

She knew he liked to take control but, dammit, this was not his show to orchestrate. She was in charge and it was time to set some clear boundaries between them. She'd dealt with alpha males in her line of work before, and she'd deal with this one too.

CHAPTER FIVE

FEELING as if the past hour had taken a day to pass, Miller unfolded a woollen blanket and laid it on the bedroom floor.

'What are you doing?'

She glanced up to find Valentino lounging against the bathroom doorway, watching her. His face was stony, but it only highlighted the chiselled jaw that was again in need of a razor. He wasn't wearing anything other than his black jeans, unbuttoned, and his biceps bulged where he folded his hands across his superbly naked chest.

'Problem with your shirt?' she said, and could have kicked herself when his mouth curled into a knowing smile.

'Only in as much as I don't wear a shirt to bed.'

Miller raised an unconcerned eyebrow. 'Lucky you wear jeans, then.'

'I don't.'

His eyebrow rose to match hers and she turned back to unfold a second blanket she'd picked up from the end of the bed. Flicking it out, she laid it on top of the first.

'I repeat—what are you doing?'

'Making up a bed. What does it look like?'

Valentino looked bored. 'If you're worried about whether or not I'm going to jump your bones now that we're alone, I doubt I could get through that passion killer you're wearing with a blowtorch.'

Miller stood up and moved to the wardrobe, where she had seen a group of pillows on the top shelf. She was glad that he didn't like her quilt-style dressing gown. It had been a present from her late father, and although the stitching was frayed in places she'd never get rid of it.

Thinking about her father made her remember the day her parents had told her they were separating. She'd been ten at the time, and while they'd talked about it calmly and rationally Miller had felt sick and confused. Then her mother had driven her from Queensland to Victoria and Miller's world had gone from cosy and safe to unpredictable and unhappy. A bit like the steely, coiled man feigning nonchalance in the bathroom doorway.

'Or are you worried you won't be able to keep your hands to yourself after that kiss?' he asked.

Miller cast him a withering look and returned to the bed she was setting up on the floor. She wasn't going to stroke his ego by responding to his provocative comments.

He'd felt her response to his kiss and it still rankled. Afterwards she'd pretended that she'd been acting for the sake of their audience, but she hadn't been, and she needed time to process that.

In the space of a short time the solid foundations of her secure life had become decidedly rickety, and she wasn't going to add to that by letting her plans for the future be derailed by a sexy-as-sin flamboyant racing car driver who treated life like a game. Because Miller knew life *wasn't* a game, and when things went wrong you only had yourself to rely on.

It had been a tough lesson she had learned hard after being sent to an exclusive girls' boarding school, where her opinion hadn't meant half as much as her lack of money. Teenage girls could be cruel, but Miller hadn't wanted to upset her mother by telling her she was having a terrible time at school. Her mother had needed to work two jobs in order to give Miller a better start in life than she'd had, so Miller had put up with the bullying and the loneliness and made sure not to give her mother any reason to be disappointed in her.

'If you think I'm sleeping on that, Sunshine, you're mistaken.'

Valentino's arrogant assurance was astounding, and Miller stared open-mouthed as he crossed to the bed and placed his watch on the bedside table.

Fortunately she had already anticipated this problem and, she thought grumpily as she fluffed up her pillows, she hoped the bed had bugs in it.

'Good to know. At least there won't be any more arguments between us tonight.'

Tino smiled. He couldn't help it. Which was surprising since he was still irritated as hell by that kiss out in the garden and the way he had become completely lost in it. Drunk on it.

He'd told himself all day to lay off the little fantasies he'd been having about her mouth, but had he listened? No.

And what was up with that? If he ignored his instincts on the track as he had out in that garden he'd have bought the farm a long time ago.

The problem was he had made her off-limits and that had spiked his interest. Stupid. But he wasn't a man who could resist a challenge. And on top of that she was clearly not fawning over him as other women did once they knew who he was. There was nothing more likely to get a woman into his bed than giving them his job title, but this pretty little ray of sunshine was not only *not* trying to sleep with him, she was making up a bed on the floor!

She couldn't have challenged him more if she'd tried, and because he had been thwarted in racing these last couple of months, first due to injury and then because his car was under-performing and causing all sorts of problems, he was more frustrated than he normally would be. Which went a lot further towards explaining his sexual fascination with her than anything else he'd come up with so far.

It was even more of a reason to keep his distance from her.

He wasn't a slave to his hormones, and he had enough complications at the moment without adding her to the list.

He yanked off his jeans and got into the king-sized bed, letting out an exaggerated sigh of appreciation as the soft mattress gave just enough beneath his body. He might as well enjoy it since he *knew* she was about to order him to sleep on the floor. He'd do it once she said please. A word she was sorely in need of learning how to use.

He grinned. He was quite looking forward to seeing how long it would take before she caved in and used it.

He watched with some satisfaction as she stalked to the main door and hit the light switch with her open palm as if she wished it was his head. Then she did something completely unexpected. She shimmied out of her robe and got into the makeshift bed on the floor.

And made him feel like an absolute idiot.

'Ever had your testosterone levels checked out?' he grumbled.

'What's the matter, Valentino? Your masculinity being challenged because I'm not falling at your feet?'

Yes, as a matter of fact it was.

'Was the kiss that good?' he purred.

'I can't remember.'

He heard her fake a yawn and shook his head. 'Sounds like you want a reminder.'

'Not in this lifetime,' she sputtered.

Her protest was a little too vigorous, which he liked.

Tino stretched out on the bed and stared at the ceiling, his eyes starting to adjust to the grey shadows cast around the room from the moonlight seeping in around the sheer curtains.

He heard the blankets on the floor rustle and his teeth gnashed together. She was being ridiculous and taking this just a little too far. He wondered if she was wearing something lacy. Something like the freshly laundered hot-pink thong hanging on the towel rail in the bathroom. The sight of those delicate panties had knocked him for a six, and he was pretty sure she hadn't left them there deliberately.

Finding out she really *did* favour sexy lingerie was a fact he could have well done without. Ball-breaking Miss Miller Jacobs was turning out to be full of contradictions. Not least of all that fiery response to his kiss in the garden.

Acting, she had said after the event. *Yeah, right.*

Acting, my ass.

Yeah, and you're not supposed to be thinking about it.

'I like the thong you left in the bathroom,' he said, unable to help annoying her as she was annoying him.

'You can't borrow it,' she said after a slight pause.

He gave a soft chuckle. *Man*, she was sassy. And, no, he didn't want to borrow it. But he wouldn't have minded stripping it down her long legs to see what he was sure would be tawny curls underneath. His heart beat the blood a little more heavily around his body and he was unable to stop his mind from imagining her naked and spread out on the four-poster bed. Imagining her soft and wet with the same need that had compelled her to wrap her tongue around his in that garden.

He breathed deep and willed his body to relax, reminding himself that he only wanted her because he'd placed an embargo around her.

The blankets rustled again as she adjusted herself on the hard floor that not even thousand-dollar-a-metre carpet could soften.

His blood was Sicilian, and if she thought he could stay sprawled out on a comfortable bed while she lay uncomfortably at his feet she had another thing coming. But he knew offering up the bed would only play into her martyr's hands and give her a reason to make him feel even more like a heel, so he stayed quiet and devised another plan that had the double advantage of allowing him to live up to his chivalrous nature and annoy the hell out of her at the same time.

Half an hour later Tino looked down on Miller's sleeping form. Her hands were tucked under her face and her shoulder-length hair was dark against the white pillow. Deep shadows beneath her eyes attested to how tired she was.

Careful not to wake her, he leaned down and pulled the meagre blanket away from her body—and instantly stilled.

She was lying half on her stomach, one leg bent to the side in an innocently provocative pose. Her pale jersey camisole top and matching three quarter length pants stretched tight over her ripe curves. As far as night attire went it wasn't the most seductive he'd ever seen, and yet as he gazed at her slender limbs, milky in the shadowy moonlight she had his full attention.

His hand itched to curve around the firm globes of her bottom while he bit down gently on the soft-as-silk skin that covered her trapezius. Would she be sensitive there? Or would she prefer him to kiss his way down each pearl-like button of her spine? Perhaps while he was buried deep inside her.

Tino groaned and closed his eyes. He felt like a randy teenager looking at a full on girlie magazine. Lust, hot and primal, beat through his body and made his legs weak. For a moment he was gripped by an almost uncontrollable urge to roll her over and wake her with a lover's kiss. Get her to open her mouth for him as she had done earlier, cup her pert breasts, shove those stretchy pants to her ankles and thrust into her until all she could do was chant his name over and over as she came for him.

Only him.

He blinked back the unusually possessive thought, the incongruity of it burning through his sensual haze and reminding him of his initial purpose in pulling the blanket from her body.

Gently, he scooped her up off the floor and carried her to the bed. She stirred and shifted in his arms, the curtain of her hair trailing down his naked arm and her orange blossom shampoo tickling his nose. His body tightened at the allure of that clean smell and he almost tumbled her onto the bed in his haste to put her down. As soon as he did she mumbled something unintelligible and sighed deeply as she curled into the soft mattress.

Tino quickly pulled the comforter up over her near naked limbs before he could change his mind about being chivalrous.

His eyes drifted to the other side of the king-sized bed. It looked vast and empty with her only taking up one quarter of it. Tiredness invaded his body, and although he had fully intended to sleep on the floor he realised he probably didn't have to. The bed was nearly as big as the infinity pool downstairs and he was an early riser. If the gods were on his side he'd be up and running along the beach before she even knew it was a new day.

Still, he laid a row of pillows down the centre of the bed. No point in tempting fate.

'Oh, yes,' Miller moaned softly as she felt the weight of a hair roughened thigh slip between her legs while a warm, callused hand palmed her breast. Her body buzzed and her nipples tightened, forcing her to arch more firmly into that warm caress. The hand squeezed her gently and somewhere above her head she heard a rough masculine sound of appreciation. Another hand was sliding confidently over her hip toward—

Holy hell!

Miller's eyes flew open and she stared straight into Valentino Ventura's sleeping face. Within seconds her brain assimilated the fact that she was no longer on the floor, but in bed and that Valentino had one of his hands on her breast and the other curved around her bottom.

Miller yelped and pushed against his impossibly hard chest, glad when he gave a grunt of discomfort, his jet-black lashes parting to reveal slate-grey eyes still glazed with sleep.

Miller pushed at his hands and scrambled backwards, her legs colliding with one of his knees as she roughly slid her leg out from between his.

Tino let out a rough expletive and moved his legs out of the way. 'Watch the knee.'

'Watch the…?' Miller had a vague recollection of the men questioning Valentino about some racing injury but she didn't care about that right now. 'Get your hands off me, you great oaf.'

She shoved harder at his immovable arm and sucked in

her tummy muscles as his steely forearm slid across her bare stomach.

Finally, fully awake, he acquiesced.

'No need to sound the alarm, I was just sleeping.'

Miller gripped the duvet up to her chin. 'You were grop- ing me.'

'Was I? I thought you'd just ruined a pleasant dream. Sorry about that.'

'Yes, I just bet you're sorry.' She saw his eyes sharpen on hers. 'How did I end up in bed with you anyway?'

Valentino casually slid his hands beneath his head and Miller swept her angry gaze over those powerful arms and that mus- cular chest. She felt her breath catch and her heartbeat speed up and berated her instant reaction.

'I don't know, Sunshine,' he answered. 'Are you prone to sleepwalking?'

Miller narrowed her gaze, her mind flashing back to last night. A vague memory of being lifted floated to the surface of her mind. 'You carried me.'

Valentino yawned and pushed up until he was leaning against the headboard. The sheet dropped down to his waist, and the morning sun fell over part of his bronzed chest and corrugated abdomen as if lighting him up for a photo shoot.

He scratched his chest and her eyes soaked him up. God, the man really did look airbrushed!

'Damn. Maybe *I'm* prone to sleepwalking,' he said.

Miller hugged the duvet closer and felt her nipples throb with awareness as her hands accidentally grazed over them. Heat immediately bloomed in her face at the memory of *why* her breasts felt so heavy and sensitive.

'This isn't funny. That's sexual harassment.'

The great oaf just rolled his eyes. 'As I recall it, it was you who cuddled up to me in your sleep—not the other way around.'

'I did not.'

'Suit yourself. But last night I put a row of pillows between us, and I know it wasn't *me* who knocked them aside. Anyway,

I disengaged my hand as soon as you asked.' He raised and lowered his knee gingerly beneath the blanket and she hoped that she *had* hurt him.

'Remind me not to do you a good deed again,' he said.

'Ha. Good deed, my foot. You wanted to…to…'

'Have my wicked way with you?' His eyes glinted. 'If that was what I wanted that's what we'd be doing.'

'You wish.'

'A challenge, Miller?'

She didn't deign to respond. Why would she? Of course it wasn't a challenge—especially when she had liked the feel of him against her a little too much.

Her breathless response reminded her of the time she'd been secretly trapped in the girls' toilets at the hideous school she'd attended while the main bullies had loitered, giggling vacuously over some boy or another.

By the time they had hit fifteen, boys had been all they could talk about. Miller had wanted to yell, *What about when it all goes wrong?* But of course she hadn't. She hadn't wanted to look more like a freak than they already thought she was. All of them had seemed content to live in the moment in a way she never could after her parents had divorced.

'There was no way I was letting you sleep on the floor. Get over it.' Valentino's gruff voice jolted her back to the present.

'Turn the other way,' she demanded, letting her painful memories slip away.

When he complied without argument she shot out of bed and snatched up her robe. Ignoring him, she grabbed her running clothes and stalked towards the bathroom.

'Just so we're clear.' She stopped in the doorway. 'This arrangement does *not* extend to sex, and even if it did you would be the last man I would choose to sleep with.'

He looked at her as if he could see right through her. 'So you keep saying.'

His intense eyes never left hers and Miller found it hard to swallow. He looked irresistible and dangerous with his untidy dark hair and overnight stubble. By contrast she was sure she looked a fright, and all of sudden it seemed imperative that she get away from him. She couldn't remember ever feeling so vulnerable.

She shook her head. 'You're too used to getting your own way. That's your problem.'

Valentino threw back the covers and stood up. He was only wearing low-riding hipster briefs and Miller quickly averted her eyes. She felt irrationally angry when he laughed. He stalked towards her and Miller deliberately held his gaze, refusing to let him see how affected she was by his potent masculinity.

He shook his head. 'Lady, you are one overwound broad. Yes, my hand was on your breast—but that little moan you exhaled before your uptight brain kicked into gear let me know that you liked it. More than liked it.'

'Well, my uptight little brain rules my body, and what you felt back there was just a physiological reaction.' Miller felt irrationally stung by his assessment, even though she had insulted him first. She couldn't help it; he just made her feel so... so...*emotional*!

'You're telling me you'd get turned on if you woke up with TJ's hand on your breast?'

Miller clamped her lips together. That was a no-win question and they both knew it. 'There's no way to answer that without stroking your mountainous ego, so I won't bother.'

'You just did.'

Oh! Miller swivelled and slammed the bathroom door in his laughing face. He was *so* arrogant and *so* full of himself.

Impossible. The most impossible and most gorgeous man she had ever come across.

She leant back against the door and sighed. No wonder he had women lining up outside his hotel rooms to get a glimpse of him. The man was sex on legs and he knew it.

Miller made a frustrated noise through her teeth and her breasts tingled with remembered pleasure as she pulled on her shorts, sports bra and top. A strenuous run would help her forget this morning before her meeting with Dexter and TJ.

Taking a fortifying breath, she decided to ignore Valentino—but that plan instantly unravelled when she opened the bathroom door and noticed him sitting on the side of the bed, tying his shoelaces and dressed as she was.

'Please tell me you're not going for a run?'

Valentino looked up. 'Is there a law against it?'

His eyes immediately dropped to her bare legs and Miller felt slightly uncoordinated as she continued across the room to the closet.

She wanted to say yes, but he would no doubt think she was being uptight again—and anyway it was petty. The man was doing her a favour by being here—albeit a reluctant one—and who was she to tell him he couldn't go for a run? She might dislike the tumultuous feelings he incited in her just from looking at him, but she was going to have to get used to it if she was going to survive the next twenty-four hours with any degree of dignity. She had already decided she wasn't going to be his weekend plaything, so how hard could it be?

'Of course not,' she said, knowing full well he was a hundred times fitter than she was and would never suggest they run together.

'You run often?' he asked.

Miller glanced his way, noting his conciliatory tone. 'A couple of times a week. You?' she added, deciding to accept his olive branch.

'Every morning except Sunday.'

She didn't want to ask what he did on Sunday mornings. She was afraid her hormones would want her to do more than just visualise it.

He tilted his head, that devilish smile playing around his lips. 'I get time off for good behaviour.'

The incongruity of that statement brought an instant grin to her face. 'Yeah, right. I'm sure you were the type of teenager who crawled out of your bedroom window when your parents were asleep and partied all night.'

'They were called study nights at our house.' His deadpan expression made her laugh.

When she realised that he was laughing too she quickly sobered. Because she didn't want to enjoy his company, and by the wary darkening of his eyes he didn't much want to enjoy hers either.

But still the light-hearted connection persisted and made her nervous. A sudden impulse to place his hand back on her breast and kiss him senseless blindsided her.

'It's a beautiful morning. Why don't we stretch on the beach first?' he suggested.

Shocked by the unfamiliar emotions driving her thoughts and desperate to break the tension that throbbed between them, Miller cleared her throat and hoped that single gesture hadn't transmitted to him just how affected she was by his presence.

'I don't think we should run together.'

Valentino eyed her dubiously. 'How will it look if you run off in one direction and I go in the other?'

Telling, probably.

Miller smoothed her eyebrows in a soothing gesture that failed dismally.

She looked down at his long muscular legs dusted with dark hair.

'Come on, Miller, what are you afraid of?'

Him, for one. Her own feelings, for two. Did he need three? 'I'll slow you down,' she mumbled.

'I'll forgive you,' he replied softly.

Miller sighed. One of her strengths was knowing when she was beaten, but still she was hardly gracious when she said. 'Okay, but don't talk to me. I hate people who run and talk at the same time.'

CHAPTER SIX

THE morning *was* beautiful. Peaceful. The air was crisp, but already warmed by the sun beating down from a royal-blue sky, and the fresh scent of saltwater was tart on the silky breeze. Seagulls flew in graceful circles, while others just squatted on the white-gold sand, unaffected by the gentle, almost lackadaisical nature of the waves sweeping towards them.

The beach arced around in a gentle curve towards a rocky outcrop, and as it was in an unpopulated area it was completely deserted at this time of the morning.

After a few quick stretches Miller set off at an easy jog along the dark, wet packed sand left behind as the tide went out, sure that Valentino would get bored and surge ahead. But he didn't. And then she remembered that he'd complained about his knee and wondered if she *had* hurt him this morning.

Feeling hot already, Miller turned her head to look at him, her ponytail swinging around her face. 'I didn't really hurt your knee, did I?' she panted between breaths.

He glanced across at her, only a light sheen of sweat lining his brow, his breathing seemingly unaffected by his exertions. 'No. The knee is fine.'

'Was the accident very bad?'

When he didn't respond, she flicked her eyes over his profile, just in time to see him tense almost imperceptibly.

'Which one?'

'There's been more than one?'

He glanced towards the ocean, and she didn't think he'd answer.

'Three this year.'

She wasn't sure if that was a lot for his profession. She imagined they must crash all the time at the speeds they drove. 'The one where you hurt your knee?'

He didn't look at her. 'Bad enough.'

His voice was gruff, blunt. Very unlike his usual casual eloquence. 'Was anyone else hurt?'

'Yes.'

'Wh—?'

'I thought you said you didn't like to talk while you ran?'

It was pretty clear he didn't want to tell her about it so she let the subject drop. But of course her curiosity was piqued. Dexter's comment about his next race being the race of the decade was making her wonder if it had anything to do with his accident. She really didn't know anything about Valentino Ventura, other than the fact that he was called Maverick and he dated legions of women, but she wouldn't mind knowing what secrets she was beginning to suspect lay behind his devil-may-care attitude to life.

Tino had never run with anyone before. Not even his personal trainer. Running was meditative, and something he liked to do alone, so he hadn't expected to enjoy Miller's company as much as he was.

Despite his large family he wasn't the type to need others to be close to him. He was a loner. Maybe not always, but certainly since his father's death. And, yeah, he knew a shrink would say the two were connected but he was happy with the way he was and saw no reason to change. If he died one day pushing the limits, as his father had, and Hamilton Jones had last August, at least he knew he wouldn't be leaving a devastated family behind him.

The image of Hamilton's wife and two young daughters—

teary and slightly accusing at the funeral, because he'd survived and their father hadn't—caused guilt to fluctuate inside him.

Survivor guilt.

The team doctor had warned him about it afterwards, and while he'd never admitted to feeling it he knew that on some level he did. But he also knew it was something that would wear off if he didn't think about it. Because the accident hadn't been his fault. Hamilton had tried to overtake on one of the easiest corners on the track, but had somehow managed to clip Tino's rear wheel and hurtle them both out of control.

Hamilton had lost his life and Tino had missed three of the following races due to injury. And he'd failed to finish the last two races due to mechanical issues.

He wasn't superstitious, and he didn't believe in bad luck, but he couldn't deny—at least to himself—that there seemed to be a black cloud, like in a damned cartoon strip, following him around at the moment.

A sudden memory of the moment his mother had returned from the bathroom and he'd had to tell her that his father—the love of her life—had just been involved in a hideous accident clamped around his heart like an iron fist. No one knew what had caused the accident that had ended his father's life—engine malfunction or human error—but the pit crew had said his father hadn't been himself that morning, and Tino remembered overhearing his mother urge his father to pull out of the race. But the old man had ignored her and gone anyway.

Tino swiped a hand through his hair. Had that been what had killed him? His mother's soft request? Tino shuddered. It was a hell of a position for a man to be put in.

Refocusing on Miller's steady rhythm, he was surprised that he didn't have to temper his speed all that much for them to remain together.

Waking up beside her, he hadn't meant to have his hands all over her, and now he decided that it would be best to play the relationship game her way. So what if Caruthers had the hots for her? It was none of his business, as she had rightly pointed out. Now that he knew he wasn't being used as a patsy to hide an affair it shouldn't mean anything to him that the other man wanted her.

Had they *ever* been lovers?

Not wanting to head down that particular track he concentrated again on the rhythmic sound of their feet hitting the sand and the crystal clear waters of the South Pacific Ocean rolling onto the beach. The coastline reminded him a little of his house on Phillip Island, near Melbourne, although he knew the water there was at least ten degrees cooler and a hundred times rougher.

Miller stopped and started walking, her hands on her hips, and Valentino joined her.

'You can keep going if you want,' she panted.

He glanced at her. He *could* keep going but he didn't want to. What he wanted was to stop thinking about the past and make her smile. Like she had back in their room. He wondered what she did for fun, and then wondered why he cared.

'You work out a lot?' he asked.

She glanced at him, and he tensed when her eyes dropped to his stomach as he used his T-shirt to wipe a line of sweat off his brow. He knew she was attracted to him, maybe even as attracted as he was to her, but he also knew it would be stupid to follow up on that attraction. Not only did *she* not want it—he didn't either. And, while his body might have ideas to the contrary, his body was just an instrument for his mind, not the other way around.

'I go to the gym three times a week and try to go for a run along the Manly foreshore on the weekend.'

She walked in a small circle to ease the lactic acid burn from her legs.

'You do weights?'

'Some. Mainly light weights. Although I missed every one of my workouts this week due to work, so no doubt when I start back Monday morning I'll be a little sore.'

'Do some now.'

She cast her eyes from the sparkling ocean to the sand dunes behind them. 'I'm sorry, but if you see a weight machine anywhere around here you're on your own.'

He laughed. 'There's a lot you can do without machines. Trust me. This is part of my day job. Why don't we start with some ab crunches?'

He lay on his back and started curling his head towards his bent knees. He'd made it to twenty when out of the corner of his eye he saw her reluctantly join him. He wasn't sure why that pleased him so much.

She kept pace for a minute, then fell back on the sand. 'I've been running for a while but I'm still pretty new at the gym thing,' she said.

'Okay, now squats.'

Miller groaned. 'I really don't like squats.'

'No one likes squats except bodybuilders.'

She laughed and the husky sound made his stomach grip.

'Come on.' His voice was gruff, unnatural sounding.

She jumped lithely to her feet and he couldn't look away from the toned muscles in her thighs as she braced her legs slightly apart.

'Raise your arms overhead as you go down. And keep your chest up.' He cleared his throat, trying to concentrate on her technique rather than recalling the feel of her peaked nipple pressing eagerly into his palm. 'Squeeze your glutes and extend through your hips as you come up.'

He'd need to dunk himself in the ocean at this rate, but at least his mind was fully focused on something other than racing again.

'Am I getting a personal training session now?' She grinned at him, but didn't stop.

'Maybe.' He returned her smile. 'I do aim to please.'

'What's next?' She breathed deep and shook out her legs.

Tino could think of a lot of 'nexts' that involved her horizontal on the soft sand without the top and shorts, but he shouldn't even be thinking like that.

He sucked in a litre of air and took her through a couple of other light exercises. 'Push-ups.'

Miller grimaced. 'Oh, great. You're hitting all my favourites.'

She got down on the sand and started pushing herself up, her knees bent.

'They're not real push-ups,' he teased.

'Yes, they are!' After twenty she collapsed and rolled onto her back. 'Okay, that's it. Those and the bench press are my weakest exercises.'

He absently noted how the sun had turned her hair to burnished copper, with some of the tendrils around her temples darkened with sweat. Her cheeks were pink from exertion, her chest heaving…

Don't even go there, Ventura.

'That just means you have to do more of them.'

Miller turned her head towards him and her eyes sparkled as blue as the ocean behind her. 'Oh, darn. No bench press. What a shame.'

Tino smiled. So she did have a sense of humour.

Lifting from his sitting position beside her, he came over the top of her, before he could talk himself out of it, his body hovering far too close to her own.

Her eyes flew wide and her hands fluttered between them, the pulse-point at the base of her throat hammering wildly. 'Valentino, what are you doing?'

He liked the way she used the full version of his name. Breathless. Husky.

'Accommodating you.' His own voice was rough again, as if he'd swallowed a mouthful of sand, and he hoped to hell she hadn't noticed that he was already fully hard. 'I'll be your bench press.'

'Don't be silly.'

He braced himself on his arms and lowered his upper body slightly over hers. 'Hands on my shoulders,' he commanded.

When she put them there he barely suppressed the shudder that ran the length of his whole body.

She shifted beneath him. Swallowed. 'This won't work,' she said, but she didn't remove her hands. 'You're too big.'

Her eyes met his and the air between them sizzled.

She was wrong. This wasn't silly. This was way beyond silly. 'Ten reps. Go.' He just wanted them out of the way now.

She pushed at his shoulders and he mentally worked his way through every component of a car engine as they moved in unison. He could feel her hot breath on his neck as she exhaled and he dared not look at anything but the sand above her head.

Of all the lame-brain things to do...

He paused when he felt her weaken, intent on pushing himself away from her, but he made the mistake of looking down into eyes that had gone indigo with desire.

The sound of seagulls squalling couldn't even distract him from the hunger that burned a hole in his belly.

Her hands slipped down his arms, shaping his muscles, and her eyes drifted to his mouth. 'Valentino...'

Her husky plea weakened him more than fifty reps with twenty-five-pound dumbbells could and, groaning deep in his chest, he lowered his head and captured her soft mouth with his own.

Miller was aware of every hard inch of Valentino's male flesh pressing her into the sand. Her own body throbbing as if it was on fire, totally drugged by his heat, his smell, his taste. She couldn't remember why this was a bad idea. No rational words remained in her head to rein in her pleasure-fuelled body. Her arousal with him in bed earlier had returned full-force.

Impatient with a need she'd never felt before, she swept her hands down his back and then smoothed them up under his sweaty shirt. He groaned approvingly and with his elbows either side of her face cradled the back of her head, angling her so that his skilful mouth could ravage her lips, his moist tongue plundering and duelling with her own in a way that made the ache between her legs become almost painful.

She felt his other hand drift over her torso, feather-light as if learning her shape, his fingertips moving closer and closer to the tip of one breast. Moaning, Miller twisted in his hold, her body begging for more of his touch. She felt him smile against her mouth, his lips drifting over her jaw and down the column of her throat.

'Please, Valentino…' she pleaded, her body craving a release she had never experienced during sex but which now seemed infinitely possible. Infinitely desirable.

Obliging her, his hand rose over her breast, cupping her, his thumb flicking back and forth over her nipple at the same time as his teeth bit down on the straining, sensitive cord of her neck.

Miller cried out, jerking beneath him. Her body was liquid with need, her hips arching towards his, her mind completely focused on one outcome.

His fingers plucked more firmly at her nipple and her fingernails unconsciously scored the tight muscles of his lower back.

He shifted sideways and she whimpered in protest. Then his hand slid lower, and she stopped breathing as he cupped between her legs.

'Miller—'

She didn't want him to speak. She just wanted to lose herself in these magic sensations. She dragged his mouth back to hers, her tongue instantly gratified by the warm wetness of his deep, soul-destroying kiss. Her body was close, so close, and she couldn't think, couldn't breathe.

'Oh!'

His hand slipped beneath the hem of her shorts and knickers and then his fingers parted her and lightly stroked her swollen flesh. He groaned into her mouth, pressed deep at the same time as Miller pressed upwards, and that was all it took for her to tumble over the edge. She gripped his shoulders and wrenched her mouth from his, gasping for oxygen as her body disintegrated into a million wonderful pieces.

For a while nothing happened, and then she became aware of the sound of Valentino's harsh breathing above her own panting breaths, the seagulls squalling overhead.

When she finally managed to open her eyes she found him looking down at her with an open hunger that made her feel instantly panicked.

Oh, God... 'What have I done?'

'I believe it's called having an orgasm,' he mocked, clearly understanding the horrified expression on her face. 'Followed closely by feeling regret.'

Regret? *Did* she regret it? She didn't even know. But all the reasons this was not a good idea rushed back like a blast of cold water from a hose.

Public beach. Playboy. Promotion.

If she could bury her head in the sand right now she would.

A seagull squawked close by and Miller jumped. 'You have to get off me.'

'I'm not actually on you.'

He was right. His body hovered beside her, shielding her from any prying eyes at TJ's house some way along the beach, but he wasn't holding her down.

Miller scrambled to a sitting position and looked over his shoulder. They were still alone. Thank God.

'I said I wasn't going to have sex with you,' she spat at him accusingly. She knew full well that she was equally responsible for what had just happened between them, but was still unable to fully take in the sensations rippling through her body. 'This never happened,' she said firmly, her emotions as brittle as an empty seashell.

His eyebrows drew together and his features were taut. 'Not part of your plan, Sunshine?'

'You know it wasn't.' She hated the sarcastic tilt to his lips.

'Believe me, it's not part of mine either.' He pushed himself to a sitting position and deftly removed his runners and socks. Then he dragged his T-shirt up over his chest and Miller's insides, still soft and pliant, clenched alarmingly.

His easy acceptance of her brush-off was slightly insulting, and the illogical nature of that thought wasn't lost on her in the heat of the moment. In fact, it only made her more irritable. But whether at him or herself she wasn't sure.

She watched him jog down to the shoreline and gracefully duck dive beneath an incoming wave. Thank God she didn't like him very much. She wasn't ready to change her life for a man, and some deep feminine instinct warned her that being with him intimately, even once, would be life-changing.

She sighed. At least for her it would be. For him life would no doubt go on as normal.

CHAPTER SEVEN

TJ TIPPED his Akubra back from his forehead and rocked forward on his chair, and Miller knew the presentation she and Dexter had just delivered hadn't gone well.

'Miller, you're a talented girl, no doubt about it,' he drawled, in a condescending tone that set Miller's teeth on edge. 'But I told Winston International I'd give their show another shot.'

What?

Miller narrowed her eyes, sensing Dexter's surprise without having to look at him.

The reason TJ had even approached Oracle was because he was disgruntled with the service he'd been receiving from Winston International.

'I was thinking about it all last night, and it doesn't seem right to trash our relationship after so many years. One of their boys is going to show me what they've got Monday morning. In the meantime why don't you fix the concerns I have with your current proposal and get it back to me ASAP?'

Miller was thankful for the years of practice she'd had at pretending she was perfectly fine when she wasn't, and schooled her features into an expression of professional blandness. Was this because she'd rejected his advances in the restaurant the week before? He might be ruthless and without morals, but he didn't strike her as the vindictive type. But he did know Oracle *was* desperate for his business, so he had them over a barrel in that regard.

She had started to hate this aspect of business. The 'anything goes' mantra Oracle had adopted as the global economic crisis had deepened. In some ways she supposed it had always been there, but she hadn't noticed it in her single-minded climb to the top.

Now that she was almost there, so close she could see her name on a corner office overlooking the famed Harbour Bridge and the soaring white waves of the Opera House, she felt unsettled. Nerves, she supposed. But also the acknowledgement that maybe she didn't have the killer instinct that was required in the upper echelons of big business. Miller cared too much about business practice, and sometimes that didn't play out very well.

'Now, if you'll both excuse me, I have guests waiting to play croquet on the south lawn.'

You could have heard a snail move as TJ pushed back his chair and ambled over to the door. 'By the way, Miller.' He stopped and held her unwavering gaze. 'Tell Maverick to quit stalling on taking the Real Sport sponsorship deal, would you? My people don't seem to be able to pin him down but I'm sure you can.'

And there it was. The real reason Winston International were *supposedly* being given a second chance.

Miller heard the door snick quietly closed but hadn't realised she was staring at it until Dexter muttered a four-letter word under his breath.

Miller swung her stunned gaze towards him.

'You didn't know?' He raised a condescending eyebrow.

Miller felt her face heat up, not wanting to add to her cache of lies. 'No,' she admitted reluctantly. She'd had no idea one of TJ's subsidiary companies was professionally courting Valentino. Why would she?

Dexter swore again. 'Some relationship you've got there. Does lover boy have any idea he's put a multi-million-dollar contract in jeopardy?'

'Valentino didn't do that.' Although she was silently spitting chips that he hadn't had the decency to inform her of TJ's overtures so she could have been more prepared. 'TJ did.'

'TJ's just doing business.'

'Unethically.'

'Stop being so precious, Miller. Business is business. Getting this account will boost Oracle's reputation—not to mention yours and mine.'

Miller's stomach felt as if it had a rock in it and she methodically stuffed her notes back into her satchel.

'So, do you think you'll be able to convince Ventura to do it?'

Miller strove for calm. 'I wouldn't even try.'

'Why not?'

'Because courting favours is not the way I do business.'

'TJ Lyons's is the biggest account in the country and you want it as much as I do. Maybe more. Why wouldn't you use your influence? It's not like it's any skin off Ventura's nose. In fact, I'm quite sure TJ is offering to pay him a pretty penny for the use of his pretty face.'

Miller tried not to let her distaste show. This was a side of Dexter she hadn't experienced before.

'Maybe you could give him a little more of what you gave him on the beach this morning. To sweeten the deal,' he said snidely.

Miller felt her whole body go rigid and knew she wouldn't be able to hide her reaction from him this time.

'You know, Miller,' he continued softly, 'I expected more from you than to see you romping on the beach with your lover in full view of the house.'

Ignoring Dexter, she slammed the lid of her laptop closed and fervently hoped she hadn't broken it.

She didn't have to explain herself to Dexter, but she knew if he repeated any of this back at the office it would jeopardise her promotion. It was hard enough being taken seriously at this level, despite the pains she took to always to appear confident and professional.

Dexter tapped his pen on TJ's antique desk. 'It won't last, you know. You and Tino.'

'Whether it does or not is none of your concern,' Miller

fumed, barely keeping a lid on her anger. 'And while we may have known each other at university, that does not give you the right to comment on my personal life. I'm here to do a job. That's all you need to think about.'

Dexter looked disgusted. 'Then do your job and remember that this isn't a school camp. And another thing.' He put his hand on her arm as she turned to leave. 'If we lose this campaign because of your lover, it will be *your* reputation that suffers, not mine.'

Glaring at him, Miller shook her head. 'You know, Dexter, earlier this week I could have sworn we were working on the same team. My mistake,' she finished coolly.

She heard something skitter across TJ's desk as she let herself out of the study—presumably the pen he'd been madly tapping the whole time.

'Miller! Dammit, we have to talk!'

Miller didn't stop. She had no idea what had gotten into Dexter, but she needed time and space to work out what to do next.

Tino was sitting on the bed when the door opened. Miller stood in the doorway like Medusa on a mission. He was on the phone to his sister Katrina, who was doing her best not to talk about Sunday's race and thereby placing it front and centre in both their minds.

Miller stepped into the room, her eyes sparking fire and brimstone in his direction.

Man, she was something else when she was riled—passionately alive—just like on the beach earlier. Not that he was thinking about that. He'd been honest when he'd told her it wasn't part of his plan, but watching her come apart underneath him had been possibly the most sensually arousing experience of his life, and as such it was damned hard to put out of his mind.

'Kat, sweetheart, I'll ring you back.' Glad of the excuse to end the conversation early, he dumped his mobile on the quilt cover beside him, reminding himself that he was supposed to be keeping his distance from Miller. 'Bad day at the office, Sunshine?'

She stalked across the room and dumped her computer bag and satchel on the small desk against the wall. Then she turned on him, hands on hips, her large aquamarine eyes shooting sparks.

Tino lounged back against the bank of pillows behind him. 'Are you going to tell me what's eating at you? Or is this one of those times when a woman tries to make a man's life truly miserable by making him play Twenty Questions?'

Her gaze narrowed. 'You've got that wrong. Women do not make men's lives miserable. People do that to each other.'

He stared at her and could see she was mentally wishing her words back. He wondered who had hurt her. It was obvious she didn't like talking about herself. Something they both shared, and that protective instinct she seemed to engender in him tightened his gut.

She drew in a breath as if preparing to go into battle, but her words were resigned when she spoke. 'It would have been nice if you'd told me that TJ was trying to recruit you to represent his Real Sport stores.'

'Ah.' *That* was where he knew TJ Lyons. TJ's people had been hassling his publicist to get him to become Real Sport's public representative for about six months now.

'First—' Miller's voice brought his eyes back to her '—you don't tell me that you're the legendary lothario Valentino Ventura and *nearly* make a fool of me. Now you neglect to tell me that my client wants your face and body for his online sports brand and *succeed* in making a fool of me.'

'Miller—'

'Don't Miller me.' She stalked towards him and stopped at the foot of the bed. 'You've been having fun with me right from the start of this silly charade and I've had enough. I am not here as your resident plaything and nor am I here to alleviate your boredom.'

Irritation blossomed inside him. 'I never said you were. And

might I remind you that this is *your* silly charade and I'm actually trying to help you.'

'Some help when TJ all but told me the only way we would
win his business is if you "quit stalling" and give him what
he wants.'

Tino rubbed his jaw. 'Sneaky bastard.'

His response seemed to knock the wind from her sails because her shoulders slumped a little and her hands dropped
from her hips.

'Quite.'

'I'm sorry, Miller. I didn't deliberately withhold that information from you. I get over a hundred requests of a similar
nature every week and my publicist handles that side of my
business. Yesterday, when I met TJ, I was aware that I knew
him from somewhere but assumed it was a race meet since he
was such a fan.'

She swore lightly and retreated to sit on the velour window
seat, and Tino found himself fascinated by the play of light on
her thick, glossy hair.

'What did you say to him?' he prompted when she remained
silent.

She scowled and he noticed that her face was slightly paler
than usual. 'Nothing yet. It was his parting volley.'

'A strategic tactic.'

She looked surprised that he would know such a thing, and
he didn't like the fact that she still thought he had the IQ of an
insect. 'You can stop looking at me as if you're surprised I can
string a sentence together.'

'I don't think that.' She paused at his disbelieving look and
had the grace to blush. 'Any more.'

He grinned at her honesty.

'Anyway.' She sighed. 'I'm not going to give him the satisfaction of acknowledging it.'

'Why not?'

'Because his weapon of choice is to ask his current consultants to re-pitch for the job, but if they had any good ideas they would have already given them to him.'

'They might have something new up their sleeve.'

'Nothing as good as mine.'

Tino chuckled. He enjoyed her superior confidence and kick-ass attitude. It reminded him of himself when a rookie tried to come up against him on the circuit.

He noticed her eyes were focused on his mouth, and when she raised them to his a spark of red-hot awareness flashed between them.

Clearly not wanting to acknowledge it any more than he did, she turned to face the window.

Silence filled the room so loudly he could hear the gentle ticking of the marble clock on the desk two feet away.

'Dexter saw us on the beach this morning.'

Her voice was soft, but he heard the disappointment edging her words.

Tino rolled his stiff neck on his shoulders and swore under his breath. That man was dogging his every step and he was getting beyond irritated with him.

'Are you telling me or the seagulls?' he asked pleasantly.

Miller swivelled her head around, a frown marring her alabaster forehead. 'I'm not in the mood for your ill-timed humour, Valentino.'

'What about my well-timed humour?'

She shook her head but a smile snuck across her face. 'How is it you can make me smile even when this is deadly serious?'

'Deadly?'

She sighed. 'Maybe I'm exaggerating slightly.'

Tino sat forward and regarded her silently for a moment. 'Relax. At least he no longer thinks we're faking it.'

Her smile disappeared. 'He's right about the fact that I should behave in a more professional manner with you.'

Tino snorted. 'Let me guess. He told you no touching?'

'He told me to keep my private life private—and he's right.'

'Of course he did,' Tino drawled, half admiring the man's

nous. He wanted Miller for himself, and he was trying to drive a wedge between them to get her.

Not that he could blame him. He'd realised this morning on the beach that Miller was one of those women who had no idea of her true appeal to men and, given similar circumstance, he might have done the same as Caruthers. Then again, he had yet to want a woman enough to actually fight for her.

'What does that mean?' Miller frowned.

'It means he wants you for himself.'

'No, he doesn't.'

She turned her face away, but he'd already seen her eyes cloud over.

'I can't work out if you're actually naive when it comes to men, or hiding your head in the sand.'

Her eyes flashed a warning. 'I do not hide my head in the sand.'

'Hit a nerve, have I?'

'If you're trying to be annoying you're succeeding beyond your wildest dreams,' she retorted pithily.

'If you're trying to avoid facing your colleague's attraction to you then so are you.'

She sighed heavily and turned away. 'I'm not naive. I just…' She stopped, looked uncertain. 'Can we talk about something else? Or, better still, not talk at all?'

Tino could sense the deep emotions rolling around inside her. He knew she would hate him to know the turmoil she was obviously experiencing. He didn't think he'd met a more self-contained woman, and it wasn't his experience that women kept such a tight lid on their emotions.

His Italian mother was a classic case in point—as were most of the females he'd dated, who had wanted more from him than he had ever been prepared to give. The fact that Miller so steadfastly *didn't* want anything from him made him feel ridiculously annoyed.

'This weekend really isn't going as you planned, is it, Miller?'

She had tucked her legs up under her chin as she gazed out of the window and now she glanced back at him as if surprised he was still in the room. Another blow to his over-inflated ego, he thought bemusedly.

'You think?'

Her eyes snagged on his and for a moment he was caught by how vulnerable she looked.

'You clearly dislike TJ's business methods so why do you want to work on his account so badly?'

'Partners are not made of people who say no to clients, no matter how distasteful they are.'

It took him a minute to decipher her meaning. 'Ah. You've got a promotion riding on this.'

'Something wrong with that?' Her voice was sharp and he realised she'd taken his words as an insult. He wondered what was behind her strong reaction.

'Only if you think so.'

'I deserve this. I've sweated blood for this company. I...' She released a long breath. 'It's not something you would understand.'

'Try me.'

He thought she would reject his offer, but she heaved a resigned sigh.

'It's not rocket science, Valentino. I grew up poor with a father who thought the grass was always greener on the other side and a mother who was uneducated. My mother had to work two jobs to put me through a private school so that I would have opportunities she never had. My making partner would mean everything to her.'

'What does it mean to *you*?'

He saw her throat move as she swallowed. 'The same.'

'So you dreamt of being a corporate dynamo when you were a little girl?'

He'd meant to sound light, friendly, but Miller didn't take it that way.

'We can't all have exciting careers like yours.'

Her sheer defensiveness made him realise she was hiding something from him. 'Interesting response.'

'I expect it was easy for you,' Miller prevaricated. 'Your father raced.'

'You think because my father was a racing champion my career choice was easy?'

'I don't know. Was it?'

'My father died on the track when I was fifteen. My mother still buys me medical textbooks for Christmas in the hope I'll change careers.'

She laughed, as he'd wanted her to do, but the pain of his father's death startled him with its intensity. It was as if the crash had just happened—as if a sticking plaster had just been peeled off a festering wound.

Ruthlessly shutting down his emotions he fell back on his raconteur style. 'Astronaut.'

'What?'

'Your childhood dream.'

'No.' She shook her head at his cajoling tone.

'Lap dancer?'

'Very funny.'

Some of the tension left her shoulders, but Tino still felt claustrophobic.

Jumping to his feet, he fetched a baseball cap from his travel bag. 'Let's go.'

'Where?'

'I don't know. A drive.' It was something that always calmed him.

She looked dubious. 'You go. I have work to do.'

'And all work and no play makes Miller a dull girl. Come on. It will refresh you.'

Miller sighed. 'You're like a steamroller when you want something. You know that?'

CHAPTER EIGHT

'SORRY, I only have one baseball cap,' Valentino said, holding the car door open for her.

'That's okay. My fame hasn't reached small seaside towns yet.'

He grinned at her lame joke and for some reason she felt better. Though she wasn't really interested in feeling better. What she wanted was TJ's signature on the bottom line of a contract and the weekend to be over. And not necessarily in that order.

She sighed, turning her mind away from work for once. 'Why do celebrities wear baseball caps to hide their identity?'

'Because Lyons bought all the Akubras?'

Miller burst out laughing, suddenly enjoying the fact that he was relaxed and casual. So much simpler than being uptight and serious. So much freer… Maybe there was something to recommend the casual approach sometimes.

She noticed people looking at the silver bullet as they drove down through the main part of the town. 'Bet you wish you'd brought my car now.'

He grinned. 'We'll park around a corner.'

'What if someone steals it?'

'Dante has insurance.'

'And Dante is…?'

'My elder brother.'

'What are your sisters' names?'

She sensed more than saw his pause. 'Katrina and Deanna.'

She was about to ask him another question when he pulled

the car into an empty car space and jumped out. Was that another topic of conversation that was out of bounds?

She wondered why he didn't like talking about his family and then decided to let it go. She had to remember that he wasn't with her because he wanted to be, and talking about their personal histories wasn't part of that. Nor was what had happened on the beach, but she didn't regret it. The way he had touched her had been indescribably good.

'Where are we going?' Better not to think about something she'd rather not dwell on.

'Window shopping.'

Miller raised an eyebrow. 'You like window shopping?'

'I'm looking for something.'

Narrow Victorian-era seaside shops overlaid with modern updates and sweetly dressed cafés advertising Devonshire teas lined the quaint street.

'Want to tell me what it is?'

'Nope. I'll know it when I see it.'

Despite the fact that her curiosity was well and truly piqued Miller decided to stem her need to know and show Valentino how well she could go with the flow when she chose to. Even if it killed her!

Glancing into tourist inspired shops displaying far too many knick-knacks no one could possibly want, she nearly walked into a small child when Valentino stopped outside an ice cream shop.

She looked at him and he raised a questioning eyebrow.

Ice cream? Really?

It was just what she needed and an ear-to-ear grin split her face.

She glanced at him, so big and handsome, standing in the queue, and her chest felt tight when he remembered her favourite flavour.

Deciding that there was absolutely nothing behind the gesture, but warmed by it nonetheless, she graciously accepted the cone and together they wandered into a small park.

By tacit agreement they veered towards a weathered picnic table and perched on it when Miller discovered the bench seat was covered in bird poop.

Valentino leant back on one hand, his T-shirt riding high enough to reveal the top button of his low-slung jeans, hinting at the line of hair bisecting his toned abs.

Miller swallowed and glanced around the pretty park, pretending rapt attention on the two toddlers shouting instructions at each other on the nearby play equipment. She really didn't want him to know that just the sight of him licking his ice cream and sprawled back like that was enough for her to instantly recall their tryst on the beach that morning in minute detail.

'Where did you grow up?'

His unexpected question brought her eyes reluctantly back to him, but she was glad of the innocuous topic to focus her attention away from the physical perfection of his body.

'Mostly in Queensland, but after my parents divorced my mother moved to Melbourne.'

He studied her and she forced herself not to squirm under his regard. 'How old were you when they divorced?'

'Ten.'

'And do you like Melbourne?'

'That's difficult to say. Whenever I came home from boarding school it seemed like my mother had moved to another suburb.'

'Why did she move so often?'

'We rented, and there's not much security in rentals. Which I found hard because I've always been the type of person who needs…' She struggled for a word that didn't make her seem boring compared to him.

'Certainty?'

'Yes.' Her lips lifted into a self-deprecating smile.

'Have you ever travelled?'

'No. I was always set on working and buying my own place. Even from a young age I knew what I wanted to achieve and set out to do it. That probably makes me boring in your eyes.'

Valentino shook his head. 'Determined. I know what that's like.'

Miller concentrated on finishing the delicious ice cream, feeling the tension ease out of her body. 'I guess you do.'

'So what was your childhood dream?'

Miller flashed him an exasperated look. So much for that fleeting moment of relaxation! 'I can see why you're going for your eighth world title,' she said sourly.

A wolfish grin split his face. 'I have been told I can be somewhat tenacious at times.'

'I think that's a polite way of saying you're pigheaded.'

He laughed and she liked the sound. Liked that he didn't take himself too seriously.

'Is it really that embarrassing?'

'No...' She scratched her head and then realised he had accurately read her body language and sighed, knowing his curiosity was well and truly piqued. And really it wasn't a huge secret, or anything to be ashamed of. 'When I was about eleven I dreamt of living on a huge country property. I always saw myself in a small circular room, overlooking a paddock full of horses and—'

'Why circular?'

'I don't know. Maybe because I loved *The Hobbit*...'

'Fair enough. Go on.'

'It's not very exciting,' she warned.

'Go on.'

'And in this dream I would divide my time between illustrating children's books and taking the horses out into the hills whenever I wanted.' She stopped, feeling silly giving voice to something she hadn't thought of in years. Of course she wouldn't tell him her ultimate dream. No one knew about that.

'Nice dream.'

She heard the smile in his voice and glanced at him reclining on the weather-beaten table, the afternoon sun gilding his features into a perfect mask of casual decadence.

Her heart caught and she cleared her throat, slightly embarrassed to have shared so much of herself. 'Yes, well, as my mother pointed out, it's almost every young girl's fantasy to own horses, and she wasn't paying for me to attend the best boarding school in the country to become an out-of-work artist.'

Miller heard the note of bitterness in her voice and wondered if Valentino did as well. It made her feel ashamed. Her mother had only ever wanted the best for her.

'So you stopped dreaming and took up a serious vocation?' he guessed accurately.

Regretting whatever tangent had got them onto this topic, Miller shifted and pulled her legs up to her chest. 'Dreams aren't real. That's why they're called dreams.'

'Following them gives you a purpose.'

'Putting food on the table gives you a purpose—as my mother found out to her detriment. She had me young and didn't complete her education. It made her vulnerable.'

He leant forward, his hands dangling over the front of his knees. 'And I can see why she wouldn't want that for her daughter. But I doubt she'd want you to give up on your dreams altogether. If we don't follow our dreams, what's the point of living?'

His voice was gentle and it annoyed her. Was he being condescending?

'You don't know my mum. She has a special bottle of champagne in the fridge for when I make partner.' And there was no way Miller could imagine disappointing her when she had sacrificed so much for her.

'But it's still *her* dream for you, not yours.'

She flashed him a sharp look but nevertheless felt compelled to answer. To explain herself. 'My mother has valid points.'

'I don't doubt she means well, Miller, but are her points really valid?'

His gentle query made her edgy, because it was the same one that had been taking up her head space since TJ had started subtly hitting on her.

Feeling slightly desperate, she jumped off the table and faced

him. 'It would have been selfish of me to pursue art when my
mother gave up so much for me.' She glanced in the direction
of the sun and wondered about the time. 'We should probably
get back.'

He cocked his head to the side and made no attempt to move.
'Maybe she shouldn't have pushed you so hard in the direction
she saw as right. And what about your father? Didn't he help
with the bills?'

She shook her head. 'I think he tried to help. For a while.
But he lived on a commune, which meant that he didn't have
the means to contribute to the private school my mother chose.'

'Lived?'

'He died when I was twenty.'

'I'm sorry.'

'Don't be. We weren't very close and…he died happy. Which
I'm glad of now. But—' She stopped and let out a long breath. 'I
don't know why I'm telling you my life story.' She *never* talked
about herself like this.

'Because I asked. Why weren't you close to your dad?'

Miller snagged her hair behind her ears, memories of her
father—fit and happy before the divorce—filling her mind.
'For years I was angry at him because I blamed him for my
world falling apart. He just seemed to give up. He didn't once
try to see me.' She swallowed past the lump in her throat. 'He
later told me it was too painful.' And she suspected he hadn't
been able to afford to visit her and had been too proud to lose
face. 'But life is never that simple, and even though it took me
a while I see now that it wasn't all his fault.'

She'd learned that one person always loved more in a relationship than the other; needed more than the other.

In this case it had been her father. Her mother's post-break-
up comments had led Miller to believe that her mother had
married her father mainly for a sense of security. Constantly
disappointed when he could never hold down a job for very long.

Her parents had never been the greatest role models, and

Miller wasn't sure what she thought about love other than it seemed like a lot of trouble for very little return.

Her eyes sought out the toddlers, but they had gone. Instead, she watched a young couple strolling hand in hand with their large dog. But she wasn't thinking about them. She was thinking about the man beside her. Was he living his dreams? And what did *he* think about love? Did he hope to find someone special one day?

Miller felt the blood thicken in her veins at the thought. No doubt the woman he chose would be beautiful beyond comprehension and have the same relaxed attitude to life that he did. She could almost see them now—lazing on a yacht in the Mediterranean, gazing adoringly at each other, a half-naked Valentino leaning across her to seal his lips to—

Miller sucked in air and hoped her face hadn't transmitted anything of what she'd just been thinking.

'What about you?' she asked brightly, desperate to get the conversation onto any other topic but herself.

CHAPTER NINE

MILLER smiled and gazed around TJ's large living room. It held twice as many guests as it was intended to house, and absently she thought she felt as if she had just stepped into the pages of *The Great Gatsby*.

TJ's fiftieth birthday celebrations were in full swing and seemingly a roaring success: elegant women and debonair men were conversing and laughing with unbridled joy as if their lives were truly as beautiful as the party they were now attending. Some were already dancing to TJ's eighties-inspired music, while others had taken their beverages outside and were soaking up the balmy night, absently batting at the annoying insects that darted around as if they were trying to zap someone.

It was a crowd Valentino fitted right in with—especially dressed as he was now, in an ice-blue shirt that hugged his wide shoulders and showcased his amazing eyes, and tailored pants that hung perfectly from his lean hips.

'You look like you're at a funeral,' the man of the moment murmured wryly, his breath warm against her temple.

Miller sniffed in acknowledgement of his comment. She *felt* as if she was at a funeral. Ever since they'd returned from the park she had felt edgy and stressed at her sudden attack of blabbermouth. Trying to turn the tables on him had been a dismal failure. As soon as she'd asked about him he'd sprung up from the table as if an ant had crawled into his jeans.

'I'm boring,' he'd said, which loosely translated to *conversation closed*.

It had almost been a race to see who made it back to the car first. But he must have sensed her childish hurt at his rebuff because he'd glanced at her when they were in the car.

'Everything you could possibly want to know about me is on the internet.'

She'd scoffed. 'The internet tells me superficial stuff, like how many races you've won and how many hearts you've broken.'

He'd seemed to get annoyed at that. 'As I told Caruthers, if I had slept with as many women as the media proclaim I'd have hardly had enough time to enter a race let alone win one. In fact, I rarely take up with a woman during racing season, and if I do it's very short lived.'

Take up? Could he have used a more dissociative term?

'Why? Because you bore easily?'

'There is that. But, no, I usually don't allow a woman to hang around long enough to bore me. Basically women want more attention than I'm prepared to give them, so if I indulge it's usually only for a night or two.'

'That's pretty shallow.'

He'd shrugged. 'Not if the woman is after the same thing.'

'And how many are?'

'Not enough, it's true. Most want more—hence my moratorium on limiting those intimacies during the season.'

'To make sure you don't have to contend with any broken hearts that might wreck your concentration?' she'd said churlishly.

He'd smiled as if he hadn't heard her censure. 'Not much can wreck my concentration, Sunshine, but a whiny woman can certainly do damage to a man's eardrums.'

'No more than your whiny cars,' she'd shot back pithily. But then she'd grown curious. 'Don't you ever want more?'

'Racing gives me everything I need,' he'd said.

His unwavering confidence had pushed her to probe further. 'So have you ever been in love?'

'Sure.' He'd glanced over at her and Miller remembered holding her breath. 'My first love was a bright red 1975 Maserati Bora.'

'Be serious,' she'd said, and that had made his eyes become hooded, his expression blank.

'The love you're talking about isn't on my radar, Miller.'

'Ever?'

'Let's just say I'll never marry while I'm racing, and I've yet to meet a woman who excites me enough to make me give it up.' His flat tone had turned grim. 'Love is painful. When you lose someone…' He'd stopped, collected himself. 'I won't do that to another person.'

Another person or himself? Miller wondered now, sensing that part of his emotional aloofness was just a way of protecting himself from pain. His words hovered heavily in her mind, almost like a warning.

Determined the best thing she could do for herself was to forget the whole afternoon, Miller sipped at TJ's finest vintage champagne and focused on the tiny bubbles of heaven that spilled across her tongue.

'What did you say?' Valentino's low voice caused the champagne bubbles to disperse to other parts of her body and she opened her eyes to find him staring at her mouth.

'I didn't say anything.'

'You…' His gaze lifted to her eyes. 'You murmured something.'

Miller's mouth went dry and she was more determined than ever to crush the physical effect he had on her. 'Just remember that tonight I need you to be totally circumspect and professional. Discreet.'

What she was really saying was that she didn't want him to touch her, and he knew it.

'Like the other patsies you date?'

'I do not date patsies,' she said, wondering how it was that he managed to push all her buttons so easily.

'Sure you do. You date men who are learned, PC at all times, and…*controllable*.'

His assessment annoyed her all the more because she knew if she *did* date she'd look for someone just like that—except for the controllable bit. You didn't have to control *nice* men.

'While *you* hunt out blondes with big breasts and an IQ that wouldn't challenge a glowworm,' she replied sweetly.

He paused, and Miller was just congratulating herself on getting the last word in when he said, 'She doesn't have to be blonde.'

His slow smile was a signal for her to back off before she got sucked under again.

'And anything more—'

'Don't say it,' she admonished peevishly. 'I'll only be disappointed.'

His soft laugh confirmed that he knew he had the upper hand, and Miller determinedly faced the crowded room, searching for any distraction. She heard Valentino let out a long, slow breath and wondered if he was annoyed with her.

'How about we call a truce, Miller?'

'A truce?'

'Yeah. And I don't mean the kind of pact the settlers made with the aborigines before marching them off the edge of a cliff. I mean a proper one. Friends?'

Friends? He wanted to be friends and she couldn't stop thinking about sex. Great.

She took another fortifying gulp of champagne and could have been drinking his motor oil for all the pleasure it now gave her. 'Sure.'

'Good.'

God, this was awful, and he hadn't called her *Sunshine* in hours. What was *wrong* with her?

Miller was saved from the tumultuous nature of her thoughts when TJ, his barrel chest bedecked in a white tuxedo jacket, approached.

'Miller. You look lovely tonight.'

Miller's smile was tight. She didn't look lovely at all. She looked boring in her long sleeved black blouse and matching suit pants. She hadn't brought a single provocative item of clothing this weekend because she had no wish to encourage TJ's attention. And possibly because she didn't actually own anything remotely provocative. It had been a long time since she had spent money on clothing for anything other than work or exercise.

'Thank you.' She responded to the comment as she was expected to and, with civilities attended to, TJ turned to Valentino—the latest object of his fickle affections.

'Maverick. I have someone who's been dying to meet you.'

Miller tried to smile as the famous supermodel Janelle, clothed in a clinging nude-coloured chiffon creation, stepped out from behind TJ and extended her elegant hand.

A sort of mini-dramatic entrance, Miller thought sourly. Which was a little unfair, because by all accounts the model was not only considered the most beautiful woman on the planet, but the nicest as well. And she looked sweetly nervous as Valentino's large hand engulfed hers.

'Mr Ventura...'

Janelle's awed exhalation promised sexual antics in the bedroom Miller had only ever fantasised about—and with the man now staring at the supermodel no less.

'This is Janelle,' TJ continued. 'Latest sensation to hit the New York runways. But I don't have to tell *you* that. You probably have her photo up on your garage wall.' He guffawed at his own tasteless humour and then seemed to remember his audience. 'No disrespect, Miller.'

'None taken,' Miller lied smoothly. Because what she really wanted to say would jeopardise everything she had worked so hard for.

She felt Valentino tense beside her and wondered if he wasn't experiencing some sort of extreme physical reaction to the beautiful blonde. Every other man in the room seemed to be.

'Janelle.' Valentino smiled and slowly released her hand. *God, they looked perfect together*. Her blonde to his dark. Feeling like a poor cousin next to the stunning model Miller excused herself and left the men to ogle Janelle alone. No need to be a glutton for punishment.

She'd veered off from her decoy destination of the bathroom and made it to the glass bi-fold doors leading outside when Dexter appeared at her side.

'You know, Dexter, I don't know if I can go another round with you,' Miller said with bald honesty.

It was another balmy, star-filled night and she just wanted fresh air and peace.

He had the grace to look uncomfortable. 'I read some of the ideas you put down this afternoon. They're good.'

She raised an eyebrow. 'The only thing bothering me with that comment is that you seem to have expected something less.'

He tugged at the collar on his shirt. 'Can we talk?'

Resignation settled like a brick in her stomach and she extended her hand towards the deck. Might as well fulfil the fresh air component of her plan at least.

'By all means.'

Dexter walked ahead of her, but when he made to continue down the steps towards the more secluded Japanese garden Miller stayed him. 'Here's fine.'

She had no wish to recall the heady kiss she had shared with Valentino the night before any more than she already had. Not with Dexter around anyway.

Winding around various partygoers, Miller found a quiet part of the deck and turned to face him. 'What did you want to say?'

'Firstly, I wanted to apologise for being such an a-hole in the meeting earlier today. My intention was only to stop you from getting hurt.'

Miller felt a sense of unease prickle the skin along her cheekbones. 'I've noticed that you haven't seemed yourself lately,' she ventured. 'Is something going on with Carly again?'

'No, no. That's well and truly over.' He gripped the wooden railing and seemed absorbed by the whiteness of his knuckles.

'I'm sorry to hear that.' Even though she had never met Dexter's wife, Miller hated to hear of the end of any marriage.

Dexter jerked back and flexed his hands before catching her eye. 'Come on, Miller. Surely you know what this is about?'

Miller stared at him. Shook her head. 'No.' But she did know, didn't she? Ruby and Valentino had already warned her...

'Okay, if you want me to spell it out I will.' He seemed slightly nervous. 'Us.'

'Us?' Miller knew her voice had become shrill with alarm.

He nodded, clearly warming to his subject. 'Or more specifically the chemistry between us.'

'Chemistry?'

'I want you, Miller. There's been something between us since the moment we met.'

He held his hand up and silenced her attempt to save them both any further embarrassment.

'I know you don't want to acknowledge it because we work together, but you know I've felt like this since university. My coming to work for Oracle six months ago has just made those feelings deepen. And, yes, I know what you're going to say.' He stopped her again. 'I'm your superior and office affairs don't work. But I know of plenty that have and I'm willing to risk it.'

Miller was speechless, and barely noticed when he took her hand in his. 'I've been behaving like an idiot this weekend because I haven't wanted to accept that you're really dating that pretty boy inside. Okay, I can see the appeal. But we both know it won't last, and I'm not prepared to hold my breath and wait around for it to fizzle out.'

'That's too bad, Caruthers. I would have enjoyed seeing you atrophy.'

Miller jumped at the sound of Valentino's deep, modulated voice and so did Dexter. She glanced up and was once again taken aback by the cold glint in his eyes—a stormy-grey under the soft external lights.

He looked relaxed as he regarded Dexter: *preternaturally* relaxed. In this mode she could easily see why he was going for his eighth world championship. The shock was in the fact that other drivers had dared go up against him in the first place.

Miller saw Dexter's chest puff out in a classic testosterone-fuelled gesture and was horrified that he might cause a scene. Because right now Valentino looked as if he wanted to chew Dexter up and spit him out sideways.

'You don't have ownership rights here, Ventura.'

Ownership rights? Miller's gaze swung back to Dexter. What was she? A car?

'Let her go,' Valentino ordered quietly, his eyes never straying from Dexter's.

Miller realised Dexter was still holding her hand and tugged it free, wondering why it was that only French champagne and Valentino's touch seemed to make her insides fizz with excitement.

'Miller is her own boss,' Dexter opined.

Now, *that* was more like it.

'Miller is mine.' Valentino's soft growl was full of menace.

The immediate warmth that stole through her system at his possessive words threw Miller off-balance. How many times had she imagined her father riding in on a white charger and restoring her torn world to rights again? To have Valentino stand up for her was…disconcerting. Unnerving. *Exhilarating.*

Dexter was the first to break eye contact in the stag competition going on, and Miller couldn't blame him. Even though he was cleanly shaven, Valentino, at least in this mood, was not a man you would cross. He was like a lethal warrior of old who would not only win, but would take no prisoners either.

'Dance.'

Valentino held out his hand for her and she felt herself bristle when he didn't even glance her way. Then his steely eyes cut to hers and she forgot about being grouchy.

'Please.'

Her heart beat as fast as his silver sports car had eaten up the bitumen on their trip down as he led her onto the parquet dance floor.

'What's with the caveman antics?' she asked softly.

Valentino stared at her, his feet unmoving, his eyes intense, seemingly transfixed by hers. 'Playing the part of the jealous boyfriend. What else?'

Playing the part of the jealous boyfriend...

It took a moment for his words to register fully, and when they did Miller felt sick. *Playing the part. Pretending. Fake.*

The skin on her face felt as if it had been whipped, and she briefly closed her eyes against his handsome face.

If she thought she'd been embarrassed spilling all her secrets to him earlier, she now felt one hundred times worse.

Miller tried to understand why she felt so miserable. So he had stood up for her and she'd felt warmed by it? So he had been hurt by the loss of his father, as she had? So he had remembered her favourite ice cream flavour.

He was a nice person. That was all that amounted to. Nicer than she'd first thought. But at the end of the day he was still no one to her. A virtual stranger.

A virtual stranger who had brought her to orgasm within minutes of touching her. And if only she could stop thinking about *that*!

Steeling herself against emotions she couldn't immediately label, and determined he wouldn't know how she had momentarily forgotten this whole thing was fake, Miller breathed deeply and slowly.

'Just be thankful this thing isn't real between us,' he growled menacingly. 'I would have decked him if it was.'

For a horrifying second Miller wondered if he'd read her thoughts. 'For challenging you?'

'For staring at your breasts as if he could already imagine touching them. He hasn't, has he?'

Miller's eyebrows shot up. 'Of course not.'

He scowled. 'You don't want him to, do you?'

'No!'

Wow! He almost had her convinced he was seriously miffed about Dexter's interest.

'Good. And don't ever walk off on me in the middle of a conversation again.'

Miller frowned. 'If you're referring to TJ and Janelle...?' She rolled her eyes. 'I was hardly required.'

'When it comes to relationships you have no idea what's required.'

His words stung because they were true. Relationships scared her. But she was too tired to argue any more, so she shut up and let him guide her around the floor, focusing all her attention on the music and not on the way it felt to be held within the tight circle of his powerful arms. She reminded herself that she was a professional woman with goals and dreams that did not include this man in any shape or form. Reminded herself that her orgasm on the beach was a one-off and not to be repeated.

'What are you thinking?' His deep voice made her stumble and his hold tightened momentarily.

Miller's eyes met his. She was thinking that despite everything she knew about herself, about life, she still wanted to have sex with him with a bone-deep need that defied explanation.

'Miller?'

His husky command made her peek up at him from under her fringe. This wasn't her. She didn't *peek*. She looked. She organised. She...she was melting as her eyes drifted over his handsome face and her body brushed his.

Her heart beat much faster than it needed to and she wondered what type of man he really was. Why he lived the life he did. Why he had chosen to work in a profession that had taken his father's life—something she was sure affected him more deeply than he let on.

'How do you do what you do?' she asked, latching onto her curiosity about his racing life to distract herself from the fact that she seriously wanted to throw caution to the winds and have sex with him. Just once. To see what it would be like to do it with a man who just had to touch her to make her burn hotter than the sun.

* * *

Tino's hand tightened around Miller's as they continued to sway to the music. He had no idea what she was on about. His one-track mind was heavily mired in defending himself against the onslaught of her slender curves, her light, mouth-watering scent.

After their talk in the park earlier, when he'd felt a strong desire to comfort her and slay all her demons, his self-preservation instincts had kicked in and warned him that this time he really needed to keep his distance.

Of course dancing with her wasn't exactly conducive to that plan, but seeing Caruthers pawing her earlier had made him see red, and he knew he couldn't just drag her off to a secluded location feeling the way he did. Dancing with her was the safer of the two options.

'You're going to have to be a bit more specific than that,' he said, telling himself to ignore the way she seemed to fit so perfectly in his arms.

He was still a little shocked by the way he had nearly put his fist through Dexter's arrogant face. He had *forgotten* that this thing with Miller was fake. Of course that had more to do with male pride than the delicate, sensual woman in his arms right now.

Yeah, and pigs might fly. You want her and there's no shame in admitting it. Just don't do anything about it.

Just when he was about to end the exquisite torture of dancing with her, she answered his question.

'Race? Don't you ever get scared?'

Ah, she'd been asking him about his *job*.

Okay, that he could talk about on a superficial level. 'Motor racing is all about pushing yourself to the limit. There's no room for fear.'

Her body swayed against his in time to an eighties love song; the room too warm with the crush of similarly entwined bodies dancing together.

'But you push yourself *beyond* the limit, don't you? Isn't that why they call you an arrogant adrenalin junkie and a shock-jock? Maverick?'

'Don't believe everything you read about me, Miller. I'm happiest living on the edge, it's true. But I don't take stupid chances with my own life or anyone else's. Fear is an emotion. Controllable like any other. And while I'm not crazy, sometimes...' He paused, his mind automatically spinning back to the race that had taken the life of his good friend and caused him to question the sport he loved so much. 'Sometimes you have to squeeze the fear a little.'

And in this game you never look back, he silently added.

'Squeeze the fear?'

She said the words as if she were savouring a new taste on her tongue, and his body burned with a restless energy at the thought of tasting *her* again. But this time not just her mouth.

'You really love it don't you?' she said, a soft smile curving her lips.

Tino's mind jerked and went blank. Then he used his formidable mental control to switch off the erotic images turning his body hard. 'I get to experience life in its most heightened and intense form. Nothing else has ever come close.'

And probably right now he was too close to *her*—both mentally and physically. He couldn't remember ever having revealed so much about why he raced, and as for talking about his reasons for steering clear of relationships...

He frowned down at her. 'You're not going to repeat what I just said, are you?'

'You mean to a journalist?' Her tone was light, almost teasing.

'Yes.' His wasn't.

'Are your illustrious words worth very much?'

He scowled and she smiled.

'Relax.'

That captivating smile grew and he knew she was thinking of all the times he had told her to do the same thing.

'I don't need the money.'

Tino was jostled from behind by an exuberant dancer and his whole body came up flush against Miller's. Foreign emotions he couldn't name and a healthy dose of testosterone heightened as the arousal he'd been holding at bay flared instantly to life.

So much for that formidable mental control, Ventura.

He stopped dancing. 'I think it's time to call it a night.'

He noticed her face was flushed, and his arms tightened around her like a steel cage.

She stood still, looking up at him. 'I had no idea your job was so fascinating.'

His eyes became hooded and he saw his own desperate need reflected back at him from her over-bright eyes. Her lips parted softly in silent invitation and he had to fight the instinct to crush her mouth beneath his.

He studied her slender hands curled around his shoulders, her fingers elegant, the nails unvarnished. They suited her serious nature and reminded him that 'serious' females were best avoided at all costs.

'Valentino, are you okay?'

Her hands slid from his shoulders to rest lightly against his chest and he felt scalded.

Deliberately slowing his heart-rate, he evened out his breathing and stepped back from her. Every minute he spent in her presence eroded his self-control and he hated that. Without self-control he was nothing. He had no choice but to sever whatever bond had sprung up between them, because right now he sensed she was more dangerous to him than a hairpin turn at three hundred clicks.

He saw the moment comprehension dawned that he was rejecting what she was unconsciously offering and silently cursed as a moment of hurt flashed across her beautiful face.

It was as if he'd betrayed her. And maybe he had. The way he'd come on to her on the beach, then taken her for ice cream, grilled her about her life, his behaviour with her boss…

Feeling as if he owed her a massive apology, he didn't know where to start. Or if it would make the situation between them better or worse.

Then she took the decision out of his hands and closed down

her emotions as effectively as he had, pivoting on her sexy heels and walking away from him.

Immediately, an image of his father slotted into his brain, but rather than shake it off straight away, as he usually did, he let it settle there for a moment. The image was always the same. A smiling, larger-than-life hero in a white jumpsuit with a cerulean-blue helmet under his arm.

Miller's eyes.

His father's helmet.

His father's death hanging over him like a sword.

In this game, you never look back.

Tino felt his old rage at his father rear up and flattened it. This weekend was supposed to be light and easy. Relaxing. But Miller was drawing something out of him he had no wish to face, and it was messing with his head.

She was messing with his head.

He wasn't supposed to want her. At least not this much. And he sure as hell wasn't supposed to want to make her world a better place.

What a crapshoot.

CHAPTER TEN

STALKING into the breakfast room the next morning, Tino plastered what he hoped was an easy smile across his face.

Miller was there, as were TJ, Dexter and another female guest decked out in a Lycra leotard.

Tino hadn't returned to the bedroom he shared with Miller for a good two hours after she'd walked off the dance floor the night before, and when he had it had been to find her curled up in the middle of the huge bed.

He'd slept on the floor.

If you could call staring at the bedroom ceiling all night sleeping. Then he'd risen early and gone for a run, so he didn't know what mood Miller was in. By the look of the dark shadows beneath her eyes she hadn't slept much either.

'Maverick. You're up early.'

Valentino's gaze turned from Miller to TJ. He hated the familiarity with which TJ addressed him but it was one of those things that came with success. Men always thought he was their best friend and women always wanted to nail him. Well, except Miller, who might prefer to put an axe through his head after last night. He poured muesli from the selection of breakfast cereal arranged on the sideboard into a bowl and pulled out the dining chair beside the woman he was supposed to act as if he was in love with. He'd been chivalrous last night—truly, unselfishly chivalrous for the first time in his life—and he had no doubt she'd thank him for it later. Hopefully more than he was thanking himself right now.

'As are you.' He glanced at Miller and her grip tightened around the shiny fork she was using as a weapon against a grapefruit.

'Habit,' TJ said. 'No sleeping in when you're raised on a cattle station. So, are you up for a game of tennis later today?'

'Thank you.' Valentino accepted hot coffee from the maid who had just materialised at his side.

'As I explained before you insisted I have breakfast, TJ,' Miller interjected, 'I have to get back to the city by lunchtime.'

'What could be so important you have to rush back on a glorious day like today?'

Covering for her slight hesitation, Tino jumped in. 'Unfortunately I have to go over a new engine with my engineers today.'

Miller glanced up at him through the screen of her sooty lashes and he was disconcerted to find that he couldn't read her expression.

'And have you given any more thought to my proposal, Mav? To represent Real Sport?' TJ asked, confidence dripping from every word.

Not expecting such a direct question, Tino hesitated. He would have liked to tell TJ what he thought of his business tactics, but Miller stayed him with her hand on his.

'I've advised Valentino to set aside any final decisions about working on your campaign until after *our* business is concluded. I wouldn't want to muddy the waters by mixing the two—as I'm sure you can appreciate.'

The skin around TJ's eyes tightened briefly before the man recovered himself. He clearly hadn't been expecting Miller to turn the tables on him so neatly. And neither had Dexter, who started choking on his eggs.

Tino had actually been considering telling his publicist to accept the Real Sport deal in a bid to help Miller win the account, but perhaps he didn't need to. It really wouldn't affect him all that much, so long as TJ's company fitted the strict criteria he insisted on and was willing to pay one of his pet charity organisations an exorbitant sum of money for the privilege.

TJ scratched his ear in a dead giveaway of his mounting tension. 'Interesting decision. Not one I would have made.'

'Nevertheless, it's one *I've* made.'

Miller had her bushfire extinguishing voice in place and Tino felt his fists clench when he caught Dexter's murderous expression.

Easing his bulk back in his chair, his face flushed, TJ fixed narrowed eyes on Miller's boss. 'I thought *you* were supposed to be the senior consultant on this account, Caruthers?'

He didn't need to say anything else to indicate how he felt, and everyone in the room held their collective breaths.

A muscle in Dexter's jaw twitched, but Tino cut off any response he might have made with a single look. 'Miller's principles are admirable,' he said. He reached for an apple from the middle of the table. 'Qualities I would expect any company I endorse to emulate.'

For a moment no one seemed to know what to say.

'Then get that final proposal to me quick-smart, young lady,' TJ snapped. 'I want everything wrapped by race day.' He stared at Tino. 'Maybe we can even announce our collaboration at your mother's bash next Saturday night.'

Damn. If Lyons was going to his mother's party, he would expect to see Miller there.

Tino shook his head. 'I play a low-key role at that event. It's my mother's show.'

Miller stopped torturing her breakfast. 'I'll make sure I have the proposal to you in time for an early decision, TJ.' She dabbed at her lips with her napkin and stood up. 'Thank you for your hospitality and, again, happy birthday.' Then, acknowledging the other occupants in the room, she walked out like a queen.

Miller sat beside Valentino in the car as they headed back to Sydney, nursing a headache to end all others and a stomach that felt as if it was twisted up with her intestines.

She'd hardly slept the night before, completely mortified that Valentino had not only read how much she had wanted him on the dance floor, but that he had not wanted her in return. Her embarrassment from the whole trying day had been absolute.

It was a cliché that pride went before a fall, but right now Miller was grateful for the extra cushioning. In fact, she felt so terrible she almost felt sorry for the way Dexter must have felt when she had rejected him. One-way chemistry was not a pleasant thing to come face-to-face with for anyone.

'Are you okay?'

Valentino's quiet concern in the stuffy little car was the last thing she needed. 'No, not really.' She was too tired to pretend any more. 'Dexter is probably going to put me on performance management for overstepping hierarchical boundaries, TJ is livid, my promotion is most likely dead in the water, and I have the mother of all headaches.'

'If it's any consolation I thought you were magnificent this morning.'

This morning—but not last night... 'I was stupid.' This morning *and* last night.

'You'll win TJ's business and save the day. You'll be a hero.'

'Thanks for the pep talk.' She rubbed her forehead and grimaced as she thought of pulling her computer out of its bag. Still, it had to be done. She had 'squeezed the fear' and stood up to TJ this morning—which she didn't regret—but she didn't want to lose her job over it, and she knew she had major sucking up to do if she wanted to get her goals back on track.

'TJ and Dexter will expect to see you at my mother's charity event next weekend.'

Miller had heard of the Melbourne gala charity night, of course, but she'd had no idea it was Valentino's mother's event. 'I don't care.'

'If you need to attend I can arrange it.'

Miller glanced at him and winced as the sun reflected off the circular speakers on the dashboard. Was he kidding? She couldn't wait for *this* weekend to be over. The thought of seeing him again was just...horrifying. 'It'll be fine.'

He sped up and passed two cars at once. Miller tensed.

'Surely you're not still nervous about my driving?'

'This isn't a racetrack. It's a national highway.'

'With lots of room to pass. How are you going to explain your absence next weekend?'

'I'll have a headache.' Something she could easily envisage right now. Then she realised why she hadn't connected the event with him. 'Why does your mother have a different surname from yours?'

'She remarried.'

His response to the personal question was typically abrupt, and it stupidly hurt. Her brain slow to accept that her feelings were as one-sided as Dexter's.

Reaching down, she unzipped her computer satchel and opened her laptop. *Squeeze the fear?* What had she been thinking?

Tino knew the conversation was at an end the minute Miller pulled her computer out and, really, short of hurling the thing out of the window, there was nothing he could do about it. Certainly she wouldn't be pleased if he told her she looked as pale as a snowflake and should just close her eyes and rest.

And what did *he* care? He was a man who had never found it necessary to encourage female conversation, and right now, with the sound of four hundred and forty-three pound-feet of torque eating up the heated tar of the Pacific Highway he was in his element. If she wanted to work her life away that was her choice.

A little voice in his head piped up, asking if that wasn't also his choice, but he sent it packing. The difference between him and Miller was that he loved his work. He didn't want to do anything else. Whereas, while she was clearly good at her job, it wasn't her first love.

And what did love have to do with anything?

Shaking his head, he shifted his thoughts into neutral and the car into top gear and just enjoyed the peace of the open highway and Miller tapping on her keyboard.

More than once he found himself distracted by those killer legs encased in black cotton leggings when she shifted in her seat, but as soon as that happened he forced his eyes to the road and his mind to think about the important round of meetings he had lined up for tomorrow.

Thankfully she fell asleep soon after that and he reclined her seat and tried to ignore the way her soft scent filled the car. The way her hair glinted golden-brown in the sun. The way her deep, even breaths pulled her shirt tight across her breasts. He merged onto the Harbour Bridge and pulled into the left lane, jerking the steering wheel sharply right when a car he nearly cut off blared behind him.

What's your day job again, Ventura?

Thank God it wasn't standard procedure to drive around a racing track with a raging hard-on. He'd be dead at the first corner.

The sharp movement jolted Miller's head against the car door and she woke up and rubbed her scalp. 'What happened?'

'Lousy driving. Do I go left or right off the bridge?'

He skilfully navigated the rest of the way through the posh backstreets of Neutral Bay to her apartment.

The weekend was just about over and soon they'd go their separate ways. A fact that should make him feel better than it did.

'Thank you for the weekend.'

She held out her hand in a show of politeness as he pulled the car up to the kerb near the entrance to her apartment building. He could tell by the wary look in her eyes that she instantly regretted the overture, which only made him perversely take hold of her hand and hold it firmly enough that if she pulled away from him it would make her movement jerky.

She swallowed—hard—and his eyes dropped to her lips. For a second he contemplated yanking her forward into his arms and kissing her, but her mouth flattened and he knew it would be a mistake.

Clean break.

Still holding her hand, he let his eyes snag hers and felt decidedly unsettled at the glazed look in her eyes. 'I hope I fulfilled my purpose this weekend?'

Okay, now he sounded like Sam. Time to go.

'Yes, thank you.'

Again with the thank-yous.

'Good luck with the coming race.'

'Thanks.'

Valentino frowned. Another thank-you from either one of them and he was likely to ignore all his good intentions and kiss her anyway.

Climbing out of the car, he grabbed her bag and met her on the sidewalk.

'I can take that.'

She held her hand out for her bag but he only stared at it grimly. 'I know you can, but you're not.'

She hesitated, her eyes briefly clashing with his. 'Well, thank—'

'Don't.' He watched her sharply as she stepped away from him. She was holding herself a little too stiffly. Was that so he wouldn't touch her? Or...? 'You look like you're burning up.'

'I'm fine. I just have a headache.'

Tino wasn't convinced, but he wasn't going to argue with her on the sidewalk even if it was basically empty; most of the residents of this upper-class neighbourhood were safely behind closed doors.

'Let's go, then.'

He felt a stab of remorse at how exhausted she looked and knew he was partly responsible for her condition. Possibly he should have told her who he was *before* he had agreed to help her on Thursday night, but it was too late now and he wasn't a man who wasted time on regrets.

The lift up seemed to take a month of Sundays, but finally she unlocked her door and stepped inside, reluctantly letting him follow.

He glanced around the stylish cream interior of her apartment, surprised by the splashes of colour in the rugs and cushions. 'Nice.'

'Thank you.'

She remained stubbornly in the doorway and he set her rollaway case near her bedroom door. Then he looked around, perversely unwilling to say goodbye just yet.

'I said thank you.'

Tino glanced at a row of family photos on her bookcase. 'I heard you—and, believe me, you don't want to know what that makes me want to do.'

She made a small noise in the back of her throat and he knew she was scowling at him.

'Don't you have somewhere to be?'

Yeah, inside you.

He ground his teeth together as his thoughts veered down the wrong track.

Really, it was past time to go. Her prickly challenges turned him on, and the only risk he was up for right now was six hundred and forty kilos of carbon plastic and five point six kilometres of svelte bitumen.

He turned and noticed that she didn't seem quite steady in the doorway, although she did her best to hide it.

Frowning, he pulled a business card out of his wallet. 'If you need anything contact my publicist. His number is on here.'

'What would I need?'

'I don't know, Miller. Help changing a tyre? Just take the card and stop being so damned difficult.'

She held his card between her fingers as if it had teeth.

'You're not going to return the favour?' he asked silkily.

'I'm all out of cards.'

Sure she was.

'And you already know how to change a tyre.'

He smiled. He did enjoy her dry sense of humour on the rare occasions she unleashed it.

Like her passion.

Her voice sounded scratchy and he studied her face. Her

eyes had taken on a glossy sheen and small beads of sweat clung to her hairline. This time he didn't ignore the inclination to reach out and lay his palm along her forehead. She jumped and tried to pull away, but he'd felt enough. 'Hell, Miller, you *are* burning up.'

She stiffened and her eyes were bleak when she raised them to his. 'I'm fine.'

Like hell.

A moment passed.

Two.

She jerked her eyes from his and swayed. Tino cursed, grabbed her, and eased her over into one of the overstuffed armchairs facing the TV.

'It's just a headache.'

'Sit.' He headed into the alcove kitchen and flicked on the electric kettle.

'What are you doing?'

'Making you a cup of tea. You look shattered.'

She didn't argue, which showed him how drained she was. He located a cup and saucer in her overhead cupboard and a teabag in a canister on the bench and waited for the water to boil. 'What's your mother's number?'

'Why do you want it?'

She had her eyes closed and didn't look at him when she answered.

'I think she should stay over tonight.'

'She lives in Western Australia.'

'Your friend, then—what's-her-name.'

She peeled her eyes open and looked at him as if he was joking. 'No man ever forgets Ruby's name. She's in Thailand.'

There was a wistful note in her voice and he paused. 'Were you supposed to go with her?'

'I…had to work.'

He shook his head. 'Who else can I call to take care of you?'

She closed her eyes again, shutting him out. 'I can take care of myself.'

He poured her tea. 'Do you take milk?'

'Black is fine.'

As he handed her the hot tea a compelling bright yellow canvas dotted with tiny blue and purple fey creatures caught his attention on the far wall and he stepped closer. 'Who did this?'

'No one famous. Can you please go now?'

He looked at the indecipherable artist's scrawl in the corner of the canvas and took a stab in the dark. 'When did you do this?'

'I don't remember.'

Liar.

And she hadn't just wanted to illustrate children's books either; he'd bet his next race on it.

'You're very talented. Do you exhibit?'

'No. Thank you for the tea, but I don't want to keep you.'

He heard the cup rattle and turned to find her leaning her head against the back of the chair. She looked even worse than before.

Making one of those split-second decisions he was renowned for on the circuit, he grabbed her suitcase and stalked into her bedroom.

'What are you doing now?' she called after him.

'Packing you some fresh clothes.'

He upended the contents of her case on the bed and then opened her wardrobe door. He was confronted by a dark wall of clothing. He knew she liked black but this was ridiculous. He had no idea where to start.

'Do you own anything other than black?'

'It's a habit.'

So was hiding herself. 'Never mind.'

'Why are you packing my things?' Her voice was closer and he glanced over his shoulder to see her leaning in the doorway. She should be sitting down, but he'd take care of that in a minute.

'Because you're coming with me.'

'No, I'm not.'

He knew he was forcing his will on her, and it totally went against his usually laid-back style, but *dammit* he just wasn't prepared to leave her here. What if she got really sick?

Then she'll call a doctor, lamebrain. And since when have you taken care of anyone other than yourself anyway?

'It's stress and lack of sleep,' she murmured.

'I can see that. And you've hardly eaten all day either. You need a damned keeper.'

'I'm fine.'

'Consider this a long overdue holiday.'

'Don't you *dare* go near my underwear drawer!'

'It's too late. I know you like sexy lingerie.'

She groaned, and he smiled.

He threw a fistful of brightly coloured underwear into the case, pulled a selection of footwear from her closet and zipped the case closed.

He wheeled it towards her and deftly scooped her up with one arm.

'I don't like all this he-man stuff,' she said, leaning weakly against his chest.

'Too bad.' He grabbed her computer satchel and her handbag, slammed her apartment door behind them. 'My instincts tell me you need someone to take care of you, and I have track practice tomorrow morning I can't miss.'

Her head dropped against his shoulder. 'I have to go to work tomorrow. I could get fired.'

'Everyone's entitled to a sick day. If you're okay tomorrow night I'll fly you back. Anyway, you could get fired for *not* coming with me. Dexter wants TJ's business, and TJ wants me. You can tell Dexter you're working on me.'

He put her down to fish his car keys out of his pocket and then gently deposited her inside the car.

'I don't think that's going to impress him.'

But she rested her head against the car seat and closed her eyes.

CHAPTER ELEVEN

MILLER knew she should probably put up more resistance to his high-handedness but she felt too weak and light-headed. And some deeply held part of herself was insanely pleased by his gesture.

But she was being a sucker again. It was obvious that his behaviour had more to do with his overdeveloped sense of responsibility than it did with her as a person and she would do well to remember that.

He expertly pulled the silver bullet into the area of the airport reserved for private planes, and Miller gave up fighting the inevitable. She was so weak she had no choice but to lean into him and soak up some of his strength as he guided her towards the steps to his plane.

It was sleek and white, and she didn't feel so unwell that she couldn't be impressed. 'You're not the prime minister, are you?' she murmured faintly.

He smiled softly. 'Sorry. I'm not that big.'

Their eyes caught and held and his smile turned devilish.

'I meant that important.'

Keeping her sheltered against his broad shoulder, he led her past wide leather bucket seats with polished trim down a narrow corridor and into a room lit only by the up-lights in the carpet.

'You have a bed?' She couldn't keep the astonishment from her voice.

'I fly a lot. Hop in.'

'Don't I have to wear a seat belt for take-off?' As she said

the words she felt the jet move slowly forward. Or backwards.
It was hard to tell.

'Not on a private plane.'

'Does it have a bathroom?'

'Through there.' He gestured towards a narrow sliding door.
'If you're more than five minutes I'm going to assume you've
collapsed and come in.'

'And you accuse me of being bossy?' She sniffed, but didn't
argue. Her back ached, her stomach hurt, and her head felt as if
it had some sort of torture device attached to the top.

When she came out he was on the phone speaking to someone in Italian. One of his family maybe?

God, their worlds were so different. She felt a pang as she
recalled watching the cool kids all eating at the same cafeteria
table at school every day while she pretended she needed to be
alone to spread out her drawing pad.

'I've ordered you a light meal. It'll be delivered as soon as
we're airborne.' He shoved his phone in his pocket and came
towards her. 'You look like you're about to fall over, Miller.
Please get in the bed.'

He might have said please but his tone implied he'd put her
there in about three seconds if she didn't comply.

Slipping off her boots, she folded herself inside the cool,
crisp sheets and laid her head on the softest pillow in the
world…

'Come on, Miller, we're here.'

Groggy from sleep, Miller allowed Valentino to lift her out
of the bed.

'Don't forget her boots,' he told someone, and Miller rested
her head against his shoulder, unable to completely pull herself
from the blissful depths of unconsciousness.

Seconds later she was placed in a car, and seconds after that
she was being lifted again.

The next time she woke the nausea had passed and so had
the headache. She stretched and felt the resistance of a top sheet.

Someone had made this bed with hospital corners. She wondered if she was in a hospital.

Opening her eyes, the first thing she noticed was that the room was in semi-darkness, with a set of heavy silk drapes pulled across the windows. The second thing was that the room was expensively furnished in rich country decor and definitely not in a hospital. She strained her ears but could only hear the faint sound of white noise. A washing machine, perhaps.

Pulling back the covers, she was pleased to see she was wearing her T-shirt and leggings from earlier. So it was still Sunday, then. She felt utterly displaced and wouldn't have been surprised if she'd slept for a week.

Feeling grimy and hot, she checked through a door and was relieved to see it was a bathroom.

Before going in she glanced around and spied her case in a corner. Flicking on the bedside lamp, she went to rummage through it for something else to put on and was surprised to discover it held only underwear and shoes.

Resting back on her heels, she let out a short, bemused laugh, remembering the exasperation in Valentino's voice when he'd asked her if she wore anything other than black.

'You're awake, then?'

Miller spun around, so startled by his voice she fell back on her bottom. Which only made him seem to fill the doorway even more. She tried not to think about how gorgeous he looked in his casual clothing. He hadn't shaved and his hair was still slightly damp from a recent shower. Then she noticed he was holding a steaming porcelain bowl.

He walked into the room and placed it on the bedside table. 'Chicken noodle soup.'

'You made chicken noodle soup?'

His lips twitched. 'My chef did.'

'You have a chef?'

'Team chef, to be precise.'

'Well...' Miller stood up, not sure what to say. 'That's very nice of you but I feel fine. Great, in fact. I did tell you I wasn't sick.'

'You *should* feel great. You've slept for nearly twenty-four hours.'

'Twenty-four hours! Are you kidding?'

'No. The doctor checked your vital signs this morning but he wasn't overly concerned. He said you might have picked up a bug and if you didn't wake properly by tonight to call him again. You spoke to him while he was here. You don't remember?'

'I have a vague recollection but…I thought I was dreaming. I know I've been pushing myself lately, but—wow. I feel fine now.'

Valentino stuck his hands into his jeans pocket. 'I'll leave you to have your soup and a shower.'

'Thanks.' Miller's mind was still reeling from the fact that she'd slept for so long. 'Oh, wait. I don't have anything to change into. You only packed…underwear and— What *is* that noise?'

He stopped at the door. 'The ocean. A cold front came through this morning so the swell is up.'

'You live on the ocean?'

'Phillip Island.'

'We're not even in Melbourne?'

'Take a shower, Miller, and join me in the kitchen. Down the hall, left and then right. There are clothes in the wardrobe. They should fit.'

Curious, Miller went to the wardrobe door and gasped when she opened it to find an array of beautifully crafted women's clothes filling the cupboard—half of them black! Wondering who they belonged to, she fingered the beautiful fabrics of the shirts and dresses, the soft wool pants and denim jeans.

But whose were they? And why did Valentino have a closet full of—she checked a few of the labels—size ten clothes?

Her size.

The thought of wearing another woman's clothing wasn't exactly comforting and her stomach tightened. T-shirts, jeans and shorts lined the shelves, and there was a grey tracksuit.

Feeling as if she was stealing the pretty girl's clothing from a school locker, Miller gingerly pulled out the tracksuit pants and a T-shirt. Thank God she had her own underwear—because there was no way she was wearing somebody else's. In fact, she'd put on her own clothes again if she hadn't slept in them for so long. The thought that she'd actually been ill was still something of a shock.

Going through to the marble bathroom, Miller quickly showered under the hot spray and opened the vanity and found the basics. Deodorant, toothpaste and a new brush, a comb and moisturiser. Brushing the tangles from her hair, Miller hunted in the cupboard for a hairdryer and came up empty.

Damn.

Without a hairdryer her hair would dry wavy and look a mess. She felt vulnerable and exposed without her things, but there was nothing she could do about it. Valentino had swooped down, got her at a weak moment, and she'd just have to brave it out. It was only clothes and hair anyway. He probably wouldn't even notice.

She walked back into the bedroom and her stomach growled as the smell of cooling soup filled her nostrils. Salivating, she perched on the bed and demolished the fantastic broth in seconds, her body feeling both clean and nourished.

But, knowing she couldn't hide out in this room any longer, she picked up the empty bowl and followed Valentino's directions to the kitchen.

His home was modern and spacious, with lots of exposed wood and a raw-cut stone fireplace that dominated a living area that was furnished with large pieces of furniture built to be used as well as to look good.

When she stepped into the modern cream and steel kitchen she was assailed with the smell of sautéed garlic and her eyes became riveted to the man facing the stove. She drank in his athletic physique in a fitted red T-shirt and worn, low-riding denims that cupped his rear end to perfection.

He was without a doubt the sexiest man she had ever seen,

and he made her forget all about being self-conscious or cautious. But she wasn't here because he was attracted to her. He'd made it perfectly clear Saturday night he didn't want her in that way, so it was time to stop thinking about the way he made her feel.

There was nothing else going on here but his over-developed sense of responsibility, and if she didn't pull herself together she'd likely make a huge fool of herself again.

Something must have alerted him to her presence because he stopped pushing the wooden spoon around the pan and turned towards her.

His eyes swept over her and she felt the thrill of his smoky, heavy-lidded gaze from across the room. She wished her senses weren't so attuned to his every look and nuance because the tension she felt in his presence made it impossible for her to relax.

Miller sensed he was holding himself utterly still, almost taut, and she was definitely using someone else's legs as she moved further into the kitchen.

'The clothes fit, then?'

She remembered the dull feeling that had washed over her when she'd first seen them. 'Yes. Whose are they?'

'Yours.'

'You bought me clothes?'

He shrugged carelessly at her stunned tone and added tinned tomatoes to the pan. 'Technically Mickey bought them.'

'Mickey?'

'My Man Friday.'

He had a Man Friday? One who knew his way around women's fashion? She hated to think how many other women Mickey had clothed at Valentino's request.

'Mickey runs interference between all the people vying for my attention and makes sure my life runs smoothly. Calling up a department store and organising a few items of clothing for a woman was a first.'

'I didn't say anything.' She felt impossibly peeved that he'd read her so well.

'You didn't have to. You're very easy to read.'

'Not usually,' she muttered.

His slow smile at her revelation made breathing a conscious exercise.

'Why didn't you just pack me something other than underwear and shoes?' Realising she was still holding the empty soup bowl she set it down on the benchtop between them. 'That would have made more sense.'

'Probably,' he said. 'But I saw all that black in your wardrobe and panicked. And I have a soft spot for your lingerie and shoes. How was the soup?'

'Divine.' Miller felt flustered by his admission about her underwear. 'I'm not keeping the clothes,' she said stubbornly. 'There's enough there for ten women.'

He leaned against the lacquered cabinet beside the stove. 'Mickey's ex-army—a complete amateur when it comes to what women need.'

'Whereas you're an expert?'

His eyes studied her in such a way that goosebumps rose up on her arms. 'So I've been told.'

Miller sighed deeply, searching around in her mind for some way to change the subject and lower the tension in the room to a manageable level. It would be too embarrassing if he guessed how disturbed she was in his presence.

'I should probably get going. I've taken up enough of your time.'

'I'm cooking dinner.'

'I thought you had a chef?' She tried to make her tone light but she wasn't sure she'd pulled it off.

'He provides the food. I cook it when I'm here.'

'What is it?'

'Not poison.'

He gave a short laugh, and she realised she'd screwed up her face.

'Relax. If you want to go home after dinner I'll arrange it.'

Just like that, she thought asininely. Did nothing faze this man?

Yes. Talking about his family. His father. The accident that had claimed the life of his friend. He had his demons, she knew, he just kept them close to his chest.

Miller nodded. She felt stiff and awkward, and when she wetted her painfully dry lips his eyes locked onto her mouth with the precision of a laser. She felt the start of a delicious burn deep inside.

So much about this man stimulated her to the point that she could think of little else. Which made staying for a meal a questionable decision. Wasn't it playing with fire to spend any more time in his company?

A vague memory of him feeling her head and administering a drink of water to her some time during the day filtered into her mind. His gentleness and consideration of her needs was breaking down all of her defences against him. Something she really didn't want. Lord only knew what would happen if he showed any indication that he wanted her half as much as she wanted him. She wasn't sure she would say no. Wasn't sure she *could* say no.

Spotting his phone on the far bench, her mind drifted to work.

'Did you happen to bring my phone yesterday?' she asked, wondering if she still had a job and if it was too late to call Dexter. She'd done nothing on TJ's account all day, so chances were slim, but she'd rather know than not.

He stopped stirring the sauce on the stove. 'It wasn't in your handbag?'

'No.'

'You can borrow mine. But if you're calling work don't bother. They know you're with me.'

'Sorry?' She forced her eyes away from the muscled slopes of his arms. 'What did you tell them?'

'That you were sick.'

Miller barely suppressed a groan. 'Why did you do that?'

'I presumed you'd want your workplace to know where you were and you weren't capable of telling them.'

Miller knew he was right, but it didn't change the fact that she was irritated. 'I have to finish TJ's proposal, and I'm still not sure Dexter isn't planning to put me under a formal performance review. Now he'll just think I'm skiving in order to spend time with you and definitely do it.'

'After his own behaviour over the weekend he'd be crazy to question yours. I'm sure your job is perfectly safe. And everyone's entitled to a sick day. I bet you have almost a year's worth accumulated by now.'

Miller blushed. He made her feel like a goody-two-shoes. But his championing of her gave her a warm glow that was hard to shake.

Something she could never rely on long term, she reminded herself. Especially with a man like him.

'You have a point.' Hopefully one Dexter recognised. 'But still, I can take care of myself.' She tried to hide her irritation but it wasn't easy. Everything about her response to him—and his lack of one to her—was just debilitating.

He flicked a knob on the stove and put a lid on the saucepan, his gaze never shifting from hers as he prowled towards her. He rounded the island bench and Miller felt her breathing become choppy. She knew it wasn't just because of her rush of irritation.

He stopped just shy of touching her, his blue-grey eyes piercing, his arms folded across his chest. *'Thank you, Tino, for helping me out Sunday night when I felt like something the cat had dragged in,'* he said mockingly.

Miller felt ashamed of her stroppy behaviour. What was *wrong* with her? 'Thank you, Tino, for helping me out Sunday night when I felt like something the cat had dragged in.' And probably looked it…

'That's better.'

His smile could have melted a glacier. Then his eyes locked onto her hair and she suddenly remembered that it wasn't straight, as usual, and probably looked terrible.

She raised a self-conscious hand. 'Wavy.'

He reached out and looped a semi-dry curl around a finger. 'Pretty.'

She shook her head and his finger snagged on the curl, pulling it tight. She shivered. 'I prefer it straight.'

His hand drifted to the side of her face, his fingers following the curve of her jaw. 'That's because it gives you a sense of control. I like it either way.'

Miller's breath stalled in her lungs at the way he was looking at her. She could read desire in his eyes. Want. Intent, even. She was shocked by it because previously she had assumed his interest in her wasn't real. But now she suspected he had just been resisting the chemistry between them on Saturday night—as she had done for most of the weekend. As she should still be doing...

Only she felt powerless to look away from the banked heat in his gaze and a thrill of remembered pleasure raced through her body. A thousand reasons as to why this wasn't a good idea pinged into her mind, but overwhelming her logical thinking was a wicked, sinful sensation that refused to go away.

All her life she'd done the right thing. The proper thing. Working hard to get good grades and make her mother proud, building a reputation at work that would ensure her future was secure, shelving the more risqué side of her nature. Until now that had been enough. Satisfying, even.

But Valentino brought out a delicious craving in her that was impossible to ignore.

CHAPTER TWELVE

TINO saw the sharp rise and fall of Miller's chest as his finger lingered on the side of her jaw, felt her tremble as he deepened the caress. He hadn't intended to touch her, seduce her, but now he could think of nothing else.

Some part of him hesitated. Really, if he had any integrity he'd stop. She'd been sick. She was a guest in his house. But none of that registered with her standing in front of him looking gorgeous and tousled, her cheeks pink, her lips softly parted. God, he wanted to kiss her. He wanted—

She swayed slightly towards him, pressed the side of her face into his palm. 'Valentino…?'

Her blue eyes were huge, shining with an age-old invitation that sent every ounce of blood in his body due south. Breathing felt like an effort, and it would have taken more strength than he possessed not to lean in and kiss her.

So he did.

Lightly. Gently. Just their mouths and his hand on her face connecting them.

And maybe he would have stopped so that they could eat the dinner he'd prepared, but after the slightest of hesitations she rose onto her toes, flattened herself against his chest and he was lost.

His hands moved to span her waist and curled beneath the fabric of her T-shirt to sweep up and down the smooth skin of her back. She whimpered. He groaned, angled his head, took the kiss deeper, his mouth hardening as the hunger inside him threatened to consume them both.

Her hands found his hair; his found her breasts. Those perfect round breasts.

'Miller…' Her name was a deep rasp and she wrenched her mouth from under his as his thumbs flicked across both nipples at once. She arched into his hands, her back curving like an archer's bow, and he growled his appreciation, pushing her bra cups down to pluck at her velveteen flesh more firmly.

Her sensitivity and responsiveness completely undid him, and he lifted her and turned to place her on the stone bench.

'Valentino.'

Her desire-laden sigh stalled him. He pulled in a tanker full of air and tried to steady himself as his eyes met hers. He flicked his tongue over his lips and saw her pupils dilate as she watched him.

Forking a hand through her thick waves, he forced her eyes up to his. 'Miller, I want to be inside you more than I've wanted anything in my life. Tell me you want the same,' he ordered gruffly.

He felt the thrill of desire race through her and her lips parted, her fingernails digging into his shoulders. 'Yes. I feel… I want the same thing.'

Tino's eyes grew heavy with fierce male triumph and his hands confidently moved to the waistband of the sweats she wore. 'Lift up.'

He dragged the pants down her legs, admiring her red lace panties before they dropped to the floor. 'God, I love your lingerie.' He spread her thighs wide and pulled her forward until her bottom was balanced on the edge of the bench. 'Take off the T-shirt and bra.'

She complied, and he leaned forward to capture one pointed nipple into his mouth. He suckled her. Bit down lightly. His hands steadied her hips as she jerked under the lash of his tongue. She was perfect.

'Beautiful,' he breathed. He switched his attention to her

other breast, loving the feel of her fingers speared into his hair, holding his head hard, her small whimpers of arousal testing his self-control.

He felt her hips push against his restraining hold and knew she was seeking pressure at her core. Pressure he couldn't wait to give her. He moved one hand between her legs and urged her thighs wider, opening her, his eyes momentarily closing as he revelled in the feel of his hand sliding through her curls and over her delicate folds. She was already wet and his middle finger slipped easily inside her. She made a sound like a sob, her hands clutching at him as he stroked her sweet spot with his thumb.

His erection jerked in an agony of wanting.

Soon, he promised himself. He curved his other hand around the nape of her neck and pulled her eager mouth back to his, adding another finger into her body and setting up a steady rhythm.

She groaned, a deep, keening sound, and ground herself against his hand. He felt the urgent lift of her body that signalled she was close to coming, but as much as he wanted to feel her orgasm gripping his fingers he wanted something else more.

'Lean back on your elbows.'

He waited while she shifted the empty soup bowl out of her way and then he bent forward and nuzzled her, his tongue stroking and teasing the bundle of nerve endings at the top of her sex.

She bucked against him so hard she nearly dislodged him, and he wound his arms around her waist.

'Damn, Miller, you taste so good.'

His husky words sent her over the edge and she came like a shot around his tongue. He nearly disgraced himself in his own kitchen.

Calling on every ounce of focus, he rode her orgasm with her. Then he stood, rose above her, pulled his T-shirt up over his head and shucked his jeans around his ankles. Her head was still thrown back on her shoulders, her breasts pushed high, her body open for his viewing pleasure. His eyes drank in the sheer beauty of her for all of two seconds and then he shifted closer, positioning himself between her splayed thighs before—

Condom.

Right. *Hell.*

He reached around and pulled one out of his back pocket, sheathed himself.

'Are you always this prepared?'

Her husky words and wary gaze stayed him. His usual approach would be to make a sarcastic quip. Keep things light. But her scent was warm on his tongue and for some reason he couldn't conjure up anything light.

'No. But after touching you on the beach Saturday I've dreamt of nothing else since.'

'Nothing else?'

Her tone was teasing and it gave him permission to tease her back. 'Maybe my mother's lasagna.'

She smiled, her eyes slumberous as she took him in. His erection throbbed under her perusal and her startled eyes flew to his.

His hands tightened on her hips. 'Do you want me to stop?' The words felt as if they were ripped out of his throat with a pair of pliers, but he needed to be sure she was totally on board with this.

Her eyes held his. 'Would you?'

'Of course.' Though it might kill him.

'No, I don't want you to stop.' She leaned forward, gripped him in her palm. She closed her eyes as her fingers explored him. 'I want to feel you inside me.'

He wanted that too—so badly his legs were shaking with need. He pulled her hands from his body before he lost it. 'Open your eyes.' His voice was a husky command and it seemed for ever before she raised her sleepy gaze to his. 'I want to see your eyes as I fill you.'

Her eyes widened and her tongue touched her lips as she nodded.

'Hold on to me.' She draped her arms along the line of his

shoulders and gripped the back of his neck. Tino pulled her firm breasts against his torso and lifted her.

He'd intended to take her hard, his instinct to plough himself into her, but some sense of civility whispered that this first time he might hurt her, so instead he lowered her with as much care as he could.

Even so, he felt the hiss of air against his temple as her body encircled him.

She was tight. So tight. He stilled. 'Are you okay?' Sweat beaded his forehead as he forced himself not to jam her on top of him.

She wriggled her hips and adjusted herself around his girth and his head nearly came off.

'Now I am.' Her voice was so damned sexy. Like her smell. 'You're just...big.'

Women had told him that before, but never had those words sounded so sweet.

'You can take me,' he growled, kissing her brow.

'I think I already have.' There was laughter in her voice and then he shifted his hips and surged forward, giving her more.

'Or not.' She groaned. 'I want more.'

God, so did he.

'Hook your legs around my waist.' He could barely speak. The urge to pound into her was overwhelming but he needed a soft surface for what he was about to give her—otherwise she'd end up black and blue.

Somehow he made it to his bed, but when he fell on top of her he was so close to coming he didn't hold back. Her body clung to his as if it had been made just to please him, and when he felt another orgasm building inside her he didn't know how he managed to hold off long enough to take them both over the edge together, but he was so damned glad he had.

God, had sex ever been this good?

Miller lay still, unable to move, and yet stricken with the urge to run for her life. She had just had wild, unrestrained sex with one of the beautiful people. Someone so far removed from her real world she couldn't even leap to see the platform he lived on.

And it had been amazing. He'd filled her so completely, so powerfully, all she'd been able to do was cling to him as he'd carried her into his room and then carried them both into a miracle of erotic pleasure.

At least it had been for her. For him it was probably run of the mill. *She* was probably run of the mill. Trying not to let her old insecurities swamp her, Miller clung to what was real. Which, ironically, was that this was fake.

Her sickness, his bringing her here—none of that had changed anything between them. And would it matter if it had? She had her goals, her plans for the future, and she wasn't looking for a relationship. She wasn't looking to fall in love with anyone yet.

She understood the fundamental rule that one person always loved more than the other, and she also knew that relationships were unstable at best and downright destructive at worst.

And it wasn't as if Valentino was going to insist on having a relationship with her! He'd probably prefer to be hit by one of his fast cars. And even if he did his job took him all over the world. She knew herself well enough to know she'd never cope with the uncertainty of having a relationship with someone who left her all the time. *Would* leave her as soon as he was bored.

But that still wasn't the scariest thought churning through her right now. No, the scariest thought had been the sense of connection she had felt when Valentino had joined their bodies together. It had been as if a missing part of herself had slotted into place. A ridiculous notion, and one that made her think that the sooner she got her life back to normal the better.

Valentino shifted beside her and Miller tuned into the laboured sounds of his breathing, the only noise in the otherwise silent room.

'You're thinking again.' His low voice rumbled from deep inside his chest.

'It's what I do best.'

'I think we've just discovered another occupation you could channel your energies into.'

Miller smiled weakly, and then gasped as he rolled on top of her and lightly pinned her to the bed. He fisted a hand in her hair and tilted her face up to his. She swallowed. He was so primal, so male. His hold was both possessive and dominant, and it shouldn't have thrilled her as much as it did.

'What are you thinking about?' he persisted.

'Isn't that my line?'

'I think it's pretty clear what I'm thinking about. What I want to know is if you're regretting what just happened between us.'

No, she wasn't regretting it. She was trying to figure it out. 'No. I probably should, but I don't.'

'I'm glad.'

He laid his palm across her forehead and Miller swallowed past the lump in her throat. 'I'm fine. I told you that.'

'I'm allowed to check.' Leaning down, he ran his tongue over her lips, stroking into her mouth as she automatically opened for him.

Miller gasped as pleasure arrowed straight to her pelvis, turning her liquid. She moaned when his knees urged hers wider and he settled himself between her thighs.

'I want you again,' he murmured roughly.

'Really?' Miller felt him hard between her legs and her trepidation at being here with him evaporated as she sensed just how wrong she had been about this chemistry being one-sided. He wanted her. Badly. And the knowledge gave her a giddy sense of sensual power that amazed her.

CHAPTER THIRTEEN

TINO woke up early, as usual, and smelt the scent of sex at the same time as he registered that Miller was no longer in his bed.

Confounded, he cracked an eye open and was even more puzzled to find the room empty and silent except for a couple of magpies warbling outside his window.

He was used to a woman clinging after a night of sex. Not that he remembered ever having a night quite like that. He'd been insatiable, and a grin split his face as he recalled how she had matched him the whole way.

He stretched his hands above his head and flexed stiff muscles. Last night had been incredible—and against every one of his rules.

Sort of.

It wasn't that he'd forbidden himself to have sex this close to race day, it was getting involved emotionally that was the no-go zone. He might have thought about Miller more than he would have liked over the past couple of days, but he knew now that he'd had her in his bed his interest would start to wane. It always did.

Which was why it was good that she would be leaving this morning. He had an enormously busy week, made even more so because he'd had to cancel yesterday's round of meetings to care for Miller.

Rolling out of bed, he pulled his jeans on and went in search of her to find out what time she wanted him to get the jet ready.

He found her outside, watching the sun rising over the ocean that stretched beyond his backyard. She was completely enveloped in his black robe—so appropriate, he mused—her hair mussed and wavy, the sun's rays highlighting the gold in amongst the brown.

She turned when she heard the sliding door open and fingered her hair self-consciously. She looked adorable. And uncomfortable.

He immediately sought to put her at ease and ignored the whisper of apprehension that floated across his mind. He didn't doubt for a minute his ability to control this situation between them.

'What are you thinking?'

'I didn't know men wanted to know what women were thinking so much.'

He studied her, feeling as if he was facing down one of Dante's highly strung thoroughbreds. 'I don't want to know what women are thinking, I want to know what *you're* thinking.'

'I'm thinking that you have a beautiful home. For some reason I took you as a city type.'

'I visit too many cities as part of my job. My mother lives on the other side of the island and I bought this place when she fell ill a couple of years ago.'

'Is she okay now?'

'Fine. Fitter than I am.'

Miller's lips twisted into a faint smile. 'Well, it's lovely here. Peaceful.' She glanced out over the lawn towards the beach and he caught the nervousness in her eyes. 'But I should probably be heading back home.'

Her lips were still kiss swollen from last night, and he noticed a slight red mark from where his beard growth had grazed her neck. He'd have to be more careful of her soft skin, though some primal part of him was pleased to see his mark on her.

'It's seven in the morning. Are you sore?'

She coloured prettily. 'That's personal.'

'Sunshine, it doesn't get any more personal than my mouth between your legs.'

She gasped. 'You can't *say* that!'

She looked mortified, and for some reason her reaction pleased him. He was so used to women preening and posing in front of him that her embarrassment was refreshing. She hadn't been a virgin, he knew that, but she wasn't a practised sophisticate either, and one of the things he loved—hell, *liked*—about her was that she was so easy to tease.

He stepped closer to her and urged her stiff body into the circle of his arms. 'I've embarrassed you?'

'Yes, but I don't know how.' She gave a deep sigh. 'I should have expected you to just say what you think. It's one of the first things I noticed about you.'

She gripped his forearms as if to hold him off, but he'd have none of it, his thumbs drawing lazy circles over the thin cotton of his robe covering her lower back, gentling her until she fitted against him as naturally as his tailor-made jumpsuit.

'What else did you notice?'

'That you had ripped jeans and needed a shave.'

Tino gave a hoot of laughter. 'Sunshine, you are hell on my ego.'

'Your ego is one area I would never worry about.'

She was watching his mouth, and his laughter dried up instantly. 'I usually start the day with a run followed by a green smoothie, but this morning I'm going to make an exception.'

Her aquamarine eyes lifted to his, her pupils expanding as he watched. 'What are you replacing it with?'

He enclosed the nape of her neck with his hand, slowly bringing her mouth to his. 'That depends on the answer to my earlier question.'

She frowned, and he pressed his pelvis into her to facilitate her memory recall. She smiled, and he felt tightness in his chest.

'Only a little.'

Her answer sent the tightness lower. 'I promise to be gentle.'

Miller must have dozed, because she awoke to the feel of Valentino spooning her from behind as he had done first thing that morning. Then she had slipped out of his bed, because the sensation of waking with his protective arm draped around her waist, his fingers resting protectively over her abdomen, had been both frightening and exhilarating. And now the same feelings were back.

He just seemed to swamp her. His warmth, his scent, her desire to burrow against him and never leave. It was as instinctive to her as breathing.

Right from the beginning she'd sensed he would have this intense effect on her, and wasn't that the reason behind her fear now? Hadn't she avoided feeling such intense emotions for another person because she knew better than most how tenuous relationships were? But how could a playboy racing car driver with a reputation for having a death wish make her feel so…so safe? So secure? It had to be straight hormones because otherwise it defied logic!

As did her current feeling of wellbeing. Something she hadn't experienced since before her parents had divorced, she suddenly realised. And hot on the heels of *that* little revelation was the unwelcome understanding that she had been trying to get this same sense of belonging from her job for years.

On some level that wasn't a total surprise, because she had always treated work as a second home, but what *was* newsworthy was that even the thought of making partner didn't give her quite the same sense of safety that Valentino did right now.

Confused, and feeling slightly exasperated with her seesawing emotions, Miller again tried to creep out from under his arm—only this time his strong fingers spread out like tentacles to cover her whole belly.

'Am I going to have to tie you to my bed to make sure you're still here when I wake up?'

His deep voice was sleep-rough, his warm breath stirring her hair.

Miller stilled, wanting to run and wanting to stay at the same time. In the end she wasn't strong enough to resist his magnetic pull and subsided back against his hard body.

'Where were you going, anyway?'

'I really need to start making tracks.'

'Now, *there's* a very Aussie expression.' He rolled her onto her back and rose up on one elbow, his gunmetal-grey eyes lazily intense between thick, dark lashes.

Feeling exposed, Miller pulled the sheet up over her breasts. His gaze lingered on the sheet and she had the vague impression that he was about to flick it off her.

Glad when he didn't, she let her breath out slowly.

'Why are you so determined to run off, anyway? You don't strike me as the one-night-stand type.'

'I'm not.'

'Then stay one more day. I have a sponsors gig tonight. You can come with me.'

Alarmed by just how much she wanted to accept what she suspected was an unplanned invitation, Miller immediately re-acted in the negative. 'I can't. I have to work.'

Annoyance flickered briefly across his face. 'Work from here. You have your computer.'

Miller smoothed her eyebrows. He was doing his steam-roller thing again, but what was one more day to him? And when would she go home? Later tonight or in the morning?'

He stroked a strand of hair back off her forehead. God, she must look a mess.

'I know what you're thinking. You don't like the uncer-tainty of it.'

Miller's eyes flashed to his. Did he really know her that well, or was she really that easy to read?

'It's not hard to figure out, Miller. I know you hate surprises so it follows that you wouldn't like half-baked plans. How about we make it the whole week?'

The whole week!

'Five days, to be exact. That way you can come to my moth-er's gala event, which TJ is expecting to see you at anyway, and watch me race on Sunday.'

Miller felt her brows scrunch together. 'Why would you want me to come to your mother's ball?'

Tino rolled onto his back and gave her a reprieve from his intense scrutiny. 'Honestly? My mother invites every debutante in the known universe to this thing and expects me and my brothers to meet every one of them in the hope that we'll fall in love.'

His apathetic attitude to falling in love stabbed at something inside her. 'Oh, poor you. All those single women in one room. I would have thought it was every man's dream.'

Her words were sharper than she had intended, but she was slightly insulted that he would talk about other women while he was in bed with her. Even if they were women he apparently didn't want.

The reminder that he would never want anyone permanently—not even her—struck a chord, because permanence was all she did seek! She'd just never sought it with a man before.

'Hardly.' His dramatic tone nearly made her laugh, despite her aggravation. 'Debutantes come with strings attached, stars in their eyes and pushy mothers. That's no dream any man I know has ever had.'

Suddenly, he lifted onto his elbow, looming over her again, and Miller caught her breath. His gaze roved over her face and he trailed a finger over the sensitive skin of her neck just below her ear, winding a slow, sensual path downwards.

'I did you a favour last weekend. The least you can do is protect me from women I'm not interested in on Saturday night.'

His voice had lowered with intent, and Miller's body responded like one of Pavlov's dogs. She pushed his hand away. 'Stop that. I can't think when you're this close.'

'That's only fair since you have the same effect on me.'

'I do?' For some reason, his admission startled her.

'Well, I *can* think, but it's usually about one thing.' His hand returned and his fingers circled her nipple, making her arch off the bed. 'Say you'll stay.'

She tried to organise her thoughts. 'Because of the sex?'

She was breathless, and his smile as he rolled on top of her was one of pure male triumph. 'The sex is phenomenal, but the more I think about you going to my mother's party the more I like it. With you there I can relax, and I might even enjoy it. And Caruthers will expect it.'

'Since when do you care what Dexter thinks?' Miller asked breathlessly, catching a moan between her clamped lips as his fingers traced a figure eight over first one breast and then the other, skimming over her nipple just a little bit too lightly each time.

'I don't.' His skilful touch became firmer. 'Say yes.'

Miller felt deliciously light-headed. 'You're steamrollering me again,' she accused, trying to hold her body still.

Valentino nipped the skin around her clavicle. 'Is that a good thing?'

Giving up on trying to resist him, she speared her fingers through his hair, enjoying the thick, weighty texture of it curling through her fingers.

'I don't know.' She groaned and dragged his mouth to her breast. 'Please, just stop talking.'

'You're so sexy.' His voice was rough, more a low growl, as he *finally* pulled her nipple into his mouth with just the right amount of pressure.

Miller felt as if she was levitating as her legs shifted helplessly under the onslaught of pleasure. She moaned his name. He nudged her legs apart, and even though her internal muscles ached from over-use the rush of liquid heat between her thighs was instant. She felt him fumbling in his side table, his mouth briefly leaving her breast to tear the condom packet open, and then he was back, pressing her into the bed.

'Now, where was I?'

God, he made her feel… He made her feel…

'Say you'll stay.'

His mouth teased the soft skin beneath her ear, and even though she knew she must have terrible morning breath she turned her face, searching for his kiss.

'Okay.'

What had she just agreed to?

'For five days.'

His fingers stroked between her legs, drawing moisture from her body in preparation for his possession.

'I…' She arched her hips, her body already balanced on a knife-edge of pleasure, desperate to go over.

'Say yes.'

'Yes—whatever.'

She was desperate, and his husky chuckle of dominance annoyed her. With a spurt of defiance at his formidable self-control in the face of her total lack of any, she wrapped her legs around his hips and tilted her pelvis so that he had no choice but to slide deep.

He swore as he plunged into her, and Miller smiled and buried her face against his straining neck. She clenched his shoulders and her internal muscles at the same time, and suddenly the balance of power shifted as he bucked in her arms before surging deep again.

She felt him groan against her hair, and then her mind closed down as he pounded into her with such primal force she thought she might break. And then she did. Into a whirlpool of pleasure that sucked her under and blew her mind. Dimly, she heard Valentino shout her name, and she could feel the power of his release as he spilled himself inside her.

It seemed for ever before either one of them moved, and even then it was only weakly.

'Are you okay?' he asked.

Miller gulped in air. 'Ask me in a minute.'

He chuckled and shifted onto his stomach beside her. 'Sorry. That was a bit rough.'

Miller stretched her arms above her head. 'It was fabulous. I may never move again.'

Groaning, Valentino dragged himself from the bed. 'I wish I had the same luxury. Unfortunately not working yesterday and spending half the morning in bed today has no doubt put the team incredibly behind.' He bent and gently kissed her lips. 'Why don't you stay in bed? Recover? I'll send Mickey with a car at five o'clock to bring you into the city.'

The city? It took a minute for Miller to remember their conversation. She watched through half-closed lids as Valentino strolled into the bathroom and turned on the shower.

She recognised that she'd just been steamrollered *again*, and that she had agreed to stay with him for five days and attend a party to help keep eager debutantes at bay.

What were you thinking?

She stared at the ceiling and tried to feel agitated, but instead all she felt was happy. Oh, not at the whole debutantes thing, but just at being here. Maybe it was called afterglow.

Otherwise it didn't make sense. Especially given her confused emotions and the fact that she still didn't know if she had a job or not. But, yes, she was definitely happy.

But she was also smart enough to know that she couldn't rely on those feelings. Reality would intrude and she would have to get herself back on track. In the meantime maybe she should take his suggestion. Call Dexter, finish TJ's proposal, and then treat the next five days as an impromptu holiday.

Valentino, she knew, would make sure she had fun—and would it be so wrong to soak up his hospitality for a little longer? To soak *him* up for a little longer?

She rolled onto her stomach and glanced at the digital bedside clock. Ten o'clock. If this was a normal work day she'd have been hard at it for three hours by now and staring down the barrel of another ten. And those were her hours during quieter periods.

She sighed and shifted her attention to the magpies hopping about and conversing with each other outside the full-length window that took up one whole wall of Valentino's masculine room.

She was under no illusions as to why he had asked her to stay for five days, and although she had never been the type to enter into a purely sexual relationship there was a first time for everything. She just had to keep things as light and breezy as he did. No intense emotions, no second-guessing herself at every turn. Just...fun.

Miller stepped from the car and smiled at Mickey as he held the door for her. Mickey was everything she'd expected—large, fit, and capable of lifting a small house with his bare hands. The fact that he was also capable of purchasing women's clothing didn't bear thinking about.

The pavement outside the swanky Collins Street retail outlet was lined with photographers and fans, all of whom quickly lowered their cameras as soon as they saw that she wasn't anybody special. Glad for once not to be part of the in crowd, Miller quickly turned her eyes to the burly security guards who stood either side of the short red carpet.

Swallowing hard, she was just contemplating how foolish she would feel if she gave them her name and they rejected her when a woman in a chic black suit rushed forward.

'Ms Jacobs?'

'Yes.'

Thank God. Someone knew her name.

'My name is Chrissie. Mr Ventura asked me to show you in.'

Miller smiled, ready to kiss Valentino's feet for his thoughtfulness. Straightening her spine, she followed Chrissie into the brightly lit store.

Faces turned towards her but she ignored everyone as the attractive aide wound a path between glamorous, laughing guests holding sparkling glasses of wine and champagne. The room was buzzing with energy and it grew steadily more frenetic the further she went—until Chrissie stepped aside and Miller knew why.

Valentino stood in the centre of a small circle of admirers wearing a severely cut pinstriped suit and an open-necked snowy white shirt. He looked so polished and poised, so sinfully good-looking, her mind shut down and all she could do was stare.

Having chosen black trousers and a gold designer top carefully from Mickey's inspired collection, and redone her hair in its normally sleek style, Miller still felt utterly exposed, stripped bare, when Valentino's eyes honed in on her like a radio device searching out a homing beacon.

God, she was in trouble. Big trouble. He was just so beautiful, with his dishevelled sable hair and five o'clock shadow, and her body knew his, had kissed every inch of him. The urge to bolt was overwhelming, but then he smiled and she exhaled a bucketload of air. It would be all right. She was fine.

Her toes curled in her strappy heels as he walked towards her, his eyes glittering.

'You look beautiful,' he murmured as he captured her hand and brought it to his lips in an age-old gesture.

Miller's stomach flipped and she couldn't tear her eyes from his. 'Funny, I was just thinking the same about you. Though I wasn't going to mention it on account of your ego and your current cheer squad, lapping you up like Christmas pudding.'

Valentino threw his head back and laughed and Miller felt riveted to the spot. Did he have any idea that he was so completely irresistible? Yes, of course he did. The people around them couldn't take their eyes off him.

'How did you spend your day?' he asked, smiling down at her.

'I worked—'

'Now, *there's* a newsflash,' he teased.

'Yes, well. I spoke to Dexter, and although he hasn't forgiven me for what I said to TJ I don't think he's going to do anything to jeopardise my promotion.'

'Good.' He grabbed a glass of champagne from a passing waiter and handed it to her. 'When are you going to start painting again?'

Miller was exasperated that he had discovered her most secret dream.

'Valentino, don't ask me that.'

'Why not?'

'Because it was a childish dream.'

'Not childish. Daring. A dream unhampered by adult limitations. Perhaps it's time you stopped hiding behind that wall you protect yourself with and go fot it.'

'I will if you will.'

The instant the words were out she held her breath, her heart hammering.

His eyes pierced her but there was no hostility behind them, just reluctant admiration. 'I forgot you were such a shrewd operator. Come on—I have to mingle.'

That easily he closed her down, and although it made her feel slightly hollow inside she refused to address the feeling.

With Valentino beside her she felt carefree, as if he had flicked a switch inside her, and as much as she fought against the uncertainty of her emotions she felt more like herself now than she ever had.

She watched him handle a group of business executives with ease and aplomb and for a moment envied him his sheer confidence and charisma. There was just something about him that was devastatingly attractive—and it wasn't just the way he looked. It was his sense of humour, his chivalry, his deep voice, his keen intelligence…

Miller sucked in a breath as a shot of pure terror made her chest hurt.

She was falling for him.

No. It couldn't be true. She wouldn't let it be true. But…

As if sensing her distress, Valentino turned to her, his eyes intense as they swept over her. Burned into her.

'Miller, are you okay?'

Miller stared up into his concerned gaze.

'I'm fine,' she answered automatically.

His gaze narrowed, sharpened, and Miller had a horrible feeling that he could see into her deepest self.

His hand reached for hers. 'You're sure?'

No, she was far from sure. But what could she say? That she

thought her feelings for him were deeper than his for her? She shook her head, and his frown deepened.

Realising she was behaving like a nutcase, Miller pulled herself together. She *wasn't* falling in love with him; she was too smart to do that.

CHAPTER FOURTEEN

He really should be worried about getting himself into the mental space required to win pole position for tomorrow's race but for some reason he wasn't. The race was less than twenty-four hours away, and he wondered if he had time to make a quick detour on his way to the track.

He probably should be worried about how he felt about Miller as well, but so far he'd refused to think about it—and he was going to continue doing so until after the race.

It was true he was starting to entertain some thoughts about not finishing things with her straight away...but the jury was still out on that one.

And it wasn't just because of the sexual pleasure she brought him—though that was astounding. It was that he liked being with her. He'd even let her convince him to try Mexican food yesterday. He smiled at the memory. He hadn't planned on eating much—his team manager would have thrown a fit if he'd deviated from his strict diet this close to a race—but he hadn't needed discipline to tell her he'd pass.

'What are you thinking about?'

He glanced at her, sitting beside him in his Range Rover, her long legs curled to the side. The question had become a running joke between them since Monday night.

'That bean mixture you tried to force-feed me yesterday.'

'Enchiladas.'

He shuddered, and she rolled her eyes.

'I did not try to force-feed you. There must be something wrong with your tastebuds.'

'I promise you there's nothing wrong with my tastebuds, Sunshine.' He watched her blush and brought her fingertips to his lips.

He grinned as she smiled, and the sudden realisation that he was relaxed and happy jolted him. Often he had to force those feelings, but right now they were as genuine as she was.

'Any news from TJ?' He knew the man had agreed to part of Miller's business proposal, but the crafty old bastard was holding back on the rest until he found out his own decision about representing Real Sport.

Miller had insisted that he not do it, but he'd turned the matter over to his publicist anyway.

'Not yet. But I'm confident he'll give us the rest of his business in due course.'

Tino was too, but talking business reminded him again of one of his own little projects that he'd neglected of late.

Deciding that he had enough time, he turned the car off the next exit ramp, just before the Westgate Bridge, that led to the backstreets of Yarraville.

'This isn't the way to Albert Park,' Miller said, curiosity lighting her voice.

'I want to show you something first.'

He pulled into a large empty car park and cut the engine.

'This is a go-carting track.'

'Yep. Go Wild.'

Miller followed him out of the car, her sexy legs encased in denim jeans and cute black boots.

'Why are we here?'

'I want to check it out.'

'I think it's closed.'

'It is.' He reached the double glass doors and used a key to open it. 'I bought the place two months ago, when I was bored convalescing. I've had a lot of work done on it, but I haven't been back for a while.'

He walked into a dimly lit cavernous room, the smell of grease, sawdust and petrol making him breathe deep. A sense of wellbeing settled over him as he took in the changes since the last time he had visited.

Miller walked past him, clearly impressed by the view of a twisting track that took up most of the space.

She wrinkled her nose. 'It smells of stale chips.'

He hadn't noticed that.

'I think the kitchen is the next thing to be overhauled. This is the little kids' area,' he explained, walking towards one of the barriers. 'The bigger kids' track is out back.'

'Do we have time to see it?'

'Sure—hey, Andy?'

'Tino. I wasn't expecting you.' A tall, lanky man in a plaid shirt that had seen better days and grease-streaked jeans loped towards them.

Tino clasped his friend's hand. 'Andy, this is Miller Jacobs. Miller, this is my centre manager and fellow visionary, Andy Walker.'

'Hello.'

Miller took Andy's hand and Tino was slightly annoyed with himself for automatically stepping into her personal space when he registered Andy's very male appraisal of her.

They might be sleeping together right now, but that didn't mean she belonged to him in any way. The words he'd thrown at Caruthers at the weekend—"Miller is *mine*!"—reregistered in his mind and pulled him up short.

'Tino?'

He blanked his expression and cast off the unsettling notion that he'd well and truly crossed into a no-go zone with Miller. 'Sorry, I missed that last bit.'

'I said the main track is finished,' Andy repeated. 'Did you get my text last Wednesday?'

'I did. That's why I thought I'd stop by.'

'Come on. I'll show you.'

Clamping down on his worrying thoughts, Tino followed

Andy towards the rear of the building and out into the bright sunshine, shielding his eyes as he took in the track.

'It's huge.' Miller exclaimed behind him. 'Like a mini-racetrack.'

Tino smiled. 'That's because it is.'

'I know that,' she scoffed. 'I just wasn't expecting it to be that big.'

'Want to go out on it?'

'You mean walk around it?'

'Not walking.' He turned to Andy. 'Any chance you can pull a couple of carts out?'

'Sure.'

Andy grinned like a happy Labrador and Tino enjoyed the look of surprise on Miller's stunning face.

'I've never driven a go-cart before.'

'There's nothing to it.'

Five minutes later they were both kitted out in helmets and gloves, and once he'd fixed Miller into her cart he climbed into his own.

'We're not racing each other,' she informed him nervously.

Wondering if she would get the bug, he smiled. 'Remember it's just like driving a normal car only the gears are on the steering wheel and there's no clutch. Right foot is accelerator and left is brake. Other than that there's nothing to it.'

He watched as she revved the engine, unexpectedly distracted when her face glowed. 'One more thing,' he called above the throaty whine of the carts. 'These engines are more powerful than the usual carts, so go easy on the first few laps. I'll go first, so you can follow my line as you learn the track.'

'Ha—you're going first because you can't stand being second.'

Valentino smiled. She'd got that right.

He gunned his engine and put the cart into gear. The carts were fixed with a side mirror, so he kept his eye on her as they did a couple of laps.

Both he and Andy had designed the carts, and he was impressed at how well they handled.

After five laps he pulled his cart to a stop near the starting line and waited for Miller to pull up beside him.

'How was it?'

Her face was flushed from the light wind and her eyes were glowing with excitement. Oh, yeah, she definitely had the bug.

'I think you could turn me into a speed demon.' She grinned. 'This is *amazing*. But they seem a bit powerful for kids.'

Valentino found himself once again captivated by her smile, those eyes that shifted from aquamarine to almost indigo when she was aroused. 'They're for big kids. Teenagers, adults. This is a specialised track.'

'Great to hire out to corporations for bonding sessions.'

'Maybe.' He hadn't thought that far ahead yet.

'I have an idea.'

She leaned towards him conspiratorially and his eyes instantly fell to the deep V the movement made in her black T-shirt.

'What?'

'I'll race you!'

It took him a second to get his mind off her cleavage, and by that time she was already two cart lengths ahead of him. Valentino felt his competitor's spirit champing at the bit.

Little witch. She had deliberately distracted him.

As he followed her the feeling that he was very much in trouble with this new, more relaxed Miller returned. In fact, possibly he'd been in trouble all along.

He'd sensed this latent fire in her nature many times over the weekend at TJ Lyons's, and after listening to her story about her childhood he could see how she had locked herself down to a certain extent to achieve her goals. Which he admired. It took a lot of fortitude to achieve what she had done, and even though he felt that her reasoning had been a little skewed by her mother's fears, he couldn't fault her execution. She'd devised a plan for herself and she'd worked diligently to achieve it. A bit like himself.

Tino kept pace with her, challenging her lead on one of the easier corners but never taking over. For once he was happy to take the back seat in a competition.

He came up beside her and signalled one more lap. He saw determination set in her face and had to smile. If she but knew it he could take her in a heartbeat.

He upped the pressure as they headed towards the home straight and his heart nearly exploded in his chest as her cart veered to the side and headed full speed towards a railing that had yet to be lined with safety material.

'The brake! Dammit, Miller, hit the brake!'

He knew she couldn't hear him, and he was powerless to do anything but watch. It was like seeing his father head towards that concrete barrier all over again. The feelings of pain and loss were so powerful, so ferocious, he tasted bile in his mouth.

By some dumb stroke of luck her car pulled up an inch before the railing. Tino vaulted out of his cart and wrenched her helmet off before he'd taken his next breath.

'What were you *thinking*?' he all but bellowed as he took in her wild eyes and laughing face.

'Oh, my God. I nearly hit the rail!' Her voice was vibrating with both adrenalin and mild shock.

'That was a bloody stupid thing to do.'

'I didn't mean to,' she said indignantly. 'My heel got caught under the brake pedal.'

Her heel… Tino glanced down at her feet and noted the delicate heels on boots he'd only seen as cute. Damn, he hadn't even considered her footwear when he'd made the impromptu decision to take her out on the track.

He swore under his breath. Ironically, he'd never felt more scared of anything in his life than seeing Miller hurtle towards that railing.

'Hey, relax.' She was still smiling as she pulled herself out of the cart. 'It was just a bit of— Oh!' She threw her hand out and gripped his forearm as her legs buckled beneath her weight. 'My legs feel like jelly.' She laughed and locked her knees. 'I think that was better than sex.'

Tino shook his head, his sense of humour gone. 'Those carts top out at sixty ks an hour. You could have been seriously hurt.'

And why was he yelling at her when it was his own fault?

'I'm sorry if you were worried.' She tightened her grip, suddenly becoming aware of his over-reaction at the same time as he did.

'Of course I was worried. I don't think we have insurance on this place yet.'

'I don't know what to say.' She looked stricken. 'Are you okay?'

Tino collected the helmets. 'Fine.' He clamped down on his emotions with vicious intent, doing his best to stanch the fierce male rage that flooded him. The desire to grab her, crush her up against the nearest wall and pump himself inside her was like a savage animal riding him hard.

Instead, he shook his head, trying to clear his thoughts, and stalked off towards the equipment room. He could see Andy striding across the track and deliberately headed in the other direction. He needed to do something. *Hit* something.

'Tino!' Miller called after him, and he could hear her clipped footsteps on the concrete behind him. He lengthened his strides. 'Tino?'

Dimly he registered that she had stopped walking, and he pivoted around and stared at her. Her beautiful face was pale with concern. She approached him with the caution of a lion tamer without a whip and chair.

'Don't walk away. Please.'

Her quiet voice set off a riot of emotions, and right up there with wanting to physically take her—to physically *brand* her—was the urge to hold her and keep her safe. For ever. And that was the moment he realised he was shaking.

With the kind of lethal precision that was used to construct one of his beloved racing cars Tino shut down everything inside him.

'I have to get to the track. I've wasted enough time here.'

CHAPTER FIFTEEN

'Ma's finally got her wish, I see.'

Valentino turned at the sound of his older brother's voice and kept his irritation in check. He'd been enjoying a moment's quiet after being inundated with well-wishers and pseudo-virgins at his mother's charity extravaganza all night, but fortunately now the guests seemed to have settled—chatting, dancing and enjoying the view from one of Dante's premier hotels.

'What's that?' he asked, feigning interest.

'One of her sons has found love at her famous event.' Dante glanced towards the dance floor where Miller was dancing.

Tino glowered at him. 'I'm not even going to pretend I don't know what you're getting at.'

'That's good. We can cut straight to what you're intending to do about it instead. Should I be shining my shoes?'

'Not unless you're planning to go back to school,' Tino said lightly. 'I'm not in love with Miller,' he added dismissively. 'In case that was your next inopportune comment.'

He'd rather Dante harangue him about the big race tomorrow than a woman who was already constantly on his mind. He glanced at the dance floor where Miller was teaching his twelve-year-old nephew to waltz, and his body throbbed at the pleasurable memory of their lovemaking an hour earlier when he had returned to their penthouse suite.

Not that he'd meant it to be lovemaking. What he'd meant it to be was rough and raw sex to put them squarely back on the footing they'd started out on.

He'd spent six stressful hours at the track, secured second off the grid for tomorrow's race, and endured a gruelling press conference that had focused as much on his new "girlfriend" as it had on tomorrow's race.

All day he'd ignored his over-reaction to Miller's near accident, and the effort it had taken to keep his emotions under lock and key and be able to perform on the track had worn thin.

When he'd returned to the room and found Miller standing beside the bed in a demi-cup bra and matching thong he hadn't even bothered to say hello.

He frowned, memory turning him hard as a rock.

No, he hadn't said hello. She'd glanced up, half startled to see him as he'd prowled silently into the bedroom, and then she'd been against the wall and he'd been between her legs before he'd even thought about it.

He'd barely leashed his violent need for her, and yet once again she'd been right there with him. And, just as she had a tendency to do, she'd managed to twist the final few minutes of their coupling so that he was no longer the one in control. This time she'd insisted that he look at her with just the whisper of his name, and they'd flown over the edge together in an endless rush of pleasure.

Her sweet mouth still looked a little bruised, and as for the dress she had on… He took back his declaration that Mickey knew nothing about women's fashion. The chocolate-brown silk and froth creation clung to every curve and set off her eyes and skin to perfection. He'd never actually seen a more beautiful woman in his life, and his latent fear of tomorrow's race paled in comparison to the feelings she raised in him.

She was in his head—hell, she had been in the car with him at the track that afternoon, and that couldn't happen.

'You haven't taken your eyes off her all night and you've barely gone near her,' Dante drawled.

Tino tipped the contents of his glass of iced water down his parched throat. 'That's your definition of love?' he mocked, forcing his tone to reflect bored nonchalance. 'No wonder you struggle to keep a woman.'

Dante laughed softly. 'That's my definition of a man who's still running.'

'Let me repeat,' Tino bit out. 'I am not in love with Miller Jacobs.'

'What's the problem with it?' Dante was watching Miller now, his eyes alight with admiration. 'It was bound to happen some day. You're a lover, Tino, not a fighter. And she *is* stunning.'

'You're calling me soft?' He ignored the instinct to go for his brother's throat.

'I'm telling you I think she's great, and if you don't go get her I might.'

Valentino knew Dante was baiting him but even so his brother's soft taunt twisted the knots in his gut.

'Okay.' Dante held up his hands in mock surrender, even though Tino hadn't moved a muscle. 'I take back the not a fighter bit... But seriously, man, why fight it?'

Tino turned his back on the dance floor. 'You know why.' He sighed. 'My job.'

'So quit.'

Tino was shocked by Dante's suggestion. 'Would you give up your multi-billion dollar hotel business for a woman?'

Dante shrugged. 'I can't imagine it, but...never say never. Isn't that the adage? You've done it for fifteen years and you have an omen flapping over your head the size of an albatross. I don't think your time will be up tomorrow, if that helps, but why risk it?'

Tino knew Dante was remembering the day his father had crashed, something neither brother ever talked about, but he felt better now, knowing the reason behind Dante's topic of conversation. 'Did Ma or Katrina put you up to this?'

'You think the girls tried to get me to stop you racing? Ma would never do that. She's always been a free spirit. No.' He shook his head. 'There was just something different about you on the track today. As if you were…'

He frowned, searching for a word Tino didn't want him to find.

'Distracted.' *Yep, that was the one.* 'I thought maybe you were thinking it was time for a change.'

'In conversation, yes,' Tino bit out tersely.

The fact that his brother had noticed his earlier tension before the qualifying session was more concerning to him than if either one of the females in their family *had* sicced Dante onto him.

'Fair enough.' Dante took the heavy silence between them for what it was—disconnection. 'I won't push it. God knows I'd hate someone to push me. But I'd avoid Katrina if I were you. She's already trying to work out who will be flower girls to Toby and Dylan's pageboys.'

Miller stood to the side of the sparkling room, only half listening to Katrina's friendly chatter, her body still tingling from Valentino's earlier lovemaking when he had returned from the track. He hadn't even greeted her when he'd walked into the room—just backed her against the wall like a man possessed and taken her.

It had been fast and furious, and although he had shown her the same consideration as always she couldn't shake the feeling that he had been treating her as just another pit lane popsy—someone to use and discard straight after.

After her near accident at the go-cart track that morning his emotional withdrawal had been handled with military-like precision.

Which on some level she understood. She had been a complete bag of nerves watching him whip his car around the track during the qualifying sessions at speeds that made the go-carts look like wind-up toys, so she could only imagine how badly he had felt when she had lost control of the cart.

What she couldn't understand—what she *hated*—was the

way he politely maintained that everything was still normal between them.

It was too much like the time her parents had sat her down to tell her they were separating, pretending that they were happy with the decision while they each seethed with anger and hurt below the surface.

Their denial of how they really felt had made dealing with the separation nearly impossible, because Miller had *known* something wasn't right, and yet the one time she had been brave enough to broach the subject with her mother she had brushed her off and made her feel stupid.

Which was why, she realised, she had let Valentino give her the silent treatment. She hadn't been brave enough to open herself up to that kind of hurt again.

Unfortunately, that wasn't a failsafe plan, because without her even being aware of it the unthinkable had happened.

She had fallen in love with him.

The uncomfortable realisation had hit her when she'd been pressed deliciously against the hotel wall with his body buried deep inside hers.

At that moment when he had looked at her a spiral of emotion had caused her heart to expand, and she'd shattered around him in an agony of pleasure and longing.

She'd told herself it wasn't possible to fall in love in such a short space of time, but her heart had firmly overridden her head—as it had always done with Valentino Ventura.

And now, feeling like a liferaft set adrift, she understood why people did crazy things for love. She understood what her father had been talking about when he'd said that it was too painful to visit her after she had left with her mother. He'd had his heart broken. The sudden wave of understanding made her eyes water.

Blinking back the memories, she smiled at Katrina and pretended she'd been listening—and then at her next words she really was.

'I never thought I'd see my brother so in love. He can't stop looking at you.'

Couldn't stop looking at her? He hadn't looked at her once.

Well, okay, she had seen him glancing her way a couple of times, but she'd have called that glowering at her, not the benign version of *looking*. And he'd turned away each time before their eyes could properly connect.

Which was ironic, because she was supposedly here to prevent him from being accosted by every unattached woman at the ball, and since they weren't behaving like a couple the women had been lining up to get to him in droves. In fact, if she'd known he was going to completely ignore her, she would have brought a numbering system to help the whole process go more smoothly. Sort of like a speed dating service. Give everyone their five minutes and wait for him to choose her replacement.

Miller felt a spurt of anger take over from the intense pain that thought engendered, and latched onto it.

He might not want to continue things with her, but that didn't give him the right to treat her so poorly. It wasn't as if she would suddenly develop into a needy person who wouldn't let him go. She had known it was going to end. What she hadn't expected was that she would enjoy being part of a couple so much. She had been so fiercely independent for so long the thought hadn't occurred to her. But with Valentino... He made her feel so much. Made her want so much. Was that why he was avoiding her so thoroughly? Had he guessed her guilty secret?

The thought that he had horrified her. She might feel as if she was ready to face a lot of things she hadn't before in her professional life, but personally she was very far from ready to "squeeze the fear". Certainly not with a man who would never feel for her the same way she felt for him.

But it was one thing to deceive her workplace about her relationship with Valentino, which she had hated doing, and quite another to deceive Valentino's loving family. She didn't think Valentino would care if she corrected Katrina.

'Actually, Valentino isn't in love with me.'

'Oh, I wouldn't be so sure. He might not have said—'

Miller put her hand on Katrina's arm. 'I only met Valentino last week. The only reason I'm here with him now is because he helped me out of a bind and pretended to be my boyfriend.' She saw Katrina's eyes widen with unbridled curiosity and shook her head. 'Don't ask—it's a long story. Suffice it to say I became unwell, Valentino helped me out, and…here I am. But I'm going home tomorrow.'

Katrina turned compelling blue-grey eyes on her. 'But you have feelings for my brother?'

Miller inclined her head. No point in denying what was clearly obvious to Valentino's sister. She shrugged. 'Like every other woman on the planet.'

'So you're going to do what he does?' Katrina gently chided.

Miller's brow scrunched in confusion.

'You're going to make light of it?'

'No, you're wrong. I don't make light of anything.' She gave a self-deprecating laugh. 'I'm way too serious; it's one of my faults.'

Katrina pulled a face. 'I know my brother can be intensely brooding and unapproachable at times, but don't give up on him. He's protected himself from getting hurt for so long I think its second nature to him now. After our father's death he changed, and not—'

'Giving away family secrets again, Katrina?'

A biting voice savagely cut through his sister's passionate diatribe and Miller cringed. He stood behind her, legs braced wide and larger than life in a superbly cut tuxedo that made him look even more like a devil-may-care bad-boy than his jeans and T-shirts.

'Hello, little brother. Are you having a good time?' Katrina greeted him merrily.

'No. And I need to go. I'll see you at the track tomorrow, no doubt. Miller?'

He held out his arm for her to take and Miller did so, but

only because she didn't want to cause a scene in front of his sister. 'It was lovely to meet you, Katrina.'

'Likewise.' Katrina leant in close. 'Don't let his scowl put you off. He's harmless underneath.'

Oh, she was so wrong about that, Miller thought miserably. Valentino had the power to hurt her like no one else ever had, and she was really peeved she had given him that power over her. Because it was her own stupid fault. He'd been honest right from the start.

Halfway across the room, Miller tugged on his arm. 'I might stay on a bit longer, if that's okay?'

God, when had she been reduced to sounding like a Nervous Nelly?

'Why?'

Because I don't want to go upstairs with you in this mood and have you rip my heart to pieces.

'I'm having a good time.'

'I don't want you talking to my family about me *or* my father.'

His voice was cold and she now wondered if he really was leaving because he needed to get sleep and prepare for the race tomorrow, or because he assumed she'd keep trying to wheedle secrets out of his family about him.

'I didn't ask Katrina anything,' she denied. 'She assumed that you had feelings for me. We both know you don't and I told her this whole thing was fake.'

Valentino grabbed her elbow and pulled her to the side of the room to let a couple pass by.

'Why would you say that?'

Miller forced herself not to be intimidated by his frown. 'Because I don't like being dishonest and I like your family.'

'This thing stopped being fake the minute we had sex and you know it,' he growled.

Miller's hopeful heart skipped a beat. Did he mean that? Could his black mood be because he had strong feelings for her and just didn't know how to express them?

'What is it, then?' She knew she was holding her breath but she couldn't help it.

He raked back his hair in frustration and glowered at the glittering crowd of doyennes behind her. 'I don't know. Good fun?'

Good fun?

Stupid, desperate heart.

'Look, I'm sorry. I've had a terrible day and I don't want you talking about my father. The man died racing a car. Everyone needs to get over it and move on.'

'Like you have?'

His scowl at her quietly voiced question didn't bear thinking about. 'Don't psychoanalyse me, Miller. You don't know me.'

'Only because you hide your deepest feelings under solid cement.'

She thought he would try and make light of her comment. When he didn't she realised how stressed he really was. She also realised that her breathing had grown harsh, and the last thing she wanted to do was argue with him the night before a crucial race.

'Valentino, your sister didn't mean any harm. She was boosting me up because she thinks that you protect yourself against being hurt.' A conclusion she had also drawn after talking to him that day in the park.

'That's ridiculous.'

'Is it?' Miller asked softly, her heart going out to this wounded, gorgeous man. 'Or is it that you believe that your father didn't love you enough to quit racing? Because I know that tomorrow's race has been playing on your mind, and I've seen enough to guess that maybe you're a little angry with him.'

A flash of insight hit her as she recalled how stiff he had been in his mother's company—a woman she knew he loved dearly.

'Maybe even with your mother—although I'm not sure why that would be.'

'Don't confuse your mother issues with mine, Miller,' he snarled.

Miller gasped. 'That's a horrible thing to say. My mother

did her best and while you've helped me see that I've blindly followed her dreams instead of my own that wasn't her fault. It was mine. I didn't *have* to give up my artistic aspirations. I *chose* to because it suited me at the time.' Miller felt as if he'd torn a strip off her and left her bleeding. 'Now, I can see I've overstayed my welcome, so if you'll ex—'

'Don't leave.'

Miller's stomach was in knots and she was shaking. She *had* to leave before her runaway mouth said anything more she might regret. 'I'm tired.'

'I don't mean right now. I mean tomorrow. Quit your job and travel with me. Come to Monaco next week.'

Miller stared at him. The tinkling chatter of happy guests faded to a low hum. He didn't look completely comfortable, but was he serious?

'Why?' she blurted out.

'Why does there have to be a reason? Haven't you had fun the last few days?'

Miller smoothed her brows. 'You know I have. But it's not enough to sustain a relationship.'

'Why put a label on what's between us?'

Miller paused, taking in the offhandedness of his question, his effortless arrogance.

Oh, God, he wasn't talking about having a relationship with her. Not a real one, anyway. *She* was the only one here with long-term on the brain.

'I...can't.'

She knew if she took him up on his offer it would mean a lot more to her than it did to him, and she knew herself well enough to know that it would be hell on her self-esteem. It would also be repeating the same mistakes she had made in the past— because following him around the world would be following *his* dreams at the expense of her own.

Reluctantly, she shook her head.

'Why not?' He sounded frustrated. 'You hate your job.'

'I don't hate my job.'

He made a patronising noise and swung his arm in an arc. 'It's not what you want to do.'

'How would you know? You never ask me what it is I want— you just tell me.' She knew that was slightly unfair but she wasn't about to correct herself right now. This was about protecting herself from his clear intent to change her mind for his own selfish purposes.

'If you don't want to come just say so, Miller, but don't use your job as an excuse.'

'What has got into you?' she fumed. 'You've been like a bear with a sore head all day, you've ignored me all night, and now you're trying to steamroller me again to get what you want.'

'Because I *always* get what I want.'

Miller rolled her eyes. 'That's arrogant, even for you.'

He shoved a hand in his pocket, pulling the divinely cut tuxedo jacket wide in a casually elegant move redolent of a 1950s film. 'You didn't seem to mind it this week.'

Didn't seem to... Miller couldn't fathom his indifference. She had feelings and he was treating her as if she was here just to please him.

'I don't know how serious your offer to travel with you was, but I'm assuming you want a relationship. I have to tell you that I would never enter into something with a man who is so stubborn and selfish and *angry*.'

'And finally she lists my faults.'

'Oh, that is *so* typical of you—to make fun of something so serious.'

'And it's so typical of you to make serious that which could be fun.'

Miller drew in a fortifying breath. 'I think we've said enough. We're too different, Valentino. You want everything to be light and easy, but sometimes feelings aren't like that.'

'I know that. It's why I refuse to have them.'

'You can't just refuse to have them. They're not controllable.' But Miller had the uncomfortable realisation that she had once believed exactly that.

Valentino rocked back on his heels. 'Every emotion is controllable.'

'Well, you're lucky if that's true, because I've just discovered that mine aren't, and I can't be with someone who only connects with me during sex because he's too afraid to share how he feels.'

'It's the damned uncertainty of it you don't like.'

Miller threw up her hands. 'And now you're going to tell me how I feel in an effort to hide your own feelings.'

'Fine—you want to know how I feel? I feel that my father made a bad choice when he married my mother. He wasn't a man equipped for having a family and he was never around for us. Hell, I was his favourite because of our shared love of adrenalin highs, but even then we hardly had any time together. And when his car hit that wall—' He stopped suddenly, his voice thick. 'I won't do that to another person.'

The words *it hurts too much* hovered between them and Miller's stomach pitched.

'Valentino, I'm so sorry.' She wanted to touch him, but his stiff countenance stole her confidence.

'You're not coming with me, are you?'

Miller swallowed heavily. If he had shown any inclination that his feelings might be even close to being as strong as hers she'd stay. She'd...

No. She couldn't stay for anything less than love. She refused to fall victim to the laws of relationships. She refused to be in an unequal partnership and watch it wither and die. Because it would take her along with it.

'I can't. I—' She hesitated, fear of being ridiculed stopping her from exposing exactly how she felt, but knowing she loved him too much just to walk away without trying. 'I want more than you're prepared to give.'

He raked back his hair in frustration. 'How much more?'

'I want love. I never thought I did, and I'm still afraid of it, but you've made me see that working so hard, cutting myself off from my true passions, from my *feelings*, is living half a life. I'm sure I won't be any good at a real relationship, but I'm ready to try.'

He turned his head to the side, his expression hard. 'I can't give you that. I don't do permanence.'

Miller smiled weakly, her heart breaking. 'I know. That's why I didn't ask it of you. But thank you for last weekend. For this week. And good luck tomorrow.'

'Fine.' His voice was harsh, grating. He cleared his throat. 'Tell Mickey when you want to organise the jet.'

Miller felt her lower lip wobble and turned away before the tears in her eyes spilled over. It didn't get much more definitive than that.

CHAPTER SIXTEEN

WHEN Miller disappeared from view Tino stalked off without a clear destination in mind, burning with anger. Didn't she know what a concession he had made for her? What he had just offered her?

Tino stopped when he found himself outside on a tiered balcony, staring sightlessly at the glittering city lights.

Thank God she *hadn't* taken him up on his offer. What had he been thinking? He *never* took a woman on tour.

'I'm probably not the best person to follow you out here, but I know at least out of respect you won't walk off on me.'

Valentino turned to find his mother standing behind him.

'Want to talk about it?'

No, he didn't want to talk about it.

'Thanks, but I'm fine, Ma.'

'Don't ask me how this works.' His mother stepped closer. 'But a mother always knows when one of her children is lying. Even when they're fully grown.'

Valentino blew out a breath and tipped his head to the starry sky. He really didn't want his mother bothering him right now, and he cursed himself for not leaving when he'd had the chance.

'Ma—'

His mother held her hand up in an imperious way that reminded him of Miller. 'Don't brush me off, darling. I once let your father go into a race in turmoil, and I won't let my son do the same if I can help it.'

Valentino stared down at the tiny woman who had the

strength and fortitude of an ox, and his anger morphed into something else. Something that felt a little like despair.

She stood beside him and the silence stretched taut until he couldn't stand it any more. 'You found it hard to be married to Dad with his job. I know you did.'

'Yes.'

'Why didn't you ask him to quit?' Valentino heard the pain in his voice and did his best to mask it. 'He would have done it for you.'

She regarded him steadily. 'You're still angry with him. With me, perhaps?'

He turned back to the lights below; cars like toys were moving in a steady stream along the throughways. Miller had said he was angry and right now he *felt* angry, so what was the point in denying it?

'I never realised just how much you closed yourself off from us after your father died.' His mother's soft voice penetrated the sluggish fog of his mind. 'You were always so serious. So *controlled*. But somehow you were still able to make us laugh.'

She offered him a sad smile that held a wealth of remembered pain.

'I can see now it was your way of dealing with your pain, and I'm sorry I wasn't there more for you right after it happened.'

Valentino raked an unsteady hand through his hair. 'He always acted so bloody invincible and I...' He swallowed the sudden lump in his throat. 'I stupidly believed him.'

'Oh, darling. I'm so sorry. And I must have only made it worse by relying on you so heavily after his death because I thought you understood.'

Valentino felt something release and peel open deep inside him. Clasping his mother's shoulders, he drew her into his arms. 'I'm not angry at you, Ma.'

'Not any more, hmmm?'

He heard her sniff and tightened his embrace. 'I'm sorry. I've been an ass to you and to Tom. I treated him appallingly when he dutifully drove me to go-cart meets every month, stood in the wings of every damned race.' He stopped, unable to express his remorse at the way he had treated his mother's second husband.

His mother hugged him tight. 'He understood.'

'Then he's a better man than I am.'

'You were only sixteen when we married—a difficult age at the best of times.'

'I think I resented him because he was around when Dad just never had been.'

'Your father took his responsibilities seriously, Valentino. His problem was that he'd grown up in a cold household and didn't know how to express love. He didn't know how to show you that he loved you, but he was torn. That morning...' She stopped, swallowed. 'We'd been talking a lot about him retiring leading up to that awful race, and I think that had he survived he *would* have quit.'

'I overheard you both talking about it that morning.'

His mother closed her eyes briefly. 'Then you must blame me for his death. For putting him off his race.'

Her voice quavered and Tino rushed to reassure her. 'No. Certainly not. Honestly, I blamed Dad for trying to have it all. I think, if anything, I was just upset that you hadn't tried to stop him.'

His mother pulled back and gave him a wistful smile. 'It is what it is. We are each defined by the choices that we make for good and bad. And it wasn't an easy decision for your father to make. He had sponsors breathing down his neck, the team owner, his fans. He did his best, but fate had other ideas.' She paused. 'But life goes on, and I've been lucky enough to find love not once, but twice in my life. I hope you get to experience the same thing at least once. I hope all of my children do.'

Jamming his hands in his pockets, Tino wished he could jam a lid on the emotions swirling through his brain.

Damn Miller. She had been right. He had been angry with his mother all this time. 'I'm sorry. Thank you for telling me.'

He caught a movement in his peripheral vision and saw Tom,

his stepfather, about to head back inside, his expression clearly showing that he didn't want to interrupt.

Valentino beckoned him and Tom approached, putting his arm around his wife, love shining brightly in his eyes. 'I didn't want to interrupt.'

Tino drew in a long, unsteady breath. 'Tom…' He searched for a way to thank this man he had previously disdained for loving his mother and always being there for him and his siblings.

Tom inclined his head in a brief nod. 'We're good.'

Tino felt a parody of a smile twist his mouth. He nodded at Tom, kissed his mother's cheek and left them to admire the view.

The urge to throw down a finger of whisky was intense. So was the need to find Miller.

Tino did neither.

Instead, he took the lift to the ground floor and hailed a cab to the only place he'd ever found real peace.

His car.

The tight security team at the Albert Park raceway were surprised to see him, but no one stopped him from entering.

Not ever having been in the pits this late at night, he was surprised with how eerie it felt. Everything was deadly quiet. The monitors were off, the cars tucked away under protective cloth. The air was still, with only a faint trace of gasoline and rubber.

He threw the protective covering off his car, pulled the steering wheel out and climbed in. His body immediately relaxed into the bucket seat designed specifically to fit his shape. The scent of moulded plastic and polish was instantly soothing.

After re-fixing the steering wheel, he did an automatic pre-race check on the buttons and knobs.

Then he thought of his father and the times he'd watched him do the same thing, remembering the connection they had shared.

He released a long breath, realising that he had always felt superior to his father because *he'd* kept everyone at a safe distance. He'd believed it to be one of his great strengths, but maybe he'd been wrong.

A faint memory flickered at the edges of his mind, and he let his head fall back, stared unseeing at the high metal ceiling. What was his mind trying to tell him…? Oh, yeah—his father had once told him that when love hit you'd better watch out, because you didn't have any say in the matter. You just had to go for it.

Tino's hands tensed around the steering wheel. His father hadn't been weak, as he'd assumed, he'd been strong. He'd dared to have it all. Okay, he'd made mistakes along the way, but did that make him a bad person?

In a moment of true clarity, Tino realised that he was little more than an arrogant, egotistical shmuck. One who didn't dare love because he was afraid to open himself up to the pain he had experienced at losing his father.

For years he'd truly believed he was unable to experience deep emotion, but now he realised that was just a ruse—because Miller had cracked him open and wormed her way into his head and his heart.

Damn.

Tino banged the steering wheel as the truth of his feelings for her stared him in the face. He loved Miller. Loved her as he'd never wanted to love anyone. And ironically he was now faced with his worst nightmare. Forced to face the same decision he'd held his father to account for so many years ago.

For so long he had resented his father for refusing to quit, but he'd had no right to feel that way. No right to stand in judgement of a man who'd been driven to please everyone.

Like Miller.

Tino felt a stillness settle over him.

He could hear tomorrow's crowd already, smell the gasoline in the air, the burn of rubber on asphalt, *feel* the vibration of the car surrounding him, drawing him into a place that was almost spiritual. But despite all that he couldn't *see* himself doing it.

He could only see Miller. Miller in the bar in her black suit.

Miller tapping her toes by the car as she waited for him to pick her up. Miller completely wild for him on the beach, in his bed, staring at him with wide, hurt eyes in the ballroom as the light from the chandeliers lit sparks in her wavy hair.

God, he was more of an idiot than Caruthers. He'd had her, she'd been *his*, and he'd pushed her away. Closed her down as he'd done all week whenever the conversation had veered towards anything too personal.

Levering himself out of his car, he knew he was saying goodbye to a part of his life that had sustained him for so long, but one that he didn't need any more.

He didn't care what the naysayers would say when he pulled out of the race tomorrow. For the first time ever he had too much to lose to go out onto the track. For the first time ever he wanted something else more.

The signs had been there. Or maybe they hadn't been signs, maybe they'd just been coincidences. It didn't matter. When he closed his eyes and thought about his future he wasn't standing on a podium, holding up yet another trophy. He was with Miller.

Miller who had stalked off with tears behind her eyes.

Where *was* she?

He doubted she'd organised the jet to fly back to Sydney at this late hour; she was too considerate to disturb his pilot.

Likely she was still at the hotel. But he'd bet everything he owned she'd arranged for another room by now.

Miller felt terrible. Beyond terrible. Walking away from Valentino's offer to travel with him had felt like the hardest thing she had ever done in her life. Even harder than leaving her father behind in Queensland all those years ago.

She was in love with Valentino and she was never going to see him again, never going to touch him again. There was something fundamentally wrong with that.

Travel with me. Come to Monaco next week.

Had she made a monumental mistake?

Miller looked down, half expecting to find herself standing

on a trapdoor that would open up at any minute and put her out of her misery, but instead all that was there was designer carpet.

She sighed. This morning she had woken in Valentino's arms and felt that life couldn't get any better. TJ had signed Oracle to consult for his company *before* finding out what Valentino's decision about Real Sport was, and the powers-that-be had requested a meeting with her first thing Monday morning. Which could only mean a promotion because, as Ruby had pointed out, no one got fired on a Monday.

But the idea of a promotion didn't mean half as much as it once might have. Not only because her priorities had changed over the course of the week, but because she felt as if all the colour had been leached out of her life. Try as she might to pull herself together, it seemed her heart had taken a firm hold of her head and it was miserable. Aching.

She'd known falling in love would be a mistake, and boy had she ever been right about that. Love was terrible. Painful. *Horrible.*

She had accused Valentino of keeping himself safe from this kind of pain, but of course it was what she had always done as well. Keeping her hair straight, wearing black, hiding herself away at her work in an attempt to control her life. None of it had been real—just like her relationship with Valentino.

Only towards the end it had felt real with him. Had *become* real without her even noticing… She'd fallen in love and he hadn't. Which just went to prove the law of relationships: one person always felt more.

And now, sitting on Valentino's plane as his pilot ran through the preflight check, still wearing her beautiful, frothy dress, she felt like the heroine from a tragic novel.

She sniffed back tears and wondered if she had time to put her casual clothes on. And then she wondered what was taking so long. Surely she'd been sitting on the tarmac for over an hour now?

The whoosh of the outer doors opening brought her head

round, and she was startled to see Valentino's broad shoulders filling the doorway.

Like her, he hadn't taken the time to change, and he looked impossibly virile: his bow tie was hanging loosely around his neck and the top buttons of his dress shirt were reefed open.

Miller swallowed, her heart thumping in her chest. 'What are you doing here?'

Valentino stalked inside the small cabin. 'Looking for you. And I have to say this is the last place I tried.'

'I told Mickey not to tell you.'

'He didn't. My pilot did.'

He looked annoyed.

'I'm sorry if you're upset about me commandeering your plane at this hour. I felt terrible doing it. But all the hotel rooms were booked and Mickey insisted...'

'I don't care about the plane. And stop moving.' Miller stopped when she realised she was stepping backwards. 'Where are you going, anyway?'

'The pilot stowed my bag in the rear cupboard. I was just going to get it.'

'Leave the damn bag.' He dragged a hand through his hair and Miller realised how tired he looked.

She swallowed heavily. 'Why were you looking for me?'

Had she forgotten something? Left something in their room?

'Because I realised after you left that I loved you and I needed to tell you.'

'You...what?'

He came towards her again and Miller's back bumped the cabin wall. Her senses were stunned at his announcement.

Valentino stepped into her personal space and cupped her elbows in his hands. 'You heard right. I love you, Miller. I've spent my whole life convincing myself it was the last thing I wanted, but fortunately you came along and proved me wrong.'

Miller tried to still her galloping heart. 'You told me that racing was all you ever needed.'

'Which shows you that you need to add stupidity to my list of flaws.'

'I might have been a bit harsh earlier.'

'No, you weren't.' He hesitated. 'After my father died I was determined never to love anyone because I convinced myself that I wanted to protect them from the hurt I had experienced. But you were right. I was protecting myself.' He shook his head. 'Until you came into my life, Miller, I truly believed that I didn't have the capacity to love anyone.'

Miller felt her heart swell in her chest. She desperately wanted to believe that he loved her but her old fears wouldn't let go.

He squeezed her hands gently. 'You're thinking something. What is it?'

'I thought you always knew what I was thinking?' Miller smiled weakly at her attempt at humour.

'Usually I do, but right now…I'm too scared to guess.'

Scared? Valentino was *scared*?

His admission was raw, and unbridled hope sparked deep inside her. 'You risk your life every time you race.'

He laughed. 'That's nothing compared to this. Now tell me what you're thinking, baby.'

Miller felt as if her heart had a tractor beam of sunlight shining right at it at the softness of his tone. 'I'm thinking that I may never outgrow my need for certainty, and I don't know if I can watch you throw yourself around a track every other week without making you feel guilty. Watching you qualify today, I thought I was going to throw up.'

'You won't have to do either. I've organised a meeting first thing tomorrow morning to announce my retirement from the circuit. Effective immediately.'

Miller didn't try to hide her shock. 'Why would you do that? You love racing.'

'I love you more.'

His words made her heart leap. 'But what will you do instead?'

'Andy and I have a patent over the new go-cart designs and we have visions of taking Go Wild global. I like your idea of turning it into a venue for corporations to use and I'm also thinking we can use it as a place to give kids interested in competing some personal coaching.'

Miller nodded. 'That's a great idea.'

Valentino blew out a breath as if her opinion really mattered. 'Good. I'm glad you like it. In fact, I was hoping to convince you to consult for us. Andy and I know a lot about cars, but we know jack about running a business.'

'You want me to work for you?' Miller knew she was smiling like a loon.

'Only if you want to—God, Miller, you're beautiful.' Valentino dropped her hands and hauled her against him, kissing her so passionately she couldn't think straight.

He drew back, shuddering. 'Where was I? Oh, yeah. Marry me.'

'Marry you?'

'I'm sorry I don't have a ring yet. Honestly, I've been fighting my feelings so hard for so long I'm embarrassingly underprepared, but I promise to make it up to you.'

Remembering how everything had gone so wrong between them just hours earlier, Miller felt some of her anxiety return.

As if sensing her tumultuous emotions, Valentino tugged her in against him again. 'If you don't like the idea that's fine. I know you have your own dreams to follow and I'll support you in whatever they are.' He smiled. 'Just so long as we find a little bit of time to have a house full of kids.'

'A house full?'

'You said you didn't like being an only child.'

'I hated it.' Miller's head was reeling.

'Then we should probably try for more than one, because chances are they'll hate it too.'

Once again happiness threatened to engulf her, but a tiny niggle of doubt still prevailed. 'Wait. You're steamrollering me again.'

'But I am wearing a suit this time. Does that count?'

Miller felt both fearful and excited in the face of his unwavering resolve. 'It does help that you look insanely handsome in one, yes.'

Valentino clasped her face in his hands. 'Okay, you're still worried. Talk to me.'

Miller wet her dry lips and took a deep breath. He'd put his heart on the line for her, was giving up his racing career to be with her. The least she could do was confide her greatest fear.

'Valentino, you can't possibly feel the same way about me as I do about you, and that will eventually ruin everything between us.'

She tried to glance away, feeling utterly miserable now, but he held her fast.

'How *do* you feel about me, Miller?'

'I love you, of course. But—'

She didn't get any further as his mouth captured hers in a blistering kiss so full of sensual passion and promise that tears stung the backs of her eyes.

'Stop.' She pushed at him weakly, her body trembling against his. 'You're too good at that, and it doesn't change the fundamental law of relationships.'

'Which one's that?' he asked, nuzzling the side of her neck.

Miller tried to put some distance between them, but his hold was implacable. 'The one that says one person will always love more than the other.'

Her voice was so anguished Valentino stopped kissing her and stared into her eyes. 'I've never heard of that law, but you'll never love me as much as I love you. I guarantee it.'

'No.' Miller shook her head. 'Your feelings can't possibly be as strong as mine are for you.'

Valentino smiled, pressed her against the cabin wall. 'Want to argue about it for the rest of our lives?'

Miller burst out laughing, radiant happiness slowly soaking into every corner of her heart. 'You're serious!'

Valentino stayed her nervous hands in one of his. 'I've never been more serious about anything. I once told you I'd never met a woman who excited me as much as racing—but, Miller, you do. I feel exhilarated just thinking about seeing you. And when I do...' He shook his head, the depth of his emotions shining brightly in his eyes.

Miller gazed back at the only man who had ever made her heart sing. 'I love you *so* much. I didn't know it was even possible to feel like this about another person.'

'Ditto, Sunshine. Now, put me out of my misery and tell me you'll marry me.'

Completely overwhelmed by emotions no longer held at bay Miller grinned stupidly. 'I'll marry you—but with one condition.'

Valentino groaned. 'I knew you wouldn't make it easy. What's the condition?'

Miller linked her hands behind his neck, deciding to have some fun with him. 'We do it at my pace, *not* yours.'

Valentino threw back his head and laughed. 'I told Sam that was my lucky shirt. Now it will be forever known as my *life-changing* shirt.'

Wriggling closer, Miller nuzzled his neck, the last of her doubts fading into nothing. 'I love you.'

Valentino's touch became purposeful, masterful. 'And I you.'

Miller smiled. How had she ever thought love was horrible? Love was *wonderful*.

* * * * *

HER SHAMEFUL SECRET

BY
SUSANNA CARR

Susanna Carr has been an avid romance reader since she read her first Mills & Boon Modern at the age of ten. Although romance novels were not allowed in her home, she always managed to sneak one in from the local library or from her twin sister's secret stash.

After attending college and receiving a degree in English Literature, Susanna pursued a romance-writing career. She has written sexy contemporary romances for several publishers, and her work has been honoured with awards for both contemporary and sensual romance.

Susanna lives in the Pacific Northwest with her family. When she isn't writing she enjoys reading romance and connecting with readers online. Visit her website at: www.susannacarr.com.

To Carly Byrne and Lucy Gilmour with thanks
for their insights and generous support.

CHAPTER ONE

Isabella Williams heard the throaty growl of an expensive sports car and lifted her head like a hunted animal scenting danger. The sudden move made her head spin. She took a step back, gripping the serving tray as she fought for her balance.

The sound of the car faded before she turned to see it. Isabella exhaled shakily, her bunched muscles relaxing. She swiped her hand against her clammy forehead, hating how her imagination ran wild. Her mind was playing tricks on her. One sports car drove past her and she immediately thought of him.

It was ridiculous to think that Antonio Rossi was in this part of Rome, or even searching for her. She rolled her eyes in self-disgust. She'd only shared a bed with him for a few glorious months in the spring. The guy would have long forgotten her. He was every woman's secret fantasy and Isabella was certain that she had been replaced the moment she left his bed.

The thought pricked at Isabella and she blinked away the tears that stung in the backs of her eyes. Glancing at the clock, she calculated how many more hours she had left on her shift. Too many. All she wanted to do was crawl back into bed, burrow under the threadbare covers and keep the world at bay. But she couldn't afford to take a day off. She needed every euro to survive.

"Isabella, you have customers waiting," her boss barked at her.

She simply nodded, too tired to give her usual sarcastic response, and headed toward one of the small tables on the sidewalk café. She would get through this day just like every other day. One foot in front of the other. One minute at a time.

It felt like she had waded through sludge by the time she got to the tiny table where the couple waited. They didn't seem to mind her slow pace. The man gently, almost reverently, kissed the woman's lips. Envy pierced through Isabella's stupor. She bit down on her lip to hold back a whimper as she remembered what it felt like to be adored and desired.

Isabella's shoulders slumped as the bittersweet memories poured over her. She couldn't recapture that kind of love. She would never be the center of Antonio's attention again, and he would no longer be her entire world. She missed his possessive kisses and the raw hunger they'd shared. But, much as she missed him, he would never take her back. Not when he discovered the truth.

Her knees threatened to buckle under the weight of her regret. She gritted her teeth and harnessed the last of her self-control. Those wildly romantic days were over, she reminded herself fiercely. It was best not to think of them.

"Are you ready to order?" she asked hoarsely in Italian. Her grasp of the language wasn't that great, despite her taking a few classes in college. Her struggle to communicate made it even more difficult to get through a day.

Once she'd had big dreams of becoming fluent in Italian, transforming herself into a sophisticated and glamorous woman and taking the city of Rome by storm. She'd wanted to find adventure, beauty and love. For a brief moment she'd had it all in her grasp, but she'd allowed it to slip through her fingers.

Now she worked all day in this dump and had no money. People either ignored her or viewed her as trash. So much for her transformation. She could have gotten that treatment back home. At least then she would know what was being said behind her back. She lived in a room above the café that didn't have running water or a lock on the door. All she had was the weight of the world on her shoulders and a deep need to survive.

As she took down the order and walked back to the kitchen Isabella realized that she was in danger of getting stuck here. She needed to work harder, faster and smarter if she wanted to return to America in the next few months. Now more than ever she needed to surround herself with the familiar. Find a place where she could keep her head down, work hard and complete her college degree. After all this time yearning for excitement, she now longed to find a safe haven.

But she didn't think she could keep this up, working long hours and barely getting by. And it was only going to get harder. The thought made her want to drop to the floor in a heap and cry.

Isabella leaned against the kitchen wall. One day she'd get out of this nightmare. She weakly closed her eyes, ignoring her boss's reprimand to hurry. Soon she'd have enough money to fly back to America. She'd start over and maybe get it right the next time. If there was one thing she could rely on it was learning from her mistakes.

Antonio Rossi surveyed the small sidewalk café. After searching all weekend he was going to face the woman who had almost destroyed him and his family. He strode to an empty table and sat down, his lethal grace concealing the anticipation of battle that was racing through his veins. This time he wasn't going to fall for Isabella's big blue eyes and innocent beauty. He would be in command.

He leaned back, his legs sprawled under the tiny table. Sliding dark sunglasses on his nose, Antonio looked at the paint-chipped, rusted furniture. Of all the places he'd thought she would be, he mused as he glimpsed the ratted, faded awning, he hadn't pictured a dirty little café on the wrong side of Rome.

Why was Isabella living in this filth and poverty? It didn't make sense. He had opened his world to her. She had lived in his penthouse apartment and shared his bed. She had had his servants to take care of her.

And she'd thrown it all away when she'd slept with his brother.

The knowledge still ate away at him. He had provided Isabella with everything, but it hadn't been enough. No matter how much he'd given, how hard he'd worked, he hadn't been able to compare with his brother. It had always been that way.

Still, he had been blindsided by Giovanni's drunken confession six months ago. Had responded by casting

Isabella and Giovanni out of his life. It had been swift and vicious, but they had deserved much worse.

Isabella stepped into his view. Tension gripped Antonio, and he braced himself for the emotional impact as he watched her precariously balance two cappuccinos on a serving tray. He had prepared himself for it, but seeing her was like a punch to his gut as she walked past him.

She wore a thin black T-shirt, a skimpy denim skirt and scuffed black flats, but she still had the power to draw his attention. His gaze lingered on her bare legs. He remembered how they'd felt wrapped around his hips as he drove into her welcoming body.

Antonio exhaled slowly and purged the image from his mind. He would not be distracted by her sexual allure or her innocent face. He had made the mistake of lowering his guard with her. He had trusted Isabella and got close to her. That wouldn't happen again.

Antonio grimly watched her serve the couple, noticing that she looked different. The last time he'd seen her, she had been asleep in his bed, flushed and naked, her long blonde hair fanning like a halo across the white silk pillow.

Isabella now looked pale and sickly. Her hair fell in a limp ponytail. The curves that had used to make him forget his next thought had diminished. She was bony and frail.

She looked terrible. A cruel smile flickered on the edge of his mouth. Antonio hoped she'd been to hell and back. He was prepared to take her there again.

He'd once believed she was sweet and innocent, but it had all been a lie. Her blushes and slow smiles had disarmed him and he had been convinced that she wanted only him. But her open affection had been a smoke-screen.

It turned out that Isabella was a master of the mind game and outplayed the most conniving women in his world, who would lie, cheat and bed-hop to get closer to Gio, heir to the Rossi fortune. Isabella had seduced Antonio with her angelic beauty. Made him believe that he was her first choice. Her only choice. But all that time she had been working her magic on Giovanni.

Isabella turned away from the table and headed towards him. Her head was bent as she grabbed her notepad and pen. Tension coiled inside him, ready to spring. He sat unnaturally still, refusing to make any sudden moves that would alert her to impending danger.

"Are you ready to order?" she asked uninterestedly.

Her hoarse voice was nothing like the husky whisper he remembered.

"Hello, Bella."

No, no, no!

She looked up sharply and her cloudy eyes cleared as she focused on Antonio. He was here. In front of her. Waiting for her to make the next move, even though they both knew it was useless.

Run. The word screamed through her brain.

Isabella slowly blinked. Maybe she was hallucinating. She hadn't been herself lately. There was no way Antonio Rossi, billionaire, member of the social elite, would be sitting in this café.

But her imagination couldn't conjure the electric current coursing through her body from his nearness. Or the panic that stole her breath. Her heart gave a brutal leap before it plummeted.

Does he know? Is that why he's here?

She couldn't stop staring at him like a deer caught in the headlights. Antonio wore a black pinstripe suit, the ruthlessly tailored lines emphasizing his broad shoulders and lean, muscular body. The hand-made shirt and silk tie offered a veneer of civility, but they couldn't mask his animal magnetism. He was the most sensual man she had ever known, and the most powerful.

Antonio Rossi was also the most callous person she'd met.

Isabella took short, choppy breaths, but she was suffocating with dread. She couldn't gauge his next move or his next thought. She only knew that it was going to be devastating.

She had been an idiot to get involved with him. He was the kind of man her mother had often warned her about. Antonio would see a woman like her only as a plaything and then discard her when something better came along. Isabella knew all this but she had still been drawn to him like a moth to a flame. Even now she felt the pull and she couldn't stop staring at him.

His eyes were hidden behind the sunglasses, but the angles and lines of his savagely masculine face were just as sharp and aggressive as she remembered. Antonio wasn't beautiful, but his dark, striking looks made women of all ages eager for another glimpse of him.

Run. And don't look back.

"Antonio?" Her voice was high and reedy. "What are you doing here?"

"I've come for you."

She shivered. She'd never thought she would see him again or hear those words. But it was too late. She couldn't go back. She wouldn't let herself think that it was possible. "Why?"

"Why?" Antonio leaned back in his chair and arrogantly studied her appearance.

Her skin tingled as she felt his lazy gaze sliding over her tired body and cheap clothes. Her pulse tripped before galloping at maximum speed. *How much did he know?*

She couldn't tell because his sunglasses hid his eyes. Was he here because he missed the sex? What they had shared had been hot, raw and primitive. It had made her wild, irresponsible and addicted to him. When they were together nothing else had mattered. And if she were smart she would keep her distance before she fell under his spell again.

Her muscles were locked, her feet were still, but her heart pounded hard against her ribs. She should tell him to leave and then get as far away as she could, but instead she was letting him take a good, long look at her.

"You need to leave. Now." She forced the words out. She needed to be harsh. In the end it would be kinder this way.

"Bella…" he warned in a low growl.

Only Antonio called her that. She'd used to love hearing him say it with a hint of a smile when he greeted her, or in awe as she brought him satisfaction with her mouth. Now, hearing him say it again, this time in anger, it brought a pang in her heart.

"I have nothing to say to you," she said in a rush.

His face hardened with displeasure. Antonio whipped off his dark sunglasses and glared at her. "How about offering your condolences?"

Her chest tightened, squeezing her lungs until she

found it difficult to breathe. His dark brown eyes ensnared her. She wanted to look away, but couldn't. She had never seen such fury or pain. It wouldn't take much to unleash it. If she moved he would pounce.

"I only just heard about Giovanni's car accident. I'm sorry for your loss."

Antonio's eyes narrowed and she could swear his anger quivered in the air.

"Such a display of grief for an ex-lover," he said in a raspy low tone. "It must have been a nasty break-up. What happened? Cheated on him, too?"

He didn't know. She breathed a little easier. "I did not have an affair with Giovanni," she said, holding her notepad and pen against her chest as if they could shield her from Antonio's wrath. She took a cautious step back.

"Bella, one more move…"

"*Signorina*," the man from the other table interrupted, "you forgot the—"

"One moment," Bella pleaded to the customer as she took the opportunity to shuffle away from Antonio. "I'll be right back."

She tried to march into the kitchen just as she felt Antonio's large hand fall on her shoulder. She still recognized his touch, she thought as she squeezed her eyes shut, fighting off the self-recrimination and longing swirling inside her.

Antonio whirled her around until she faced him. If he hadn't been holding her so tight she'd have collapsed. She felt so sick. So tired. Of worrying. Of barely surviving.

Isabella tilted her head back to look him in the eye. She had forgotten how powerfully tall he was. His height and strength had used to make her feel safe and protected. Now it made her feel extremely vulnerable.

"I've been looking for you," Antonio said. His voice was soft and dangerous. He lowered his head until he blocked out the rest of the world. "You were surprisingly difficult to find."

Isabella's stomach twisted with fear. Antonio placed both hands on her shoulders, his fingers digging into her like talons. He surrounded her. She felt caged. Trapped.

"What's going on here?" Her boss's harsh voice sounded close. "Isabella, what have you done?"

"I'll take care of it," she promised the older man without taking her eyes off Antonio. One touch, one look and she was his. It had always been that way.

The world started to spin and she swallowed roughly. She was mentally and physically exhausted. She wasn't at the top of her game when she needed to be the most. Why did Antonio have to reappear in her life when she was so fragile?

"I don't know why you bothered." Isabella took a quick glimpse and saw her boss next to the stove, saw his undisguised interest in the rich customer in his café. "You still think I was having an affair with Giovanni when I was with you."

Antonio's eyes darkened and his harsh features tightened with anger. "Oh, I *know* you were."

He hadn't forgiven his brother. Or her. He never would. Isabella swallowed hard, tapping into the last of her strength. She felt wobbly and weak, but the fight hadn't quite left her.

She just wished Antonio would take his hands off her. Her skin stung with awareness as tension whipped between them like a lash. She couldn't think straight when he touched her. She'd never been able to.

"I know you were his mistress," he drawled softly. "Why else would he leave you something in his will?"

Isabella cringed. That couldn't be good. She had thought Giovanni was her friend, letting her stay with him and helping her out. He hadn't revealed his true nature until it was too late. "Go away, Antonio. You don't know anything."

"I'm not leaving without you. You have to sign some documents in the law office as soon as possible."

Panic bloomed inside her. She wasn't going anywhere with Antonio. Isabella tried to show no expression, but she knew she'd failed when she saw the glint of dark satisfaction in Antonio's eyes. He wanted to make her uncomfortable. He wanted to see her suffer.

"Tell your family that you couldn't find me." She took a step away from Antonio and was relieved when he let go. "Give the money away to charity."

Antonio eyed her with disbelief. "You don't know how much it is."

"It doesn't matter." She could use the money, but she didn't trust this gift from Giovanni. There would be a price to pay if she accepted.

"Isabella!" her boss yelled. "Get the food on the table before it gets cold."

She turned abruptly and her head spun. She reached for the wall but her fingers gripped Antonio's strong arm. She battled desperately for her balance. She couldn't show weakness—or any other symptoms. She sensed Antonio's stare and held back a groan.

"You're ill?" he asked sharply.

"I didn't get much sleep last night," she replied in a rough voice.

She refused to look at him, not wanting him to see just how weak she truly felt. She could tell that he was assessing her and that made her worry. Antonio was smart and he'd made a fortune on intuitive connections. It wouldn't take him much longer to figure out what was wrong with her. She had to get away before he discovered the truth.

"Isabella!" her boss barked out.

"Let me serve this," Isabella told Antonio as she grabbed the tray of food. "Then we won't be interrupted again."

She didn't wait for his answer as she hurried out to the sidewalk. She served the food quickly, almost spilling it. She recovered just in time, murmuring her profuse apologies, but her mind was on possible escape routes. Isabella moved slightly until she was in a blind spot from the kitchen. This was her last chance to make a run for it.

Isabella placed the serving tray on one of the empty tables. She kept her casual pace until she turned the corner. Then she ran as fast as she could down the alley to the back stairs.

As her feet slapped against the pavement her lungs felt like they were going to explode—but she couldn't stop. Time was of the essence. Isabella reached the stairs and climbed them, two steps at a time. She tripped and bruised her knee. For a moment her world tilted, but she got back up and kept going.

Her legs burned and shook, but she pushed herself to go faster. Antonio would now have realized that she'd escaped. Any minute he'd start looking for her.

She reached the door to her room, but didn't stop to take a breath. She felt nauseous and her body ached. It didn't matter. She needed to get far away and then she would rest.

Swinging the door open, Isabella saw her backpack on the top of her lumpy mattress. She stepped into the small room and lunged for it. As she grasped the shoulder strap she heard the door bang shut.

Isabella turned around and the room moved. She saw Antonio resting against the door. He didn't look surprised or out of breath. From the glimmering rage in his dark eyes, she thought he had probably been waiting there for her the moment she stepped out of the kitchen.

"I'm disappointed, Bella," he said in a dangerously soft tone. "You're becoming so predictable."

"I—I…" She blinked as dark spots gathered along the edges of her eyes. She felt light-headed, but her arms and legs were unusually heavy. She couldn't move.

He stepped away from the door and approached her. "I don't have time for your games. You're coming with me *now*."

"I…" She needed to move. Run. Shamelessly lie.

But just as Antonio reached for her her head lolled back and she fainted, collapsing at his feet.

CHAPTER TWO

"BELLA!" Antonio sprung into action and caught her as her backpack fell onto the wooden floor with a thud. He lifted her and couldn't help noticing how light and delicate she was. *Fragile*. The word whispered in his mind like a warning.

She slumped against his arm and he held on tight as alarm pulsed through his veins. He swept the wisps of hair from her face. Her eyes were closed and her complexion was very pale. He laid her carefully on the mattress. Crouching down next to her, Antonio took a quick survey of the tiny room. The beige paint was peeling off the walls in chunks and a faint scent of rotting garbage wafted through the small open window. There was nothing else. No sink or refrigerator so he could get her water. There was hardly enough space for the mattress. How could she live like this? Why was she living here when she had a life and a future in America?

"Bella?" He tapped her cheek with his fingers. Her skin was soft and cold.

Isabella frowned and pursed her lips. She murmured something but it was incomprehensible. She didn't open her eyes.

Antonio started to get suspicious. His first instinct

had been to take care of Isabella. *Some things never change,* he thought bitterly. But what if this was an act? Did she hope that he would back off? Not a chance.

"Isabella," he called out sharply.

"Go away," she said drowsily. She turned to her side and curled her legs close to her chest.

"No." He grabbed her shoulder and gave her a shake.

"I'm serious." She squeezed her eyes shut and weakly tried to push his hand away. "Leave me alone."

He wished he could. He wished he had left her alone when he'd first seen her. It had been early March. The sun had been shining but there had been a chill in the air as he'd left his office. He had just pocketed his cell phone when he'd seen a young woman standing a few feet away on the sidewalk.

Antonio had done a double-take and halted.

"Is everything all right, sir?" his assistant had asked.

No. His world had taken a sudden tilt as he'd stared at the blonde, dressed simply in a fitted leather jacket, skintight jeans and knee-high boots. The violent kick of attraction had made him take a staggering step back.

He knew many beautiful young women, but there had been something different about this one. He had wanted to accept her silent challenge. It could have been her don't-mess-with-me stance or the jaunty tilt of her black fedora. Maybe it had been the bright red scarf draped around her neck that hinted at attitude. Whatever it was, he had found it irresistible.

"Sir?" his assistant had prompted.

Antonio had barely heard him. His attention had been on the blonde as she'd turned a map upside down, clearly hopeless at navigating. Then suddenly she'd shrugged her shoulders and stuffed the map carelessly into her backpack. Antonio had watched as the blonde had started walking away as if she was ready for whatever adventure she faced.

Her beauty and vitality had intrigued him, and her bold spirit had captured his imagination. He'd known he had to meet this woman or regret missing the opportunity.

"Cancel my meeting," he had said to his stunned assistant.

Following an elemental instinct he had not wanted to question, Antonio had ignored the chauffeured car waiting for him and followed the blonde.

His pulse had quickened as he'd watched the swing of her long blonde hair and the sway of her hips. She'd looked over her shoulder, and as their gazes connected he had seen the flare of attraction in her blue eyes. Instead of looking away she had turned and approached him.

"*Mi scusi*," she had said, her voice strong and clear as she'd met his gaze boldly. "Do you speak English?"

"Of course," he had said, noticing she was American. There had been no light of recognition in her eyes—just lust. She'd had no idea who he was.

"Great. I'm looking for the Piazza del Popolo," she had said, her attention clearly drawn to his mouth. She had absently swiped the tip of her tongue along her bottom lip.

Antonio had clenched his jaw. He had wanted to know how her lips tasted, but it had been too soon, too fast. The last thing he'd wanted to do was scare her off. "It's not far," he had replied gruffly as attraction pulsed between them. "I can show you where it is."

He had been fascinated as he'd watched her cheeks

turn pink. She hadn't tried to hide her interest, but she'd been fighting an internal struggle. He had seen the rise and fall of her chest and the eagerness in her expression. She had been tempted to explore whatever was happening between them.

"Wouldn't it be out of your way?"

"Not at all," he had lied. His voice had softened as his chest had tightened with growing excitement. "I happen to be going in that direction."

"What luck!" Her broad smile had indicated that she didn't believe him. She could have said she was going to Venice and he would have given the same answer. "By the way, I'm Isabella."

He had taken Bella to bed that night. There had been no games, no pretense. There had also been no indication that this American student on Spring Break would twist him in so many knots that he would never be the same again. She hadn't been very experienced, but a generous and affectionate lover.

Giovanni had thought so, too.

The reminder burned like acid, eating away at him.

Antonio stood up and shoved his clenched fists in his pockets. "You told me you weren't sick."

"I'm not sick," she countered faintly.

The Isabella he knew was full of life and ready to take on the world. This Isabella looked like a strong gust of wind would knock her over. "You need to see a doctor."

Isabella suddenly opened her eyes wide. She blinked a few times and darted a quick look at him before keeping her gaze on the floor. She rose, resting awkwardly on her elbow and pushing the wayward hair out of her face. "I've seen a doctor. I'm not sick. Just exhausted. All I need is to eat and sleep properly."

Antonio cast her a look of disbelief. "I would ask for a second opinion."

"I don't need one. Now, go away," she ordered with the flutter of her hand.

"I'm not leaving here without you."

"You have to," she urged as she held her head in her hands. "Tell everyone that you couldn't find me. Tell them that I'm back home."

It was tempting. He wanted to leave and not look back. Purge her from his memories. Do anything that would erase Isabella from his world. But he knew that was impossible.

"Sorry. I'm not like you. I choose to tell the truth whenever possible."

She lifted her head to glare at him. "I never lied to you. I never—"

He turned away and checked his watch. "I don't have time to rehash the past."

"Rehash?" Isabella's voice rose angrily. "When did we discuss it the first time around? I thought we were happy. We had been together for weeks and going strong. We had made love throughout the night. The next morning your security woke me up to kick me out. My bag was packed and you wouldn't take my call. You didn't tell me why you did that, and you never gave me a chance to talk about it!"

Antonio leaned against the wall by the door. The room felt like it was getting smaller. "I wasn't in the mood to hear your excuses. I'm even less inclined to now."

"There was nothing to excuse," Isabella argued as she rose slowly.

Her movements were wobbly and awkward. Antonio folded his arms so he wouldn't reach out and help her. He already regretted holding her close. He didn't like how much effort it had taken to pull away. His fingertips still stung from where he had touched her face.

Isabella looked him in the eye and jutted out her chin. "I did not have an affair."

He held up his hand. "Enough! I will not discuss it."

"Typical," she said with a sigh. "You don't like to discuss anything. Especially if it's personal. No matter how hard I tried, you wouldn't share how you felt. The only time I knew exactly what you were thinking was when we were in bed."

An intimate and very inconvenient image bloomed in his mind. Of Isabella, naked in his bed, eagerly following his explicit demands. When they'd been alone together he had held nothing back. He had demonstrated how much he wanted Isabella and how much her touch had meant to him. There had been many times when it hadn't been certain who was in command.

A muscle bunched in his jaw and ferocious energy swirled around him. "We are leaving," he announced in a gravelly tone. Antonio thrust the door open and waited for Isabella.

"No," she said firmly. "I'm not signing any papers. I don't want Giovanni's money."

"I'm sure you earned it." He didn't want her to know what was at stake here. All he wanted was to end this errand as soon as possible. By whatever means necessary. Antonio walked over to her.

Isabella's eyes widened. "Don't you dare touch me!"

"How times have changed," he said silkily as he wrapped his hand around her wrist. He ignored her racing pulse under his fingers as he picked up her backpack. "I remember when you begged for my touch."

Isabella tried futilely to pull out of his grasp. "I thought you didn't want to talk about the past? Let go of me."

"I will when we get to my car." If it was still where he had parked it. Trust Bella to find the most dangerous neighborhood to live in.

"I'm not going anywhere with you!" Isabella declared as she tried to grab onto the doorframe—but she couldn't hold on.

"Think again." He headed for the stairs, dragging her behind him.

"Pushy and selfish," she muttered. "It must be a Rossi trait. You are just like your brother."

Antonio stilled as the accusation lashed at him. He slowly turned and faced Isabella. He saw the wariness in her eyes as she backed away. She didn't get far as his grip tightened around her wrist. "*Don't.*"

Isabella's gaze fell to her feet. "All I meant—"

"I don't care what you meant." Her words had clawed open a wound he had valiantly tried to ignore. Were he and Gio interchangeable in Isabella's mind? How often had she thought of his brother when she'd kissed *him*? Had she responded the same way in Gio's bed?

His thoughts turned darker, piercing his soul. Antonio didn't say anything as he took a step closer to Isabella, backing her against the wall. Why had she chosen Gio over him? Everyone else he knew made that choice, but why Isabella? He had thought she was different. Was it because Gio had been the handsome and charismatic one? Had his brother fulfilled her deepest, darkest fantasies? Or had she actually fallen in love with his brother?

"Antonio?" she whispered with uncertainty.

He stared at Isabella. Her angelic beauty hid a devious nature. Her bold spirit and breathtaking innocence had led him straight to a hell that he might never escape. He blinked slowly as he battled the darkness enveloping him. He wouldn't let this woman destroy him again.

Antonio released her wrist as if her touch burned. He took a deliberate step back but met her eyes with a steady gaze. "Don't compare me with my brother. *Ever.*"

Isabella couldn't move as she stared into his brown eyes. Her heart twisted and her breath snagged in her throat. Antonio was always so careful not to show his thoughts and emotions, but now they were laid bare before her. The man was in torment.

But just as quickly as he'd exposed his pain his eyes were shuttered. When he opened them again he was back in control, while *her* emotions were in a jumbled mess.

Antonio turned away from her and Isabella sagged against the wall. She slowly exhaled as her heart pounded in her ears. She felt shaky, her limbs twitching as she watched Antonio take the stairs.

"I'm sorry."

Her words were just a whisper but she saw Antonio's rigid stance as he silently deflected her apology.

She hadn't meant to compare Antonio to his brother. They had very different personalities. It was impossible to confuse the two. Giovanni had been a charmer, with movie star looks, always the life of the party. He'd been entertaining—but not fascinating like Antonio.

The moment she had met Antonio she'd known he was out of her league. She didn't have the sophistication or sexual knowledge to hold on to him. It hadn't mattered. She'd only wanted to be with him. Just once.

Isabella remembered when they had first met and he had offered to show her Piazza del Popolo. The sight of him had jolted her as if she had woken from a deep slumber. Her heart had started to race when she saw him.

She knew she had projected an image of being bold and strong. Tough. It had all been an act. It had been her way of protecting herself as she went through the world alone. But the way the man had been looking at her—she had felt brazen. She had wanted to hold on to that feeling.

"I'm Antonio," he had said, and offered his hand.

She had hesitated at the sight of his expensive cufflinks. It had only been then that she'd noticed he wore a designer suit. His silk tie had probably cost more than her round-trip ticket to Italy. She didn't know anyone who had that kind of money.

Be careful of the rich ones. Her mother words had drifted in her head. *They only want one thing from women like us.*

Isabella had smiled. She had decided that it was okay because she was after the same thing.

She had reached for Antonio's hand and felt a sharp tingle as her skin had glided against his. She hadn't been able to hide her gasp of surprise. When she had tried to pull away Antonio had wrapped his long, strong fingers around her hand.

Instead of making her feel trapped, his touch had pierced through the gray numbness that had settled in her when she had nursed her mother through her final illness. Her breath had locked in her throat as he'd raised her hand to his mouth.

The earthy colors of Rome had deepened and the sun had turned golden. The blaring sound of traffic had faded as Antonio had brushed his lips against her knuckles. She had known that this man would be the highlight of her vacation. She hadn't expected to fall in love—and into his bed—with such wild abandon.

She hadn't expected that she would never be the same again.

Isabella jerked her mind to the present as she saw Antonio disappear from the stairwell with her backpack. Everything she owned—her passport, her money—was in there.

"Wait!" she called out, and hurriedly followed him. She rounded the building and saw Antonio striding down the block. Isabella ran after him. "Antonio, stop!"

He walked to his sports car—a menacing-looking machine that was as black as night. He punched a button on his keyring and the small trunk popped open. Isabella watched in horror as he tossed her backpack in and slammed it shut.

"Give me back my bag," she said as she reached the car.

"You'll get it after we visit the lawyers."

"You don't understand, Antonio. I have to work." She gestured at the café on the other end of the block.

"Who cares?" He walked to the driver's side. "This is more important."

Spoken like a man who had never had to scrape by

or go hungry. "I'm already going to get in trouble for taking an unscheduled break."

"Unscheduled break? You made a run for it and you weren't planning to return."

"I can't afford to lose this job." She rubbed her hand over her forehead as she tried to maintain her composure. "If I get fired I lose my room."

He glanced up at the broken rusted window of her room. "It won't be that big of a loss."

Isabella put her hands on her hips. "Maybe not to you, but this job is the only thing that is keeping me from becoming homeless!"

Antonio's eyes narrowed. "Is this about money?"

"What?" She stared at him across the car.

"Of course it is."

"It's about my *livelihood*," she corrected him through clenched teeth. Antonio wouldn't understand about that, having been born into wealth and status. She needed her job because she had no other form of support or resources. Why couldn't he see that? "Listen, let's make a compromise. I will go to the lawyers with you once I finish my shift at the café."

Antonio took another look at his watch. "That's unacceptable."

"Seriously? How is that unacceptable? You asked for a favor from me and I just agreed to do it."

"We both know you are prolonging the inevitable and will try to avoid it. Although I find it very curious that you aren't asking how much money you will get. Unless, of course, you already know."

"There's nothing curious about it," she said as she folded her arms protectively around her. "The only thing I know is that any money will come with strings attached. I don't want anything—especially if it means dealing with you or your family."

Antonio chose to ignore her comment. "I'm not willing to wait around and watch over you until your shift ends."

"Do you even know how to compromise?" she asked, tossing her hands up in frustration. Of course he didn't. The world bowed down to him. Just as she had done, once upon a time.

"This is what I know," he said as he slipped on his sunglasses. "The will was read three days ago. The contents will soon become public."

Isabella frowned. "What are you talking about?"

He opened the door and sat down in the driver's seat. "It won't take long before the paparazzi find you."

She jerked her head back in surprise. "Paparazzi? What would they want with me?"

"You're kidding, right? The woman who slept with the Rossi brothers has wound up with a fortune."

She stared at him with wide eyes. "There is no need to make it sound so salacious."

"I'm just telling it like it is," he said impatiently. "Now, get in."

Isabella hesitated. Giovanni had left her a fortune? That couldn't be right. Antonio must be exaggerating. If only she *could* accept the money. But even if she did it would take ages to go through the legal and financial systems and get the cash she so desperately needed.

What would happen to her after she'd signed the documents? She had no home, no money and no protection. She had been working for months to raise the money to get back to California and she didn't think she would make enough before the paparazzi found her. Could she ask Antonio for help?

She bit her lip as she weighed the pros and cons. *Could* she ask him? Was she willing to stoop that low? Antonio could easily afford the price of a plane ticket, probably had the cash in his wallet, but it felt wrong.

Antonio leaned back in his seat. "What do you want?"

She took a deep breath. "I need a plane ticket to Los Angeles. For tonight."

He nodded sharply. "What else?"

She was already regretting her request. She didn't want anything from Antonio. His presence reminded her of the poor choices she made because she'd been in love. She had fought for him, for them, and he had discarded her without a second thought. As much as it pained her to think about it, her mother had been right. She hated it when that happened.

"That's it."

He tipped his sunglasses and studied her face. "I don't believe you."

"That doesn't surprise me," she replied. "But I mean it. I don't want anything else."

"That will change soon," he said as he started the engine.

"Maybe I didn't make myself clear. I shall consider this a loan," she said as the car purred to life. "I'll pay you back once I get settled."

"It's not necessary."

"It is," she insisted. "It wouldn't be right to take your money."

"I don't care about the money." Antonio said. "Get in the car."

Isabella hesitated. Was that wise? The man hated her. He thought she'd betrayed him. Then again, he probably wanted her out of Italy and out of his life as soon as possible. She had nothing to worry about.

"Bella…" Antonio's tone warned of his growing impatience.

Isabella opened the door and sat down before she changed her mind. "Don't expect me to stay long," she said as she reached for the seatbelt. "I'll sign the papers and then I'm gone."

And if she were lucky she would never see Antonio again.

CHAPTER THREE

"THIS is a law office?" Isabella asked as she studied the old building. "I haven't seen one like this before."

Antonio glanced up and saw that the façade was pale, almost pink-gold. He noticed the faded mosaics next to the arched windows and pillars. It was strange that he'd never really looked at the building before.

"Where did you think I would take you?"

"You don't want me to answer that," she muttered.

They entered the dark and musty building. It was unnaturally quiet and the only sound was their footsteps as they climbed the stairs. The silence Antonio shared with Isabella felt strange but he was grateful for it. He didn't need to think about the easy conversations they'd once had that would last throughout the night. He didn't want to remember how he'd used to call her up during the day just to hear her voice. He wanted the barrier of silence. Needed it.

The receptionist took one look at Isabella and sniffed with disapproval. Antonio glared at the dour woman, letting her know that he wouldn't tolerate that kind of behavior. The woman bent her head from the silent reprimand and icily escorted them to the conference room.

When the door opened Antonio saw his mother, sitting regally next to the ornate rosewood table. Dressed severely in black, Maria Rossi was as elegant and private as always. She was trying to hide her distress, but he instantly saw it in her face.

"Mother, why are you here?" Antonio asked. "Your presence isn't required."

His mother's expression darkened when she saw Isabella at her side. "Is this the woman?"

"This is Isabella Williams," Antonio said with a hint of warning.

He reluctantly introduced Isabella to his mother. He had hoped to prevent these two women from meeting. With one wintry glance Maria made it clear what she thought of Isabella. She knew this blonde beauty was the reason her sons had been estranged.

Antonio's first instinct was to protect Isabella from the slight. But that didn't make sense. She was in the wrong and should suffer the consequences. She had created a scandal when she'd started living with Giovanni. The paparazzi had gone into a feeding frenzy, and had Antonio borne the brunt of the gossip. But he still couldn't stand by and watch Isabella receive this treatment.

Most socialites he knew would have wilted under his mother's apparent disgust. To his surprise, Isabella tilted her head proudly. She wasn't going to back down or hang her head in shame. She stood before this doyenne of high society in her cheap clothes, with her tarnished name, and held her gaze unflinchingly.

His mother was the first to break eye contact. She

turned to him. "I can't bear to be in the same room with her."

Isabella showed no expression as she watched Maria Rossi leave the room and closed the door with a flourish.

"I apologize for my mother's behavior," Antonio said, fighting back anger. "I'll see that it doesn't happen again."

"No need," Isabella crossed her arms and walked to the large window. "I know you feel the same way."

Antonio watched her as she stared at the view of the Pantheon. He suspected she wasn't really looking at anything. It was as if she was in another time, another place, trapped in a memory.

If only he could do the same. His mind was always racing, predicting problems and creating solutions. He required an outlet for his inexhaustible energy and found it in his work. The money and power that came along with it wasn't important. Antonio needed the challenge, to push himself to the razor's edge.

There had been one time when he hadn't felt that drive, and that had been when he was with Isabella. When they'd been together nothing else had existed. Isabella Williams had been his escape. And eventually his downfall.

"What did you tell your mother about me?" Isabella grimaced as the question sprang from her lips. She hadn't meant to ask, but it was obvious that her reputation had preceded her. Isabella knew she shouldn't care but it bothered her.

There was something about Antonio's mother that intimidated her. The woman was beautifully groomed, from her coiffed hair to her pedicured feet, but she also had an aura of power. No one would treat Maria Rossi with anything less than respect. Isabella had felt grubby next to her.

"We never discussed you," he said stiffly.

She wouldn't be surprised if that were true. Antonio rarely discussed his family. Everything she knew about his mother and his late father had come from Giovanni. And he'd probably been just as private about his love life with his family.

Isabella turned and approached Antonio. "But she knows you and I were once together?"

"Not from me."

"Giovanni?" No wonder his mother hated her.

"My mother was prying into the reason why her sons weren't on speaking terms again." Antonio crossed his arms and looked away. "I'm sure Gio concocted some story that made him look like the innocent victim."

"Again?" Her tired brain caught onto that word. "You and Giovanni had been estranged before?"

Antonio's jaw clenched. "Yes."

She felt the weight of guilt lift a little. All this time she'd thought she had ruined the strong bond between brothers. "But how could that be?" she asked as she remembered Giovanni and Antonio together. They'd had a tendency to use the same expressions, finish each other's sentences. "You two were close."

Antonio shrugged. "Gio had been trying to make amends and was on his best behavior. It was one of the few times we got along."

"Why did you accept him back into your life?" That didn't seem like something Antonio would do. You screwed up once and you were banished from Antonio's life. You didn't get another chance.

"I thought he had changed." He sighed. "I wanted him to change."

She saw the grief in his expression. She wanted to reach out and bring him comfort, but she knew Antonio would not appreciate the gesture. "How old were you when you first stopped talking to each other?"

His harsh features tightened. "I don't want to discuss it."

"Why not?"

"I answered your questions, now it's my turn."

Isabella jerked her head back. She saw the intensity in his eyes, the determined set of his jaw. Was he really trying to deflect her questions or had this all been a technique to draw her closer? Make her think he was opening up to her so she would feel obligated to do the same?

Isabella braced her shoulders. "I didn't agree to that."

"Why did Gio include you in his will?"

"I have no idea. I didn't ask him to." But she suspected she knew the answer. Giovanni had been playing games and now she was going to lose everything.

"The lawyers say that Gio changed his will a month ago."

Isabella paled. That could not be a coincidence. "S-so?"

Antonio tilted his head to one side as he studied her face. "You know why. No one else does. No one knows why he gave you millions."

"M-millions?" she whispered. "That doesn't make any sense."

"And half the shares in Rossi Industries."

"What?" The shock reverberated through her body.

"He gave you half my birthright," Antonio said in a growl.

She clapped her hand over her mouth. *Oh, Giovanni. What have you done? Why did you do this?*

"I lost part of my birthright once before," his said, his voice a harsh whisper. "I have no intention of losing it again."

Isabella frowned. She felt like she was missing crucial information. "What are you talking about?"

Antonio didn't hear her. "Why did Gio give all this to *you*? Why not the woman he was dating? Why not a woman who meant something to him? Why *you*?"

"Antonio…" She braced her legs and held her clenched hands at her sides. She didn't have the nerve to tell him. She didn't want to face the consequences.

"Was it so I would be required to work with the woman who had cheated on me?"

Had Giovanni done this out of spite? For his own perverse pleasure? It was possible…

"Or did you seduce it out of him? I admit you're good in bed—but *that* good?"

Isabella felt the heat in her cheeks. If only she could run away. The moment she uttered the next words everything would change. Everything would be lost.

"It's because I'm p-pregnant."

He stared at her in shock. Isabella hunched her shoulders, preparing for the world to fall around her as struggled to get the words out.

She nervously licked her lips before she added, "And Giovanni *is* the father."

Antonio staggered back as if he had been punched. His body went numb and his mind whirled. His world tilted and he swayed. He wanted to grab hold of something so he wasn't brought to his knees, but that meant reaching out to Isabella. The one woman who still had the power to hurt him.

"You…"

Isabella was having his brother's baby. Gio had known and hadn't told him. The pain radiated through his body.

"But I didn't have an affair with him. I swear."

An affair. A fling. Sex. It was all the same.

Antonio held up his hand. Rage billowed through him, crimson, hot and bitter. "You're pregnant," he said, as if he was in a daze. "How many months?"

She held her hands in front of her stomach. "I'm just past the first trimester."

"Three months?" he muttered as the fury seized his throat.

"Antonio, you have to believe me," she pleaded. "I only slept with him one time."

He fought back the red mist that threatened to overtake him. "*Only?* Is a one-night stand supposed to make me feel better?" he asked in a low, biting tone. Was he supposed to believe that when she had lived with Giovanni for *weeks*?

Isabella's face tightened with anger. "How many women have you slept with since we broke up?"

"That's not the issue. Those women were not the *reason* we broke up." He would not allow Isabella to distract him. "I kicked you out because you were sleeping with my brother. Now you're telling me you're carrying his child."

"It happened the night I heard on the news that you

were going to marry someone else." Isabella spoke haltingly, as if the memory still tormented her.

"And that's your excuse?" He stared at her. He didn't know if she was feeding him lies or if she was planning to thrust another knife in his back.

"No. I'm trying to explain." She covered her face with her hands. "I was emotional and I drank far too much. I had been like that for weeks. I was self-destructive and I made a lot of poor choices during that time. I'm not proud of what I did."

But she had done it. Would she have told him about Giovanni if she wasn't pregnant, or would she have taken her secret to the grave?

"Do you wind up in the nearest bed whenever you drink?"

She slowly lowered her hands. "I'm not sure what happened that night."

"How convenient."

She glared at him. "All I know is that I was an emotional mess. You had kicked me out, you didn't want to have anything to do with me, and then I heard you were planning a future with another woman."

"And what better way to get back at me than by sleeping with my brother?" He'd used to think Isabella was sweet and innocent, but she had hidden a vengeful streak. The people closest to him had warned him about Isabella, but he hadn't listened. He'd thought he knew everything about her. But it turned out he didn't know her at all.

"I didn't know about your history with Giovanni." Isabella stood rigid in front of him, her clenched fists at her sides. "I didn't know you had discarded me like a piece of trash because you thought I'd had an affair with your brother."

"And look at what you did," Antonio said. The red mist was creeping in and he was feeling dangerous. Out of control like never before. Antonio shoved his shaky hands in his pockets.

"Giovanni planned this!" she blurted out. "He took advantage of me."

"I'm sure he got you into bed in record time." Bile rose from his stomach and he wanted to be violently ill.

She thrust out her chin. "I'm not like that," she said in a trembling voice.

"Yes, you are," he said with a sneer. "You were with *me*."

Isabella eyes widened as if she'd been hit. "You throw that back in my face?" she asked in a shocked whisper. "What we had was different. It was special. It was—"

"Part of your routine," he finished coldly. "Only Gio got you pregnant. Was that planned or an unexpected bonus? Is that why he kicked you out?"

"He didn't kick me out. I left the next morning," she told him, her voice wobbling with emotion. "I didn't feel safe there anymore. I ran as fast as I could."

Antonio frowned and he crossed his arms. Her explanation niggled at him. Something didn't add up. "Then how did he know about the baby?"

"I told him when I found out. That was a month ago."

And his brother had changed his will a month ago. "What did Gio say?"

"Not much." Isabella looked away abruptly.

"Isabella," he warned in a firm tone, "tell me."

Her shoulders sagged in defeat and her expression

turned grim. "He laughed," she answered. "He said, 'Antonio will never touch you now!' and he laughed like a madman."

Antonio took a step back. He shouldn't be surprised, but he was. He hadn't fully appreciated the depth of his brother's hatred.

"And he was right." She gestured at him, the simple movement indicating her disappointment. "He knew exactly how you'd react if you found out the truth."

"That's why you ran away at the café?" Isabella had been afraid of how he would react. And she was smart, because right now he wanted to lash out. He wanted to smash and destroy everything around him. "You are not the woman I thought you were."

"That's not true," she spat angrily. "You just want to hear bad things about me. It's easier for you because you're looking for my faults."

Easier? He felt like he had been ripped apart. He was never going to be the same again.

She gulped in a ragged breath. "I want you to know that I didn't cheat on you."

"How can I know that? How can I believe you weren't sleeping with my brother from the first day you met him?"

"I have no way of proving it. Why can't you—?"

A polite knock on the double doors interrupted them. Isabella jumped back and pressed her lips together as a withered old man with snowy white hair in a black three-piece suit entered the room.

Antonio tried to rein in his emotions as he tersely introduced the lawyer to Isabella. The older man invited her into his office and she silently followed. As she passed Antonio he grabbed Isabella's wrist, forcing her to stop.

"This discussion isn't over," he said.

"Yes, it is," she said coldly as she pulled away from his grasp. "I don't have to explain myself to you. You have no rights over me *or* my child."

Isabella walked through the door and the lawyer followed. Antonio stared at the closed door, his body rigid as an idea formed.

"Not yet," Antonio murmured. "But I once I do there will be hell to pay."

CHAPTER FOUR

"I'M GOING to be a grandmother." Maria Rossi sighed and clasped her hands together. "Gio's child. Oh, I hope it will look just like him."

"I'm glad to see you're taking this well," Antonio muttered as he'd paced the floor of the conference room. He should have left his mother in the waiting room but he had to tell her that their situation had changed. Their strategy had been blown apart by Isabella's bombshell.

"I admit Gio had no business putting her in the will." His mother's voice was thick with annoyance. "Giving money and power to *that* woman."

"He did it to cut me out."

"No, Gio wouldn't do that to you. He wouldn't," she insisted as he made a face. "That woman bewitched him. He wasn't thinking straight. I can understand making provision for the child—but all that money?" Maria shuddered delicately. "We don't know if it's even his."

"We'll find out." But Antonio's instincts told him that the baby *was* Gio's. His brother wouldn't have pulled this stunt unless he had been absolutely sure. Gio wanted his child to inherit and gave Isabella the power over the money and shares until the child comes of age.

"Gio told me himself that that Jezebel seduced

him," his mother continued. "You both should have known better. I don't know what either of you saw in the woman."

He could easily make a list of things he had seen in Isabella, but it would scandalize his mother. Antonio raked his hand through his hair. "I don't want to hear it."

"There's only one way a girl like her can land a rich man. She has to get pregnant."

Antonio slammed his hand against the mahogany table so hard that Maria jumped. "That's enough." It also wasn't true. Isabella had had *him* wrapped around her little finger without an unplanned pregnancy.

"Temper, temper," Maria said as she patted her chignon. "If you plan to get full control of the Rossi fortune you need to show some patience."

Antonio walked to the window and leaned against the pane. "I have one or two plans," he admitted. He wasn't happy about either of them. Both required him to get very close to the woman who betrayed him.

"How many months along is she?"

He had been reluctant to ask for details, but at the same time his mind was filled with questions. "She says she's at least three months pregnant. I kicked her out the last week of May, so I know the baby isn't mine. She left Gio on the first of July and that fits the timeframe."

"You need to do something."

"I know. It leaves me two options. I can seduce her into giving up her inheritance and leaving the country for good."

But history had proved that he didn't have an infinite amount of sexual power over her. Isabella had left his bed to go into Gio's. He wasn't sure if he could seduce Isabella knowing she was carrying his brother's child.

"No," his mother said firmly. "That child is the only thing I have left of Gio. I want it to be part of my life."

Antonio inhaled sharply as jagged pain burned through him. His mother had had no problem banning *him* from her life when he had needed her the most. But then she'd still had Gio around.

"What is the second option?" she asked.

"Marry her and adopt the child as my own. That way I would have full control over the Rossi fortune."

He had never thought about becoming a father. As the second son, he'd felt no pressure to sire an heir. Now he might be required to accept Gio's child as his own. That baby would be a constant reminder of betrayal.

"That would be perfect," his mother said. "We wouldn't have to give up anything."

Just his freedom, Antonio thought he looked out of the window and gazed at the Pantheon. *And his peace of mind*. If there had been any other way he wouldn't have gone looking for Isabella. Now he might have to bind himself to the cheating vixen for the rest of his life.

"I really don't think this is a good idea," Isabella said as she entered Antonio's penthouse apartment. She heard the door close behind her and flinched when she heard it lock.

"I agree," Antonio said, "but the paparazzi have already found out about your windfall and my home is the safest place. Anyway, it's only for one night."

Isabella scoffed. As if that meant anything. She had slept with Antonio within hours of meeting him. But she wasn't going to tumble into his bed again, she reminded herself. He didn't want her anymore. He had someone else in his life.

But, to her shame, she knew that fact wouldn't stop her from falling into his arms. Despite everything—despite the way he'd discarded her and cast her out of his life—she still longed for Antonio's touch.

Isabella rubbed her bare arms as she stepped into the drawing room. She looked around and noticed that not much had changed. In fact the only thing different about the apartment was her. She was no longer the carefree and impetuous girl who'd seen the beauty in this room but not the power behind it. Back then she had put her dreams on hold for the man she loved. These days she had to play it safe. She would hold back instead of brazenly going forward. She had to protect herself and her baby's future.

She frowned when she noticed how quiet the apartment was. No music. No easy conversation. No laughter. The room was modern and dramatic. The sleek contemporary furniture and bold artwork were at odds with the panoramic view of Rome's ancient ruins. Isabella had always thought the apartment suited Antonio, a self-made man who bridged innovation and tradition. He'd conquered the business world with cutthroat strategy, but there was a dark sensuality about him that he contained ruthlessly. Yet *she* had seen it. In the artwork he was drawn to, in his movement, in his eyes.

She knew Antonio wanted a showdown, and he had brought her here because he wanted it on his territory. This place held wild memories. Did he think it would distract her? Or would he use their past as a way to seduce the truth out of her?

"The housekeeper has made up the guestroom for you," he said as he walked across the room.

"Thank you." She wished the housekeeper were here.

She didn't want to be alone with Antonio. She didn't trust him. She didn't trust herself.

She watched him as he strode to a table that held drinks. She tried to look away, but she couldn't. His striking features were so harsh and aggressive. Her hands tingled as she remembered brushing her fingertips along his slanted cheekbones and angular jaw. He radiated masculine power and raw sensuality. He had discarded the suit jacket that had cloaked his lean, muscular build. She dragged her gaze away so she wouldn't stare at his broad shoulders or sculpted chest.

"Would you like a drink?" he asked as he grabbed a decanter from the table. He froze and stared at the crystal in his hands. "I forgot. You can't drink alcohol."

"It's not just because I'm pregnant." She returned her attention to the window and looked out onto the night sky. "I don't drink anymore."

She heard Antonio pause in pouring a glass of whiskey. "Why is that?"

When she had stayed with Giovanni she had gotten caught up in his party circuit. She'd drunk to dull the pain. To forget. She hadn't realized she was out of control until she woke up in Giovanni's bed. "I overindulged one night and swore I wouldn't drink again."

"That often happened when you socialized with Gio and his friends."

"Yes, I found that out." She couldn't hide the bitterness in her voice.

"You couldn't keep up with his wild ways?" he asked as he took a sip of his drink.

Isabella breathed deeply and leaned against the cold glass. She had to control her temper. Had to keep her wits about her. She knew Antonio was going to interrogate her. "I thought you didn't want to talk about this?"

"I don't."

She believed that. He didn't want to know, but he had to find out. The curiosity was killing him. "Did you think for a minute that Giovanni might have lied to you?" Isabella asked. "That I might have been faithful to you?"

He stilled. "Yes," he said slowly.

The surprised her. Antonio didn't second-guess himself. "When was that?" she asked, watching him down his drink in one swallow.

"The day after you left." He curled his lip and set his glass down. "I considered the possibility that I made a mistake."

Isabella pulled away from the window. "And?"

"I made some enquiries." His expression darkened and he braced his hands on the table. "Only to discover that you had rolled out of my bed and into my brother's."

Isabella closed her eyes as she heard the raw pain in Antonio's voice. "It wasn't like that," she whispered.

"Right." His voice was low and biting as he glared at her. "You had already been in his bed before you left mine."

Isabella rubbed her forehead as tension pulsed underneath her skin. "I went to Giovanni because you had thrown me out. I had nowhere to go."

Antonio snorted with derision. "Hardly. You were right where you wanted to be."

She shook her head. "I wanted to be with you."

"Until you met my brother." Antonio walked over to where she stood. "You used your relationship with me so you could get closer to Gio and his money."

"I have never been interested in that!" Isabella said. She was surprised that he would think that of her, and she was also hurt that he didn't really know her at all.

"I thought I knew you." Antonio rested his arm against the window.

"You knew everything." But either he hadn't listened or he didn't care to remember. "Unlike you, I didn't hold anything back."

"Is this another stab at how I don't communicate?" He leaned forward, towering over her. "I disagree. We talked all the time."

She flattened her hand against her chest. "I did the talking. You didn't share anything. I didn't know about your hopes and fears. Your family life. You told me nothing."

"We're talking now," he said softly. "Tell me, how long were you sleeping with my brother when we were sharing a bed?"

"I was always satisfied in your bed. I didn't need to look elsewhere."

Isabella bit her lip, knowing she shouldn't have spoken so boldly. She saw the sensual heat flare in Antonio's eyes. Her skin tingled in response as a kaleidoscope of images swirled in her head. Tension curled around her. It was dangerous to bring up those memories. Isabella nervously cleared her throat.

"If that was true, why did you go to my brother in the first place?" he asked. "Why didn't you go back to California?"

Isabella sighed. She had asked herself that many times in the past three months. "I should have gone back home, but I thought we could get back together. I hoped it was a rough patch we could work through."

Antonio's eyes widened with disbelief. "Work through the fact that you were sleeping with my brother?"

"I didn't know you thought that I had!" she said in a raised voice. "How could I? You didn't share your suspicions with anyone. I didn't know anything. I only found out about Giovanni's lies three months ago."

Antonio's eyes narrowed as he watched Isabella's face. Impatience scratched at him. "Why did you think I dumped you?" he asked as he tugged his silk tie loose.

"I thought you had found someone else. When your security kicked me out, I tried to get in touch with you," she said coolly. Her eyes were blank, her composure restored. "You were blocking my calls. I went to your office and couldn't even get through the door."

He had cut her out of his life ruthlessly. He wouldn't deny that. It had been the only way he could get through the day. The nights had been the worst. He hadn't thought a man could crave a woman so strongly until Isabella had gone out of his life.

Isabella shrugged. "So I called Giovanni."

"You had his number?" Antonio gritted his teeth. He knew he was being possessive, but he didn't like the idea of Isabella having had *any* man's phone number.

"I told him what had happened and he invited me to his place." Isabella looked down and whispered, "I thought he was my friend."

"You two got along very well whenever I was around."

"Giovanni got along with everyone. But I wasn't interested in him," she said. "The only thing we had in common was you. When we talked, it was always about you."

"Why does that send a chill down my spine?"

Her mouth tightened into a straight line as she struggled with her temper. "I didn't know what your relationship was like. And when I accepted his invitation to stay I thought it would only be a day or two before you came to your senses. I kept trying to contact you but you blocked me in every way."

If she hadn't been living with his brother he would have crawled back and grovelled. But she had shown her true colors too early.

"Then, about the third day I stayed at Giovanni's, he told me that you had cut him out of his life because he'd taken sides."

"I cut him out of my life because he slept with *you*."

"Like I said," she bit out through clenched teeth, "I had no idea you thought that. I felt incredibly guilty for causing a rift between two brothers."

"Which you decided to fix by staying with him?" he asked, poking holes in her story. "How would that repair anything?"

"Giovanni told me it would all blow over and I believed him." She shook her head at her obvious mistake. "And, like a fool, I kept trying to contact you. He convinced me that I wasn't going to get you back by crying myself to sleep every night. He suggested I go out, act like I was having a good time, and remind you of what you were missing."

She'd done that very well. It had been difficult for him, coming back to this apartment every evening and knowing she wouldn't be there. Knowing she was in another man's bed. "You went out with Gio every night."

She nodded and slumped against the window.

"There were pictures of you and Gio in the papers. Every day." She had looked happy, relaxed and very sexy.

"I wasn't trying to make you jealous," she insisted. "Since I couldn't see or talk to you, it was my way of reminding you that I was still around."

"Clinging to his arm?" he added sharply.

Isabella scowled at him. "I did no such thing."

Antonio remembered how she'd used to cling to *him*. She'd curled up against him whether they were walking along the street, sitting on the sofa, or making love. It had been as though she couldn't get close enough. And he had welcomed the warmth and affection.

"In those tiny dresses."

Isabella blushed. She looked away and turned until her back pressed against the window. "That was probably a bad idea."

"Dresses that Gio bought you." They had been short, tight and revealing. The kind of dresses a man gave his mistress. "When you wouldn't accept any gift from me."

"I didn't have anything acceptable to wear to those events," she mumbled as she flattened her hands against the glass pane.

"And I didn't take you anywhere but to bed?"

She looked up sharply. "That's not true! We had so much fun exploring the city. I got to see Rome through your eyes."

"Obviously that wasn't enough." *He* wasn't enough, no matter what he had done and what he had given. "But you made up for lost time by attending every nightclub."

"I wasn't interested in those parties. Or those people. I preferred the places we went to alone."

He'd like to believe that. When he had learned she

was an art history student he had gone out of his way to take her to see private art collections and participate in specially guided tours. He had ignored all invitations to dinner parties and exclusive events because he hadn't wanted to share Isabella.

He'd thought she had felt the same. Isabella had never complained, or asked to go dancing. Isabella had never felt a need to dress up or entertain. The only other person who'd spent any time with them was his brother.

"If any of this is true, what made you leave Gio?"

She pressed her lips together. "I discovered that Giovanni was not my friend. He pounced when I was at my most vulnerable."

Antonio waited, but she didn't reveal any more details. "You'll have to do better than that."

Isabella exhaled slowly. "And then I found out about the lies he had spread. I was not unfaithful to you, and I don't know why you would have believed him. You should have confronted me," Isabella said, her voice wavering with emotion. "You should have told me about your suspicions."

He should have, but he knew what would have happened. He would have accepted her version because he'd wanted to believe her. He had wanted to be with her at any cost. Even now her story seemed plausible, even though she was carrying his brother's baby.

"But you cast me out." She gestured to the front door with a flutter of her hand. "You had your security staff do your dirty work. I would never have thought you'd take the coward's way out."

He had been cold and ruthless, but it had been an act of self-preservation. Isabella would have wrapped her magic around him, distracted him from the truth and made him believe anything.

Like she was doing now.

Right now he wanted to lean into Isabella. Sink into her soft, warm curves. Erase the past and drag her back to his bed. He was fighting her lure, but it was a losing battle. Her power over his senses, his mind, was humbling.

"How am I the coward?" he asked. "You ran away when you saw me."

"Why do you seem so surprised? I knew that seeing you again would destroy everything I've done so far to recover."

Her actions had caused her downfall, not his. "And that's why it's imperative that you return to America?" he asked. "Why do you need to leave immediately?"

"I want to go home and start over again." Her mournful voice pulled at him. "I want to forget Italy and everything that happened here."

Her words tore at him. Isabella had been the most important part of his life. Everything had fallen by the wayside when they were together. He had treated her like a queen and put her needs first, but it hadn't been enough for her.

Now she wanted to forget all that. She would move on while he stayed behind, haunted by memories wherever he went.

"I want to forget you."

He flinched as if he had been stabbed. No, he wouldn't let that happen. They'd shared heaven together and now they would share hell. He wasn't going to be the only one in torment. He would not carry the burden alone.

"I won't let you," he said. He stood in front of her, trapping her against the window. "I'm going to make you remember what we had and you will regret everything you did to destroy it."

CHAPTER FIVE

ANTONIO'S kiss was hot, hard and possessive. Isabella felt the kick of exhilaration before it rushed through her bloodstream. Her skin heated as she softened against him.

The flare in his dark eyes had been her only warning before his mouth claimed hers. At first she didn't fight it. She'd never thought she'd get the chance again, and his kiss was just as magical as she remembered.

Raw emotions crashed through her as she responded to his rough, hard mouth. He tasted of sensual, masculine power and a secret part of her wanted to surrender. Her heart pounded against her chest. Her flesh prickled with anticipation.

Isabella knew she needed to pull away. She had to stop this madness before she passed the point of no return. Had to break the spell. She had to find a way to keep her distance from Antonio.

Following her most primal instinct, Isabella sank her teeth into his bottom lip.

Antonio reared back. The red mark on his mouth should have made her feel guilty, but it gave her a dark satisfaction seeing her brand on him. She felt the angry puff of his breath and risked a look at his eyes.

An unholy glow leapt in them, and his face was taut with lust. Excitement lit through her body. She had unleashed something wickedly sensual she didn't think she could control.

Antonio crushed her against him, his strong arms caging her. She gasped as her breasts pressed hard against his chest. He plowed his hands into her hair, pushing the rubber band free before tangling his fingers into the long tresses. There was no escape, she realized as he kissed her.

Antonio easily broke through her resistance as his tongue plunged into her mouth. She had physically ached from the loss of this passion. This was what she wanted back in her life, whatever the consequences.

Isabella surrendered and sagged against Antonio. She grabbed onto his shoulders, needing to hold something solid as her world spun crazily. Her hands skimmed his back and she clutched his shirt, bunching the fine linen in her fists.

Antonio's growl of triumph vibrated deep in his chest. The sound tugged deep inside her as she rolled her hips restlessly against him.

Isabella skimmed her hands over his broad chest, shoving his tie to one side. Her fingers fumbled with urgency against his strong neck before she speared her fingers through his thick hair. She ground her mouth against his, craving another taste of him.

Antonio groaned with pleasure as he delved his tongue past her lips. Her skin tingled with anticipation as she drew him in deeper. He dominated and conquered her mouth, leaving her breathless.

He leaned in and trapped her firmly against the window with his body. Isabella wanted to feel his hands all over her, wanted him to pleasure her as only he could. She rubbed her hips against his thick arousal, teasing him until his fingers clamped down on her waist. Antonio held her still, the strength and size of his hands sending a thrill down her spine.

Tearing his mouth away from hers, Antonio muttered something in Italian against her cheek that she didn't catch. He slanted his mouth against her throat and laved her heated skin with the tip of his tongue. Isabella fisted his hair and tilted her head back, offering him free rein.

As he caressed her neck with his lips Antonio brushed his fingertips against the hem of her T-shirt. Her breath caught in her throat as he glided his hands along her ribcage. Isabella pressed her hands flat on the window behind her, arching her spine, brazenly offering herself to Antonio as he grazed his fingers along the underside of her breasts.

Isabella swallowed hard as impatient need swirled inside her. Her legs trembled, her heart raced and desire clawed through her. She felt a hint of feminine pride as she watched his chest rise and fall rapidly as he fought for restraint. She knew then that he too felt the relentless compulsion, but he was trying to control it.

Isabella didn't want him to hold back. She needed Antonio to act on the wild desire that pulsated between them. She had to relive this feeling one more time.

She reached for Antonio's necktie and pulled it free. The silk hadn't landed on the floor before she tore at his shirt buttons, her fingers scrabbling with haste. She parted the fine linen, exposing Antonio's golden-brown chest. Clutching the shirt with both hands, Isabella dragged him closer, until the hard, aching tips of her breasts rubbed against the coarse black hair on his chest.

Isabella moaned as her nipples tightened against the soft cotton of her T-shirt. She wanted to feel his skin on her. Isabella shoved Antonio's shirt off his powerful shoulders, desperate to feel more of him. She wanted all of him.

"Say my name," he said roughly as he dragged her shirt up.

"Anto—" Isabella frowned, momentarily confused, until it dawned on her why he'd made that request. Did he believe she was thinking of Giovanni? She gasped against his mouth as hurt ricocheted inside her. Flattening her hands against his hard chest, she tried to push him away. "How dare you?" she said in a whisper.

"Your eyes were closed," he mocked. "And you weren't saying anything. I wanted to make sure you knew which brother you were kissing."

Her palms stung with the need to slap him hard. She had surrendered to Antonio against her better judgment, but he'd seen it as another way to insult her. She shook with anger as she curled her hands into fists. "Get away from me."

Antonio ignored her command and grabbed her wrists. She tried to break his hold but he easily raised her hands high above her head. He held her captive and she was at his mercy.

He leaned against her until his body was flush with hers. As much as she tried to fight it her body softened, welcoming him closer. His heat, his scent clouded her mind. The fierce pounding of her heart matched his.

"Were you thinking of him when you kissed me?" he asked in a drawl.

"No!" How could he think that? Couldn't he tell that all she wanted—all she had ever wanted—was him? She rocked against Antonio in an attempt to break free.

He captured her earlobe between his teeth. Isabella stilled as the nip sent a shower of sensation through her veins.

"Does he kiss like me?" he whispered in her ear. "Do we taste the same?"

Fury and lust whipped through her body. "You are disgusting." But most of all she was disgusted with herself. How could she respond to his touch so immediately while he said those hurtful words?

"Did you think of me when he was deep inside you?"

"Stop it!"

Antonio rested his forehead against hers. "I want to erase his claim on you," he confessed in a harsh whisper. "I want to take you to bed and make you forget Gio."

"I am not going to bed with you." She wanted to. Oh, how she wanted to drag him to his bed and make love all night long. But her heart would never recover. Isabella knew he would kick her out in the morning. The hurt, the pain of his rejection, would overshadow any pleasure he'd given her.

He didn't reply. Instead he dipped his head and trailed a row of soft kisses along the line of her clenched jaw. Isabella shut her eyes, her anticipation escalating as intense sensations billowed through her.

"I mean it, *Antonio*," she said, emphasizing his name. "I will not sleep with a man who thinks so little of me."

She felt his mouth curve into a smile. "Bella, we both know that's not true."

He was right, and his certainty was humiliating.

Antonio knew the power he held over her. One touch, one kiss and she wouldn't deny him. She would make love to him anywhere, at any time. And she had.

Antonio met her gaze, his dark eyes blurred with desire. "I only have to say the word and you would surrender completely."

Her skin flushed hotly. The only thing that kept her glaring right back at him was the reminder that there had been times when *he* had surrendered. When she had tapped into his fantasies. Once she'd had this power over *him*.

Antonio claimed her mouth with his. Just when she thought she couldn't take it anymore Antonio captured her tongue and drew on it hard. She moaned as she felt the pull go deep into her pelvis. Pleasure spilt through her.

"So responsive," he murmured against her mouth. "You must have learned a lot in my brother's bed."

She turned her head sharply and avoided his mouth. If only she could avoid his words. She couldn't protect herself from his anger. From his accusations. He wanted to get close enough so she could share his pain, but she suspected he was getting caught in his own trap. And, even though he treated her like the enemy, she still clung to him.

"I could take you right here against this window, but I can't be sure whose name you'll cry out."

Isabella flinched. She desperately wanted to retaliate. Make wild comparisons between Antonio and his brother. Call out Giovanni's name. She wanted to hurt him so badly he would never recover.

But she wouldn't. His torment was hers. She was still

in love with Antonio and had already caused him so much pain. She couldn't forgive herself for that.

"Are you done with this little demonstration?" she asked brokenly as she fought back the tears. "I'm tired and I want to go to bed. *Alone*."

"You don't have to worry about that, Bella." Antonio slowly let go of her hands and took a step back. "What we had was good, but I've never been interested in my brother's cast-offs."

That burned. Isabella bolted away from him. Her movements were awkward and shaky as she walked across the room and grabbed her backpack. She wanted to keep walking. Out the door. Out of Antonio's life.

Let him think the worst of her. It didn't matter anymore. They had no future together. She had already wasted so much time trying to get him back. What they'd had was a dream, and the beauty and magic were fading every minute she tried to hold onto it.

"Leave and I'll drag you back in here," Antonio warned. "You are carrying the Rossi heir."

How could he be like this? So ruthless and hard after the kiss they'd just shared? And why couldn't she be just as unemotional?

She whirled around and glared at Antonio. His shirt was unbuttoned, his hair mussed, but he still had a commanding presence. He was in control while she felt like she was being tossed from one crashing wave after another.

"I was in love with you," she announced bitterly.

Antonio didn't show any sign of surprise. That rankled. He knew how she'd felt. He had always known. And it didn't make a difference.

"I was so deeply and so foolishly in love," she said. "It was the reason that I put my future on hold."

"I never asked you to do that."

"I changed the course of my life to be with you," she said as she walked across the length of the room to the doorway, avoiding Antonio. "And right at this moment I regret it."

His eyes glittered with anger. "You regret getting caught. You didn't expect Gio to tell me the truth."

"I regret *you*," she retaliated. She wasn't sure if it was true. Her emotions were running high. Frustration billowed through her chest. "You were the biggest mistake of my life. But don't worry, Antonio. I learn from my mistakes and I never repeat them."

CHAPTER SIX

MORNINGS were the worst.

Isabella groaned as she sat on the bathroom floor, her bare legs sprawled on the cold linoleum. She had to get up and get dressed. She wished she could sit here until her stomach settled, but she didn't have the luxury of time.

How was she going to get through this pregnancy? Hell, how was she going to get through this morning?

Another question slipped into her mind and she couldn't push it away fast enough.

How was she going to be a mother?

A heavy ache settled in her chest. She was scared of going through this alone. She wasn't ready to be a parent. A single mom. Isabella had always assumed she would be a mother one day. Far, far in the future. But in the meantime she'd had other plans. A few goals she'd wanted to accomplish. She had promised her mother.

Isabella weakly closed her eyes. If her mother were alive, she would be devastated by the news. Before Jody Williams had become ill she had done everything possible to give her daughter the opportunities she hadn't had. Isabella remembered the litany of advice and warnings. *Finish college before you have a child... Never rely on a man... Protect yourself...*

At the time Isabella had thought her mother had a bitter view of the world, but her negativity was understandable. Jody's dreams had been cut short when she'd become a teen mother. Everyone had turned her back on her. The first one to walk away had been the father of her child. *Stay away from the rich ones*, her mother had said frequently. *They have so many choices that they don't know how to commit.*

Isabella wiped a tear from the corner of her eye. She had been so certain that nothing could sidetrack her from her dreams. No man would stand in her way.

She had been so arrogant. So naïve. But she couldn't dwell on that anymore. Now she needed to protect herself and her child. She would be as strong and resilient as her mother had been for her.

She slowly stood, her legs shaky and weak. Her stomach churned and she tried desperately to ignore it. Clutching the rim of the sink, Isabella turned on the faucet and rinsed her mouth out with water. She splashed her face and glanced up in the mirror.

Her hair, which had once been her glory, fell limp against her shoulders. She was pale, her eyes dull and her lips colorless. She saw the strain tightening her features. She was a mess. It would take hours to make her appearance presentable. Normal. Even longer until she felt that way.

The morning sickness was worse today, Isabella decided as she reached for a towel. Was it from the lack of sleep? The stress? Why did it have to be today, when she needed to be strong as she faced Antonio and demanded her plane ticket? She couldn't show any weakness around him.

"Bella?"

Panic radiated from her chest to her arms and legs when she heard the authoritative knock on her bedroom door. *No!* He couldn't come in here. He couldn't see her like this. Bella propelled herself forward just as Antonio entered her bedroom.

She slammed the bathroom door closed but it was already too late. He had seen her. He had stopped in mid-step at the sight of her in a T-shirt and panties. She could only hope her skimpy sleepwear had distracted him from the dark circles under her eyes and the greenish cast of her complexion.

"Why are you hiding in the bathroom?" he demanded.

"I'm not dressed," she said.

"I'm well aware of that." His voice was close and she knew he stood on the other side of the door. "But I've seen you in a lot less. Come out."

"No." She rested her head against the door and fought the urge to slump to the floor. Her body was punishing her for the sudden movement and the jolt of panic.

"Is this because of last night?"

"Maybe." She took a few shallow breaths but her stomach still threatened to revolt.

"I told you, I'm not interested in my brother's castoffs," he taunted.

"Yes," she said, and swallowed hard, "you really proved that last night."

Antonio sighed and she pictured him raking his hair with his hand. "We need to meet with the doctor in an hour."

"That isn't necessary," she insisted. "I've been to a doctor recently and everything is fine."

"You may be okay with that but I want a second opinion. Why wouldn't you want to visit one of Italy's top obstetricians?"

Isabella's shoulders sagged in defeat. When Antonio explained it like that, she really didn't have a reason to decline. "I'll be ready soon." *If she was lucky.*

"You still need to eat breakfast."

The idea made her gag, which she tried to cover up with a loud cough. "No, thanks. I'm not hungry."

"Then eat dry toast. Or have a cappuccino."

She grimaced as she pictured the milky drink. Oh, God. She was going to be sick again.

"Bella?" He turned the doorknob.

"Fine," she said in a high, urgent voice. She didn't care how it sounded. The less she argued, the faster he would leave.

She fought against the nausea, her skin going hot and cold, as she listened to Antonio's familiar footsteps. When he closed the bedroom door she ran to the toilet and vomited.

That had been too close, she decided as she lay on the floor. If Antonio had known she had been sick he wouldn't have left her alone. While she wouldn't mind having someone take care of her, Antonio would have seen how weak she felt. She couldn't allow that.

She was no longer his lover and was now a hindrance. An inconvenient obstacle. She was the reason he wouldn't inherit what was rightfully his. Isabella couldn't forget that. If she showed a chink in her armor, if she revealed any vulnerability, Antonio would take advantage. It was his nature.

She had to get out of here.

And I will once I've visited the doctor, Isabella thought as she turned on the shower. She would demand a plane ticket and deal with any paperwork through the lawyers. She couldn't be around Antonio anymore. Especially after last night. Because if he didn't suspect already Antonio would soon realize that *he* was her only weakness. And he would use that information ruthlessly to get what he wanted.

Weak and shaky, it took her much longer to get ready than she'd anticipated. She pulled her damp hair back in a tight ponytail and dressed simply in a gray T-shirt, jeans and her scuffed-up flats. Looking in the mirror, she wondered how she'd ever gained Antonio's attention. She wasn't beautiful or sexy. There was nothing special about how she looked. She had nothing to offer someone as rich and worldly as Antonio.

Maybe he'd slept with her because she was different from the women he normally had in his life. She was earthy compared to those glamorous creatures. Isabella grabbed her backpack and strode across the bedroom. Or maybe it was because she'd made it known that she found him desirable. That was more likely. Isabella swung open the door and jumped back when she saw Antonio standing in front of her.

"Here—eat this." He offered a piece of dry toast.

Isabella reared her head back. The bread did nothing to whet her appetite. "I was heading for the dining room."

"Where you would have found an excuse not to eat breakfast," he predicted. "I know you don't believe me, but you will feel better after you've eaten."

Once she would have found comfort in the fact that

Antonio knew her so well. Now it made her feel vulnerable. She snatched the toast from his hand, deciding she needed to pick her battles. She didn't want to argue with him when she needed to get her plane ticket.

She looked at the toast with hesitation and then glanced up at Antonio when she noticed he wasn't walking away. "Are you just going to stand there and watch me eat?"

"It's the only way I'll know you've been fed."

Isabella frowned. Why did he care? "I can take care of myself."

"I've already caught you once when you fainted," he reminded her as he crossed his arms as if ready for battle. "I don't want to make it a habit."

"It won't be," she said as she leaned against the wall and nibbled on the toast. She hated being an inconvenience. Or, worse, an obligation. She always toughed it out on her own, took care of her problems alone, and promptly repaid any favor or debt. She didn't accept charity and she wasn't going to start now.

"Can you give me the address of the doctor's office?" she asked Antonio, avoiding his intent gaze as she took another bite of toast.

"No need. I'm coming with you."

She almost choked on the bread. "Why? It's a simple examination and a blood test. You don't need to be there."

"Why do you hate the idea so much?" he asked, and his gaze narrowed on her face. "Do you have something to hide?"

"No, but I don't need to be watched like a hawk." She wanted to handle this alone. Antonio would immediately take over and she knew she would lose the power struggle.

"We'll need to do a DNA test to prove paternity," he explained.

"I'll sign a release form and the lab will send you the results," she promised as she finished the last of the toast. "Or are you afraid I might tamper with the procedure?"

"Are you always this suspicious when someone tries to help you?" he asked as he arched an eyebrow.

"Yes." Because no one offered help unless there was an agenda. The last time she'd accepted assistance she had become a pawn in Giovanni's games.

Antonio took a step forward. "Then you need to work on that, because from now on I'm going to be with you every step of the way."

She should take that as a threat, but she felt her body soften and warm at the promise. "We both know that's the last thing you want to do," she muttered.

"You are carrying the Rossi heir." He gestured at her stomach. "This is my concern as much as yours."

Isabella automatically wrapped her arms around her belly. "You can't possibly want to have anything to do with me or my child. You think this baby is proof that I cheated on you."

"I wouldn't blame a child for his parents' sins."

Isabella stilled as Antonio's words stung. She took a deep breath. "I'm not willing to test that out."

Antonio flattened his hands against the wall as a dark, unpredictable energy swirled around him. "Do you think that I'm the kind of man who would mistreat a child?" he asked in a low, biting tone.

Her instincts said no. She knew Antonio would use

all his power and resources to protect a child. But this was Giovanni's baby. She didn't know much about the history between the brothers, but she knew it was filled with pain and betrayal. Could Antonio separate his feelings for Giovanni from the feelings he had for the baby?

"I don't know," she admitted, tilting her head up to meet his angry gaze. "I've never seen you around kids."

"I haven't seen *you* around children, either," he said as he leaned in, "but I know enough about you to know that you would be a good mother. I don't need a blood test to know that this child is family."

Family. She really wanted her child to grow up with a sense of belonging and surrounded by unconditional love. Her mother had given her those things, but there had been times when she had wanted acceptance from the family that had shunned her. There had been times when Isabella had wondered what was wrong with her that her relatives should withhold their love and approval.

"I take care of my family," Antonio said, his voice strong and clear, "and I will take care of this child."

Isabella blinked slowly as she listened to his vow. Why was he claiming this child? She hadn't expected that. But then why would she? Her own father hadn't claimed *her*. Giovanni had only claimed his baby because he could use the information to hurt Antonio. What did Antonio expect to get from all this? What was his end game? Whatever it was, she didn't think she could afford the price.

"My baby doesn't need your financial support," she declared huskily, and tried to move away. Antonio settled his hand against her shoulder and she stopped.

"It's not just money," he explained. "Your child will

one day head the Rossi empire. He will be part of this world. He needs me to guide him through it," Antonio said as he removed his hand from her shoulder. "Unless you think you're up for the challenge?"

Isabella felt her skin flush. She was an outsider while Antonio's family ruled high society. "Who says my child will want this world?"

"That should be his decision, not yours. Your child will need to be groomed from the beginning. He will need to attend the best schools, train—"

"I can provide that now. I am *not* a disadvantage to my baby," she insisted, hating how her voice shook.

She was surprised when Antonio hooked his finger under her chin and guided her face up so she could look into his eyes. "Your baby is already lucky to have you as a mother," he assured her softly. "You are very nurturing and affectionate."

Maybe too much so. During their affair she hadn't held back on her embraces and caresses. She'd always been touching Antonio. Holding on. Clinging. It had led him to think that she was like that with everyone.

"But you don't think I can give this child the sort of life that befits a Rossi heir?" she said.

Antonio dropped his hand and took a step back. "That's where I can help."

It was too good to be true. There must be some strings attached to his offer. An expectation of good behavior or a short expiration date.

"For how long? Until it's no longer in your interest? When you start a family of your own?" With that fiancée of his. The thought of the other woman made Isabella want to crumple up in pain. She'd seen pictures of the sophisticated lady. She was beautiful, from a prominent Italian family. She would be an asset to Antonio while Isabella had been a liability.

"I am committed to being in this child's life. From this moment on. Whenever I am needed I'll be there."

"Antonio, you don't know the first thing about commitment."

"How can you say that? I have always met my obligations. I have a duty to—"

She raised her hand to stop him. "I am *not* your obligation and you have *no* duty to my child," she said fiercely. "I am solely responsible for my baby and I don't want your help."

He gave an arrogant shrug. "Too bad because you already have it."

"Your type of help will be more like interference and influence." She stopped as she thought of her words yesterday. *You have no rights over me or my child.* That was what this was all about. Isabella closed her eyes as anger washed over her. Oh, she was so stupid for not realizing it sooner. "You want to control the power and the money Giovanni gave to me."

"No," he said through clenched teeth.

"Are you worried that I would squander the family fortune? Or that I will abuse my power?" She shook her head. "Don't worry. I didn't ask for this kind of responsibility. I don't even want it. But I'm doing it to protect my child's interests."

"If you don't want the responsibility I can help you with that. If the tests prove that this child is Giovanni's I'll pay you a lump sum in exchange for your interest in the Rossi empire. You will have millions more dollars at your fingertips instantly and you won't have to make any business decisions."

Isabella noticed he'd come up with the alternative quickly. It was almost as if he'd been waiting to present it. "And you won't have to deal with me or my baby," she pointed out sweetly.

Antonio's nostrils flared as he reined in his temper. "My commitment to you and the baby would remain the same."

"It's a tempting offer," she said with exaggerated politeness, "but I'll have to think about it."

Isabella turned away as she battled conflicting emotions. She'd known Antonio had an ulterior motive, but she was filled with disappointment because she was right.

She knew better than to accept Antonio's help. He'd said he was fully committed, but what he really meant was that he would be committed until he could get full control of the Rossi money. The minute he got what he wanted Antonio would discard her from his life with the same ruthlessness as before.

"Committed? Yeah, right."

"What was that?" Antonio was right behind her. She felt his heat and his towering strength.

Isabella knew she should let it go, but the anger was building up inside her. She slowly turned around, wondering if this was the smartest move, and confronted Antonio. "I think your definition of commitment is different from mine. You couldn't commit to me, but now you'll pledge a lifetime of commitment to a child?"

Antonio clenched his teeth and a muscle bunched in his jaw. "You question my ability to commit when *you* are the one who cheated?" His harsh voice was almost a whisper.

"I didn't cheat," she said with a weary sigh. "Not

that it matters. If Giovanni hadn't come up with that story I'm sure you would have found another reason to dump me."

Antonio's eyes darkened as tension crackled around them. "That's not true."

"It is. Men like you don't *do* relationships." She had been warned, but she hadn't listened. She'd thought what she'd had with Antonio had been different. Special. That it would beat the odds.

"Men like me?"

"You have money, power and so many choices." And she'd had nothing to offer to make him want to stay. "Why make a commitment when something new and exciting, something better, is just around the corner?"

Antonio grabbed her wrist and pulled her close. "I wanted you and only you."

She believed him. But she also believed the feeling had been temporary. "And how does your fiancée feel about that?" Isabella asked as she pulled from his grasp.

"So that is where all this is coming from?" Antonio exhaled sharply and rubbed his hand over his face. "Let me assure you, Bella, I do *not* have a fiancée."

"Isn't that just a technicality?" she asked as she rubbed her wrist, hating how her pulse skipped and her skin tingled from his touch. "You haven't put a ring on her finger yet, but there is an agreement."

"I was engaged, but that was before I met you."

He had been engaged? Maybe he did know how to commit, but just not to her. "To the woman they mentioned in the news? Aida?"

Antonio nodded. "Her parents were good friends with mine. It was to be an arranged marriage."

Isabella's mouth parted in surprise. "Why would you

do something like that?" Antonio was the most sexual man she knew. Passionate. He would have suffered in a paper marriage.

"We came from the same world, had the same interests, and the marriage would have been advantageous for both families. Aida would have made a good wife."

Aida clearly offered everything she could not. Isabella tried not to think about that. "If it was such a good match, why aren't you married?"

He rubbed the back of his neck and looked away. "Before we announced our engagement Aida decided she couldn't bear the idea of getting married to me when she had fallen in love with Gio."

"Oh." Isabella's eyes widened. "Is *that* why you and your brother were estranged?"

Antonio shook his head. "Gio never knew, thank God. He had no interest in Aida. She might as well have been invisible to him."

Isabella wondered if this was why Antonio was so quick to assume she'd used him to get to Giovanni. His own fiancée had rejected him for his brother. It would have been hard to get over that, arranged marriage or not. "I'm sorry."

"Why? I wasn't in love with Aida, but I would have taken my wedding vows seriously. I know how to make a commitment and how to honor it." He took a step back and glanced at his watch. "That's all you need to know."

"No, it's not," she said with exasperation. Typical of Antonio. If he felt he'd revealed too much, or if it veered into uncomfortable territory, he shut the conversation down immediately.

"Then let me be clear," he said in a clipped tone. "It doesn't matter whether you accept your inheritance or let me buy you out. This is still Gio's baby and I'm still going to be part of this child's life. Get used to it."

He was in hell.

The white walls of the doctor's office were closing in on him. His hands were cold, his chest clenched and he wanted to walk away. Instead he stood by the door, arms folded, as the amplified sounds of an infant's heartbeat filled the examination room.

He watched Isabella as she listened. Her face softened and she pressed her lips together as she listened to her baby. The child might have been unplanned, but Isabella had already bonded with this child and wanted it fiercely.

The ultrasound technician invited him to come closer. Antonio declined with a shake of his head and didn't move. He felt like he shouldn't be there, that he was intruding on a very private moment. He'd promised to look after Isabella and her child, but that didn't erase the fact that he was standing in for his brother. *Again*.

And Isabella had made it clear she didn't want him around. Her instincts were right on target. He *was* doing all this to gain control of her. She wasn't going to give up her fortune—that had been a long shot. Which meant marriage. He could make her fall in love with him, but that wouldn't be enough. He needed to demonstrate that he could accept the baby as his own.

"Everything looks fine and your baby has a strong heartbeat," the lab tech said as she got up from her chair. "You can get dressed now and go to the lab to get your blood taken."

"How long will it take to get the results?" Antonio asked.

"I'll ask them to hurry," the woman said as she approached him, "but it can take up to a week."

A week was too long. He wasn't thinking only about the legal aspects of confirming Gio's heir. Having Isabella in his life, in his home, was already placing a strain on his self-control. She had only been under his roof for a few minutes when he had pounced.

He thanked the technician, ignoring the flirty promise that lay beneath her fluttering eyelashes. He closed the door firmly behind her and turned around when he heard Isabella's deep sigh.

"This is why I wanted to come alone to this doctor's appointment."

"Why?" Antonio asked as he watched Isabella sit up and swing her bare legs over the edge of the examination table. "What did I do?"

"She was paying more attention to you than the screen."

"You're exaggerating," he said. Her comment surprised him. Isabella wasn't the jealous type, but then he had never given her reason to worry. His adoration had been painfully obvious.

Isabella hopped down from the table and her paper gown rustled loudly. "I'm going to get dressed."

Antonio retrieved his phone from his jacket and leaned against the door. He scrolled through a few messages before he glanced up again. Isabella was tapping her bare feet impatiently and had her hands on her hips.

"I'd like some privacy."

He raised an eyebrow. This from the woman who had once given him a striptease so erotic that his body still clenched from the memory of it? "You can't be serious."

She glared at him. "Will you at least turn your back?"

"No." He pocketed his phone and crossed his arms. He should probably be a gentleman and allow her to get ready in private, but he didn't like being relegated to the status of an acquaintance. A stranger. They had once been lovers and he didn't want her to forget it.

"Fine. Hold this while I dress." She thrust the ultrasound printout in his hand.

He automatically looked down at the black and white image of Isabella's baby.

Gio's baby.

His fingers pinched the edge of the picture.

Antonio braced himself for searing pain as he stared at the image. But all he felt was curiosity and regret. He wished Isabella were carrying *his* child.

What kind of father would Gio have been? Antonio wondered. Would he have been a disciplinarian, like their father, or would he have been an absent parent? He didn't think Gio would have offered stability or comfort. His brother had been famous for his playboy lifestyle and wouldn't have changed his ways to accommodate a baby.

Antonio, on the other hand, was already prepared to make changes for this child. He frowned at the picture, noticing how small and innocent the baby appeared. He could offer the child a stable environment. Protection. But love? *That* he didn't know.

"Is something wrong?" Isabella asked softly.

Antonio realized he had been staring at the picture all this time. "I think it's a girl," he said gruffly.

"I haven't asked about the sex of the baby," Isabella said. She turned around and walked to the chair that held her clothes. "All I care about is the baby's health."

Antonio glanced at the paper gown that fell onto the

floor. A kick of anticipation heated his blood. His gaze trailed from Isabella's bare feet to her slender legs. He wanted to let his eyes roam, to memorize every line and bend of her body, but that would be dangerous. Antonio knew once he did that he wouldn't be able to keep his hands off Isabella.

"Was your assistant able to find a plane ticket for me?" she asked as she stepped into her panties. The cheap cotton didn't detract from the gentle curve of her hips, and his hands stung with the need to drag it down her thighs.

"Plane ticket?" he asked in a daze. He remembered the warmth and softness of her skin. The way she'd nestled perfectly against him when they slept.

"To Los Angeles," she said as she hooked thin bra straps over her shoulders. "That was the deal."

He watched the muscles in her back move sinuously as she hooked her bra. Her fingers fumbled on the last hook and Antonio stood very still as desire whipped through his body. He wasn't going to offer any assistance. He would not brush her hands away and let his fingers graze her skin as he unhooked the bra and peeled it off...

Antonio cleared his throat. "That was before I knew you were carrying the Rossi heir."

She glanced over her shoulder. "A deal is a deal, Antonio."

He could argue, point out that she had withheld important information. Instead he watched, fixated, as Isabella bent from the waist. Her long blonde hair swayed along her shoulders as she shimmied into her jeans.

"Wait until the results are back?" he suggested. It

wasn't a great idea. For his own preservation it would be better if Isabella was far away.

"There is no need," Isabella said as she hastily put on her shirt. "I know what the results are going to say."

"But you don't know what you plan to do. If you want to support your interest in the Rossi fortune then *you* need to learn the business, too. That means staying here."

"And you're going to teach me? Is that right?" she asked as she straightened the hem of her shirt. "And eventually my child. That way you can wield influence even if you *don't* have all the power."

He gritted his teeth. "Your child needs to grow up here in Rome. She needs to understand where she comes from and who her family is. Then she will know what to do when she takes charge of the family business."

"Heritage?" Isabella paused in slipping her foot into her shoe. "She needs to know her heritage?"

Antonio was surprised by the longing in Isabella's voice. "She can only do that around her remaining family," he added. He needed to keep a close eye on Isabella. The last thing he needed was another man in the picture. Antonio's stomach twisted violently at the thought.

"It's a good point." Isabella said, her gaze on her feet. It was obvious that she was having second thoughts. "I need to think about this."

"Think about it here in Rome," he urged.

She nodded slowly. "I'll stay until the test results are ready."

"Good." Antonio felt a hint of relief. He had a week to seduce her. Considering their history, she would capitulate sooner than that.

Isabella reached for the sonogram printout. "Once

we're done here I'll move into a hotel. I don't have the money right now, but maybe I can work something out with the lawyers dealing with the will."

Hotel? He couldn't let that happen. "I have no problem with you staying in my apartment."

"I don't want to take advantage of your hospitality," she replied. "I think I've already overstayed my welcome."

"Not at all. In fact I won't be in Rome for the rest of the week. I have business to attend to in Paris," Antonio lied.

Isabella bit her bottom lip. "I don't know…"

"Stay. I insist." His strategy would only work if she remained in his home and in his control. "It will put my mind at ease knowing that you are cared for while I'm gone."

"Okay, thank you," she said with a grateful smile. "By the time you come back I'm sure I'll have made my decision."

And Antonio was determined to do everything in his power to have the decision work in his favor.

CHAPTER SEVEN

FIVE days later Isabella sat in Maria Rossi's grand home just outside Rome. She perched on the edge of a sofa and silently accepted a fine china teacup. She winced when the cup rattled on the saucer.

Do not drop it. The tea set looked like it had cost more than her entire college tuition fees. The rug beneath her feet had to be obscenely expensive. It didn't take any expertise in antiques to know that everything in the room was priceless. She needed to keep her hands in her lap and refrain from making any sudden movements.

She and Antonio's mother made an odd tea party. Maria wore a silk dress and pearls, while Isabella wore dime-store denim and cotton. Her skin prickled as she remembered the disapproving look from the butler when she had arrived. She fought the urge to tug at her skirt, which was several inches above her bare knees.

Isabella wasn't sure what the protocol was for tea, so she waited for the older woman to drink from her own cup, then took a polite sip from her tea and carefully set the cup and saucer down gently on the table in front of her.

"It was kind of you to invite me to your house, Mrs.

Rossi," Isabella said, hoping to get through this quickly. "I'm wondering what the occasion is."

"Please, call me Maria."

The woman must want something if she was trying to be friendly, and Isabella felt a stab of guilt. She didn't know anything about Maria Rossi. It was possible that she was a kind soul who only turned into a lioness when she felt her family was being threatened. It was highly unlikely, but anything was possible.

"It must be important," Isabella continued. "I know you aren't entertaining while you're in mourning."

"This isn't entertaining," Maria corrected her. "You're practically family."

She was glad she wasn't holding the china cup when Maria said that. Unsure how to respond, Isabella smiled tightly and glanced around the room. Her eyes bulged when she recognized a painting from one of her art history classes.

Her fingers tightened and she pushed her elbows in closer to her body. She'd never seen a home like this, even when she'd used to clean houses with her mother. It made her uncomfortable. Nervous.

"I understand you took a DNA test to establish paternity?" Maria said.

Isabella slowly returned her attention to Antonio's mother. "Just a formality." She was sensitive about the fact that she had been made to take the blood test. She wasn't a slut who didn't know the father of her baby.

"Have you received the results?"

Please. Isabella narrowed her eyes at Maria. She'd got the call this morning and an hour later had been summoned to the Rossi family estate. That was no coincidence. Maria had probably known the results before she had. "Yes, I have."

"And?" Maria prompted as she took another sip of tea.

Isabella took a deep breath, knowing that Maria was going to be a part of her life once she gave the answer whether she liked it or not. "Giovanni is the father."

To her surprise Maria's eyes dulled and a sad smile flickered across her lips. "It's a shame he will never be able to see his child," she said softly.

Isabella tried to remember that this woman was grieving for her son. Maria had been rude and hurtful to her, but she was suffering. Isabella remembered how it had felt when her mother had died, and tried to find some compassion.

At least Maria had Antonio, Isabella reminded herself. She wouldn't feel lost and alone. Unlike her, Maria had other family to rely on.

Maria regained her composure and took another fortifying sip of her tea. "Anything else?" she asked briskly.

Isabella wasn't sure what she was asking. Did Maria know something she didn't?

Isabella shrugged. "Antonio thinks it's a girl."

"I'm only going by the ultrasound." Antonio said as he entered the room.

Isabella heart lurched when she heard Antonio's deep voice. She whirled around and saw him striding toward her. He was a commanding figure, his confidence and energy crackling into the stifling atmosphere. Although he was dressed casually, in faded jeans and a long-sleeved shirt, Antonio looked like he ruled the world.

She didn't know why she had such a fierce reaction

from seeing him again. It had only been five days. It wasn't as if she'd been out of contact with him. She had spoken to him daily on the phone while he was gone. He had also sent links throughout each day to websites about pregnancy and maternal health. Only this morning she had discovered he had been in contact with the doctor's office, asking advice about her debilitating morning sickness.

This was a side to Antonio she hadn't expected, Isabella realised as she watched Antonio greet his mother with brief kiss on the cheek. He was her fantasy lover and a fascinating man—but thoughtful and protective…?

She saw Antonio pause as a shadow passed along his face. Isabella immediately knew he had caught a glimpse of Giovanni's photo next to Maria's chair.

He was being a picture of strength and power for the sake of his mother and the employees who depended on him, but she knew he was hiding his own suffering. Giovanni had been his brother. Isabella wanted to offer him comfort, but he was too proud for that. She would lighten his burden if she could, but Antonio wasn't someone who shared his thoughts or his pain.

Oh, damn. Isabella closed her eyes weakly as the truth hit her. She was still in love with Antonio. She had never stopped loving him. For months she had wished for reconciliation, with the loss of what she'd had with Antonio almost driving her mad. She'd tried to be practical, tried to move on, but she couldn't extinguish that whisper of hope.

Rubbing her aching head, Isabella wondered if she'd ever learn. This was why she needed to keep her distance. She wasn't going to start up again with Antonio.

It didn't matter how much they wanted each other or how much she loved him. Nothing would change the fact that he still believed she had been unfaithful.

"What are you doing here?" Isabella blurted out.

Antonio faced her, his gaze warming as it traveled from her face to her bare legs and back to her eyes. "I was going to ask you the same."

"I invited her to tea," Maria explained. "She told me the blood test results are in and Gio is the father."

Isabella saw a stealthy look pass between mother and son. She didn't know what it meant. Had they seriously questioned the paternity of her child?

"And," Maria continued, "I was hoping to know what her plans are now."

The two looked at her expectantly and Isabella felt her nervousness spike. She knew they weren't going to like her decision, but she had to be strong.

"I'm leaving Rome. Today," she added. She had to leave before Antonio discovered her weak points. Had to get out before he talked about family and heritage. Before he made seductive promises he had no way of keeping.

She sensed Maria's disappointment. She tried not to look directly at Antonio. She couldn't determine his re-action. Was he surprised? Did he know how much she had wrestled with this decision? Had he been hoping she would stay?

Maria frowned. "But…"

Isabella raised her hand to hold off any arguments. "I plan to visit Rome frequently. I want my child to know his or her family. But it's best for me to return to Los Angeles and finish my degree."

Maria tilted her head to look at Antonio. "Talk to

her," she said in Italian. "Take her into the gardens and convince her to stay in Rome."

Isabella lowered her head and kept her gaze on her hands. Did Maria think she didn't understand *any* Italian? How did she think she had been able to live in Rome all these months? She pressed her lips before she corrected the older woman. She knew some Italian, but not enough to speak fluently.

Isabella's pulse quickened as Antonio approached her. She glanced up and her heart did a slow tumble when she saw his weary face. She didn't think she'd ever seen him like this. She wanted to smooth away the lines and hold him tight.

"Bella, let's discuss your travel arrangements," he said in English. "Would you like to join me in the gardens?"

Isabella nodded and rose from her seat. She quietly followed him to a door that led out to the magnificent garden. It was as large as a public park, artfully designed with statues and fountains. The lush green lawn was beautifully maintained, and contrasted against the crimson and gold leaves on the large, solid trees.

She shouldn't be doing this, Isabella thought as she walked alongside Antonio. She was obediently following him just to *be* with him. Her chest tightened as she realized this was the last time they would be alone together. Instead of getting closer, she needed to start creating distance.

"You don't need to pretend, Antonio," she said. "I understood what your mother told you."

"I know," he said with a hint of a smile. "But I didn't want to have this conversation in front of her."

"There's nothing to talk about. I thought about staying here in Rome, so my child would know his family and his heritage, but I think it's best for me to return to Los Angeles and finish my college degree."

"You can always finish your degree here."

She shook her head. "My Italian isn't good enough."

"Those are obstacles we can easily overcome. Tell me what you need and I'll make it happen."

Isabella stared at the pale stonework under her feet. No one had offered that kind of support for her while she'd pursued her education. She had done it all on her own. She was proud of her accomplishments, but she'd love to share her future ups and downs with Antonio. Have someone at her side during the journey.

But she couldn't rely on him. If she accepted his help he would expect something in return. Something like allegiance and obedience when it came to matters concerning the Rossi fortune.

"I appreciate the offer," she said woodenly. "I really do. But—"

"What is the real reason you're leaving Rome?" he interrupted. "It's not because you want to continue your education. The academic year has already started and you can't re-enrol for another couple of months. So what is the urgency?"

"Once I make a decision I act immediately."

"No, that's not it." He dismissed her answer with the flick of his hand. "You're leaving because of me."

"You are so—" She stopped herself. What did it matter if he knew how she felt? "Okay, fine. *Yes*, Antonio. It's best for me to leave Rome because of *you*. You think I cheated on you. I gave you no reason to be jealous, and there is no evidence that I cheated, but you're determined to believe the worst about me."

He took a deep breath. "I regret letting Giovanni get between us."

Isabella stopped walking and closed her eyes as old pain washed over her. "But you believed him. You *still* believe him."

Antonio took a step closer. "If I could do it all over again I would do it differently," he said softly. "I should have confronted you. I should have told you about the history between Gio and me. I regret allowing his accusations to ruin what we had."

Isabella noticed he no longer called it Gio's *confession*. She wondered if she was investing too much significance in Antonio's word choice. She opened her eyes and turned to him. "Do you believe me? That I was faithful?"

She saw the struggle in his eyes before he answered. "I want to," he answered slowly. "I'm trying to believe it."

But he couldn't. Disappointment welled up inside her. "Why can't you? What is it about me that makes it so hard to believe?"

He shook his head and tossed his hands up in frustration. "I don't know."

Isabella pressed her lips together as she considered a few possibilities. "Is it because I wasn't a virgin when I met you?"

"No!" Antonio looked surprised by the suggestion.

She squinted as she watched his face. "Or because we fell into bed the day we met?"

"No..."

She heard the moment's hesitation. "Don't you *dare*." She pressed her finger against his chest. "Don't tarnish that memory."

"I'm not," he insisted. "You are bold and passionate. Adventurous and trusting. I'd like to think you were only that way with me."

"I have never fallen that hard or that fast for anyone," Isabella said fiercely, and immediately dropped her hand. She took a step back and pursed her lips. She felt exposed and uncertain, but Antonio needed to hear this. He had to understand just how important he was to her. "And I never will again."

His eyes darkened. "Because you regret it?"

"No," she said, realizing he had gotten it all wrong. "Because the next time it won't be *you*."

Antonio stilled. He didn't speak or move. He stared at her with quiet intensity.

"You know what?" she said, feeling foolish as a blush crept up her cheeks. "It doesn't matter anymore. For one reason or another you can't believe that I was faithful. Tonight I'm out of here and I will be just a memory."

Her words jerked him out of his stupor. "About that…"

She didn't like the sound of that. "About what?"

"Bella…" he said softly.

"No." He wasn't going to give her the ticket. She shook her head and sliced her hands in the air in case she wasn't getting her point across. "No, no, *no*. You promised."

He bent his head and shoved his hands in his pockets. "I'm aware of that."

She pressed her hands against her head as frustration billowed through her. "I need to get back to where I belong. To be in familiar and comfortable surroundings. I have some big changes ahead of me and I need to be ready."

"I understand. I think it's the nesting instinct. But that shouldn't occur until around the fifth month of pregnancy."

Isabella forgot what she'd been going to say next. She stared at Antonio as if he was speaking a different language. "What are you talking about?"

"It's in this book I'm reading about pregnancy and labor."

"You're reading a book about *pregnancy*?" His admission astounded her. She hadn't expected him to have an interest. When they had visited the obstetrician it had looked as if Antonio had wanted to be anywhere but in that examination room. "If you understand why I need to leave, then why are you asking me to stay?"

Antonio swallowed, opened his mouth and stopped. He clenched his jaw and looked away.

Isabella watched with growing concern. She had never seen him hesitant.

"Antonio?" Isabella prompted. "What is it?"

"Gio left a mess." The words came out in a rush. "It's a nightmare."

"Okay." What did that have to do with her? Did it have something to do with the will? Wouldn't the lawyers inform her if so?

He squeezed his eyes shut and raked his hand through his hair. "Never mind. Forget I said anything."

She watched Antonio walk away abruptly, his shoulders stooped as if he was carrying the weight of the world. He was a dark, solitary figure among the bright colors of the garden.

He wasn't *really* alone, she told herself.

But who was there for him?

He was grieving for his brother, but he couldn't show

it while he took care of everyone else. His mother was leaning on him and no one was offering support while he had to move into his brother's role. He'd almost swallowed his pride and asked her to stay.

But why? Why *her*? Was it because there was no one else? He didn't trust her. He still suspected the worst of her. She was not the ideal candidate to stay by his side.

Damn. She wanted to stomp her foot. Why did he have to do this to her? Now? She was so close to leaving. She was almost home.

It wasn't like he'd asked her to bed. He was simply asking for support, right? She could do that. She wanted to do that.

"Antonio, just ask," she called out.

He stopped but didn't turn around. "I understand if you can't," he replied stiffly. "We didn't part on good terms."

Maybe that was why her resolve was weakening. Isabella reached his side and placed her hand on his arm. She couldn't recapture what they'd had, but she could change the ending of their relationship.

"What do you need?"

"You."

Her heart lurched to a stop and then pounded violently. Was he asking for something more than emotional support? Why did she feel that kick of excitement? Almost a week ago she'd told him she wouldn't sleep with a man who didn't trust her. But he wasn't asking to sleep in her bed. He was putting his trust in her hands as he asked for her help.

Isabella nervously swiped her tongue along her bottom lip. "Could you be more specific?"

"I need you at my side," Antonio admitted. He looked

down at her, his eyes stormy and troubled. "Just for a few days while I deal with some competitors. They are circling Rossi Industries hoping to find a weakness. It would help if we looked like a united front. Once that's accomplished then I'll send you home."

Antonio could handle his enemies without her at his side. Isabella suspected this was not really about business or about his mother's request. He was reaching out in his own way. He was taking a risk, knowing she had every right to reject him.

"Do you still want me to stay at your apartment?" she asked calmly as her mind raced. Had Antonio figured out that *he* was her weakness? That, despite her better judgment, she couldn't stay away?

He frowned as though he'd made it obvious. "Yes."

"And I stay in the guestroom?" She didn't know why she'd said that. She didn't want to be there.

"Yes, of course."

She saw that glint in his eye. He had no intention of having her stay in the guestroom. He wanted comfort and support in the most basic form. Antonio wanted a few hours to forget—a few nights where he could lose himself.

And she wanted it, too. She knew his trust in her was fragile, that his motivations had nothing to do with love. She was willing to risk it all if it meant having another night with the man she couldn't stop loving. If he propositioned her, would she reject him? She didn't know.

But she was tired of playing it safe. And she didn't want this affair to have ended when he'd kicked her out of his bed. This time she would walk out when she was ready.

"Sure, Antonio," she said calmly as her heart started to race. "I can stay for three more days. But that's all I can promise."

CHAPTER EIGHT

ISABELLA was relieved when she and Antonio left the Rossi estate a short time later. Once they'd told Antonio's mother that she was extending her stay for a few more days Maria had sent them on their way with barely disguised haste. It was as if Maria had got the result she desired and wanted Isabella gone.

Antonio guided her to his black sports car with a large hand at the small of her back. Her skin tingled from the gentle touch. She knew he didn't mean anything by the gesture, that it was something he did automatically, but she liked it. It made her feel like he was looking after her.

Once Antonio had helped her into his low-slung car, he slid into the driver's seat and checked his watch. "There is a party that I have to attend."

Disappointment filled her. She knew what that meant. When they'd been together Antonio had rarely accepted invitations to a party or event, but there had been times when it was required. He would dress up in a suit or tuxedo, looking so devastatingly handsome that it almost hurt to look at him, and then he would go alone and she would stay at home and wait for him.

In the past Isabella had told herself that she was glad

she hadn't had to go to those parties. She wouldn't know anyone, struggled with the language, and wouldn't feel comfortable in extravagantly luxurious settings. But there had been times when she'd wondered *why* Antonio didn't include her. Was she not good enough to be seen with a Rossi? Had he only wanted her for sex?

She wasn't his lover anymore, but the old insecurities were still there, along with her desire to be with him. She hadn't seen him for days and now he was going out for the night. Only this time she didn't have a claim on him. She wasn't sure she ever had.

But she wasn't going to make the same mistake this time. She was in the city of Rome. There was beauty and excitement all around her. She wasn't going to stay at home in hopes that Antonio would return earlier than planned. She had wasted too much time waiting for him and putting her life on hold. Isabella wanted to make the most of her time in this vibrant city.

"Okay," she said, and she stared straight ahead at the Rome skyline, her gaze focused on the famous dome of St. Peter's Basilica. "I might be home late tonight too."

Antonio started the ignition and paused. "Where are you going?"

Isabella had no idea, but she was sure there were many choices. Maybe she would go to the Piazza di Spagna. She didn't care so long as she wasn't home alone. "I've always wanted to experience Rome at night," she said. "I never really got the chance."

"You were out every night with Gio," he muttered darkly as he sped the car down the wide lane that was flanked by big trees.

"I'm not talking about nightclubs. When you've seen

one, you've seen them all," she said. "I want to explore the city and see a different side of it."

"Can't you postpone that till tomorrow?" Antonio asked as they passed the intimidating iron gates that barred ordinary people from the Rossi world. "I promise I will make it worth the wait and show you Rome under the stars. Tonight I want you to come with me to the party."

"You do? Why?" What had prompted the invitation? Was it because he knew she wasn't going to stay at home and he wanted to keep an eye on her? "I've never gone to a social event with you before."

She knew why. It simply wouldn't have *done* for her to be at his side. He was sophisticated, powerful, part of prestigious family. She, on the other hand, had had no money, no connections, and hadn't known the secret handshakes of high society. She had been a disadvantage. A liability.

"I wanted you all to myself," he confessed. "I know it was selfish but I didn't care."

Isabella jerked her head and stared at Antonio. *That* was why he'd kept her from his world? "I thought it was because you were embarrassed by me."

"Why would you think that? Hell, I would have shown you off, but that would have encouraged an invasion of our privacy. I didn't want anyone intruding on us. But I went too far. It was only this week that I realized how isolated you must have been. That was not my intention."

"I see," she said softly. Why hadn't he told her that earlier? But then, why didn't she insisted that he take her along? Because she had been afraid of making demands. She hadn't felt secure in her relationship with Antonio and hadn't wanted to start a battle.

"Would you *like* to go to this party with me?" Antonio asked as he shifted gears. "I think you'll enjoy it."

She didn't know why he was making the effort now, when she was leaving in a couple of days. Was it an apology or did he really want her to accompany him? She admitted that she was curious about Antonio's life. What was he like when he was around friends and acquaintances? Antonio didn't need to grab the spotlight like his brother, but he wouldn't stay in the shadows, either.

Isabella wanted to accept his invitation, but one thing was holding her back. "I don't have anything to wear. And my hair…" She threaded her fingers along the ends of her hair, certain it was a tumbled mess. She didn't usually style her hair, but she needed to go all out if she wanted to make a good impression.

"You don't need to change," Antonio assured her. "It's a casual party."

"We may have different definitions of *casual*." She remembered Giovanni's circle of friends. *Casual* had meant preparing all day at the spa and wearing outfits that cost the same as a car.

Antonio cast her an appreciative look that made her blush. "Trust me, Bella. You'll fit right in."

Isabella couldn't believe what she was seeing. She couldn't pull her gaze away from Antonio as he leapt into the air. His strong arms were reaching, stretching as he dove for the soccer ball. Isabella's stomach clenched and her skin felt flushed at the sight of his vigor and masculinity. Just when Isabella thought he would grab it, the ball zoomed past him and Antonio tumbled to the ground, rolled and shot to his feet.

A group of young boys cheered as the ball hit the net.

Unbelievable, Isabella thought. She'd never thought Antonio could be having fun at a child's birthday party. He should look out of place among the colorful balloons, party hats and streamers. Instead the children gravitated toward him, eager for his attention. He gave it freely and didn't refuse when several boys asked him to play.

"I have told Antonio a thousand times that he shouldn't let Dino win," said Dino's mother, Fia, as she stood beside Isabella, bouncing baby Giulia on her hip. "But at least he makes my son work for it."

"Maybe soccer isn't Antonio's sport."

"Ha!" Fia said as she tried to give a pacifier to her grumpy baby. "He was one of the best athletes in school. Football, swimming, skiing. He could do it all. He needed a sport for every season to expend his energy."

"I had no idea." She should have known. Antonio was lean and muscular and moved with enviable grace.

"Really?" Fia gave up on the pacifier and shifted baby Giulia onto her other hip. "How long have you known him?"

"A few months." But she hadn't known that he loved sports. There were no trophies or sports equipment in his home. He didn't tell stories about his adventures or his triumphs. Was it really a passion of his or did his abilities come to him so easily that he didn't think much about it? "How about you?"

"My husband has known him since their schooldays, and they've been together through the good times and bad." Fia raised her voice over Giulia's tired cry. "That's why Antonio is Dino's godfather."

Isabella watched Antonio ruffle Dino's hair. His affection for the boy was apparent. "He takes that role seriously."

Fia nodded. "We couldn't have asked for anyone better."

"I've never seen him around children," she murmured as she watched Antonio approach her. Her heart began to beat fast. "He's completely different."

"Not different," Fia said. "More like he's…"

"Unguarded?"

"Exactly." Fia patted Giulia's back but the baby continued to fuss. "I think it's the little one's bedtime."

"Here—let me hold her," Antonio said, and reached out for the baby.

Isabella couldn't hide her surprise as he cradled Giulia in his arms. The baby stopped fussing and stared at Antonio with wide eyes as he spoke softly to her.

"How did you do that?" Isabella asked. She couldn't soothe a baby that quickly even after years of babysitting.

Antonio smiled. "I have this effect on all women."

Fia laughed and lapsed into Italian. She spoke fast and Isabella struggled to keep up with the conversation. Eventually she allowed her gaze to fall on the baby, who was now falling asleep in Antonio's arms.

He was good with children and he liked being around them. How had she not known about this side of Antonio? Before she would have described him as sexy, powerful and remote. But today, as she watched him around his friends and their children, she knew there were many sides of him she had yet to discover. She needed to dig deeper to understand him.

When they left the party it was late at night and the

birthday boy had been asleep for hours. Isabella had enjoyed visiting Antonio's friends. She could tell they were curious about her but they'd made her feel welcome.

She'd noticed how open and relaxed he was with his friends. He was much more formal with his mother, and had been watchful and cautious with his brother. If she wanted to understand Antonio she needed to know the source of the strain between him and his relatives.

But Isabella was hesitant to ask. She bit her bottom lip as Antonio drove back to his apartment in comfortable silence. She didn't want to ruin a perfect evening, but she didn't have a lot of opportunity to find out before she left Rome.

"Antonio, why did you have such a difficult relationship with your brother?"

Antonio frowned, and she felt the mood shift in the small confines of the car. "It's not something I like to talk about."

"I know, but I feel like I'm missing a huge piece of the puzzle." If she had known their history she could have avoided so much heartache. But some instinct warned her that Antonio would have kicked her out sooner or later even without his brother's interference. "What happened between you two?"

Antonio felt Isabella looking at him, curious and expectant. He knew he owed it to her. It wasn't just about him and his brother. Isabella had been affected, too.

"My brother and I were close when we were young," he said, looking straight ahead as he drove through the busy streets. A smile tugged at the corner of his mouth as he remembered how much fun he'd once had with his brother. "My parents didn't have any more children so it was just the two of us. I often heard us described as the heir and the spare."

"Ouch. That's not very nice. Did they said that to *you*?"

He didn't care about the label anymore, but he found Isabella's indignation a comfort. "The servants or guests would say it when they didn't think I understood. Or when they thought I was out of earshot."

"Still, that's not something anyone should say about a child. It's something he'd carry with him. Either he tries to live up to it or fight against it. It would have the power to define him."

"I knew there was some truth to it," he admitted. "My parents loved me, and I was cared for, but Gio was the center of attention. There were times when I felt envious and resentful, but as I got older I realized I was the lucky one."

"Lucky? How can you say that?" she asked. "Your parents played favorites."

Antonio glanced at Isabella. She was curled up against the passenger side door with her arms crossed. If she was trying to keep her distance she was failing miserably. Isabella was already taking sides in his story.

"I was lucky because I wasn't pressured to perform better. My parents had high expectations for both of us, but I was lazy and unfocussed. Everyone knew that Gio was smarter, faster and better than me," he said matter-of-factly.

"That's not true," Isabella said.

"It was at the time," he said, frowning as he noticed how Isabella leapt to his defense. She'd used to do that when she read an unflattering news item about him, even when she didn't have all the facts. "Or it could have been my family's mindset. He was firstborn. He was the heir. Of course he was the best at everything."

"That is *so* unfair," she muttered. "I don't know how you could have stood it."

"Don't worry, it didn't last long," Antonio said. He glanced at Isabella as the streetlights flickered through the window. She looked upset for the child he'd used to be. "I hit my stride in my late teens."

"Uh-oh," she said. "You shook up the status quo?"

He nodded. "We started getting competitive. Gio needed a challenge, but he never thought I would eclipse him. I was tired of hearing, 'If only you were more like your brother…' I wanted someone to say that to Gio. And they did, but not in the way I wanted."

Isabella leaned closer. He caught a faint hint of her scent.

"What happened?"

Antonio shifted uncomfortably in his seat. "One day my father told us that he thought the Rossi empire was going to the wrong brother."

Isabella's gasp echoed in the car. "Why would he say that?"

"I think he said it to make Gio work harder. It made *me* work harder. I openly gloated, but I was secretly horrified." He hated how he had felt. How he had acted. Antonio closed his eyes, wishing he could forget the devastation in Gio's face. "For once I wasn't the other brother. The spare. And I wasn't going to have that taken away from me."

Isabella scooted closer. "But being the heir was part of Giovanni's identity?"

He nodded. "My father unintentionally created a

chasm between Gio and me. Our competition wasn't so friendly anymore. Gio saw me as a threat."

She reached over and placed her hand on his arm. "Did he hurt you?"

"No, there wasn't any physical fighting. And we were a team when we needed to be. But I learned to keep my thoughts private. I could never show what I wanted or what was important to me. Otherwise Gio would go after it."

"Like what?" Isabella asked.

He shrugged. "It was little things at first. I saved up and bought a motorcycle, but I didn't have it for more than a week before Gio stole it one night and wrecked it. Stuff like that."

"I don't consider that as *little* stuff," Isabella said. "He destroyed your property. It was vandalism. It was *wrong*. Why didn't your parents intervene?"

"At first they just believed that boys would be boys. Then they decided that it was a phase we would grow out of."

"It sounds like they just didn't want to take sides. Or deal with it," she said, and gave a sympathetic squeeze on his arm.

"Probably." He wanted to cover her hand with his and enjoy the feel of her. "Then it started to escalate. Sometimes I felt I was being paranoid. I had no proof he was behind the sabotage and the thefts, but I had my suspicions. And then we were in the running for the same honor at university. I knew he was going to pull something, but I didn't think he would get me expelled."

"He got you kicked out?" Isabella's voice trembled with outrage. "That's horrible. How did he do that?"

"He told the dean at the university that I was cheating and he manufactured evidence." His voice was calm and controlled, but cold anger weighed heavily against him as he remembered the injustice. No one had believed him. And to add insult to injury Gio had been commended for making the difficult decision to reveal the deceit of his own brother.

"Couldn't you have proved otherwise?" Isabella asked. "What about your parents? Didn't they defend you?"

He shrugged his shoulders, hiding the hurt. "My mother believed I was set up, but not by Gio." She had refused to hear a bad word about her firstborn, and Antonio still felt the sting of betrayal.

"And your father?"

The sting intensified. "He believed that I was cheating and that I had shamed the family," he said quietly. It was hard to get the words out. "I was disinherited."

"You were punished and Giovanni got away with it? Did you retaliate?"

"I wanted to, but my friends talked me out of it. They told me I was lucky to get out of that poisonous atmosphere and I needed to move on or it would destroy me. I knew they were right but I was still bitter."

"Something tells me that's an understatement," Isabella said. "Now I understand what drives you to work so hard."

It did have something to do with his success. He had something to prove. "Eventually my father welcomed me back into the family." He smiled as he remembered the awkward reconciliation. "After I made my first million. My father was very proud of what I had achieved without his help."

"And Giovanni never confessed?"

"No." He didn't know if Gio had kept silent because he'd wanted to enjoy the spoils of war or if he'd been afraid of what their disciplinarian father would have done if the truth came out. "I didn't speak to Gio for years. Not until I saw him at my father's funeral almost two years ago. He asked for forgiveness. It was sincere and genuine."

That was what his instincts had told him, but now he wondered if he had gotten it wrong. Maybe he'd wanted to believe Gio and have his brother back.

Isabella pulled her hand away from him. "And were you able to forgive?"

"Not forgive so much as move on," he admitted. "Gio should have felt secure. I didn't think we were in competition anymore. But for some reason I didn't trust that the treaty would last."

"He was your competitor for longer than he was your friend?"

Antonio nodded. That was why he'd he still been cautious around his brother. "I knew I had to keep my guard up. But I made a mistake." He paused, unsure if he wanted to reveal this to Isabella. "I couldn't hide how I felt about *you*." He felt Isabella's tension.

"So you think Giovanni went after me and I wasn't able to resist his charms? That's why you were so quick to believe him?"

"It fit his pattern. He went after something, or in this case someone, who was important to me."

Isabella leaned back in her seat. "Why didn't you tell me about this? You could have shared your concerns."

"I didn't think I had to." He had trusted Isabella, but he'd seen how close she'd become with Gio. He'd thought that Isabella wouldn't choose his brother over him. That she wasn't capable of crossing that line. But Gio's charm had been too seductive for her.

"It would have helped knowing that I was a target," Isabella said. "Or maybe you wanted to test me?"

"Why would I do that?" he asked, suddenly weary.

"Did you ever consider that your brother knew he could sabotage our relationship with just a lie? All he had to do was raise suspicion." She tossed her hands in the air. "He knew you wouldn't open up and talk about it. That your suspicion would fester until finally you couldn't trust me anymore."

"That's not what happened," Antonio said as anger curled inside him. Why was he telling her any of this? He should have kept quiet.

Isabella crossed her arms. "Your brother's ploy worked better than he could have imagined."

Antonio gritted his teeth. "You're giving Gio far more credit than he deserves."

"Giovanni played on the weakness in our relationship," she pointed out. "He was around enough to see what we couldn't. He knew you wouldn't talk about what was on your mind, and he knew I would do anything to get you back."

Isabella's words pricked at him. There was some truth in them. Hadn't he learned anything from the past?

"You kept making the same mistakes with your brother," Isabella accused. "But don't worry, Antonio. I've learned *my* lesson. We weren't meant to be together. I'm not fighting for us anymore."

Her words were like a punch to his chest. He wanted to say something sarcastic. Something biting. But it would only reveal how much he felt the loss. Instead Antonio stared straight ahead and pressed his foot harder on the gas pedal. Isabella might not like it when he went quiet, but he had learned that silence was his best shield.

CHAPTER NINE

ISABELLA lay in bed wide awake and restless. Her bedsheet was tangled around her legs from her tossing and turning. The silence in Antonio's apartment made her tense. She stared at the ceiling, wondering if she had made the right decision to come back here. Lately she'd made the wrong choices. Like Giovanni.

When she had slept with Antonio's brother she had been drunk and deeply hurt. She blamed the alcohol, Giovanni—and herself. She didn't remember a lot about that night, but she knew she had made the choice. She could have stopped it anytime.

But she hadn't. Because she had been acting out. She had lost Antonio, allowed her dream to slip through her fingers, and she hadn't known why. She had tried to blunt the pain with drinking and partying. She'd sought comfort where she shouldn't have.

She couldn't change the past, but Isabella knew she wouldn't make those choices again. Next time she would recognize the warning signs of her own behavior. She'd have to; her baby was relying on her.

Isabella rubbed a protective hand over her stomach and heard a noise in the hallway. She lifted her head from the pillow and looked at the door. Her pulse skipped a beat when she saw a shadow underneath the door.

Antonio. He was coming to her. *Finally.*

She exhaled slowly as she stared at the strip of light underneath the door. She had been getting mixed signals from Antonio. He had refrained from touching her but she had felt his heated gaze. He had been the perfect gentleman but she sensed his self-control was barely contained.

Her restraint had been shaky, too. She wanted to be with him, but would it send her into a tailspin like last time? Did she want to be with him because she felt alone and scared of her future? Or did she want a do-over and nothing more?

Isabella watched the door as her heart pounded in her ears. Her chest was tight with anticipation. When she heard him mutter something softly in Italian and walk away, she bit her lip to prevent herself from calling out.

Antonio might want to relive the memories, but he obviously didn't think it was worth the risk. He still didn't trust her. Isabella sank back onto her pillow, disappointed.

She didn't trust her decision-making. What if she had invited him into her bed? Would it have taken her down the same path and brought the same outcome? Would she have regretted it?

No. She would regret not giving herself another chance.

"Antonio?"

Antonio felt his shoulders bunch when he heard Isabella's soft voice. He had tried to banish all thoughts of her by working, but his legendary focus was absent tonight. He needed to lose himself in reports and e-mails. It had almost worked. He hadn't heard Isabella enter his study. He didn't have a chance to put up his guard.

He glanced up from his laptop computer. His chest tightened when he saw her at the doorway. Her long blonde hair was tumbled, her face free of make-up. She wore only a white T-shirt and panties.

Isabella was a tantalizing mix of innocence and sin. Antonio clenched the edge of his desk, his fingers whitening as he struggled for control. The shirt barely skimmed the tops of her thighs. The thin cotton couldn't hide the shape of her breasts or the dark pink of her nipples. He didn't know why she bothered wearing it. It would take only a second to tear it off her body.

Don't do it. The words reverberated in Antonio's head as his gaze focused on her long, bare legs. His study was in the farthest corner of her apartment from the guestroom. It was his sanctuary and no one disturbed him when he was working. Antonio had thought he would be safe from temptation tonight. He hadn't thought she would seek him out.

"Yes?" he said, his voice hoarse.

She looped her long hair over her ear. "It's late."

It *was* late. Too late to stop what he had put into motion. When he'd asked her to stay for a few more days he had been looking for more than a shoulder to lean on. He needed Isabella to return to his side—and also to his bed. But when she had asked about the guestroom, he'd known she wasn't ready for them to become lovers again. After the way he'd treated her, the things he'd said, he couldn't blame her.

But it didn't stop him from hoping. Planning. Strategizing. He shouldn't consider getting her back. He should send Isabella away once and for all so he could focus on his responsibilities. Now that his brother had died Antonio needed to fix the mess Gio made of the family's fortune.

Yet all he could think about was Isabella.

"You shouldn't be working," she said as she leaned against the doorframe. The movement caused her T-shirt to hike up, offering him a glimpse of her tiny white panties.

He pulled his gaze away but it didn't stop the desire heating his blood. Antonio cleared his throat and pulled at the collar of his shirt. "I have a lot to do."

"Do you need any help?" Isabella offered.

He imagined Isabella assisting him. Leaning over his shoulder as her T-shirt gaped. Sitting primly on the edge of his desk, her legs brushing against him as she inadvertently offered a glimpse of white silk. Antonio swallowed back a groan as his imagination went wild. Isabella would be more distraction than help.

Distraction. That was putting it mildly. As he silently declined Isabella's offer with a shake of his head Antonio realized that Isabella had become an obsession. Thoughts of her interrupted his daily life. She invaded his dreams. He was addicted to her touch to the point that nothing else mattered.

This woman had destroyed him once. Yes, she had sent him soaring to the heavens, but she had also sent him crashing into hell. And he was willing to risk going through all that again if it meant one more night together.

What was it about this woman that made him so reckless? Was it how she had fit so perfectly in his arms? Was it her soft curves or the warmth of her smile?

No, it was more about how she had brightened his day. Just her presence had transformed his mausoleum of an apartment into a home.

But was that enough to make him forget that this woman had been unfaithful to him? That she'd cheated on him with his brother?

That reminder should have burned like acid, erasing any desire for her. He waited for dark emotions to wrap around him like a heavy cloak. But they didn't this time. He felt conflicted because he wasn't sure if she *had* cheated on him.

What is it about me that makes it so hard to believe?

"Excuse me?" Isabella frowned and pushed away from the doorframe.

Damn. He hadn't realized he had spoken out loud. "I was thinking about what you asked earlier. Why I have a difficult time believing you."

"You never gave me an answer." She crossed her arms and the cotton strained against her full breasts.

Antonio's mouth went dry. "I don't think I have one," he answered gruffly.

"You never asked me about my sexual past, but maybe that's because you didn't think you would like the answer."

He'd never asked because he didn't like the idea of her with another man. He had struggled with the unfamiliar possessiveness. Had he been willing to believe she was unfaithful because she was so incredibly sensual and eager? Had he assumed she was like that in bed with any man?

"I kind of have a reputation back home—but I didn't earn it," she said. "A lot of guys brag that I slept with them, but it isn't true."

It seemed Isabella was *always* struggling with her reputation. She was beautiful and sexy, and she wasn't cautious. The girls in her youth must have been jealous, but he also suspected that a few teenage boys had misread her friendly smile and bold attitude.

"I want you to know that I only had three boyfriends before I met you. And there was never any overlapping between. I also think you should know that I never had a one-night stand. I don't jump into bed with just anyone."

Three? That was it? Antonio was deeply grateful she didn't ask how many sexual partners *he* had had. He wasn't surprised that she had fallen into his bed the first day they'd met. They'd had an instantaneous connection and it had been so powerful she'd done something she wouldn't normally do.

"That day we met was special. Perfect," he said in a husky voice. "Too perfect."

"Too perfect?" She raised her eyebrows. "Is there such a thing?"

"Yes, because I always knew something that perfect couldn't last." He had often thought that Isabella had broken down his barriers, but now he realized that wasn't true. She had knocked some of them down, but he hadn't been as unguarded as he'd thought.

"It was supposed to be a fling," Isabella said. "It lasted longer than it should have because... Well, I held on longer than I should have." She looked away as she blushed. "I didn't mean to do that. I pushed too hard and I clung on tight when I should have let go."

"No, that's not true." When she'd pushed, he'd known she cared. When she had deferred her college education, he hadn't taken it for granted. He wasn't used to his loved ones choosing him first. It had felt strange and temporary. As if somehow he would mess it up and her loyalty would be taken away from him. That was why he had always been on his guard. "Maybe you should have pushed harder."

Isabella couldn't hide her surprise. "Are you kidding me?"

Antonio wasn't sure how to explain why he'd acted the way he had. He wasn't comfortable exposing this side of him. "We had a whirlwind affair. Everything was fast and furious."

"What's wrong with that?" she asked with a smile.

"I tried to shove a lifetime of memories into a few months, knowing it couldn't last." He frowned as he thought about what he had just said. "*Expecting* it wouldn't last."

"I don't understand," Isabella said, her smile fading. "*Why* couldn't it last? Did you *expect* me to cheat on you?"

"No, not exactly. I expected that it wouldn't take much for you to leave my side," he said. "I had nothing to hold you. You didn't want my money or enjoy high society. The sex was amazing, but I didn't think it was enough to keep you in my bed. For all I knew it was always like that for you."

"I was interested in *you*, Antonio," Isabella said. She looked stunned, with wide eyes and parted lips. "You were my world. I thought it was obvious. I would never have chosen your brother over you."

"But I didn't know that." He sighed and rubbed his face with his hands. Isabella had been faithful. He, however, hadn't shown any faith in her. "You were right: all Gio needed to do was plant a kernel of suspicion. I took care of the rest."

"Because you don't think anyone can be loyal to you. I understand that now." She rested her shoulder against the doorframe and sighed. "I wish I had known that a long time ago. I should have seen it."

"But you *were* loyal," he insisted. "You always took my side when you read the news or when my brother tried to rile me up. I noticed, but I didn't trust it. It was too good to be true. Even after all I did you didn't give up on me. You stayed here. You kept fighting for us."

But he had refused to see it that way. When she had remained in Rome with Gio he'd thought it was evidence of her infidelity. He had twisted her actions into proof that she'd betrayed him.

"Yeah," Isabella muttered, "that wasn't one of my better ideas."

Antonio barely heard her as he accepted he had been wrong. He'd allowed his insecurities to poison something beautiful. His actions sickened him. Isabella hadn't destroyed him. *He* had destroyed everything. He was his own worst enemy.

"I'm sorry, Isabella." His throat felt tight, but he had to get the words out. "What I put you through was unforgivable. None of this was your fault. I'm to blame."

She stared at him in surprise. It was obvious she'd never expected an apology and that shamed him even more.

Isabella nervously darted her tongue along her lips. "It's not *unforgivable*."

"I don't deserve your forgiveness. Your kindness," he said slowly. "Even now, after all I've said and done, after I promised you a ticket back to Los Angeles, you're still here. Simply because I asked."

"Well…" She nervously pressed her hand against her

chest and cleared her throat. "My motivations aren't *that* pure."

Antonio heard the sensual promise in her voice and his heartbeat began to gallop. His gaze slowly traveled from her eyes to her feet. "So I gather."

Isabella didn't know what she was doing. No, that wasn't quite true. She had plans to seduce Antonio. She had done it dozens of time before without second-guessing herself. But this time she wasn't sure. Would he reject her out of guilt? Bed her and then have a change of heart once the sun came up? He'd asked for forgiveness, but would he cruelly kick her out of his bed again?

His reaction could be even worse. What would Antonio think of her if she propositioned him? She had told him the truth about her sexual past, but did he believe her? Her brazen act could blow up in her face. He could twist it around and believe that her passionate nature couldn't be contained. That she wanted a man—any man. He might even believe that she'd seduced Giovanni in the same manner.

That thought made her want to run back to the safety of her room. But she didn't want to play it safe anymore. She didn't want to stand on the sidelines and wait for permission. She wanted to live again. Love. Be with Antonio once more.

She took a step forward. Her legs shook, but there was no way she could hide it. Isabella knew she should have worn something different. She wished she had sexy lingerie or something more feminine. She shouldn't attempt to seduce someone as sophisticated as Antonio wearing an oversized T-shirt. In the past it hadn't mattered what she wore, but then she had been confident of the outcome. This time she needed all the help she could get.

She shouldn't even attempt this, she decided as she took another step forward, but she knew she hadn't been bold since the moment Antonio had kicked her out of his bed. She had lost everything that was important to her and become too afraid to make a move. Those days were over. She wanted to be her old self again.

Antonio closed his laptop computer, his eyes never leaving hers. He rose from his chair and walked around his desk. He was silent and his movements were deliberate, reminding her of a hunter circling his prey.

Isabella's stomach clenched as her gaze traveled down the length of him. Antonio Rossi was effortlessly sexy. His shirt accentuated his broad shoulders and muscular arms. She shivered as she remembered what it was like to be held in his embrace.

She had always felt safe and secure when she was in his arms. She could go wild with lust and still know Antonio would take care of her. He would take to the heights of ecstasy and hold her when she felt like she would shatter into pieces. And then he would curl her against his chest and hold her all night long.

Desire, thick and overpowering, coiled tight in her belly as her gaze traveled from his flat stomach to the dark jeans that emphasized his powerful legs. She noticed his bare feet and her mouth twitched into a small smile. She always liked it when he was casual and barefoot. It didn't make him any less intimidating. Instead it stripped away another layer of civility and gave her a glimpse of the earthy man underneath.

Isabella slowly raised her gaze back to his face. Her skin went hot when she saw the lust in his dark eyes.

She didn't have to worry whether or not her seduction was going to work. He was going to take her to bed before she could make a move. He was going to make love to her. Hard, fast and wild.

She could barely catch her breath as the excitement pressed against her chest. Antonio would make love to every inch of her. She shook with anticipation and her knees threatened to collapse.

The baby.

Isabella lowered her gaze, shielding her thoughts from Antonio. What would he think about the gradual changes in her body? Her breasts already seemed larger and more sensitive. Her belly wasn't as flat as it used to be. And what if she woke up in his bed and had morning sickness? That would permanently ruin the mood.

Maybe she was taking too much of a risk. She should back down. Accept that what they had was truly over. Run away. Go back to her room and lock the door.

Isabella hated that idea. Her feet refused to move. She didn't want to give up Antonio. It was time to reclaim him and the woman she'd used to be. It was time to be bold and grab her dreams before they got away from her.

She wanted this. She raised her lashes and looked directly in his eyes. She wanted Antonio. She would regret not having this one last time with him. She couldn't get back what they'd used to have, but she could end this relationship with a happy memory.

"I need to know something first," Isabella said in a rush as emotions swirled around her so fast that she could barely speak. What she was about to ask could ruin the moment, but she needed to know. "Do you trust me?"

"Yes."

He didn't hesitate or embellish. She saw the certainty in his eyes. One little word and he had given her something she'd never thought she'd have again. He trusted her.

That was all she needed to know.

CHAPTER TEN

ISABELLA had longed for Antonio for months. His touch had haunted her and she knew she would never have the same experience with another man. She trembled before him, eager to touch him again—but what if they couldn't recapture the magic? What if everything that has happened between them cast a dark shadow and she could never reach that pinnacle of beauty and love again?

Their gazes clashed and Isabella felt the anticipation stirring deep inside her. From the look in his eyes, Antonio had no qualms. He knew what he wanted and he wasn't going to wait anymore.

Isabella's gasp was muffled as he claimed her mouth with his. He demanded entry and she kissed him hungrily, matching his aggression. She couldn't fight her shameful response to his forceful nature.

He bunched her cotton T-shirt in his hands. Isabella wanted him to wrench it from her body. Tear it off. She felt the tremor in his fingers as he peeled the shirt over her breasts and shoulders. When he pulled it over her head and tossed it on the floor Isabella knew he was trying to slow down. Hold back. He didn't want to scare her with the intensity he felt. Didn't he realize that she felt the same?

Antonio gathered her close against him. She sighed when he wrapped his arms around her. His shirt rasped her tight nipples and she moaned against his mouth. His hands slid down her body as he roughly caressed her curves. He impatiently shoved her panties down her legs. When she kicked them aside, he grabbed her waist and pressed her against his erection.

Isabella felt her desire heat and thicken as it flared low in her pelvis. She knew this was going to be fast and furious. She already felt out of control. Her world tilted and she grabbed onto Antonio's shirt.

She felt Antonio lower her onto the floor. Their kisses grew untamed. She pulled him closer as he knelt between her legs. Isabella felt surrounded by Antonio as she inhaled his scent and felt masculine heat coming off him in waves. All she could see and feel was him, but it wasn't enough. She needed him closer. She needed him deep inside her.

Isabella jerked her mouth away, her lips swollen, her lungs burning for air. She grabbed the back of his head, clutching at his dark, thick hair as he licked trail down her neck.

His hands were everywhere and she offered no resistance. He knew what she liked. Antonio remembered her pleasure points, teasing and stroking her until she didn't think she could take it anymore. Antonio's touch was merciless as he wrung out every bit of pleasure.

Her defenses were crumbling. She couldn't wait, and the forbidden thrill chased through her blood. She wanted to see Antonio in his conquering glory. She wanted him to claim her heart and soul.

As Antonio drew her nipple deep in his mouth he boldly cupped her mound with his hand. She bucked against his possessive touch, moaning as Antonio dipped his fingers into her moist heat.

Isabella stretched her arms on the floor in surrender. She was his for the taking. He gently massaged her sex, teasing her as he kissed along her hipbone. She bucked her hips restlessly. She thought she was going to go out of her mind with wanting.

"More." Her breaths came out in short pants. She wanted it all, and she wanted it right now, because she didn't think she'd get another chance.

Antonio didn't respond, but she knew he wouldn't deny her. She could ask for anything and he'd give it to her. He always fulfilled her deepest needs. He parted her legs wider with a forceful hand and lowered his mouth against her sex. Isabella cried out in ecstasy at the first flick of his tongue.

His touch was just as addictive as she remembered. Antonio swiftly took her to the edge and then held back. She begged for his touch, pleaded for satisfaction as he took her pleasure to another level. Just when she thought her mind would shatter, Antonio granted her the sexual release she craved. He ruthlessly drove her over the edge and a white-hot climax consumed her.

She was shaking with the aftershocks when she heard the rustle of his clothes and felt the tip of his penis pressing against the entrance to her core. Isabella groaned when he gave a savage thrust. She tilted her hips to accommodate his heavy thickness and curled her fingers into his shoulders, digging her nails into his shirt.

Antonio withdrew almost completely. Isabella cried out as her core clenched. She then saw the look on

Antonio's face. His features were blunted with lust and his eyes glittered with need.

"I can never get enough of you," he growled as he plunged into her.

His thrusts were long and measured. It was testament to his willpower. But as Isabella went wild underneath him his relentless rhythm broke free. He grabbed her hips, his fingers digging into her skin, and sank deep into her heat. He tensed and shuddered as she let out a hoarse cry of triumph.

He collapsed onto her. Isabella wrapped her arms around him as his choppy breath warmed the crook of her neck. Antonio didn't say anything as they tried to catch their breath. She felt small tremors rocking her heated body as Antonio raised his head.

"Don't fall asleep on me now, Bella." He looked down at her face, his eyes gleaming with sensual promise as he picked her up and carried her out of the room. "The night has just begun.

Isabella gasped and her eyes widened as she escaped from a bad dream. She jackknifed into a sitting position and looked around, ready to escape. Her heart was racing. She was shivering but her skin felt hot and sweaty.

It took her a few moments before she recognized her surroundings. It was turning dawn. In Rome, she noticed as she glanced through the window. She was in Antonio's bedroom. Not Giovanni's.

She was with Antonio. Isabella studied him in the shadowy room as he lay sleeping. He was sprawled across the bed, naked and glorious. She wasn't reliving that horrible moment three months ago. It was just a bad dream mixed with a bad memory.

Isabella instinctively reached for Antonio to rouse him. She needed to be in his strong arms. There she would feel safe and secure. Her fingers slowly curled against his shoulders and she stopped herself.

What was she thinking? She couldn't tell Antonio about her bad dream. She couldn't discuss Giovanni. Not while they were sharing a bed. Not when they just had made love. Antonio would think she was comparing him with his brother.

Isabella pressed her hand against her head. She felt a little dizzy from moving so fast. She lowered herself carefully, gently resting her head on the pillow, and faced Antonio.

When would she stop having these dreams? Isabella cautiously closed her eyes, hoping she didn't fall into a troubled sleep again. She had heard that pregnant women often had strange dreams and nightmares. Something about worry and hormones colliding. Isabella really hoped that wasn't the case. She didn't think she could take another six months of this.

Isabella stilled when Antonio shifted. His arm draped over her side and he nestled her against his chest. She pressed her lips together as she resisted temptation to melt against him. As Antonio cradled her his large hand spanned her abdomen.

Her breath caught in her lungs as the protective gesture nearly undid her. Even in his sleep he was fulfilling his promise. He would look after this baby. Emotions stung her eyes and clogged her throat. She didn't move and she kept her eyes closed.

Had he noticed the changes in her body? She didn't think he had. Throughout the night he had shown his appreciation for her body. He had been fascinated and had paid particular attention to her breasts. Isabella blushed at the erotic memories. From what she remembered, he'd made no mention of any changes.

She waited for Antonio to move his hand. Nothing happened. He continued to sleep soundly as she rested her head against his bare chest. His warm breath wafted over her skin and his broad chest rubbed against her back. Isabella slowly exhaled, but the tension didn't leave her body.

Isabella reached for Antonio's hand and carefully removed it from her stomach. She couldn't let him get this close. She couldn't get used to this. She had already taken too many risks. All for the sake of being with Antonio one more time.

It had been worth it, but she couldn't indulge in this kind of recklessness. The child was reality and Antonio was fantasy. She needed to remember that.

She didn't want to hide anything from Antonio, but she had to protect herself. She wasn't going to look for emotional support from him only to feel the sharp sting of rejection. It was only a matter of time before Antonio would move on and find a suitable woman. A society wife. She needed to rely on *her* strength and not his when that happened.

Isabella squeezed her eyes shut as tears burned. She took a choppy breath and slowly turned around, her back facing Antonio. She wanted to talk through her fears about being pregnant and share her dreams for her child. But she couldn't. She had to go through this alone.

She needed to start making plans. Although she had only promised a few days, Isabella knew she was taking a step back. If she weren't careful she would promise a few more days, and then a few weeks. She wouldn't find the strength to break away. She'd be clinging onto this relationship again.

It was time to create some distance. Isabella slowly moved from Antonio's embrace. She suddenly felt cold. She wanted to return to Antonio's bed and curl up against him.

It was tempting. Isabella wavered for a moment, and was about to lie back down when she felt a wave of nausea. It was a sign of morning sickness she couldn't ignore. Pressing her hand against her mouth, Isabella hurried back to her room.

Antonio stretched his tired muscles as a satisfied growl rumbled in his chest. He finally had Isabella back in his bed. All was right with the world, he thought with a lazy smile. He reached for Isabella, wanting to hold her against him and enjoy the feel of her warm skin against his.

His hand touched the bedsheet. Antonio blinked and opened his eyes. Isabella wasn't there. The pillow still held an indentation, but the wrinkled sheets were cool. She had slipped out of his bed hours ago.

What the hell was going on here? Antonio jumped out of bed, his feet hitting the floor as he strode to the door. Isabella had never left him while he slept. If she didn't wake him up with the sweetest kisses and caresses, he was the one to wake *her*, in the most wickedly erotic ways. He was getting hard just remembering.

He reached the guestroom in record time and opened the door without knocking. Isabella was curled up in her bed, sound asleep. "Bella?"

She raised her head with a start. Her hair was still damp from a shower and a bathtowel was wrapped around her. "Oh, I lay down and fell asleep again," she said groggily. "What time is it?"

"Why are you sleeping here?" he asked as he towered over her. "Why did you leave my bed?"

"Uh, because I wanted to get some rest." Her eyes widened as her gaze traveled down his naked body. He saw the flare of desire in her eyes and couldn't hide his response.

But it didn't change a very important fact. She'd had sex with him and then she had left. That wasn't like Isabella. She'd used to burrow as close as she could and cling to him throughout the night. Now she couldn't get away fast enough. "Bella, do you see me as a one-night stand?"

"Um…" She shoved her tangled hair from her face.

"You just wanted one more time before you left? Needed to scratch an itch and nothing more?" He wouldn't allow it. When they'd been together it had been wild and mind-blowing because there had been no games or limits. Just pure sensation and emotion.

"What if it was?" she asked with a hint of defiance.

He was no one-night stand or meaningless fling. Antonio wanted to be the most important person in her life. He was used to being second choice, but not with her. He wanted their past and their future to be inextricably linked. He was prepared to bind her to him in any way possible.

"Then I will change your mind," he said, and he flipped the bedsheet over and crawled into her bed.

CHAPTER ELEVEN

ISABELLA tightly held the edges of the towel as she scooted to the edge of the mattress. "Antonio, don't pretend that this is anything more than what it is."

He slid his hands underneath her and pulled her close to him. She wanted to push him away but that would mean losing the towel.

"Why did you leave our bed?" he asked.

His tone was firm and it held a dangerous edge that made her hot.

"Your bed," she corrected him. They didn't share anything. Not anymore. It would be good to remember that.

"*Our* bed."

No, it had never been theirs. It was his bed, his apartment, his world. She was a temporary guest. She didn't belong here and probably never had.

"Really? Our bed?" she asked. She struggled to hold her towel in place as he placed a kiss against her collarbone. She felt his smile against her quickened pulse. "How many women have slept there since I've been gone?"

He lifted his head and held her gaze. "Don't even

try," he warned softly. "I know you want to create a barrier between us. I won't let you."

Isabella gritted her teeth. He had no right. She needed to place a short expiration date on this relationship. If she could even call it that. This time she couldn't get caught up in a whirlwind affair. She needed a stable environment for her baby.

She would love to think that they could try again and their affair would last longer. But who was she kidding? Would he want her when she was heavy with child? How long would it be before he needed to marry and have children of his own? She didn't fit any of the requirements he had for a wife and there was no getting around that.

"I left because it's not our bed anymore," she said. "We are no longer a couple."

"We have a connection that can't be broken." He threaded his hands through her hair and spread it across her pillow.

She winced when his fingers got tangled in her hair. "That doesn't make us a couple."

Antonio smoothed his fingertips along the side of her face before cupping her jaw with his strong hand. He tilted her face so she couldn't look away from his serious gaze. "Why do you think I asked you to stay?"

"For the sex." She knew that was the truth. He couldn't argue with that.

"And that's all?" he asked lightly as his hand drifted down her throat to her chest.

Her skin tingled from his touch and she was having difficulty remembering what they were talking about. She should get out of this bed and into some clothes, but she couldn't move. She didn't want to.

"When we're together you have the ability to shut out the world," she said. They both did. Time stood still when they were making love. "You want to do that because you're dealing with a family crisis. That's why you want me around. So you can take me to your bed and lose yourself."

"I want to make love to you," he admitted. His fingers dipped behind her towel.

Isabella's chest rose and fell as she felt his fingers graze her breasts.

"But I also want more from you."

She swiped her tongue along her bottom lip "More?"

"I need you at my side," he confessed in a low, husky voice. "When you're there, I feel like I can conquer the world."

Isabella wanted to believe she had that kind of influence in Antonio's life, but she knew it wasn't true. She was an ordinary girl with no special skills or powers. "You don't rely on anyone, Antonio."

"It may not look like it, but I do," he said as he gently tugged the towel from her slackened grasp. "It meant a lot to me when I could wake up and see you in my bed. When you shared how you felt and what you thought. When you changed the course of your life to be with me."

"That was then." She couldn't make those sacrifices again.

"But you're still looking after me," he pointed out as he parted the towel and revealed her body to him. Her nipples puckered and his eyes darkened with pleasure. "You delayed your trip back to Los Angeles to be with me. You had no trouble sharing your feelings and thoughts, even though I might disagree. But when I woke up you weren't in my bed."

He hadn't noticed. He didn't realize that she was having trouble sharing her fears and dreams. She wasn't going to tell him. This time she was holding back. She wasn't giving him everything because she didn't want to get hurt again.

"Your bed?" she teased, determined to distract him from the truth. Let him think she was the same as before. It was only for a few days. "I thought it was *our* bed."

Antonio wrapped his hands around her wrists and lifted her arms above her head. She twisted her body in protest, her skin tingling as she thrust out her chest.

"Stay next time," he ordered softly.

"I can't promise you that." She wanted to bite her tongue. She should have just agreed. He wasn't going to let this go until he got his way.

"There was a time when you never wanted to leave my bed," Antonio said as he dipped his head and took her tight nipple in his mouth.

Pleasure, white-hot and blinding, crackled through her body. "Antonio!" she exclaimed. She tried to pull away, but he held onto her wrists. She arched against him, trying to get closer.

When he turned his attention to her other breast his touch was just as ruthless as he took her almost to the height of ecstasy. Just when she thought she would shatter he pulled back, denying her release.

"Please, Antonio," she said in between gasps as hot pleasure pressed just under her skin. "Let go of me. I want to touch you."

Antonio raised his head and she saw the glitter in

his eyes. He bestowed upon her a hard, almost brutal kiss before he let go her wrists. She greedily clasped her hands on the back of his head and pressed his mouth on her breast.

He teased her nipple with the edge of his teeth and grabbed her hips. Her fractured sigh echoed in the quiet room as he urgently caressed her body.

Antonio pulled away and gazed down at her. His features were carved and taut with desire. "So beautiful," he murmured as though he were mesmerized.

He surged forward, capturing her mouth with his, and gently parted her legs with his hands. Antonio pressed his hand against the apex of her thighs and growled his appreciation. She was so aroused that she couldn't hide it even if she wanted to.

Antonio plunged his tongue into her mouth and caressed her swollen clitoris. Isabella rocked against his hand as she chased the pleasure coiling low in her pelvis. The sensations were so exquisite that it almost hurt.

"Now, Antonio," she said against his mouth. "Take me now."

She reached for him, but Antonio ignored her hands. His face was grim as he grasped her waist. He lifted her hips slightly and nestled his erection at the juncture of her thighs.

Isabella felt the rounded tip of his penis prodding against her. She wrapped her legs around his waist and held on tight. She took a deep breath just as he slowly penetrated her.

Isabella closed her eyes and bit her bottom lip as he stretched and filled her to the hilt. Antonio paused and she felt his muscles twitch as he fought for self-control. His fingers trembled as they dug into her hips.

Antonio retreated and gave a deep thrust. Her pulse skipped a beat and her breath hitched in her throat as pleasure tightened inside her, ready to spring wildly and explode. He bucked against her and sensations showered through her like fireworks.

Antonio withdrew slightly before driving into her wet heat. Isabella gasped and dug her nails in his shoulders. One more deep thrust and she knew she would climax hard. She would need Antonio to hold her tight as she splintered into pieces.

He gave a shallow thrust.

"More," she whispered urgently. But Antonio didn't move. He held her tightly, his muscles shuddering as his restraint started to slip.

She opened her eyes and his gaze ensnared hers. The stark need in the dark depths was raw and elemental. More powerful than she'd ever seen.

"First," he said in a gravelly voice, "tell me why you won't share my bed."

Her eyelashes fluttered as she tried to hide her eyes. Why wouldn't he let the matter drop? Why did he find it so significant? "What did you say?" she asked as she frantically tried to come up with a believable excuse.

"I can take you against the window." He rocked against her tauntingly, reminding her of the pleasures he could give her. "Or on the floor. But you won't stay in my bed?"

She shook her head, refusing to meet his eyes that willed her to answer. Need pulsed inside her. "It's not important."

"I disagree. I think it's very important." Determination rang clearly in his raspy voice.

"Please, Antonio." She desperately bucked her hips, hoping his willpower would give away. "Don't stop."

Tension rolled through him, but Antonio didn't move. "That's up to you."

"I don't have a reason," she said on a sob. She was shaking and her body burned for satisfaction. He couldn't be this cruel.

"It's because you don't trust me like you used to." He reached down to where they were intimately joined and pressed his thumb on her clitoris. She shuddered, gasping for air as white-hot pleasure streaked through her. "I'm not going to kick you out of my bed again. I promise."

"You can't give me that kind of guarantee," she said between gasps. Was that why she'd had the bad dream? Because he had kicked her out of bed once before and knew he could do it again? She couldn't think straight, was tempted to tell him anything he wanted to know. Her body demanded release.

"Bella," his voice was thick and uneven. "Promise me—"

"Yes! Yes!" she cried out recklessly. "I'll share your bed."

She was rewarded with a series of deep, plunging thrusts. Her body accepted each stroke with unrestrained hunger. She writhed against Antonio, her movements frantic. His unforgiving rhythm made her delirious. Her breath snagged in her chest and a hush blanketed her mind as a violent climax lashed through her.

Her core clenched and squeezed Antonio. His muscles rippled with a hard tremor and his thrusts were suddenly wild and untamed. Antonio tilted his head back, his eyes shut, the tendons of his neck straining, as he unwillingly surrendered to the demands of his body. His hoarse cry tore at her heart and he gave one final, powerful thrust before tumbling on top of her.

As she clung to Antonio, Isabella tiredly stroked his sweat-slickened back. She didn't know if she'd made the right decision. She'd always thought that she learned from her mistakes, but she was right back where she had started. Only this time she wasn't so naïve. Not that it would help. She was still hopelessly in love with Antonio.

If only she had more willpower. She shouldn't have made that promise.

She didn't protest when Antonio rolled on his back and gathered her in his arms. She relaxed as she listened to his strong heartbeat. It felt right being with him. She should enjoy it while it lasted. What could possibly happen in two more days?

"The other bed is so much better," he said.

Was he wondering if she would follow through on the promise she'd made in the heat of the moment? "I agree. Much more room."

"You should move your things into the master bedroom," he said as he stroked her back with his strong fingers. "No point in keeping them here."

He wasn't giving her any room to retreat and hide. Antonio was making it clear that they were going to resume where they'd left off.

"I'm only going to be here for two more days. It's not worth the effort."

His fingers went still against her spine. "Two days?"

No, no, no. She recognized his tone but was not ready

to renegotiate. "Antonio, I'm not staying here any longer. We agreed."

Antonio rolled over and braced his arms on either side of her. His abdomen rested lightly against hers as he settled his hips between her thighs. He surrounded her, and she hated how her body softened and yielded to his.

"About that…" he drawled.

CHAPTER TWELVE

ANTONIO entered his apartment and heard Isabella's laughter coming from another room. He imagined the way she would toss back her head and her blonde hair would cascade over her shoulder. She put her whole body into it. It was always a beautiful sight and he couldn't get enough of it. He did everything he could to keep her laughing.

He paused at the threshold and allowed the joy of his home to wash over him after a stressful day. The music that blared from Isabella's MP3 player was fun, vibrant and very American. It should be at odds with his apartment's décor, but he liked it. It reminded him of Isabella.

Antonio closed the heavy front door and heard Isabella's footsteps. She rounded the corner with her usual exuberant style and Antonio stilled at the sight of her. Her hair was pulled back into a high ponytail and she wore one of his sweaters. It was too big, but the colour brought out the blue in her eyes. The sleeves were folded up and the hem went to her knees. It also concealed her curves. He liked seeing her in his clothes and in his home, but he wanted to see more of her. *All* of her.

His gaze traveled down and he gave an appreciative

whistle when he saw her legs encased in form-fitting black leggings. "I see you went shopping."

"I did," Isabella said as she draped her arms over his shoulders and leaned into him.

His hand automatically rested on the small of her back and he drew her close. He took a moment to savor her softness and warmth as she kissed him.

Antonio deepened the kiss and she matched his eagerness. They hadn't seen each other all day and all he wanted to do was take her to bed, shut out the world and reacquaint himself with Isabella's body.

But he couldn't do that anymore, Antonio reminded himself and reluctantly pulled away. He'd promised he wouldn't be selfish and isolate Isabella. He had been good on his word for the past month. Antonio had introduced her to his friends and important business associates. It had been a pleasant surprise to discover that not only was Isabella a natural hostess, but that she had already become close with his friends.

"What did you do today?" Antonio asked as he smoothed his hand along the curve of her hip.

"Fia came over for lunch and she took me to some great shops. I needed a couple of things to replace my old clothes. What do you think?" She raised her arms and spun around.

Antonio saw how his sweater draped over her stomach. His heart skipped a beat as he noticed the small bump.

Giovanni's baby.

He had dreaded this moment because he'd been unable to predict how he would respond. Isabella was now noticeably pregnant with his brother's child.

"Well?" Isabella asked warily.

He took a step forward and placed his palm gently over her stomach. His large hand rested perfectly against the baby bump. "You look beautiful."

She blushed and dipped her head. "Are you sure?"

Her shyness surprised him. It wasn't like her. He suddenly understood Isabella's concern. Did she think she would be less attractive to him? Or that the baby would be a constant reminder of her one night with his brother?

He didn't know how to reassure her. The baby wouldn't come between them. It would bind them closer together. Antonio was about to remove his hand but Isabella placed hers over his fingers. He held her gaze but she didn't say anything.

She didn't have to. At this moment nothing else existed. They were sharing this journey as parents together.

"I can't wait to meet this baby," he confessed. "She's going to look just like you."

"That would be unfortunate if 'she' turns out to be a boy."

Antonio watched her smile and his heart did a slow tumble. He loved Isabella. Deeply, madly and irrevocably. He wanted to be with her forever—and not because of the baby or the terms of Gio's will. He wanted to share every moment with her, starting now.

Antonio must have had an intense look. Isabella frowned and took a step back. "I shouldn't have stolen your sweater, but it's so soft and cozy."

"What's mine is yours," Antonio said, and he meant it.

Isabella's eyelashes flickered with uncertainty. Was

she uncomfortable because she didn't think she had anything to give *him*?

Then she was wrong. Isabella had made his apartment a home once again. The music, color and laughter seemed brighter this time around. His life had been stagnant and bitter after she had gone. Lonely. Now he felt surrounded by her love.

Isabella chuckled nervously and pulled at the collar of the sweater. "That's very generous of you, but I'll start with the sweater."

"You need to think bigger," he encouraged. "It's time to make some changes around here."

He looked around the apartment and saw the small additions Isabella had made. The big bouquet of yellow and orange flowers made him think of her bold personality. A small picture frame held a photo of the two of them when they'd visited the Trevi Fountain late one night. A bright red throw was casually draped on a chair and he imagined Isabella there moments ago, curled up and waiting for him.

He also noticed something else. This apartment wasn't ready for a child. "We need to baby-proof this place. And turn the guestroom into a nursery. Don't worry about the cost," he said when he saw Isabella's eyes widen. "Only the best for this baby."

Isabella knew her mouth was hanging open as she stared at Antonio. Had he just said the word *nursery*?

"You…you want to do what?"

"We haven't done anything to prepare for the baby," Antonio said as he curled his arm around her shoulder.

"There's no need to worry about that," she said as she

looked around the room. She couldn't imagine a child growing up here. *Her* child. "I've got plenty of time."

Antonio's hand tensed at her choice of pronoun. "The baby arrives in four months."

"No, that's not right. The due date is in late March."

"Right. Four months," he repeated patiently. "It's already November."

Oh, my God. Isabella went rigid as she recalled the date. How had that happened? She had been staying at Antonio's for more than a month. She'd only been supposed to stay for a few days and then Antonio had suggested she extend it for a weekend. And then another week. After a while she'd stopped asking about the plane ticket. But she couldn't believe over a month had already passed.

She was enjoying her stay with Antonio. It was better than anything she had hoped for. In some ways she felt their relationship was much stronger than when she'd first met him. She knew him better and had had a glimpse of his world. She also believed that he would be there for her when she needed him.

But it was time for her to go. What had started out as a vacation fling had derailed her from her goals. And, as much as she hated to think about it, she was keeping Antonio from what he needed. One day he would have to find a suitable wife.

"Antonio, I would enjoy tackling that project, but I'm not going to stay here for much longer. In fact, I think I should leave by the end of the week."

"I don't understand," Antonio said with a fierce frown. "I thought you were happy here?"

"I am," she quickly assured him. "These have been the happiest days of my life. But I've taken a huge detour from my future plans and it's time for me to return home."

"Is this about returning to college?" he asked. "Because you don't need a degree. I can take care you and the baby. I want to."

But she didn't want to be a kept woman. She needed to stand on her own two feet and take full responsibility for her child. "I made a promise to my mom. And, actually, it was also a promise to myself. I have to do this."

Antonio sighed. "I can't talk you out of it, can I?"

He could. That was part of the problem. She hugged him tightly and rested her head against his shoulder. "I'm going to miss you."

"I want you to visit Rome during your next Spring Break."

"I can't travel that late in my pregnancy." And she was worried that if she returned to Rome she would be reminded of everything she'd given up and wouldn't finish her college education.

"Then I will visit Los Angeles and be there for the birth," he promised.

"Sure." But she wouldn't hold him to his promise. He led a busy life that offered a great deal more than she could. She wasn't naïve. Long-distance relationships didn't work with someone like Antonio. Once she left Rome she would be out of sight and out of mind.

"I mean it, Bella. Whenever you need me, I'll be there."

CHAPTER THIRTEEN

TODAY was her last day with Antonio.

It hadn't quite sunk in, Isabella thought as she lay in bed watching the sunrise over Rome. She wanted to create some lasting memories. She wanted to remember Antonio's passion and heat. She needed to touch and taste him one last time. It was her wish to end the relationship on a kiss and then she could say goodbye.

Isabella reached out and cupped Antonio's jaw. The dark stubble was rough against her soft palm. She stroked the sharp angles and hard planes of his face, remembering the lines fanning his eyes when he smiled and the grooves bracketing his mouth when he frowned. She was going to miss his scowls as much as his sexy, slow smiles.

She lowered her head and brushed her lips against his. Isabella didn't know how she was going to live without Antonio's kisses again. Whenever he claimed her mouth with gentle seduction, or with hot, pulsing need, it was like an electric current snaked through her veins. She felt wildly alive each time Antonio touched her.

Isabella lips grazed Antonio's mouth again and she felt his body shift. "Bella…" he said in a sleepy growl.

Her breath hitched in her throat as a bittersweet ache filled her chest. She loved the way he said her name. It was a mix of masculine satisfaction and adoration. She hoped that it would always be that way when he thought of her.

Isabella trailed her hand down the thick column of his neck and memorized the strong lines and bronze skin. She gave a start when Antonio draped his arm around her waist and his fingers spanned her side. She felt the possessiveness in his touch through her T-shirt.

She glanced up at his face and her gaze collided with his. The sleep faded from his eyes and he studied her face with serious intent.

Isabella lowered her lashes, veiling her eyes from him. She didn't want him to read her thoughts. Her sadness.

Her hand stilled against his chest as Antonio bunched her T-shirt in his fist. "Why," he asked softly, "do you hide underneath this when you know I want you naked in bed?"

She smiled at the teasing quality in his voice. "I wear it so you will have the pleasure of taking it off me." That was partly true. What she didn't add was that she wore an oversized T-shirt to conceal her baby bump.

"No, you do it because you want to tease me." He let go of the cotton and tucked both his hands under his head. "This time I want *you* to take it off."

A wicked curl of excitement unfurled low in her pelvis. Antonio didn't simply want her to strip for him. He wanted her to express how she was feeling—or rather how he made her feel.

Isabella knelt beside Antonio on the mattress, her gaze never leaving his. She reached for the hem of her shirt. Her fingers flexed against the cotton. Today she wouldn't hold back.

She slowly raised the shirt, sensuously rolling her hips and arching her spine as anticipation sizzled in her veins. She felt Antonio's hot gaze on her skin. It made her feel scandalous and beautiful. She wasn't worried about her pregnant belly. Isabella thrust her breasts out and stretched as she freed herself of the shirt.

Antonio didn't move but watched in intense silence as she tossed the shirt onto the floor. She was naked before him. Instead of feeling shy, she felt gloriously alive.

Heat suffused her skin as she caressed her collarbone and shoulders. He was unnaturally still as he watched her. His harsh features and radiating tension were subtle responses. She didn't want that. She wanted to shatter that self-control once and for all.

Isabella massaged the tips of her breasts just like Antonio would. She bit her lip and moaned as her nipples stung. Antonio's chest rose and fell as he watched her hands trail down her body. Isabella felt like a harem girl pleasing her master. She felt powerful but submissive. Daring yet obedient. She wanted to give Antonio his fantasy, but at the same time she wanted to make him beg.

She skimmed her fingers along her pelvic bone. Just when she was about to cup her sex with her hand she changed her mind. She grasped Antonio's hard erection that angled toward his flat stomach. Antonio gasped, his hips vaulting off the mattress as she curled his fingers around his thickness.

Isabella pumped her hand with slow deliberation. She watched Antonio's eyes squeeze shut as his mouth slackened. His big hands clenched the pillow under his head. She was fascinated as she watched pleasure and agony chase across his face.

She bent down and wrapped her lips around the tip of his penis. Antonio's jagged breath was the sweetest sound to her ears. She sighed with delight as his large hands knotted in her hair. His fingers twisted with every swirl of her tongue and the deep draw of her mouth.

Isabella felt the tremors storm through his hard body and heard his uneven breath. He was so close to surrendering to her. She felt his hands dig into her shoulders as he urgently dragged her up his body.

She gave a cry of complaint. As much as she wanted to lie with him naked, she was determined to give him everything he desired. She wished she was bold enough to show him, tell him how she felt.

Driven by an urgency that scared her, Isabella pressed her mouth against Antonio's ear. Her heart was pounding against her ribcage and her nerves tingled just under her skin.

"I love you," she whispered.

Antonio didn't move. Isabella's heart lurched and plummeted. At that moment she felt more exposed than when she had stripped off her clothes. She was glad she'd had the courage to finally tell Antonio, and she refused to regret her impulsive words, but she didn't dare look at him.

She flinched when he cradled her jaw with unsteady hands. She kept her gaze lowered, not willing to see if there was rejection or indifference in his eyes. She was unprepared when Antonio covered her mouth with his. The kiss was raw and untamed. Isabella felt weak as the heat rushed in her blood.

Antonio's hands were everywhere, drawing her

closer, molding her body against his. She wanted to melt into him. She wanted to be a part of him forever.

When he anchored his heavy leg against hers Isabella knew Antonio was about to take all control away from her. She was tempted to be swept away one last time, but today she wanted to focus all her love and attention on Antonio.

Isabella moved swiftly and escaped Antonio's embrace. Before he could protest or pin her down she straddled his hips. His hands fell on her waist, his fingers digging into her skin as she slowly sank down on his erection.

She closed her eyes as Antonio's groan echoed around her. Hot pleasure bloomed inside her, pressing heavily until she thought every inch of her skin would blister. She tentatively rolled her hips and was immediately rewarded with a deep thrust from Antonio.

He gained a firmer hold on her hips and lifted her slightly before he bucked hard against her. White-hot sensations rippled through her center, zooming to the top of her head and the soles of her feet.

She rocked her hips faster, compelled to follow an elemental rhythm. She couldn't get enough of Antonio writhing underneath her. She felt like she was harnessing his power and making it hers. No, she realized as she swiped her hair from her eyes. She was making Antonio hers.

He sat up and her eyes were level with his. Antonio guided her hips to counter each savage thrust. She placed her hands on his jaw and kissed his mouth.

"I love you so much, Antonio," she said against his lips.

His fingers bit into her skin as he ground his mouth

against hers. She matched his raw passion with every kiss, every touch and roll of her hips. The need clawed inside her, stripping her control to ribbons. She arched her spine and tilted her head back just as a ferocious climax screamed through her. Her body clenched, her mind went blank and her skin went hot and cold. Antonio burrowed his face against her breasts, his stubble rasping against her as he let out a hoarse cry of triumph.

Time stood still for Isabella. She wanted to hold on to this moment but it was already slipping away. She clung to Antonio as he guided her back onto the mattress. She curled up next to him and pressed her face against his sweat-slicked chest. She inhaled his scent and closed her eyes.

This was how she wanted to end their affair. No tears, no drama. This was how she needed to say goodbye.

But she had to say it one more time, even if Antonio's breathing indicated he was falling back to sleep. She had to do it now because she wouldn't get another chance.

Isabella looked up at Antonio. His eyes were closed and his features were softened in sleep. "I love you, Antonio," she whispered. "I will always love you."

Hours later, Isabella stood on Antonio's balcony which overlooked Rome. The November breeze was crisp but she didn't go back inside. Her mood was quiet and reflective as she waited for Antonio to finish his phone call and leave his study. She knew he was a busy and important man, but she resented how his business intruded. She didn't want to share Antonio's time and attention while they were leaving for the airport.

Isabella glanced down at her clothes, wishing she had something sleek and sophisticated to wear. Something glamorous that he'd always remember instead of her usual jeans and T-shirt. The sweater did nothing to add to her appearance. It was black, bulky, and it hid her baby bump.

She absently rubbed her belly, excited and nervous about her growing baby. The changes in her body were a physical reminder that it was time to move on. She had been greedy and stayed longer than she should. She didn't want to outstay her welcome and ruin these memories.

"Bella, you must be freezing," Antonio said as he stepped onto the balcony. "What are you doing out here?"

"I just wanted one more look," she said. To her horror, she felt her eyes water and her throat constrict with emotion.

Isabella ducked her head and reached for her backpack. She tried to focus on something else and keep her hands busy. She checked once again that she had her passport, ticket and money. As she was about to put them away something caught her notice.

"Antonio?" Isabella frowned as she read the printout in her hand. She straightened to her full height and looked at him. She tried not to think how masculine and powerful he looked in his dark suit and tie. "Is this a first-class ticket?"

"Yes," he answered abstractedly as he looped a wayward strand of her hair behind her ear. His fingertips brushed her throat and lingered.

Isabella took a step away as dread settled in her stomach. That had to have cost thousands of dollars.

Money she didn't have yet. Money she'd need for her baby. "You shouldn't have done that," she admonished in a hushed tone.

He shrugged and reached for her free hand, slid his fingers between hers. "You wouldn't accept my private plane," he reminded her as his thumb caressed her skin.

"I can't accept it, Antonio." It was going to take a long time before she would have the money from Giovanni's will. There were strict rules about how she could spend the money. She could use it to raise her baby but not repay a personal debt. "It's going to take me forever to pay off this ticket."

"I don't want you to repay me." He raised her hand to his mouth and pressed his lips against her knuckles.

She sighed and rested her head against his shoulder. It was tempting to accept his offer. She was going to be a poor student for a while. She needed all the help she could get. But she'd made a deal and she wanted to honor it. "It's too expensive."

His hand tightened against hers. Isabella flinched and lifted her head to look at him. His expression was closed and she couldn't tell what he was thinking.

"Then don't use it," he said.

Isabella blinked and gave him a small smile. "And do what instead? Swim my way back to Los Angeles?" she asked lightly.

She felt the nervous energy simmering in Antonio as he braced his shoulders. "You could stay."

She stared at Antonio's profile. He wasn't looking at her but she saw the ruddy streaks against his cheekbones and the tension in his jaw. If she didn't know any better she'd think he was feeling shy.

Stay? Hope blossomed through her body. She tried

to tamp down her growing excitement. She could have misunderstood his offer, but was he offering something more than affair? More than a duty to her and her child?

"Here? With you?" she clarified, her breath lodging in her throat.

"Yes." He risked a glance in her direction. "If that's what you want."

Antonio appeared vulnerable. His muscles were stiff and his dark eyes were hooded. He was reaching out, uncertain of her answer. He knew she loved him, but he wasn't sure if she would make the same sacrifices again.

She shouldn't. She had put her life on hold to be with him and then, when he had dumped her, she'd had nothing. Working in that café, with no money or opportunities, she'd sworn she would not put herself in that situation again. She would protect herself and not rely on any man. Especially not Antonio, who had the power to destroy her.

So why was she even considering his offer? Hadn't she learned anything? But this time it was different. This was not a vacation fling or an affair. Or was it?

Her chest squeezed with dismay. He had asked her to stay—something she'd needed to hear after he'd kicked her out all those months ago—but he hadn't said that he loved her. He wasn't offering anything more.

Isabella felt tears burn her eyes. "I want to," she said in a raspy voice. "But I can't."

Antonio closed his eyes briefly. His throat tightened as he swallowed. "Why not?"

She pressed her hand against his cheek. Oh, how she wished she didn't have to reject him. It hurt her just as much as it hurt him. "It's complicated."

He placed his hand on hers, trapping her against

him as he opened his eyes and held her gaze. "It's actually very simple. I want to be with you. You want to be with me."

Was that enough? It hadn't been enough last time. And this time she had a baby to consider. She needed more. She needed to know that he was going to be with her no matter what.

"You shouldn't make big changes when you're still in mourning," Isabella decided. She had learned that after her mother's death. Antonio had had a complicated relationship with his brother and needed time to come to terms with Giovanni's death.

"You think I'm doing this out of grief?" His eyes glittered with annoyance. "Do you believe that because I no longer have my brother I feel alone in the world?"

"Well, yes. It's possible." Isabella hoped it wasn't. She wanted to believe that the bond they shared was deep and powerful, but knew his feelings might only be temporary. She wasn't going to stay only to discover that Antonio had made this choice because he was bereaved.

"I'm not trying to fill a void," he said, his voice low and rough. "If anything I've realized how I want to spend the rest of my life. I want to spend it with you."

Isabella froze. Had he really said that or was she hearing what she wanted to hear? She was almost too scared to move. "What are you saying?"

"I love you, Isabella." He turned his head and pressed his mouth against the palm of her hand. "I want to be with you. Always."

Isabella inhaled a jagged breath. *He loved her.* She wanted to fling herself into his arms but something was holding her back. She was scared to trust his words. Scared to find out that her idea of love wasn't his.

"This is moving too fast." She snatched her hand away from him and clenched her fists, her pulse skipping erratically. "I...I need to think about this."

Antonio moved closer. His harsh features were sharp and there was a predatory gleam in his eyes. He didn't like her answer and was determined to make her yield. "What's there to think about? Why do you need to think about it in Los Angeles instead of here with me?"

"I.... It's just that..."

There was an apologetic knock on the balcony door. Isabella whirled around and saw the housekeeper standing in the doorway. She was wringing her hands in her starched apron.

"I'm sorry to interrupt," Martina said, trying not to make eye contact, "but your mother is here, sir."

Antonio closed his eyes and took a deep breath. He didn't hide the displeasure on his face as he held his temper firmly in check.

"Why is your mother here?" Isabella said. She couldn't imagine that Maria wanted to see her off to the airport. She had not spoken to Maria since the day she had been invited for tea.

"I don't know," he said as he reluctantly moved away. "I'll be right back."

She didn't say anything as she watched him leave. Antonio loved her and wanted her to stay. But as what? His girlfriend? His mistress? His wife?

And would he love her child?

She tried to imagine Antonio as a father.

He would be loving and affectionate. She knew that deep in her bones. He would be firm but gentle. He wouldn't make the same mistakes as his own parents. He would encourage and support his child no matter what challenges they faced. Antonio would give his child unconditional love, but would he give it to *her*?

Her opinion was swift. Yes, he would love her child. She didn't know why she was even questioning it. Antonio was already a part of her baby's life. He'd been there every step of the way.

Isabella felt as if a weight had been lifted off her. She was willing to take the risk and tell Antonio that she'd stay. She knew they could be a family. She didn't need to hear a marriage proposal. She wanted one, but she didn't need it to make her decision. Antonio loved her and cared about her baby. He proved it every day.

They could have a wonderful future together, Isabella thought as she grabbed her backpack and strode across the balcony. She was prepared to live and love boldly, without a safety net.

Isabella stepped into the apartment but didn't see Antonio or his mother. She heard voices coming from the study and hesitated. She didn't really want to see Maria Rossi. The woman intimidated her. But she was Antonio's mother and the grandmother of her child. Isabella gritted her teeth and threw back her shoulders before marching over to the study.

"Why is she leaving?" Isabella heard Maria ask in Italian. "You were supposed to convince her to stay."

"She hasn't left yet," Antonio replied. "And she can always come back."

"Yes, yes, yes. She *says* she'll visit so the child can know his heritage and his family, but there's no guarantee."

Isabella frowned as she listened by the study door.

Did Maria still think she would prevent her from knowing her grandchild? That she had no intention of keeping in contact?

Isabella was about to step into the study, but froze mid-step when she heard Maria's next words.

"You were supposed to marry her and adopt the baby so we can gain full control of the Rossi shares." Maria's tone was sharp. "What happened?"

Isabella went cold. Antonio had said he wanted her. That he wanted to look after the baby. That he loved her. Her stomach made a sickening twist. It had all been lies.

"I *will* marry Isabella," Antonio told his mother.

His confident tone scraped at Isabella. There was no question that she would have accepted his proposal. Hell, she would have jumped at the offer with pathetic eagerness. She loved him and had been about to give up everything again to be with him.

"And adopt the baby?" Maria asked.

Isabella gasped as pain ricocheted in her chest. She clasped her shaky hand against her mouth. How could Antonio have devised such a diabolical plan? And how could she have fallen for it so easily?

She should have known he wasn't going to accept Giovanni's baby into his heart. This was why he'd said he wanted to take care of them and show full support. So down the line he could win full custody of Gio's child.

Isabella pressed her hand against the wall as her knees threatened to buckle. It would have worked. If she had married Antonio she would have wanted him to adopt the baby. She would have encouraged it!

And he would have stolen her child away from her. The cold-hearted bastard.

Isabella thrust out her chin and took a deep breath. She wasn't going to let that happen. She didn't care that Maria intimidated her or that Antonio wielded enormous power. She would protect her child from the Rossi family.

Isabella stepped into the study, prepared for battle.

CHAPTER FOURTEEN

When Antonio saw Isabella enter the study a sense of dread shrouded him and weighed heavily on his shoulders. Isabella's complexion was pale and her posture was rigid. Her hands were clenched at her sides but it was her eyes that gave her away. She looked wounded. He knew she'd heard his damning words.

Antonio prided himself on his quick thinking. He was usually a man of action. Yet at this moment he couldn't move. His mind went blank as blinding panic flared inside him. There was no way he could recover from this.

His mother frowned as she watched his expression transform from annoyance to caution. She turned to the door and saw Isabella. Maria immediately pasted on a polite smile and acted as if nothing had been said. After years of gossiping and backbiting with her social circle Maria Rossi wasn't flustered. She was in her element. The only sign that she was taken by surprise was the way she fiddled with her pearl necklace.

"Isabella," his mother greeted her in English. "I wanted to see you before you left for America. I hope you will return soon."

"I have no intention of coming back," Isabella replied in Italian, "I am not giving you the opportunity to steal my child."

Maria flinched and her face went a mottled red. Her movements were choppy as she turned his attention to Antonio. "You told me she didn't speak Italian," she hissed.

"I said no such thing," Antonio replied, his gaze firmly on Isabella's trembling jaw. "Gio probably gave you that impression but he was wrong."

Unfortunately for him. How could he convince Isabella that he had abandoned his plans? Would she believe that now he really wanted to marry her and adopt her child? No. She would never trust his motivations. He didn't blame her.

"Isabella—" his mother began, but faltered to a stop as Isabella glared at her.

"Mother, I think it would be best if you left. Bella and I need to talk."

Maria looked uncertain as she glanced at Isabella and then back at him. She was very aware of Isabella's unpredictable anger quivering in the air.

"I don't think that would be wise."

Antonio sighed softly. Of all the times his mother chose now to give him support. She knew she'd made a big mistake, and he appreciated her need to back him up, but he didn't need her here. This was between him and Isabella. "Please?"

Maria's shoulders sagged in defeat. She grabbed her purse from his desk, patted her chignon to make sure every hair was in place, and gave Isabella a wide berth as she walked out of the study.

Antonio held Isabella's furious gaze but they didn't exchange a word. The moment they heard his mother leave the apartment and shut the door Isabella took an angry step forward.

"Was *anything* we shared true?" Her tone was low and fierce. "Or was it all a lie?"

Antonio saw the pain and the rage in her eyes. He wanted to wrap his arms around her, hold her close and take the hurt from her. He knew how she felt. He had wrestled with that very question when he'd thought she had cheated on him. It ate away at him to the point where he didn't think he would be whole again.

"You still believe I cheated on you," she said, her eyes narrowing into slits. "You told me you believed me so I would get closer to you."

"No, I believe you." She had been innocent, and he had renewed this affair under false pretenses. She would never forgive him and he had to live with the fact that he'd ruined their second chance for happiness.

"I don't think so. You will say anything to get what you want. You'd even go so far as to marry me if it means getting control of the family fortune. Why, you'd even say you love me when you can't stand the sight of me."

"That's not true." Antonio moved and stood in front of her. "I do love you. You don't have to question that. I have proved it every day since we got back together."

"No, you've proved that you're a very good actor. You've pretended to look after me when what you were really doing was looking after your own interests." Her hand shook with fury as she pointed accusingly at him. "You said you wanted to give me everything, but once you'd got what you wanted you would have taken it all away."

Antonio reared back as if he'd been hit. How could

she say that? Did she think him that low? "I would never do that and you know it."

"I thought I knew you, but obviously I don't." She shook her head in disgust. "I was thrilled when you finally opened up to me, but that was part of the plan, wasn't it? Were the stories even true?"

"Of course they were." Her accusations stung. He had shared those memories knowing he could trust them to Isabella. "I told you things I haven't told anyone else."

She wasn't listening. "But the *pièce de resistance* of your plan was pure genius," she declared with the sweep of her hand. "Proving that you could be a good father to my child. Only it was all a show."

"No, it wasn't," he said through clenched teeth.

"You even got your friends involved so that you could demonstrate how good you are with children. And I fell for it!"

"That's not true," he insisted. "I didn't fake anything with my friends. I adore those kids and you have no right to question that."

She thrust out her chin. "And *you* had no right seducing me," she said in a growl, her eyes flashing with ferocious anger. "Making me believe that you wanted a second chance. I knew you wanted to control my child's inheritance but I didn't think you'd try to take my child as well."

"That was not my intention." Antonio said coldly. He needed his words to pierce through her tumultuous emotions. "I would never separate you from your child."

"I heard what your mother said."

"Yes, my mother said it. Not me."

"Then what *was* your plan?" she asked, placing her fists on her hips. "I know you had one. You set it in motion when you found me at that café. Why would you come looking for me when you could have had someone else do the job?"

Antonio couldn't deny it. Isabella knew him well. That hadn't been a disadvantage in the past. She'd known his good and bad sides and still fallen in love with him. He had destroyed that love once before but this was different. There was no hope after this.

He wanted to lie. He should lie if he wanted to save what they had together. But he couldn't. It was time he owned up to his plan. Isabella deserved to know the truth and understand what he was capable of doing.

"I didn't know why Gio named you in the will. I thought it was to remind me of what he could steal away from me—you *and* my birthright. I wasn't going to let that happen and I planned to take back the power he'd given you."

She crossed her arms and glared at him. "I've already figured that out. What did you plan to do?"

Antonio looked away guiltily. Maybe it was best if he didn't tell her *everything*.

"Oh, my God," Isabella whispered and dropped her hands to her sides. "You were going to seduce me so I would give up my child's claim to the Rossi fortune."

Isabella took a cautious step back as she realized Antonio's plan. *That* was why he'd wanted more than a one-night stand. *That* was why he had been insistent on sharing his bed. It wasn't because he found her irresistible. He had been manufacturing emotional intimacy before he moved in for the kill.

She blanched as she remembered how open and trusting she had been in Antonio's arms. "Giovanni said you wouldn't touch me once you found out I was pregnant with his child," she said in a broken whisper. "I thought that was true until you kissed me...." She had thought Antonio couldn't help himself despite everything that happened between them.

"I always wanted you," he confessed. "Even when I thought you were sleeping with my brother. I can't stop wanting you."

His raw tone revealed how much he loved *and* hated the power she had over him. She knew the feeling. Antonio was her weakness, her vice. Only he'd used it against her.

"I knew early on that you weren't going to accept any financial settlement," Antonio said. "I *didn't* have sex with you to regain power over the family fortune. I made love to you because I wanted to be with you."

Despite the anger and pain pouring through her, Isabella wanted to believe him. And that scared her. She wanted desperately to believe that their relationship was as straightforward as it had been in the beginning. It hurt even to think about how beautifully simple their love affair had been.

Pain seeped into her bones. Her limbs felt heavy and she wanted to lean against the nearest wall before sliding down to the floor. She refrained from wrapping her arms around her middle or curling into a protective ball. She would not show any weakness or tears in front of this man. He would use her feelings to his advantage, just as he'd used her attraction and seduced her back into his bed.

"So," she said, her voice rough as her throat tightened, "you had to go with a Plan B. You needed to marry me. That would have been very difficult for you.

Antonio Rossi making a commitment? Especially to a nobody."

"I have never thought of you as a nobody."

"No, you saw me as the woman pregnant with the Rossi heir. That's the only reason you'd consider marrying me. You certainly weren't thinking that when we were together the first time."

Antonio shoved his hand in her dark, thick hair. "I admit that my reason for restarting our affair wasn't honest, but that changed. *I* changed."

Isabella snorted. "How convenient."

He grabbed her arms and forced her to face him. She met his gaze head-on. She wasn't afraid. She wasn't going to back down. Nothing he said or did could make her feel any worse.

"I want a future with you, Bella. When you came back into my life I knew that I couldn't let you go. It isn't about the money or the baby. It's about *us*."

Isabella slowly raised her hands and flattened them on his solid chest. She felt the strong beat of his heart. Antonio was telling her everything she needed to hear. Just like he had week after week. And somehow she was supposed to believe that the lies had become the truth?

Isabella pushed him away and he reluctantly let go of her arms.

"You have to believe me," Antonio said. "I don't know how to prove it to you. How can I show you how much I love you?"

"You can't." It was over. She couldn't make it work by clinging on to him, on to the promise of this relationship. Isabella turned around and headed for the door. She had to get out of here before she found a reason not to.

"I'm not going to let you walk out of my life again," he warned her.

"Yes, you are," she said hoarsely as emotion clawed at her throat. She didn't dare face him. "Last time you dumped me. This time I'm making a run for it."

She felt Antonio follow her. Isabella wanted to hurry and hide. She had to get out before her resolve weakened. Before she allowed herself to believe anything he said. She grabbed her backpack and swung it over her shoulders. Ducking her head and keeping her eyes straight ahead, she reached the front door in record time.

"We are a part of each other's lives," Antonio said. "You can't shut me out."

"Antonio, soon you will be a distant memory. Ancient history." She wrenched the door open. "A cautionary tale I'll share with my daughter."

"You're forgetting something."

Antonio's harsh voice was right behind her. She felt him tower over her, inhaled his scent that invaded her senses.

"We share power over the Rossi empire. That means we'll have to work together. We will be in constant contact."

Isabella's hand flexed on the doorknob. What he said was true. Antonio would be part of her life from now on. She would need to deal with him on a daily basis. She would have to watch from the sidelines as he got on with his life while she was once again picking up the pieces.

"I'll give you power of attorney, or whatever they call it," she said impulsively. "You can make all the decisions without having to discuss it with me."

"That's not how it works and it's not what I want."

Antonio cupped his hand over her shoulders and turned her around. "You can't throw me out of your life that easily."

Why not? He'd done it to her and he would have done it again. "I don't want to have anything to with you or the Rossi business."

"Too bad. I'm going to be with you every step of the way whether you like it or not. You're angry with me now—"

"Angry? Try furious. Try homicidal."

"But soon you will realize that everything we shared was true. That I wasn't pretending and that I am committed to you and the baby."

"I can't take that chance." She had taken too many risks only to have them blow up in her face. She couldn't trust Antonio at his word only to have him try to take her child away.

There was only one way she could protect her baby and her future. Her heart started to pound and she felt her skin flush. The idea was crazy, and she should think it through, but it was the only way she would get Antonio out of her life for good.

"I'm giving up my child's claim to the Rossi fortune," she said in a rush. "I don't want the shares or anything. It's all yours."

Antonio's eyes widened and his hands tightened on her shoulders. "Are you crazy? What are you talking about?"

She pulled away from him. "When I get back to Los Angeles I will have a lawyer draw up the paperwork. All the money, all the shares—everything will belong to you."

"You can't do this."

"Yes, I can," she said defiantly. The more she thought about it, the more she knew it was the right decision. This was the only way she'd be free.

"You can't give away a fortune. What about your child? It should belong to him. This is part of who he is."

It didn't have to be. "I don't want him to know anything about his heritage or his family. I need to protect him from becoming someone like Giovanni or you."

Antonio's eyes flashed with anger. "Bella, I won't let you do this. You're making a big mistake."

"Why are you fighting me, Antonio?" she asked as she crossed the threshold. "You're getting everything you want without making any sacrifice."

"Not everything," he told her. "I want *you*."

"Don't worry, Antonio," she said as she walked away. "I'm sure the feeling is temporary."

CHAPTER FIFTEEN

Four months later

ISABELLA gripped onto the wall railing and paused. She was shaky and she felt sweat bead on her forehead. She had tried to do too much, determined to heal quickly after the Caesarean. After all, she was going home alone with her baby girl in a couple of hours. She needed to be able to move.

Glancing around the busy maternity ward, she saw that her room was at the end of the hall. Isabella was tempted to give up and ask for a wheelchair, but she wasn't a quitter. She had become a fighter. There'd been plenty of days when she'd survived on grit alone.

After she had returned to California she'd ignored the desire to curl up in a ball and cry. She'd had to get on with her life and take care of her baby. It had not been easy, but she now had a tiny apartment, a few friends, and a job at an art gallery. Soon she would return to college and complete her art history degree.

Now if only she could erase Antonio from her mind... If she could stop dreaming about him, that would be great. Those dreams reminded her of what she had lost, what she would never have again. One day she would be rid of the empty hollowness inside her, but until then she needed to stop thinking about the past and focus on the future.

When she stepped into her room Isabella swore she would never take walking for granted again. All she wanted to do was get back into bed and rest. Intent on putting one foot in front of the other, she didn't realize she had a visitor.

"Bella."

Only one person called her that. Isabella glanced up, the movement so sharp and sudden that she almost lost her balance. She flattened her hand on the wall when she saw Antonio standing by the window.

Her heart did a slow and painful flip as she greedily took in the sight of him. She must be imagining things. Isabella blinked but the vision of Antonio didn't go away. He looked exactly as he had when she'd left him. Powerful, harsh and incredibly sexy. His scowl and the tailored business suit made him even more intimidating.

Isabella knew she looked a mess, with her limp hair and voluminous hospital gown. "What are you doing here?" she asked weakly.

"I'm here for you."

Damn, those words still sent a shiver of excitement down her spine. Antonio was always going to have this effect on her. It wasn't fair. She didn't need this in her life. She didn't need *him*.

"You need to leave." She wished she could leave, but she knew she wouldn't get far. Gathering all the strength she could muster, Isabella pushed one foot in front of the other. She needed to get to the bed before she collapsed.

Antonio frowned as he saw her awkward gait and

was suddenly at her side. "Let me help you," he offered as he gently placed a hand on her back.

She would have shrugged him off if she'd trusted her balance a little more. "I can do it myself. I need the practice," she insisted.

Antonio dropped his hand but walked with her to the bed. The journey was slow and painful, and she knew Antonio was tempted to pick her up and carry her. She increased her speed, finding it easier to walk having someone nearby. Antonio might have betrayed her, but she knew he wouldn't let her fall.

Once she'd sat on the bed Isabella gave a sigh of relief. She lay down, wincing and hissing a breath between her clenched teeth. Antonio didn't say anything as he pulled the blanket over her and tucked her in.

She didn't want his kindness. She might read too much into the gesture. "Now tell me why you're here," Isabella said as she sank into her pillow.

"I saw your daughter," Antonio said, his voice low and husky. "She's beautiful."

Antonio had already seen Chiara? She stiffened as the need to protect her child crashed through her like violent wave. She hadn't been prepared for that. She hadn't thought Antonio would be interested.

"She looks like her father."

He nodded. "Yes, she does. But I also see a lot of you in her."

She glanced at his face, but Antonio showed no sign of resentment. He had simply stated a matter of fact. It was as if Chiara's parentage didn't bother him. How was that possible? Was she seeing what she wanted to see?

Isabella closed her eyes. "Antonio, I'm really not up for visitors."

"You haven't been for four months," he said in a growl.

She wouldn't apologize for that. The first time he'd called her Isabella had recognized the number and hadn't picked up. She had spent the rest of the day alternating between tears and stone-cold anger. But she'd also known that she wanted to talk to Antonio, hold on to that connection. And that had scared her. How could she move on if she still felt like that?

"I've been busy," she said. "My life has gone through a lot of transitions."

"I tried to contact you."

"Yeah, I know." She had blocked his calls and texts, deleted his e-mails without opening them, and trashed the flower bouquets that had appeared on her desk at work. Anything related to her child's inheritance had been directed to her lawyer, whom she could barely afford. She had to avoid anything that reminded her of Antonio.

She'd wanted to give him full power over the Rossi shares, but he had refused to accept it. He still acted as if he needed her approval over every decision. Isabella wasn't sure why he was trying to include her in everything. He didn't need to keep in contact with her. He no longer had to pretend that he could love her and her child.

Disappointment coiled tightly in her chest. So, if he had everything he wanted, why was he here? Today of all days? She didn't want to talk to Antonio about her baby.

"I don't have the money yet to pay you back for the ticket," she said in a rush. "We'll have to make a payment plan. It'll take a while because—"

"I don't want your money. That ticket was a gift," he interrupted, annoyed. "I'm here because I heard you were in labor. Unfortunately I didn't get here in time. If I had I would have found you better accommodations."

She opened her eyes and looked around the room. It was clean, simple and private. It was better than she had hoped. What more could she possibly want? "This is fine. I won't be here for much longer. They are sending me home in a couple of hours."

Outrage flickered in his dark eyes. "That is unacceptable. You can barely walk. I will speak to the doctors immediately."

"Wait a second." She weakly lifted her hand as she realized what he had said a few moments ago. "How did you know I was in labor? Are you having me watched?"

"Of course. I was worried about you. I remember that room you had over the café when I found you." He suppressed his shudder of distaste. "I didn't want that to happen again."

"I don't like being watched or followed," she told him. "I can take care of myself. I don't need your help."

"Then why did you put me down as emergency contact on your medical forms? Why did you make me the guardian to Chiara if anything happened to you?"

Isabella cringed. She had wrestled with that choice. She could have named a friend, but in the end she'd wanted Antonio to look after Chiara. "You know about that?"

"I do." Triumph flared in his eyes. "You know deep down that I would take care of you and the baby. That I would treat your daughter as my own."

She felt the heat crawl up her neck. "You shouldn't

read anything into those decisions. I was required to give a name."

"And you chose mine. Because you know I want to be here. That I want to help."

He said that now, but how long would it last? "No, you don't want to help. Not unless you get something in return. I can't figure out your ulterior motive, but I know you have one."

Antonio sighed. "I regret that. At the time I made promises that I wasn't planning to keep."

"Just as I expected."

He shoved his hand through his hair. "But that changed once we were back together. I started to believe that this was our second chance. I wasn't thinking about gaining control as much as I was thinking about recapturing what we'd once shared."

"And when did that change of heart happen?" Isabella asked, her voice filled with skepticism.

"When you handed me the sonogram." Antonio said, his voice fading as he recalled that moment. "I looked at it and I didn't see the baby as an obstacle or a sign of betrayal. I saw this small, innocent child that was part of *you*. And I knew I wanted to go on this journey with you."

Isabella stared at him as the sincerity in his voice tugged at her. She wanted to believe him, but what if this was another act? How could she trust her instincts when he had played her so well before?

Antonio cleared his throat and awkwardly rubbed the back of his neck. "Once I found where you had gone I tried to reach out. I wanted to talk to you."

"You were very persistent."

Antonio reached out and covered her hand with his.

"I now know how you must have felt when I kicked you out. I was desperate and out of control. No matter how hard I tried, you wouldn't talk to me."

"I still don't want to talk to you." As much as she wanted to hold onto his hand, she purposely removed her fingers from his grasp.

"I understand, but I should have been here. You shouldn't have gone through this alone."

"I wasn't alone. I have friends." Friends who would adore her and her baby, no matter what her shortcomings were.

"Yes, I know," he said, the corner of his mouth slanting up in a smile. "They gathered around you in a protective circle. My security team could take a few lessons from them."

"Considering our history," Isabella said gently, "it's better if I don't accept your help."

"No, it's not." Antonio leaned over Isabella, bracing his arms on the bedrails. "If you don't want me by your side then I'll help you behind the scenes. I want to give you every opportunity to finish your college degree. I will support your dreams and goals. I'm not asking for your permission, Bella. I'm doing this because I want to."

Isabella fought back the hope that pressed against her chest. "And Chiara?"

"I want to take you and Chiara back to Rome," Antonio replied.

She frowned. "Why would you do that?"

"So we can be a family." Antonio leaned in closer. "These months have been hell, knowing that I've lost you again."

Family. There was that word again. It was as if he

knew her weakness and understood her deepest desire. "You can't just walk in here and expect me to change my life again so we can have another affair. My situation has changed. I have a child I need to think about."

"I said a family." Antonio's gaze held her immobile. "I want us to get married."

Married?

"You don't need to marry me," she said, her eyes wide and her heart starting to pound. "I offered you full control of the Rossi shares."

"I love you."

His sincerity tugged at her heart.

"And I know you love me."

"I... I..." She couldn't deny it. She loved Antonio and wanted to be with him—but love wasn't enough.

"Marry me, Bella." He rested his forehead against hers. "I want to be with you and Chiara. Always."

She slowly exhaled and looked away. There had to be another reason. An ulterior motive. Why would he want her as his wife if she didn't meet any of his requirements?

"No," she whispered.

Antonio froze. "Excuse me?"

"I'm sorry, Antonio. I can't marry you."

Antonio drew back. Isabella had said no. *No.* The word sliced through him like a knife. He gripped the bedrail as hurt bled through him. Had he ruined what they'd shared? Was it beyond repair?

He wouldn't accept that. They loved each other and they would get through this. He needed Isabella. His life was dark and empty without her and he didn't want to go through another day apart from her.

He should have come for her earlier. Antonio bowed his head with regret. He had stayed in Rome to fix the financial mess his brother had left. Not only had Gio been deeply in debt, but the Rossi family fortune was at stake. If Antonio hadn't stepped in Chiara would have inherited nothing.

And he had also stayed in Rome to make some changes in his life. He'd scaled back on his work significantly so his focus could be on his family life. He'd also found a house that would be perfect for raising children. Now that he had suffered twice from being separated from Isabella, he didn't want to miss out on another moment.

But Isabella didn't see it that way. She didn't want him to be a part of her life.

A horrible thought occurred to him. His stomach twisted with dread as he asked, "Do you want to be with me?"

"Yes," Isabella said. She wiped the tears from her eyes and sniffled. "But it's not possible."

"Of course it is," he insisted as relief poured through him. "We are free to get married. I don't want anyone but you. I know you haven't dated anyone since you were with me. There is no one holding us back."

"I don't trust you," she said. "You say everything I want to hear, but you did that before and it was all lies."

He took a step back as hurt seeped into him. "It wasn't all lies."

"You showed interest and concern because you wanted control of the money. What do you want from me now?"

"I wasn't faking it."

"Why are you still around?" Isabella asked. "I tried

to transfer my interest in the Rossi empire but you won't sign the paperwork. Just take it. You'd have full control with my blessing."

"I don't want your blessing," he said in a growl. "I want you and the baby."

"That doesn't make sense. I would not make you a good wife. I don't have the right background, the right—"

"You *are* good for me," he insisted. "You're generous and affectionate. You're bold and adventurous. You nurture and protect the ones you love. You love ferociously and you are deeply loyal."

"There's nothing special about that."

"You have no idea how rare that is." He crossed his arms and began to pace the room. "I know what it's like to grow up in a family and feel like an outsider. I'm not going to let that happen to Chiara. She won't have to earn my love or my affection. She already has it."

"How can she have it?" she threw back at him angrily. "You think I was being unfaithful to you when she was conceived."

"I did at first. I can't deny it." He rubbed his hands over his face. "It destroyed me. But that was when I thought you had cheated on me. I don't care that she's Giovanni's daughter or even that she's a Rossi. She is *your* child and I want to raise her with you."

"That doesn't change anything," she said slowly, as if she'd been taken by surprise. "I won't marry you."

"I won't stop asking," he said as he stalked back to the bed, unable to hide his frustration. "I am bound to you whether or not we're married."

"And if I keep refusing?"

"That won't change how I feel. You walked away

from me but I kept my commitment to you. I will make sure you and the baby are getting the best care," he confessed. "I will always take care of you and Chiara even if we don't marry. Never question that."

He didn't know how he could prove his love for her and Chiara. He had demonstrated it when they had been together, but those actions had been tainted with his original plan. If Isabella returned to him she'd been taking a great leap of faith.

"I'm asking you to trust me," he said as he took her hand again. This time she didn't pull away. "I will show you, Bella. You once gave everything to make our relationship work and I have the same commitment to you and Chiara."

"You say that now…"

"I will prove it every day," he vowed. "Starting today. I'm taking you to my hotel and I will look after you and the baby."

She pressed her lips together as she considered his offer. "I'm not sure about this," she said nervously.

It wasn't quite a yes, but she hadn't said no. Antonio smiled triumphantly.

"I'm still not marrying you," Isabella warned him.

"You will," he said as he raised her hand to his lips. "When you trust me. You will."

EPILOGUE

ISABELLA stirred awake and instinctively reached for Antonio. Her fingers brushed against the warm, crumpled bedsheet. She frowned and slowly opened her eyes, her gaze focusing on her hand. The diamonds on her wedding ring caught the faint light and sparkled in the shadowy bedroom.

Propping herself on her elbow, Isabella squinted at the bedside clock and saw that it was a little after three in the morning. She glanced around the large room. The curtains were still pulled back and she saw the Rome skyline glittering in the distance.

"Antonio?" she called out softly, her voice husky with sleep.

She rose from the bed when she didn't receive an answer. Grabbing her discarded nightgown that was lying on the floor in a pool of satin, Isabella slid it over her body. The hem skimmed her thighs.

She tiptoed barefoot out of the bedroom and paused at the threshold when she heard faint whispering. It sounded like Antonio's voice, and it came from the direction of the nursery. Isabella felt a flicker of worry. Had Chiara cried out and she hadn't heard it?

Isabella reached the door to the nursery and peered

inside. She saw Antonio, wearing a dark pair of pajama bottoms slung low on his lean hips. The sight of him gently cradling her fussy baby in his arms made her breath hitch in her throat.

Antonio should look out of place in the pink and green nursery. He was too sexy, his looks too darkly erotic, to sit in a rocking chair. He was known for his power and ruthlessness, but one year-old Chiara had already wrapped him around her tiny finger.

"Chiara, listen to your papa," Antonio said in a hushed, mesmerizing tone to the infant snuggled against his bare muscular chest. "We had an agreement. You are to sleep when the moon is out."

Isabella leaned against the doorframe as she watched her husband and her child. They had an agreement? She bit back a smile. How frequently did Antonio and Chiara have these late-night heart-to-hearts?

It shouldn't surprise her. From the moment she and Chiara had left the hospital Antonio had gotten into the habit of long talks with her daughter. He would encourage Chiara to reach for a toy, he would read the newspaper to her as if it was a children's fairytale, and he would soothe her when she cried loudly during her bath.

"A Rossi always honors his word," he murmured as he stroked the baby's back.

Chiara sighed and her tiny body relaxed against Antonio's chest.

"Remember," Antonio said softly as he laid the baby in her crib, "you get your mama's undivided attention during the day while I'm at work. I get your mama at night."

"Did you ever think," Isabella whispered as she walked into the nursery, "that Chiara gets up in the middle of the night so she can have *your* undivided attention?"

"Then she's a smart girl." He tucked a light blanket around the infant.

Isabella was enamored of the depth of patience and tenderness Antonio demonstrated. He always had words of praise and optimism, whether Chiara had an accomplishment or a setback. She knew Antonio would be a great father.

Antonio turned and Isabella could see his exaggerated scowl in the faint moonlight. "That nightgown looks familiar. Didn't I strip it off you earlier tonight?"

"You did," Isabella said with a smile as sexual excitement bubbled inside her. "I thought I should wear something special for our wedding night, but you ripped it right off me."

"And now you've put it back on?" His voice was low and playful. "You should be punished."

"You need to catch me first." She hurried out the door and got all the way to the hallway before she felt Antonio's arm wrap around her waist. Isabella bit back a squeal as he flattened her spine against his chest.

"I've got you," he said triumphantly against her ear as he pushed the straps of her nightgown past her shoulders. "And I'm not letting go."

She sensed a deeper meaning in his words. The nightgown slid past her hips and onto the floor. She turned and looped her arms around his broad shoulders, the tips of her breasts grazing his chest. "I'm not letting go, either. You can count on that."

* * * * *

ISLAND OF SECRETS

BY
ROBYN DONALD

Robyn Donald can't remember not being able to read, and will be eternally grateful to the local farmers who carefully avoided her on a dusty country road as she read her way to and from school, transported to places and times far away from her small village in Northland, New Zealand. Growing up fed her habit. As well as training as a teacher, marrying and raising two children, she discovered the delights of romances and read them voraciously, especially enjoying the ones written by New Zealand writers—so much so that one day she decided to write one herself.

Writing soon grew to be as much of a delight as reading—although infinitely more challenging—and when eventually her first book was accepted by Mills & Boon she felt she'd arrived home. She still lives in a small town in Northland, with her family close by, using the landscape as a setting for much of her work. Her life is enriched by the friends she's made among writers and readers, and complicated by a determined Corgi called Buster, who is convinced that blackbirds are evil entities. Her greatest hobby is still reading, with travelling a very close second.

To six Aussies and a Kiwi—thank you!
I had so much fun writing this continuity with you.
And to Meredith Webber, an amazing writer,
fabulous mentor and generous friend. Your
down-to-earth advice always keeps me grounded and
your encouragement has led me into new worlds.

CHAPTER ONE

IN A VOICE that iced through the solicitor's office, Luc MacAllister said, 'Perhaps you can explain why my stepfather insisted on this final condition.'

Bruce Keller resisted the urge to move uncomfortably in his chair. He'd warned Tom Henderson of the possible repercussions of his outrageous will, but his old friend had said with some satisfaction, 'It's time Luc learned that life can mean dealing with situations you can't control.'

In his forty years of discussing wills with bereaved families Bruce had occasionally been shocked, but he'd never felt threatened before. The familiar sound of the traffic in the street of the small New Zealand town faded as he met the hard grey eyes of Tom's stepson.

He squared his shoulders, warning himself to cool it. MacAllister's formidable self-possession was a legend. 'Tom didn't confide in me,' he said steadily.

The man on the other side of the desk looked down at the copy of the will before him. 'So he refused to give any reason for stipulating that before I attain complete control of Henderson Holdings and the Foundation, I must spend six months in the company of his—of Joanna Forman.'

'He refused to discuss it at all.'

MacAllister quoted from the will. '"Joanna Forman, who has been my companion for the past two years."' His mouth twisted. 'It wasn't like Tom to be so mealy-mouthed. By *companion* he presumably meant mistress.'

The solicitor felt a momentary pang of pity for the woman. Thanking his stars he was able to be truthful, he said austerely, 'All I know about her is that her aunt was your stepfather's housekeeper on Rotumea Island until she died. Joanna Forman cared for her during the three months before her death.'

'And then stayed on.'

The contempt in Luc's voice angered the solicitor, but he refrained from saying anything more.

Whatever role Joanna Forman had played in Henderson's life, she'd been important to him—so important he'd made sure she'd never want for anything else again, even though he'd known it would infuriate his formidable stepson.

MacAllister's broad shoulders lifted in a shrug that reminded the older man of Luc's mother, an elegant, aristocratic Frenchwoman. Although Bruce had met her only once he'd never forgotten her polished composure and what had seemed like a complete lack of warmth. She couldn't have been more different from Tom, a brash piratical New Zealander who'd grabbed the world by the neck and shaken it, enjoying himself enormously while setting up a worldwide organization in various forms of construction.

Bruce had done his best to convince Tom that this unexpected legacy was going to cause ructions, possibly even cause his will to be contested in court, but his friend had been completely determined.

Anyway, MacAllister had no reason to be so scornful. The solicitor could recall at least two rather public liaisons in his life.

A just man, Bruce accepted that a relationship between a sixty-year-old and a woman almost forty years younger was, to use his youngest granddaughter's terminology, *icky*. Involuntarily his mouth curved, only to vanish under another cold grey stare.

Luc said crisply, 'I don't find the situation at all amusing.'

In his driest tone, Bruce said, 'I realise this has been a shock to you. I did warn your stepfather.'

'When did he finalise this will?'

'A year ago.'

MacAllister pushed the document away. 'Three years after he had that ischaemic stroke, and a year after this Forman woman moved in.'

'Yes. He took the precaution of having a thorough check—both physical and mental—before he signed it.'

In a clipped voice MacAllister said, 'Of course he did. On your recommendation, I assume.' Without waiting for an answer he went on, 'I won't be contesting the will—not even this final condition.'

The solicitor nodded. 'Sensible of you.'

MacAllister got to his feet, towering over the desk, his arctic gaze never leaving Bruce's face.

Bruce rose also, wondering why the man facing him seemed considerably taller than his height of a few inches over six feet.

Presence...

Luc MacAllister had it in spades.

MacAllister's lip curled. 'Presumably this Forman woman will play along with Tom's condition.'

'She'd be extremely stupid not to,' Bruce felt compelled to point out. The other man's intimidating glance made him say bluntly, 'However difficult the situation, both you and she have a lot to gain by sticking to the terms Tom set out.'

In fact, Joanna Forman had the power to deprive Luc MacAllister of something he'd worked for all his adult life—complete control of Tom Henderson's vast empire.

Which was why the younger man's face looked as though it had been carved out of granite.

Once more MacAllister glanced down at the will. 'I assume you tried to persuade Tom not to do this.'

Bruce said crisply, 'He knew exactly what he wanted.'

'And like a good solicitor and an old friend, you've done your best to see that this is watertight.'

Luc didn't expect an answer. He'd get his legal team to go through the will with a fine-tooth comb, but Bruce Keller was a shrewd lawyer and a good one. He didn't expect to be able to challenge it.

He asked, 'Does Joanna Forman know of her good fortune yet?'

'Not yet. Tom insisted I tell her in person. I'm flying to Rotumea in three days.'

Luc reined in his temper. It was unfair to blame the solicitor for not preventing this outrageous condition. His stepfather was not a man to take advice, and once Tom had made up his mind he couldn't be swayed. He'd been a freebooter, his recklessness paying off more often than not until that tiny temporary stroke had messed around with his brain.

Which was the reason, Luc thought grimly, he and Joanna Forman would be forced to live in close proximity for the next six months.

Not only that, at the end of the six months she'd make the decision that would either hand him the reins of

Tom's empire, or deprive him of everything he'd fought for these past years.

One thing he had to know. 'Will you tell her that she'll decide who controls Henderson's?'

And watched closely as the solicitor expostulated, 'You know I can't reveal that.'

Luc hid a bleak satisfaction. When required, Bruce Keller could produce a poker face, but Luc was prepared to bet that Tom had stipulated Joanna Forman not be told until it was time for her to make her decision.

Which gave him room to manoeuvre. 'And if her decision is against me, what will happen?'

Keller hesitated, then said, 'That's another thing I can't divulge.'

Well, it had been worth a try. Tom would have organised someone he trusted to take over, and Luc knew who that would be—Tom's nephew.

He'd fought Luc for supremacy in various overt and covert ways, culminating a year previously in his elopement and subsequent marriage to Luc's fiancée. Who just happened to be Tom's goddaughter.

Damn you, Tom.

Jo stood up from the desk and stretched, easing the ache between her shoulder blades. After two years in the tropical Pacific she was accustomed to heat and humidity, but today had left her exhausted.

The last thing she wanted to do was play gooseberry to a pair of honeymooners, but her oldest friend had brought her new husband to stay one night at Rotumea's expensive resort so her two favourite people could meet...

And Lindy and she had been best friends since they'd

bonded on their first day at school in New Zealand, and it would be lovely to see her again.

Also, she was eager to meet the man who'd generated Lindy's rave reviews during the past year. A non-existent bank balance had prevented Jo from accepting her friend's request to be maid of honour, and the current recession meant there wasn't much chance of things improving financially for her for a while.

Not that she was going to dim the couple's happiness with any mention of her business worries. But the sooner she got home and made herself ready, the better.

Several hours later she realised she was wishing she'd made an excuse. The evening had started well; Lindy was radiant, her new husband charming and very appropriately besotted, and they'd sipped a champagne toast to the future as the sun dived suddenly beneath the horizon and twilight enfolded the island in a purple cloak shot with the silver dazzle of stars.

'You're so lucky,' Lindy had sighed. 'Rotumea has to be the most beautiful place in the world.'

Before she'd had a chance to do more than set down her glass, Jo heard a familiar smooth voice from behind, and the evening immediately lost its gloss.

'Hi, Jo-girl, how're things going?'

Jo froze. Of all the people on the island, Sean was the one she least wanted to see. Only a few days after Tom's death she'd refused his suggestion of an affair. His reaction had left her nauseated and furious.

However, she wasn't going to let his presence spoil the evening for her friends. She turned, wishing she'd chosen to wear something a little less revealing when Sean's gaze immediately dropped to her cleavage.

'Fine, thanks,' she said calmly, trying to convey that

she didn't want him there without making it obvious to her companions.

Sean lifted his eyes to give the other two a practised smile. 'Hi. Let me guess—you're the honeymooners Jo's been looking forward to seeing, right? Enjoying your stay in the tropics?'

Seething, Jo wished she'd had the sense to realise what sort of man he was before she'd told him about Lindy.

Sure enough, her friend beamed at him. 'Loving everything about it.'

His smile broadened. 'I'm Sean Harvey.' Glancing at Jo, he drawled, 'A friend of Jo's.'

So of course Lindy invited him to sit down. Jo cast a harried look around the open-air restaurant, her gaze colliding with that of a man being seated at the next table.

Automatically she gave a brief smile. Not a muscle in his hard, handsome face moved and, feeling as though he'd slapped her, Jo looked away.

Fair men usually looked amiable and casual—surfer-style. Well, not always, she admitted, the most recent James Bond incarnation springing to mind. In spite of the sun-bleached streaks in his ash-brown hair, this stranger had the same dangerous aura.

Surfer-style he was not...

Tall and powerfully muscled, good-looking in an uncompromising, chiselled fashion, he had eyes like cold grey lasers and a jaw that gave no quarter. He also looked familiar, although she knew she'd never seen him before.

Perhaps he *was* a film star? He wasn't the sort of man anyone would forget.

As though that moment of eye contact somehow

forged a tenuous link between them, Jo's pulses picked
up speed and she rapidly switched her gaze to Lindy.

Don't be an idiot, she told herself, and concentrated
on ignoring the stranger and enduring the evening.

Not that she could fault Sean's behaviour; he was
gallant with Lindy, man-to-man with her husband, and
managed so well to indicate his interest in Jo that when
he eventually left Lindy challenged her.

'You haven't mentioned him at all—is he your latest?'

'No,' Jo said shortly.

Her friend had spoken in a rare moment of general silence, and the man at the next table looked across at her.
Again, no emotion showed in the sculpted features, yet
for some reason an uneasy shiver skated across her skin.

All evening she'd been aware of him—almost as
though his presence indicated some form of threat.

Oh, don't over-dramatise, she scoffed. The stranger
didn't deserve it; she was still—unfairly—reacting to
Sean's intrusions. Because of him she was totally off
good-looking men.

For the rest of the evening she kept her gaze scru-
pulously away from the grey-eyed newcomer. But that
sense of his presence stayed with her until she left the
hotel and walked into the car park, stopping abruptly
when a dark shadow detached itself from the side of
her car.

'Hi, Jo.'

She froze, then forced herself to relax. On Rotumea the only danger came from nature—seasonal cyclones, drownings—or the very rare accident on the
motor scooters that were everywhere on the roads.
There had never been an assault that she was aware of.

Nevertheless, Sean's presence jolted her. She asked
briskly, 'What do you want?'

This time he didn't bother smiling. 'I want to talk to you.'

Without changing her tone she answered, 'You said everything *I* needed to hear the last time we met.'

He shrugged. 'That's partly why we need to talk.' His voice altered. 'Jo, I'm sorry. If you hadn't turned me down so crudely, I wouldn't have lost it. I really thought I was in with a chance—after all, if old Tom had been able to keep you happy you wouldn't have made eyes at me.'

It wasn't the first time someone had assumed that Tom had been her lover, and each time it nauseated her. As for *making eyes*...

Jo reined in her indignation. Distastefully she said, 'As an apology that fails on all counts. Leave it, Sean. It doesn't matter.'

He took a step towards her. 'Was it worth it, Jo? No matter how much money he had, sleeping with an old man—he must have been at least forty years older than you—can't have been much fun. I hope he left you a decent amount in his will, although somehow I doubt it.' His voice thickened, and he took another step towards her. 'Did he? I believe billionaires are tight as hell when it comes to money—'

'That's enough!' she flashed, a little fear lending weight to her disgust. 'Stop right now.'

'Why should I? Everyone on Rotumea knows your mother was a call girl—'

'Don't you dare!' Her voice cut into his filthy insinuation. 'My mother was a model, and the two are not synonymous—if you understand what *that* means.'

Sean opened his mouth to speak, but swivelled around when another male voice entered the conver-

sation, a crisp English accent investing the words with
compelling authority.

'You heard her,' the man said. 'Calm down.'

Jo jerked around to face the man who'd sat at the next
table as he finished brutally, 'Whatever you're offering,
she doesn't want it. Get going.'

'Who the hell are you?' Sean demanded.

'A passing stranger.' His contempt strained Jo's
nerves. 'I suggest you get into your vehicle and go.'

Sean started to bluster, stopping abruptly when
the stranger said coolly, 'It's not the end of the world.
Things have a habit of looking better a few weeks down
the track, and no man's ever died just because a woman
turned him down.'

'Thanks for nothing.' Sean's voice was surly. He
swung to Jo. 'OK, I'll go, but don't come running to
me when you find yourself kicked out of Henderson's
house. I bet anything you like he left everything to his
family. Women like you are two a penny—'

'Just go, Sean,' she said tensely, struggling to keep
the lid on her embarrassment and anger.

He left then, and when his footsteps had died away
she dragged in a breath and said reluctantly, 'Thanks.'

'I suggest you let the next one down a bit more tactfully.' A caustic note in the stranger's voice was overlaid with boredom.

Jo caught back a terse rejoinder. In spite of his tone
she was grateful for his interference. For a few moments
she'd almost been afraid of Sean.

'I'll try to keep your advice in mind,' she said with
scrupulous politeness, and got into her car.

Once on the road she grimaced. The spat with Sean
had unsettled her; she'd totally misread the situation
with him.

Like her he was a New Zealander, in Rotumea to manage the local branch of a fishing operation. Although from the first he'd made it clear he found her attractive, he'd appeared to accept the limits she put on their contact with good grace. Several times she'd searched her memory in case something she'd said or done had given him the idea that she wanted to be more than friendly. She could recall nothing, ever.

Frustrated, she swerved to avoid a bird afflicted with either a death wish or an unshakeable sense of its immortality. Naturally, the bird was a masked booby...the clown of the Pacific.

Concentrate, she told herself fiercely.

After Tom's death, Sean's suggestion of an affair had come out of the blue, but she'd let him down as gently as she could, only to be shocked and totally unprepared for his sneering anger and contempt.

She didn't like that he'd lain in wait for her to deliver that insulting apology. His belief that she and Tom were lovers still made her feel sick. It seemed that Sean believed any relationship between a man and a woman had to have a sexual base.

Neanderthal! In a way Tom was like the father she'd never known.

That night she slept badly, the thick humidity causing her to wonder if a cyclone was on its way. However, when she checked the weather forecast the following morning she was relieved to see that although one was heading across the Pacific, it would almost certainly miss Rotumea.

Then her shop manager rang to apologise because a family crisis meant she wouldn't be in until after lunch, so Jo put aside the paperwork that had built up over the month since Tom's death, and went into the only town on the island to take Savisi's place.

And of course she had to deal with the worst customer she'd ever come across, an arrogant little snip of about twenty whose clothes proclaimed far too much money and whose manners reminded Jo of an unpleasant animal—a weasel, she decided sardonically, breathing a sigh of relief when the girl swayed, all hips and pout, out of the shop.

But at least Savisi arrived immediately after midday to relieve her. She drove back to the oasis of Tom's house, yet once she'd eaten lunch she paced about restlessly, unable to draw any comfort from its familiarity.

In the end, she decided a swim in the lagoon would make her feel more human.

It certainly refreshed her, but not enough. Wistfully eyeing the hammock slung from the branch of one of the big overhanging trees, she surrendered to temptation.

Her name, spoken in a deep male voice, woke her with a start. Yawning, she peered resentfully through her lashes at the figure of a tall man with the tropical sun behind him. She couldn't see his features, and although she recognised his voice she couldn't slot him into her life.

Groggy from sleep, she muttered, 'Go away.'

'I'm not going away. Wake up.'

The tone hit her like an icy shower. And the words were a direct order, with the implied suggestion of a threat. Indignant and irritated, she scrambled out of the hammock and pushed her mass of hair back to stare upwards, her dazed gaze slowly travelling over the stranger's features while she forced her brain into action.

Oh. The man from last night...

Feeling oddly vulnerable, she wished she'd chosen a bathing suit that covered more skin than this bikini.

Not that he was showing any interest in her body. That assessing stare was fixed on her face.

'What are you doing here?' she demanded. 'This is a private beach.'

'I know. I came to see you.'

Although Jo just managed to stop a dumbfounded gape, nothing could prevent her jerky step backwards. Shock, and a strange feverish thrill shot through her, dissipating when she realised who he had to be. Hastily she shoved on her sunglasses—a fragile shield against his penetrating survey—and blurted, 'You're the solicitor, right?' Frowning, she added, 'I thought you weren't coming until tomorrow.'

Not that he looked anything like a solicitor. Nothing so tame! Pirates came to mind, or Vikings—lethal and overwhelmingly male and almost barbaric. And very, very vital. It was hard to imagine him sitting behind a desk and drawing up wills...

'I am not the solicitor,' he said curtly.

Her eyes narrowed. 'Then who are you?'

'I'm Luc MacAllister.'

Like his face, the name was familiar, yet her groggy mind couldn't place it. Warily, she asked, 'All right, Luc MacAllister, what do you want?'

'I've told you—I came to see you.' Again he seemed bored.

Before she could organise her thoughts he spoke again, each word incisive and clear.

'My mother was Tom Henderson's wife.'

'Tom?' she said, everything suddenly clicking into place with ominous clarity. Heat stained her face.

So this large, brutally handsome man was Tom's stepson.

And he was angry.

OK, so after Sean's sneers last night Luc MacAllister probably believed she'd been Tom's lover. Even so, there was no need for that scathing survey.

Humiliation burned through her. It took a few seconds for pride to come to her aid, stiffening her backbone and lifting her chin sharply, and all the while, Luc MacAllister's gunmetal gaze drilled through her as though she were some repulsive insect.

An explanation could wait. This man was part of Tom's family. He'd taken over Tom's empire a few years previously, after Tom's slight illness. According to Tom, it hadn't been an amiable handing over of reins...

One glance at Luc MacAllister's arrogantly honed features made that entirely believable. Yet, although Tom had been manipulated away from the seat of power, he'd still seemed to trust and respect his stepson.

Fumbling for some control, Jo fell back on common courtesy and held out her hand. 'Of course. Tom spoke of you a lot. How do you do, Mr MacAllister.'

He looked at her as though she were mad, his grey gaze almost incredulous. At first she thought he was going to ignore her gesture, but after a moment that seemed to stretch out interminably, he took her hand.

Lightning ran up her arm as long steely fingers closed around hers, setting off a charge of electricity that exploded into heat in the pit of her stomach. Startled, she nearly jerked away. He gave her hand a brief, derisory shake before dropping it as though it had contaminated him.

All right, so possibly it hadn't been the most appropriate response on her part, but he was rude! And he couldn't have made it plainer that he'd swallowed Sean's vicious insinuation hook, line and sinker.

Disliking him intensely, she said crisply, 'I suppose you're here to talk about the house.'

Without waiting for an answer, she stooped to pick up her towel and draped it sarong fashion around her as she turned her back.

'This way,' she said over her shoulder, and led him through the grove of coconut palms.

Luc watched her sway ahead of him, assessing long legs and slender curves and lines, gilded arms and shoulders that gleamed in the shafts of sunlight, toffee-coloured hair tumbling in warm profusion down her back. Unwillingly his body responded with heady, primitive appreciation. Tom had good taste, he thought cynically; no wonder he'd fallen for such young, vibrantly sensuous flesh. Even in her prime, long before her death, his mother would never have matched this woman.

That thought should have stopped the stirrings of desire but not even contempt—now redirected at himself—could do anything to dampen the urgent hunger knotting his gut. He'd never lost his head over a woman, but for a moment he got a glimmer of the angry frustration that had driven the man last night to bail her up in the car park. She must have trampled right over his emotions…

But what else could you expect from a woman who'd chosen to sleep with a man old enough to be her grandfather? Generosity of spirit?

No, the only sort of generosity she'd be interested in would be the size of a man's bank balance—and how much of it might end up in hers.

Bleak irony tightened his mouth as the house came

into view through the tall, sinuous trunks of the palms. One of these trees had killed Tom, its loosened fruit as dangerous as a cannon ball. He'd known the risk, of course, but he'd gone out in a cyclone after hearing what he thought were calls for help.

It had taken only one falling coconut to kill him instantly.

Luc dragged his gaze from the woman in front to survey Tom's bolthole. It couldn't have been a greater contrast to the other homes and apartments his stepfather owned around the globe, all decorated with his wife's exquisite taste.

A pavilion in tropical style flanked by wide verandas, its thatched pandanus roof was supported by the polished trunks of coconut palms. With no visible exterior walls, privacy was ensured by lush, exuberant plantings.

The woman ahead of him turned and gave a perfunctory smile. 'Welcome,' she said without warmth. 'Have you been here before?'

'Not lately.' In spite of the fabled beauty of the Pacific Islands, his mother had found them too hot, too humid and too primitive, and the society unsophisticated and boring. As well, the climate made her asthma much worse.

And once he'd retired Tom had made it clear that his island home was a refuge. Visitors—certainly his stepson—weren't welcome.

For obvious reasons, Luc thought on a flick of contempt. With Joanna Forman in residence Tom had needed no one else.

His answering nod as brief as her smile, he followed her into the house and looked around, taking in the bamboo furniture and clam shells, the drifts of mosquito netting casually looped back from the openings. A black and white pottery vase on the bamboo table was filled with ginger flowers in gaudy yellows and oranges that would have made his mother blink in shock. Although the blooms clashed with an assortment of brilliant foliage, whoever arranged them had an instinctive eye for colour and form.

Luc found himself wondering whether perhaps the casually effective simplicity of the house suited Tom better than the sophisticated perfection of his other homes...

Dismissing the foolish supposition, he said coolly, 'Very Pacific.'

Jo clamped her lips over a sharp retort. Tom had loved this place; in spite of his huge success he'd had no pretensions. The house was built to suit the lazy, languorous climate, its open walls allowing free entry to every cooling breeze.

It would be a shame if Tom's stepson turned out to be a snide, condescending snob.

Why should she care? Luc MacAllister meant nothing to her. Presumably he'd come to warn her she had to vacate the house; well, she'd expected that and made plans to move into a small flat in Rotumea's only town.

But Luc had bothered enough to defuse that awkward scene with Sean. And at least he was staying at the resort.

Still, she counted to five before she said levelly, 'This *is* the Pacific, and the house works very well here.'

'I'm sure it does.' He looked around. 'Is there a spare room?'

His dismissive tone scraped her already taut nerves. *No*, she thought furiously, you don't belong here! Go back to the resort where your sort stay...

Forcing her thoughts into some sort of order, she asked, 'Are you planning to stay *here*?'

He gave her a cynical smile. 'Of course. Why would I stay anywhere else?'

Sarcastic beast. Stiffly, she said, 'All right, I'll make up the bed for you.'

Dark brows lifted as he looked across the big central room to a white-painted lattice that made no attempt to hide the huge wrought-iron bedstead covered by the same brilliantly appliquéd quilting he'd noted on the cushions.

'Are there no walls at all in the place?' he asked abruptly.

Jo managed to stop herself from bristling. 'Houses here tend to be built without walls,' she told him. 'Privacy isn't an issue, of course—the local people wouldn't dream of coming without an invitation, and Tom never had guests.'

His black brows met. In a voice as cold as a shower of hail, he demanded, 'Where do you sleep?'

CHAPTER TWO

SOMETHING IN THE crystalline depths of Luc MacAllister's eyes sent uncomfortable prickles of sensation sizzling down Jo's spine. Trying to ignore them, she said shortly, 'My room's on the other side of the house.'

His frown indicated that he wasn't happy about that. Surely he didn't expect her to move out without notice? Well, it was his problem, not hers.

It would have been nice to be forewarned that he expected to stay, but this man didn't seem to do *nice*. So she said, 'I assume you won't mind sleeping in the bed Tom used?' And hoped he would mind. She wanted him to go back to the resort and stay there until he took his arrogant self off to whatever country he next honoured with his presence.

But he said, 'Of course not.' So much for hope.

She gave the conversation a sharp twist. 'I presume you flew in yesterday?'

'Yes.' Which meant he wouldn't be accustomed to the tropical humidity.

Good manners drove her to offer, 'Can I get you a drink? What would you like?'

Broad shoulders lifted slightly, sending another shimmering, tantalising sensation through her. Darn it, she didn't want to be so aware of him... Possibly he'd noticed her sneaky unexpected response because his reply came in an even more abrupt tone. 'Coffee, thank you. I'll bring in my bag.'

Jo nodded and walked into the kitchen. Of course coffee would be his drink of choice. Black and strong, probably—to stress that uber-macho personality. He didn't need to bother. She knew exactly the sort of man Luc MacAllister was. Tom hadn't spoken much about his family, but he'd said enough. And although he'd fought hard to keep control of his empire, he had once admitted that he could think of no one other than Luc to take his place. A person had to be special to win Tom's trust. And tough.

With an odd little shiver, she decided Luc MacAllister certainly fitted the bill.

If he preferred something alcoholic she'd show him the drinks cupboard and the bottle of Tom's favourite whisky—still almost full, just as he'd left it.

A swift pang of grief stung through her. Damn it, but she *missed* Tom. Her hand shook slightly, just enough to shower ground coffee onto the bench. In the couple of years since her aunt's death Jo had grown close to him. A great storyteller, he'd enjoyed making her laugh— and occasionally shocking her.

Biting her lip, she wiped up the coffee grounds. He'd been a constant part of her life on and off since childhood. Sometimes she wondered if he thought of her as a kind of stepdaughter.

When she'd used up her mother's legacy setting up a skincare business on Rotumea, he'd advanced her money to keep it going—on strictly businesslike terms—but even more valuable had been his interest in her progress and his helpful suggestions as she'd struggled to expand the business through exports.

A voice from behind made her start. 'That smells good.' One dark brow lifted as Luc MacAllister looked at the single mug she'd pulled down. 'Aren't you joining me?'

A refusal hovered on her lips but hospitality dictated only one answer. 'If you want me to,' she said quietly.

Following a moment of silence she swivelled, to meet a hooded, intent survey. A humourless smile curved the corners of a hard male mouth that hinted at considerable experience in...in all things, she thought hastily, trying to ignore the sensuous little thrill agitating her nerves.

'Why not?' His voice was harsh, almost abrupt before he turned away. 'I'll unpack.'

Strangely shaken, she finished her preparations. He'd probably prefer the shaded deck, so she carried the tray there and had just finished settling it onto the table when Luc MacAllister walked out.

He examined it with interest. 'Looks good,' he said laconically. 'Is that your baking?'

'Yes.' Jo busied herself pouring the coffee. She'd been right; he liked it black and full-flavoured, but unlike Tom he didn't demand that it snarl as it seethed out of the pot.

Sipping her own coffee gave her something to do while he demolished a slice of coconut cake and asked incisively penetrating questions about Rotumea and its society.

She knew why he was here. He'd come to tell her he was going to sell the house. Yet, in spite of his attitude, his arrival warmed her a little; she'd expected nothing more than a businesslike message ordering her to vacate the place. That he should come out of his way to tell her was as much a surprise as the letter from Tom's solicitor suggesting the meeting tomorrow.

Leaving the house would be saying goodbye to part of her heart. *Get on with it*, she mentally urged him as he set his cup down.

'That was excellent.' He leaned back into his chair and surveyed her, his grey gaze hooded.

It looked as though she'd have to broach the matter herself. Without preamble, she said, 'I can move out as soon as you like.'

His brows lifted. 'Why?'

Nonplussed, she answered, 'Well, I suppose you plan to sell this house.' He'd never shown any interest in the place, and his initial glance around had seemed to be tinged with snobbish contempt.

He paused before answering. 'No.' And paused again before adding, 'Not yet, anyway.'

'I wouldn't have thought—' She stopped.

He waited for her to finish, and when the silence had stretched too taut to be comfortable, he ordered with cool self-possession, 'Go on.'

She shrugged. 'This was *Tom's* dream.' Not Luc MacAllister's.

'So?'

The dismissive monosyllable sent her back a few years to the awkwardness of her teens. A spark of antagonism rallied her into giving him a smile that perhaps showed too many teeth before she parried smoothly, 'It doesn't seem like your sort of setting, but I do try not to make instant judgements of people I've only just met.'

'Eminently sensible of you,' he drawled, and abruptly changed the subject. 'How good is the Internet access here?'

'Surely you knew your father better than—'

'My stepfather,' he cut in, his voice flat and inflexible. 'My father was a Scotsman who died when I was three.'

In spite of the implied rejection of Tom's presence in his life, Jo felt a flash of kinship. Her father had died before she was born.

However, one glance at Luc's stony face expelled any sympathy. Quietly she said, 'There is access to broadband.' She indicated the screen that hid Tom's computer nook. 'Feel free.'

'Later. I noticed as I flew in that the island isn't huge, and there seems to be a road right around it. Why don't you show me the sights?'

Hoping she'd managed to hide her astonishment, she said, 'Yes, of course.' Her mouth twitched as she took in his long legs. 'Not on the scooter, though, I think.' Why on earth did he want to see Rotumea?

His angular face would never soften, but the smile he gave her radiated a charisma that almost sent her reeling. He was too astute not to understand its impact. No doubt it had charmed his way—backed by his keen intelligence and hard determination.

'Not on the scooter,' he agreed. 'I wouldn't enjoy riding with my knees hitting my chin at every bump in the road.'

Taken by surprise, she laughed. His brows rose and his face set, and she felt as though she'd been jolted by an electric shock.

So what was that for? Didn't he like having his minor jokes appreciated?

Black lashes hid his eyes a moment before he permitted himself another smile, this one marked by more than a hint of cynicism.

Sobering rapidly, Jo said, 'We'll take the four-wheeler.'

'What's a four-wheeler?'

Shrugging, she said, 'It's the local term for a four-wheel drive—a Land Rover, to be exact.'

An old Land Rover, showing the effects of years in the unkind climate of the tropics, but well maintained. Jo expected Luc to want to drive, but when she held out the keys he said casually, 'You know the local rules, I don't.'

Surprised, she got in behind the wheel. Even more surprised, she heard the door close decisively on her, penning her in. Her gaze followed him as he strode around the front of the vehicle, unwillingly appreciating his athletic male grace.

Once more that provocative awareness shivered along her nerves.

He was too much…too much man, she thought as he settled himself beside her. All the air seemed sucked out of the cab and as she hastily switched on the engine she scolded herself for behaving like a schoolgirl with a crush.

'Basically the road rules here amount to *don't run over anything*,' she explained, so accustomed to the sticking clutch she set the vehicle on its way without a jerk. 'Collisions are accompanied by a lot of drama, but traffic is so slow people seldom get hurt. If you cause any damage or run over a chicken or a pig, you apologise profusely and pay for it. And you always give way to any vehicle with children, especially if it's a motor scooter with children up behind.'

'They look extremely dangerous,' he said.

His voice indicated that he'd turned his head to survey her. Tiny beads of sweat sprang out at her temples. Hoping he hadn't noticed, she stared ahead, steering to miss the worst of the ruts along the drive.

She had to deliberately steady her voice to say, 'The

local children seem to be born with the ability to ride pillion without falling off.'

Her reaction to Luc meant nothing.

Or very little. Her mother had explained the dynamics of physical attraction to her when she'd suffered her first adolescent crush. And her own experience—limited but painful—had convinced Jo of her mother's accuracy.

She set her jaw. Sean's insinuations about her mother had hurt some deep inner part of her. Even in her forties, Ilona Forman's great beauty and style had made her a regular on the Parisian catwalks, and she'd been one great designer's inspiration for years.

To her surprise, the tour went off reasonably well. Jo was careful not to overstep the boundary of cool acquaintanceship, and Luc MacAllister matched her attitude. Nevertheless, tension wound her nerves tighter with each kilometre they travelled over Rotumea's fairly primitive road.

Luc's occasional comments indicated that the famous romance of the South Seas made little impression on him. Although, to be fair, he'd probably seen far more picturesque tropical islands than Rotumea.

Nevertheless she bristled a little when he observed, 'Tom once told me that many of the Rotumean people live much as their ancestors did.'

'More or less, I suppose. They have schools, of course, and a medical clinic, and a small tourist industry set up by Tom in partnership with the local people.'

'The resort.'

'Yes. Tom advised the tribal council to market to a wealthy clientele who'd enjoy a lazy holiday without insisting on designer shops and nightclubs. It's worked surprisingly well.'

Again she felt the impact of his gaze on her, and her palms grew damp on the steering wheel. She hurried on, 'Some islanders work at the resort, but most of them work the land and fish. They're fantastic gardeners and very skilled and knowledgeable fishermen.'

'And they're quite content to spend their lives in this perfect Pacific paradise.'

His tone raised her hackles. 'It never was perfect,' she said evenly. 'No matter how beautiful a place is, mankind doesn't seem to be able to live peacefully. A couple of hundred years ago the islanders all lived in fortified villages up on the heights and fought incessantly, tribe against tribe. It's not perfect now, of course, but it seems to work pretty well for most of them.'

'What about those who want more than fish and coconuts?'

She glanced at him, caught sight of his incisive profile—all angles apart from the curve of his mouth—and hastily looked back at the road. So Tom hadn't taken him into his confidence—and that seemed to indicate something rather distant about their relationship.

'Tom set up scholarships with the help of the local chiefs for kids who want to go on to higher education.'

He nodded. 'Where do they go?'

'New Zealand mainly, although some have studied further afield.' With the skill of long practice she negotiated three hens that could see no reason for the vehicle to claim right of way.

'Do they return?'

'Some do, and those who don't keep their links, sending money back to their families.'

He said, 'So if you don't buy the tropical paradise thing, why are you here?'

'I came here because of my aunt,' she said distantly.

'She was Tom's housekeeper, and insisted on staying on even after she contracted cancer. Tom employed one of the island women to help her, but after my mother died she asked me to come up.'

He nodded. 'So you took her place after her death.'

An ambiguous note in his voice made her hesitate before she answered. 'I suppose you could say that.'

Tom hadn't employed her. He'd suggested she stay on at Rotumea for a few months to get over her aunt's death, and once she'd become interested in starting her business he'd seen no reason for her to move out. He liked her company, he told her.

Luc MacAllister asked, 'Now that Tom's not here, how do you keep busy?'

'I run a small business.'

'Dealing with tourists?'

It was a reasonable assumption, yet for some reason she felt a stab of irritation. 'Partly.' The hotel used her range.

'What is this small business?' he drawled.

Pride warred with an illogical desire not to tell him. 'I source ingredients from the native plants and turn them into skincare products.'

And felt an ignoble amusement at the flash of surprise in the hard, handsome face. It vanished quickly and his voice was faintly amused when he asked, 'What made you decide to go into that?'

'The islanders' fabulous skin,' she told him calmly. 'They spend all day in the sun, and hours in the sea, yet they never use anything but the lotions handed down by their ancestors.'

'Good genes,' he observed.

His cool comment thinned her lips. Was he being

deliberately dismissive? She suspected Luc MacAllister didn't do anything without a purpose.

And that included passing comments.

Steadying her voice, she said, 'No doubt that helps, but they have the same skin problems people of European descent have—sunburn, eczema, rashes from allergies. They use particular plants to soothe them.'

'So you've copied their formulas.'

His tone was still neutral, but her skin tightened at the implication of exploitation, and she had to draw breath before saying, 'It's a joint venture.'

'Who provided the start-up money?'

It appeared to be nothing more than an idle question, yet swift antagonism forced her to bite back an astringent comment. Subduing it, she said politely, 'I don't know that that's any of your business.'

And kept her eyes fixed on the road ahead. Tension—thick and throbbing—grated across her nerves.

Until he drawled, 'If it was Tom's money I'm interested.'

'Of course,' she retorted, before closing her mouth on any more impetuous words. Silence filled the cab until she elaborated reluctantly, 'It was my money.'

Let him take that how he wanted. If Luc MacAllister had any right to know, he'd find out about Tom's subsequent loan to her from the solicitor—the man arriving tomorrow.

Was that why Luc had come to Rotumea? To be told the contents of Tom's will?

Immediately she dismissed the idea. Luc was Tom's heir, his chosen successor as well as his stepson, so he'd already know.

Possibly Tom had mentioned her in his will; he might even have cancelled her debt to him. That would have been a kind gesture. And if he hadn't—if Luc MacAllister inherited the debt—she'd pay it off as quickly as she could.

A coolly decisive voice broke into her thoughts. 'And are you making money on this project?'

For brief moments her fingers clenched around the steering wheel. For a second she toyed with the idea of telling him again to mind his own business, but it was a logical question, and if he did inherit the debt he had a right to know.

However, he might not have.

'Yes,' she said, and turned off the tarseal onto a narrow rutted road that led up into the jungle-clad mountains in the centre of the island.

A quick glance revealed Luc was examining a pawpaw plantation on his side. He didn't seem fazed by the state of the road, the precipice to one side or the large pig that only slowly got up and made room for them.

'This is the area we're taking the material from now,' she said. 'Each sub-tribe sells me the rights to harvest from the plants on their land for three months every year. It works well; the plants have time to recover and even seem to flourish under the pruning.'

'How many people do you employ to do the harvesting?'

'It depends. The chiefs organise that.'

She stopped on the level patch of land where the road ended. 'There's a great view of this side of the island from here,' she said, and got out.

Luc followed suit, and again she was acutely aware of his height, and that intangible, potent authority that seemed to come from some power inside him. The sun-streaks in his hair gleamed a dusky gold; his colouring must have come from that Scottish father. The only inheritance from his French mother was the olive sheen to his skin.

Did that cold grey gaze ever warm and soften? It didn't seem likely, although she could imagine his eyes kindling in passion…

Firmly squelching an odd sensation in the pit of her stomach, she decided that from what she knew of him and the very little she'd seen of him, softness wasn't— and never would be—part of his emotional repertoire. It was difficult to imagine him showing tenderness, and any compassion would probably be intellectual, not from the heart.

So, after an hour or so you're an expert on him? she jeered mentally, aware of another embarrassing internal flutter. *Remember you're totally off good-looking men!*

Although *good-looking* was far too weak a word for Luc MacAllister's strong features and formidable air of authority. Composing herself, she began to point out the sights, showing him the breach in the reef that sheltered the lagoon from the ever-present pounding of the ocean waves.

'The only river on the island reaches the coast below us, and the fresh water stops the coral from forming across its exit,' she said in her best guidebook manner. 'The gap in the reef and the lagoon make a sort of harbour, the first landing place of the original settlers.'

Luc's downward glance set her heart racing, yet his voice was almost casual. 'Where did they come from, and when was that?'

Doggedly, she switched her attention back to the view below. 'Almost certainly they arrived from what's now French Polynesia, and the general opinion seems to be it was about fifteen hundred years ago.'

'They were magnificent seamen,' he observed, looking out to sea. 'They had to be, to set off into the unknown with only the stars and the clouds to guide them.'

The comment surprised her. Like all New Zealanders, she'd grown up with tales of those ancient sailors and their remarkable feats, but she remembered that Luc had been educated in England and France. She wouldn't have thought he had a romantic bone in his big, lithe body, and it was unlikely he'd been taught about the great outrigger canoes that had island-hopped across the Pacific, even travelling the vast distance to South America to return with the sweet potato the Maori from her homeland called kumara.

'Tough too,' he said, his eyes still fixed on the lagoon beneath them—a symphony of turquoise and intense blue bordered by glittering white beaches and the robust barrier of the reef. Immense and dangerous, the Pacific Ocean stretched far beyond the horizon.

'Very tough,' she agreed. 'And probably with a good reason for moving on each time.'

'They must have had guts and stamina and tenacious determination, as well as the skill and knowledge to know where they were going.'

Yes, that sounded uncompromising and forceful—attributes as useful in the modern, high-powered world Luc moved in as they would have been for those ancient Polynesian voyagers.

'I'm sure they did,' she said. 'Over a period of about four thousand years they discovered almost every inhabitable island in the Pacific from Hawaii to New Zealand.'

She pointed out the coral *motu*—small white-ringed islets covered in coconut palms, green beads in the lacy fichu of foam that the breaking combers formed along the reef.

'When the first settlers landed there,' she told him, hoping her voice was more steady than her pulse, 'they didn't know whether there were any other people on Rotumea so they anchored the canoe in the lagoon, ready to take off if a hostile group approached.'

'But no one did.'

'No. It was uninhabited. Virgin territory.'

And for some humiliating reason her cheeks pinked. Hastily she kept her gaze out to sea and added, 'It must have been a huge relief. They'd have carried coconuts with them to plant, and kumara and taro, and the paper mulberry tree to make cloth. And of course they brought dogs and rats too.'

'You've obviously studied the history,' Luc said sardonically.

I don't like you, Jo thought sturdily. *Not one tiny bit. Not ever.*

Buoyed up by the thought, she turned and gave him a swift challenging smile. 'Of course,' she said in her sweetest tone. 'I find them fascinating, and it's only polite to know something of the history of the place, after all. And of the people. Don't you think so?'

'Oh, I agree entirely. Information is the lifeblood of modern business.'

Her heightened senses warned her that his words and the hard smile that accompanied them held something close to a threat.

Stop dramatising, she told herself decisively. He was just being sarcastic again.

Yet it was dangerously exhilarating to fence with him like this. Anyway, he'd soon leave Rotumea. After all, she thought irritably, there must be rulers all over the world desperate to speak to him about matters of national interest, earth-shattering decisions to be pondered, vast amounts of money to be made. Once he'd shaken the white sand and red volcanic soil of Rotumea from his elegantly shod feet, he'd never come back and she wouldn't have to deal with him again.

Cheered by this thought, she said, 'We'd better be going. I want to call in at the shop before it closes.'

And she hoped it bored the life out of him. She knew most men would rather chance their luck in shark-infested waters than walk into the softly scented, flower-filled shop that sold her products.

She turned to go back to the car, only to realise he'd done the same. Startled, she pulled away at the touch of his arm on hers, and to her chagrin her foot twisted on a stone, jerking her off balance.

Before she could draw breath strong hands clamped onto her shoulders and steadied her. Jo froze, meeting glinting eyes that narrowed. Her heart somersaulted under the impact of his touch, his closeness. Every cell in her body was suddenly charged with a fierce awareness of his potent male charisma.

His grip tightened for a painful moment, then relaxed.

But, instead of letting her go, he drew her towards him. His face was set and intent, his eyes molten silver.

Something feverish and demanding stopped her from jerking backwards, from saying anything. Helpless in a kind of reckless, fascinated thraldom, she forced herself to meet that fiercely intent gaze. In it she read passion, and a desire that matched the desperate impulse she had no way of fighting.

No, something in her brain insisted desperately, but a more primal urge burnt away common sense, any innate protectiveness, and when his mouth came down on hers she went up in flames, the blood surging through her in response to the carnal craving summoned by his kiss. Her lashes fluttered down, giving every other sense free rein to savour the moment his mouth took hers.

He tasted purely male, clean and slightly salty, with a flavour that stimulated far more than her taste buds. The arms that held her against his powerful body were iron-hard, yet somehow made her feel infinitely secure. And mingling with the tropical fecundity of the rainforest around them was his scent. It breathed of arousal and a need that equalled the heat inside her. She wanted to accept and unleash that need, allow it to overcome the faint intimations of common sense, surrender completely...

And could not—*must* not...

Before she could pull away, he lifted his head. Her lashes fluttered drowsily up, but when she saw his icily intimidating expression, all desire fled, overtaken by humiliation.

He dropped his hands and took a step backwards.

'A bit too soon—and very crass—to be making a move like that, surely?' he said in a voice so level it took her a second or two to register the meaning of his words. 'After all, Tom's barely cold in his grave. You could make *some* pretence of missing him.'

The flick of scorn in his last sentence lashed her like a whip.

Damn Sean's sleazy mind and foul mouth, she thought savagely.

But the brutal sarcasm effectively banished the desire that had roared up out of nowhere. Defiantly she angled her chin and forced herself to hold Luc's unsparing arctic gaze.

In a voice she struggled to hold steady, she said, 'Tom and I didn't have that sort of relationship.'

He shrugged. 'Spare me the details.'

'If you spare me your crass assumptions,' she flashed, green eyes glittering with some emotion.

After a charged pause, he nodded. 'I'm not interested in your relationship with Tom.'

He registered the slight easing of her tension. It seemed she was prepared to believe that.

Not that it was exactly the truth. For some reason the thought of her in Tom's bed sickened him.

But with a mother who'd made no secret of her affairs, Joanna Forman undoubtedly had an elastic attitude to morality.

As she'd just shown. Hell, she'd been more than willing. He could have laid her down on the grass and taken her.

Mentally cursing his unruly mind as it produced an image of her golden body beneath him, of losing herself in her carnal heat, he quenched his fierce hunger with the sardonic observation that possibly her response was faked.

Had she realised that giving away her lovely body might not be sensible at this time? Sex would mean she'd lose any bargaining power...

'For your information,' she said now, her tone crisp and clear, her eyes coldly green and very direct, 'when I was a child I spent quite a few of my holidays here, staying with Aunt Luisa. My mother travelled a lot, and Tom didn't mind me coming even when he was in residence.'

His brows lifted and she waited for some comment. None came, so she resumed, 'We always got on well.'

She stopped, then in an entirely different tone, the words a little thick as though fighting back a surge of grief, she finished, 'That's all there was to it.'

Cynically Luc applauded that final touch. She also made the whole scenario sound quite plausible; Tom had a history of mentoring promising talent.

However, he'd mentioned none of his other protégées in his will.

But her statement certainly fitted in with the information he had about her. She'd attended excellent private schools—paid for probably by the succession of rich lovers her mother had taken. However, she hadn't followed her mother's choice of career. At university, she'd taken a science degree and a lover, graduating from both just before Ilona Forman had developed the illness that eventually killed her.

Joanna had left a fairly menial job at a well-connected firm to care for her mother, and then found herself with an ill aunt who'd refused to leave Rotumea. Either she had a sense of responsibility for her family, such as it was, or she'd seen an opportunity to get closer to Tom and grabbed it.

No doubt it had seemed a good career move.

And it had paid off.

Luc let his gaze roam her face, unwillingly intrigued by the colour that tinged her beautiful skin. Perfect skin for a woman who made skincare products. Yet, in spite of that betraying blush, her black-lashed eyes were steady and completely unreadable.

Was she wondering if he accepted that her relationship with Tom involved nothing more than innocent pleasure in each other's company?

Tamping down a deep, unusual anger, he reminded himself that he had to live with her for the next six months. And that he needed her approval before he could assume full control of the Henderson organization.

You cunning old goat, Tom, he thought coldly, and held out his hand. 'Very well, we'll leave it at that.'

Surprised, Jo reluctantly put her hand in his. A rush of adrenalin coursed through her when long fingers closed around hers, a thrill that coalesced into a hot tug of sensation in the pit of her stomach. Her breath came faster through her lips, and she had to force herself not to jerk free of his touch.

OK, so he hadn't said he believed her. Why should she care?

Yet she did.

However, she wasn't going to waste time wondering about the reason.

But at the shop she was surprised. Tall and darkly dominant, Luc examined the fittings, and even took down and read the blurb on a package of her most expensive rehydrating cream.

She had to conquer a spasm of irritation at her manager's admiring glances. This was her domain, and he had no right to look so much in charge, she thought crossly, and immediately felt foolish for responding so unreasonably.

But something about Luc MacAllister made her unreasonable. Something more than his assumption about her and Tom. Something she didn't recognise, primal and dangerous and…and idiotic, she told herself bracingly.

Face it and get over it. He has a bewildering effect on you, but you can cope. He's not really interested in either you or your product, and you don't want him to be.

Back in the Land Rover, he commented, 'You need better packaging.'

She knew that. Though what made him an expert on

packaging skincare products? 'That's all I can afford right now,' she said evenly, turning to take the track that led to Tom's house.

'You haven't considered getting a partner?'

'No.'

He said nothing, but she sensed his examination of her set profile as she negotiated the ruts. When she pulled up at the house he asked, 'And your reason?'

'I want to retain control,' she told him, switching off the engine and turning to meet his gaze with more than a hint of defiance.

His dark brows lifted, but he said, 'Fair enough. However, unless you're happy with your present turn-over—' his tone indicated he considered that likely to be peanuts '—you're going to have to bite that bullet eventually.'

'Right now, I'm happy with the way things are going,' she told him, a steely note beneath her words.

When Tom had suggested exactly the same thing she'd refused his offer of a further loan without any of the odd sensation of dread that assailed her now.

Luc's kiss had changed things in a fundamental way she didn't want to face. His hooded eyes, the autocratic features that revealed no emotion and the taut line of his sensuous mouth—all combined to lift the hairs on her skin in a primitive display of awareness. He looked at her as though she was prey.

And that was ridiculous! He'd taken over Tom's huge empire, and had built it up even further. He was accustomed to organising and managing world-spanning enterprises. He wasn't interested in her piddling little business.

Or her, she thought, feeling slightly sick. There had

been something about that kiss—something assessing, as though he'd been testing her reactions…

And, like a weak idiot, she'd gone up in flames for him. So now, of course, he'd be completely convinced that Sean's insulting accusation was the truth.

Well, she didn't care. Neither Sean nor Luc meant anything to her, and anyway, Luc would be gone as soon as he'd organised the sale of the house.

She said, 'I have no illusions about how far I can go.'

Without moving, he said, 'It sounds as though you're planning to stay in Rotumea for the rest of your life.'

She shrugged. 'Why not? Can you think of a better place to live?'

'Dreaming your days away in paradise?' he asked contemptuously.

CHAPTER THREE

'I PRESUME YOU have no idea of how patronising you sound.'

It didn't need the subtle ironic uplift of Luc's dark brows to make Jo regret she'd voiced her irritation.

How did that slight movement give his handsome face such a saturnine aspect?

But he said levelly, 'I didn't intend to be. Rotumea is a very small dot in a very empty ocean, a long way from anywhere. If your stuff's any good, don't you want to take it to the world?'

Torn, she hesitated, and saw the corners of his mouth lift, as though in expectation of a smile—a triumphant one.

Goaded, she said explosively, 'Not if it means handing over any control to anyone else. I have an arrangement with the local people and I value the ones who work with me—I feel I've established a business that takes their ambitions and needs seriously. I don't believe I'd be any happier if I were making megabucks and living in some designer penthouse in a huge, noisy, polluted city.' She paused, before finishing more calmly, 'And my product is better than good—it's *superb*.'

'If your skin is any indication of its effect, then I believe you.'

Delivered in a voice so dispassionate it took her a second to realise what he'd said, the compliment disturbed her. Uncertainly, she said, 'Thank you,' and opened the door of the Land Rover, stopping when he began to speak again.

'Although if you were making real money you could choose wherever you want to live,' he said coolly. 'Modern communications being as sophisticated as they are, no one has to live over the shop any more.'

'Agreed, but apart from liking Rotumea, in Polynesia personal relationships are important in business.'

Another lift of those dark brows. 'No doubt.'

After an undecided moment she ignored the distinctly sardonic note to his words. Instead she said, 'I like to keep a close watch on everything.'

Luc's nod was accompanied by a measuring glance. 'How to delegate is one of the lessons all entrepreneurs have to learn.' He looked at his watch. 'When do you eat at night? I assume I'll have to reserve a table for us at the resort.'

Relieved, Jo permitted herself a wry smile. She'd been wondering whether he'd expect her to cook for him. 'It's sensible to do so.' But something forced her to add, 'We don't have to go there if you don't want to. I'm actually quite a good cook. Basic, but the food's edible, Tom used to say.'

'I'm sure he didn't employ you for your prowess in the kitchen,' Luc said smoothly.

Something about his tone set her teeth on edge. She opened her mouth to tell him Tom hadn't employed her at all, then closed it again.

The arrangement she had with Tom was none of Luc's business, and anyway, he wouldn't believe her.

Taking her silence for agreement, he said, 'Then I'll reserve a table. Eight tonight?'

Jo hesitated, then nodded. 'Thank you,' she said and got out of the Land Rover.

Inside the house, she opened a wardrobe door and stared at its meagre contents. Her one good dinner dress had been aired the previous evening in honour of Lindy and her husband.

Of course it didn't matter what she chose. After all, she wasn't trying to impress anyone.

In the end she pulled on a cotton voile dress that floated to her ankles, its pale yellow-green background printed in the gentle swirls of colour that suited her colouring. In her hair she tucked a gardenia flower.

Once ready, she examined her reflection critically. Yes, it looked good, fresh and tropical and casual—and not, she hoped, as though she'd gone to any trouble... Deliberately she'd kept her make-up low-key and simply combed her hair back from her face.

When she emerged from her room he was standing on the terrace but he turned immediately and gave her a cool, speculative survey.

'If you say I'm looking very Pacific,' she said before she could stop herself, 'I might start to think you have a bias against Pacific style.'

His smile was brief. 'Not guilty,' he said. 'You look charming, as I'm sure you know.'

'I intend to take that as a compliment,' she said coolly.

'It was meant to be.'

A compliment with a sting, she thought with a mental grimace.

It set the tone for the evening. Not that he was overtly antagonistic; in fact he was an excellent host. Before long she was laughing, and his conversation both stimulated and challenged her. If Luc had been any other man she'd have enjoyed the occasion, yet she had to keep telling herself to relax. She was far too conscious of his hard-edged control and the coolly unreadable composure that set every nerve jangling.

Too aware of the man himself.

And made uncomfortable by the covert observation of others in the restaurant. Especially the women casting envious looks her way.

Of course the resort advertising hinted at the possibility of a romantic experience, enticing guests with the allure of the tropics—the seductive, languorous perfume of frangipani and gardenia floating on the breeze that played lazily across bare skin, the promised glamour of a lover's moon rising over the reef.

And in spite of its exclusive guest list, tonight Luc was definitely the dominant male in the open-air lanai, radiating that indefinable thing called presence.

However, vitally masculine though he was, she wasn't interested in Luc MacAllister.

In any way, she told herself trenchantly.

So her reaction to those appreciative feminine glances bewildered her. A spiky, territorial instinct, it was an emotion she'd never felt before, and her unusual susceptibility sharpened her voice with a brittle, almost aggressive note.

Luc's voice broke into her thoughts. She looked up, meeting his narrowed grey eyes with something close to defiance.

'Something wrong with the fish?' he drawled.

'Of course not,' she said swiftly, attacking it with what she hoped looked like relish. It seemed to lack flavour, as though by Luc's mere presence he over-whelmed any other sensory input.

And that was just plain ridiculous.

Thankfully the evening seemed to race by, but the unusually significant tension that twisted through her increased. By the time they returned to the house she was so tense she flinched when a blur of movement shot up from the sandy ground as they walked the few steps from the garage.

'It's only a bird,' Luc said, sounding surprised.

'I know.' She was being idiotic. Completely, fool-ishly, *childishly* over the top—behaving like an ado-lescent in the first throes of a crush.

She didn't even *like* Tom's stepson, she thought re-sentfully, invoking Tom's name as some sort of talisman while she showered in the tiny bathroom off her room.

And he certainly didn't like her. He'd listened to Sean's poison and chosen to believe it, convinced she was the sort of woman who'd sleep with a man for money.

When he didn't even know her...

It hurt. Snorting at her stupidity, she turned off the unrefreshing lukewarm water and resolutely switched her mind to other things.

And failed. In bed she lay open-eyed, wooing sleep. For once the dull roar of the waves against the reef didn't work its usual soothing magic. Wild, baseless forebodings swirled through her head, playing havoc with her thoughts.

Eventually she slipped into a doze, waking to the sound of gulls squabbling on the beach and the gleam of the sun through the curtains. The angle of its rays told her it was well above the horizon.

Jerking upright, she glanced at her watch, gave a startled exclamation and leapt out of the bed.

In a couple of hours she had to be at the resort to meet the solicitor from New Zealand. The uneasy chill that tightened her skin was because the solicitor would probably tell her she had to pay back the loan Tom had made to her.

And that would be extremely difficult.

Actually, right now it would be impossible.

Every cent she possessed was invested in her business. She had already approached the small local branch of the bank, but after consulting his superiors on the main island the manager had indicated they weren't inclined to take over the loan.

Oh, Tom, she thought, aching with sudden grief, why did you have to die…?

She missed him so much. In his gruff, cynical way he'd taken the place of the father she'd never known.

Telling herself to toughen up, she raced through her morning rituals before walking into the kitchen. The house was as silent as it had been since Tom died, and even before she saw the note on the bench she knew Luc MacAllister wasn't in it.

She stood for a moment, looking down at the writing. Just as she'd have imagined it, she thought a little caustically. Bold and black and clear; a very incisive, businesslike—not to say forthright—hand.

It announced, *Back at eight a.m.* and was signed with his initials.

She crumpled it up and glanced at her watch again, then rummaged in the refrigerator. Most men his height and build probably ate a cooked breakfast, but this morning he could have the same as she did—cereals and a bowl of fruit—and if he needed more to fuel that big streamlined body, there were eggs in the fridge for him to cook.

She ate breakfast too fast, decided against coffee and glanced again at her watch. Half an hour to fill. It stretched before her like an eternity. The sea always calmed her—perhaps it would work its magic now.

But her stomach remained a refuge for butterflies even after she'd walked through the sighing palms and stopped in the heavy shade of the trees lining this part of the beach. A towel on the sand drew her gaze out over the lagoon.

Sunlight glittered across the water, bestowing heat to the sand and weaving radiance through the great rollers as they dashed themselves in a fury of foam against the obstinate reef. On the calm waters inside its shelter, a small canoe carrying two boys danced its way down the coastline.

Squinting against the brilliance, Jo spotted Luc swimming towards the shore, powerful arms and shoulders moving easily, soundlessly through the warm waters. An unexpected heat banished the dark cloud of worry; her breath locked in her lungs as he stood up, water streaming down to emphasise bronzed shoulders and chest and long, strongly muscled legs.

For such a sophisticated man he looked magnificently physical, like some ancient god of the sea—compelling and charismatic as he strode towards the shore.

Startled by a fierce stab of sensation in every nerve, her senses on full alert, Jo looked away and pretended to watch the little canoe darting across the water. It seemed intrusive to stare at Luc when he had no knowledge of her presence and she disliked feeling like a voyeur.

Her stomach clenched with a different sort of apprehension as he came closer. She stiffened her shoulders, turning to face a survey that held a cool enquiry. Every traitorous nerve in her body tightened in a brief, shocking acknowledgement of his compelling male magnetism.

Without smiling, Luc nodded and said briefly, 'Good morning.'

At least he hadn't noticed her wildfire reaction. She returned the greeting, her mouth drying when he stooped and picked up his towel. How on earth had he developed the muscles so lovingly highlighted by the sun?

Working out, she told herself prosaically, adding a wry addendum, *Lots and lots of it.* And weights. Very heavy weights...

After drying his face he said, 'Kind of you to come down, but I could have found my way back.'

'I hope so,' she said, hoping she sounded amused. 'But I always walk down to the beach in the morning.' And because it was important to make sure he realised she hadn't followed him, she added, 'I didn't know you were swimming.'

He draped the towel around his taut waist and came towards her, big and male and overwhelming. 'Do you swim?'

'Every day.' She turned to go back to the house.

He fell in beside her. 'Not afraid of sharks?'

'Tiger sharks—the ones to be scared of—don't come into the lagoon much, if at all,' she told him, glad to be able to change the subject. 'And they're usually night feeders, so daylight swimming is pretty safe. Besides, the islanders say they're protected from them.'

He was too close. She felt an odd suffocation as they walked along the white shell path beneath the palms, and increased her pace.

Shortening his long stride to match hers, he asked, 'How are the islanders protected?'

So she told him the ancient story of the son of the first chief of the island who saved a small tiger shark— son of the chief of the sharks in the ocean around Rotumea—from a fish trap. 'For his compassion, the chief of all the sharks gave the islanders the right to be free of attack for ever. But only in the waters around Rotumea.'

He said, 'A charming story.'

Mischief glimmering in her smile, Jo looked up and said demurely, 'In all recorded history there's no account of any Rotumean being attacked by a tiger shark.'

His answering smile set off alarm bells all through her. *Stop it this moment*, she told her unruly emotions, tearing her gaze away to frown at the path ahead.

But that smile was a killer...

Hastily she said, 'I've left the makings for breakfast out, but if you want any more than cereal and fruit you'll have to get it for yourself. I have an appointment with Tom's solicitor at the resort at nine.'

And glanced up at his features for any hint that he knew of this.

Of course there was no alteration in the hard male contours of his face, and his eyes were hooded and unreadable. 'We'll talk when you've come back.'

Talk? About what?

The loan, she thought sickly.

Luc said, 'And I can get my own breakfast. I don't need looking after.'

An equivocal note in his voice kept her silent. She glanced at her watch. 'I don't imagine this meeting will last long. I assume it's to tell me what Tom wanted done with the house, so I'll go straight on to the shop afterwards.'

And spend the rest of the day trying yet again to work out how she could pay back that loan and still retain ownership of her fledgling business—an exercise she knew to be futile, as she'd already tried everything she could think of.

Think positively, she adjured herself robustly. Tom was too much of a realist not to know that his health was—well, not precarious, but the stroke had been a definite warning.

Surely if he felt anything at all for her beyond a mild affection for his housekeeper's niece he'd have made a fair provision for repaying the loan?

Bruce Keller looked up as Joanna Forman came into the room. Although he prided himself on his professional attitude, it took quite an effort to hide his curiosity.

He glanced at the documents on the table that served him as a desk. Joanna Forman, aged twenty-three, a New Zealand citizen, was not exactly how he'd imagined her. Tall, she had an excellent figure—she wasn't stick-thin like so many girls nowadays. And she had that intangible thing his daughters called style.

He wouldn't call her beautiful, yet as a man he could appreciate the subtle attraction of hair the colour of toffee and exquisite skin that seemed to radiate a softly golden glow. Not at all flamboyant—in fact, she should have looked out of place in the full-on exuberance of the tropics. That she didn't was probably due to her direct green gaze and softly sensuous mouth.

Yes, I see, he thought, and got to his feet, holding out his hand. 'Ms Forman?'

'Yes, I'm Jo Forman.' Her voice was steady, its slight huskiness adding to the impact of her mouth and her slender, curvy body.

He introduced himself, mentally approved the firmness of her handshake and said, 'Do sit down, Ms Forman. You do know why you're here?'

'You have something to tell me about Tom—Mr Henderson's—affairs. I presume it's that I need to vacate the house and pay back the loan he made me.'

Bruce blinked. She wasn't in the least what he'd imagined, and he needed to marshal his thoughts.

Tom Henderson had ignored his old friend's shocked cautions and flatly refused to discuss the arrangements he'd made for his mistress in his will, beyond making sure they were watertight.

The solicitor felt a twinge of professional pride at just how watertight they were.

No one would be able to break the terms of that will, not even Luc MacAllister—who'd almost certainly put a team of high-powered lawyers onto it once he'd learned what was in it.

After a slight cough Bruce said, 'No, there's nothing like that in his will.'

Surely she had some idea of the provision Tom had made for her?

She frowned, then seemed to relax a little. 'In that case, why am I here?'

Perhaps not...

Well, he'd soon see how that mouth looked when it smiled. He said, 'You're here because in his will Mr Henderson left you shares in his business enterprises worth several million New Zealand dollars.'

To his astonishment the soft colour fled her skin and she looked as though she might faint. No, he thought, wondering if he should offer a glass of water, modern young women didn't faint; that went out with the Victorians.

But after several moments of staring at him as though

he'd grown horns, she regained her composure. *'What did you say?'* Her voice was low and intense, almost shaky.

Clearly she'd had no idea. The solicitor leaned forward and told her the amount of money Tom Henderson had left her, finishing with, 'However, there are conditions to be fulfilled before the inheritance becomes yours.'

The muscles in her throat moved as she swallowed. Huskily she asked, 'Why?'

He started to tell her why Tom had made the conditions, but before he'd got far she cut him short. 'Why did he leave me *anything*?'

Startled, he felt his skin heat. 'I…ah, it seems that he felt—' He stopped, cleared his throat and resumed, 'That is, his affection for you made him want to…to make sure you were cared for.'

She frowned. 'Why?'

Her response showed a brutal understanding of her position. Clearly she was no romantic, and under no illusions as to her place in Tom Henderson's life. It was true very few men left their mistresses a fortune—even though in Tom's eyes this had been only a small fortune—so she should be elated.

Instead, she seemed aggressively astonished, if those two emotions were compatible.

Feeling his way, he asked, 'Does his reason matter?'

'Yes,' she told him unevenly. 'I think it does matter. He never said anything about this to me.'

Once more he cleared his throat and tried to steer the meeting back on track. 'I don't know his reasons, I'm afraid. And as I said, there are conditions to this legacy.'

Breathless and dazed, Jo felt as though she'd been snatched from ordinary life and transported to an alternate universe. It took all of her energy to say, 'All right, tell me about them.'

And listened with mounting bewilderment and shock while he obeyed. He was careful to explain the legal jargon to her but, even so, it was too much to take in.

She took a ragged breath. 'Let me get this straight. You're saying that to inherit this…this money…I have to spend the next six months living with Luc MacAllister. Here, in Rotumea.'

And waited, almost holding her breath and hoping she'd got it terribly wrong.

The elderly solicitor nodded. 'That is so.'

Colour flooded her skin. Sitting upright, she said fiercely, 'Surely it must be illegal to make such conditions.'

'I thought I'd made it clear that Mr Henderson intended only that you occupy the same house,' the solicitor pointed out, not unsympathetically. He gave a little cough. 'Nothing more was intended than that.'

Fragments of thought chased each other fruitlessly through Jo's brain. She grabbed at one of them and blurted, 'I don't understand it. Why make such an imposition on me—on Mr MacAllister?'

'Mr Henderson didn't tell me, I'm afraid, but I imagine it was to safeguard you.' He paused, then added, 'It is a lot of money, Ms Forman, a lot of responsibility—' *more than you've been accustomed to*, his tone implied '—and there will be pitfalls. Mr MacAllister can help you manage this unexpected windfall and make sure you're aware of things that could go wrong.'

He'd sooner see me in hell, she thought trenchantly. Of course she'd need professional help to deal with so much money, but what had made Tom think his stepson would take on such a responsibility? Was this outrageous proviso some sort of revenge on Luc for ousting Tom from Henderson Holdings—and so successfully expanding it?

No, vengefulness didn't square with her knowledge of Tom. A sudden thought struck her. 'I don't have to accept this...the legacy, do I?'

After a shocked look, the solicitor said, 'Think about it carefully, Ms Forman. Mr Henderson wanted you to have this inheritance. His reasons for putting in such a condition are unknown, but it was important to him. He insisted on it being there, and he certainly felt it would be best for you.'

'That might be so but it's a complete imposition on L—Mr MacAllister.' Jo shivered, feeling the jaws of a trap close around her. She resisted the urge to wring her hands, and said bleakly, 'I can't believe Tom did this—or that Luc will accept such a charge.'

'He has already accepted it.'

Confused, she asked, 'He *knows* of this?'

'Yes.'

Well, of course he did. No wonder he'd believed Sean's assertion! He probably thought she'd weaselled her way into Tom's life in the hope of getting money, and now he was lumped with her for the next six months.

Her chin came up but, before she could speak, the elderly man on the other side of the table said gently, 'If you refuse Mr Henderson's legacy, your debt to his estate will have to be paid. And as he knew there will be occasions when you need money for various things, he set up an account for you with a monthly increment. But it cannot be used to pay off the loan.'

Her stomach clamped in a twist of pain. 'I don't want it,' she said automatically.

'Nevertheless, it is there.'

If Tom had wanted to help her from beyond the grave, why hadn't he just forgiven her the debt?

What had been in his mind...?

Stop asking why, she ordered, because now she'd never know. *Concentrate on the facts*.

If she turned Tom's legacy down she wouldn't be the only person to suffer. So would the people who grew the ingredients for her lotions and creams on their small plantations, who relied on her business to pay for their children's education and medical care.

She could sell the fledgling business and pay off the debt. There had been tentative offers from a couple of big skincare firms who'd wanted to get their hands on a reliable source of several of the plants she used...

Even as the thought came into her mind she rejected it. When she'd first started using the islanders' recipes and plants for her skin products she'd promised the chiefs that if it became a success the business would stay in her hands.

She couldn't sell out and turn her back on them.

Her deep breath hurt her lungs. When she could speak again she said harshly, 'All right, I accept.'

And felt a clutch of fear at the prospect of what lay ahead.

Bluntly she asked, 'But what if Mr MacAllister changes his mind and refuses?'

There was a moment's silence. 'Then he loses something that means more to him than money.' And when she opened her mouth to ask him what, he held up a hand. 'I can't reveal to you what that is. But be assured, he will not refuse.'

CHAPTER FOUR

SAFELY PARKED BEHIND the shop, Jo switched off the Land
Rover engine and sat with her hands gripped together
in her lap, trying to stop shaking.

It had taken all her powers of concentration to ne-
gotiate the road between the resort and the town. Now
her eyes stung with sudden tears, and she had to fight
off a catch in her chest that threatened to turn into sobs.

Why had Tom left her such an enormous amount
of money and burdened her with this weird condition?
Why force her to live with Luc MacAllister for six
months?

Biting her lip, she scrabbled in her bag for her hand-
kerchief and wiped her eyes, dragging in a long shuddering breath.

Stop feeling betrayed, she told herself trenchantly,
and work things out sensibly.

Tom knew she was intelligent and a quick learner,
but he had a practical man's contempt for her degree.
And of course it would be no help in dealing with that
sort of fortune. She'd learned a lot from him, but the
solicitor was probably right on the mark when he'd suggested Tom saw her as too young and inexperienced to
be able to cope, so he'd made sure she couldn't do anything foolish with the legacy.

But *why* insist she spend the next six months with Luc MacAllister? Even before they'd met, Tom's unexpected legacy must have made Luc very ready to believe the worst of her. Sean's malice had only cemented that conviction in place.

The prospect of living with a man who thought she was little better than a tramp sent chills down her backbone.

Oh, Tom, she thought wretchedly, what were you thinking?

The car door swung open, and Savisi Torrens, the shop manager, leaned down to demand, 'Jo, are you all right? What's the matter?'

'I'm fine,' she said automatically, grabbing her bag.

Savisi scanned her face. 'You look pale. Are you sick?'

'No, no, I'm all right. Sorry, I was just thinking about things.'

'Have you had lunch?'

Surprised, Jo glanced at her watch. 'Not yet. I didn't realise it was so late.' She'd spent well over two hours with the solicitor. 'I'll get something from the café over the road.'

'Let me order that, and you can sit down while it's coming.' Savisi urged her into the relative coolness of the shop.

After she'd eaten a sandwich and drunk some coffee Jo felt better, although her stomach was still churning. It was a relief to discuss the monthly returns.

'The recession's hit us quite hard,' Savisi said succinctly. 'Not so many tourists this year.'

Jo scanned the figures again. 'Actually, we're doing better than I thought we might. Well done.'

The older woman disclaimed the praise. 'A good product always sells well.'

Jo said, 'I've been thinking that we might be able to set up some sort of sales outlet at the resort. Or a spa...'

'A spa? Oh, yes!'

Jo said quickly, 'It would cost a lot, but we might be able to swing it.' Even though Tom's legacy wouldn't be hers for six months...

'Meru's sister works at the resort—she might be able to tell you if the management would consider it.'

'I'd planned to see what she thinks.' Jo glanced at her watch. 'I'm due at the factory in half an hour. But another thing I'm pondering is the packaging.' She mentally grimaced at the memory of Luc MacAllister's insultingly casual comment. 'Changing it would cost plenty too, but if we do go into the resort we'll need something more sophisticated.'

They discussed ideas over more coffee before Jo left to visit the small building where her range was manufactured.

Meru Manamai bustled out to greet her with her usual hug. Her reaction to Jo's idea was the same as Savisi's—and even more enthusiastic. 'I'll see what my sister thinks,' she said, 'but a spa sounds like a really good idea. I wonder why it wasn't part of the original plan?'

'Tom wasn't a spa person—he liked swimming in the sea.' Words wouldn't come until Jo pushed the sad memories away. 'Some of our skincare products would be useful there, but I'd need to develop others—massage oils, that sort of thing. I know mothers here massage their babies with coconut oil, so that would be a logical base.'

At Meru's nod she warmed to her theme. 'And if there's enough interest from the guests we could organise small tours of the factory. We could perhaps give free samples?' She grinned. 'Small ones, just enough to make a difference so they'd come back for more.'

Meru laughed, but said practically, 'It might work—people love to get something for free.' She gave Jo an anxious look. 'But a spa would cost a lot of money so perhaps now is not the time to consider it...'

But in six months' time Jo would have a lot of money... Everything seemed to be pushing her into accepting Tom's legacy.

'It would be really good for Rotumea,' she said thoughtfully. 'We'd probably have to import people who know different sorts of massage, but the Rotumean way of massaging would be a point of difference. Before we make any decisions I'll have to talk it over with the resort management.'

A spa would certainly get her product known internationally, and Luc's query about taking her line to the world tantalised her. Expansion would mean more jobs in Rotumea, the exhilaration of working to grow her business...

And huge risks, she reminded herself gloomily.

Later, driving home in the rapidly falling dusk, she braced herself to overcome her wary apprehension. Luc had every reason to profoundly dislike the position he'd been forced into.

At the house she switched off the engine and sat for a moment trying to ignore the tension knotting her stomach. She wouldn't—couldn't afford to—let herself get worked up about the situation, so when she discussed Tom's crazy scheme with Luc she'd be reasonable and tactful and practical. She would not, not, *not* allow her mind to be scrambled by the memory of the minutes she'd spent in Luc's arms, and the sensual impact of his kisses.

An impact she still felt, keen and precise like a dagger through armour, so that her blood throbbed thickly through her veins and she had to take several deep breaths before she could persuade herself to climb out of the vehicle and walk briskly into the house.

Only to realise that Luc wasn't there. Trying not to feel that she'd been given a reprieve, she set about preparing the dinner she'd bought at the market. Tom had always enjoyed the coconut and lime risotto cakes she made to go with fish, so fresh it still smelt of the sea, that she'd bought from a fisherman on her way home. It should please anyone but a certified carnivore who demanded red meat.

If that was Luc, tough.

She'd just put the mixture for the cakes into the fridge when instinct whipped her head around to meet a steel-grey gaze, hard as glacier ice and every bit as cold.

'Oh,' she said involuntarily. Her heart jerked violently, then seemed to skid to a stop for a second. She pulled herself together enough to say, 'I didn't hear you come in.'

'So I gather.' His tone was completely neutral, but she caught the darkness of contempt in his eyes, the same contempt she'd noticed when he'd held her and asked her what she wanted.

Still watching her, he leaned a hip against the counter that separated the kitchen from the rest of the house. Spooked by that unnerving survey, she said pleasantly, 'I usually have dinner in about half an hour's time. Is that all right for you?' And turned away.

'It's fine.' He glanced at his watch. 'Do you mind leaving the room? I need to talk to someone back home.'

'Of course. I'll go outside.' The telephone was an old handset, placed where any conversation could be heard right through the house.

Tom had rarely used it, so its position had caused no problems. Jo walked across the garden to pick a couple of Tahitian limes from the tree. Warned by the distant sound of Luc's voice that he was still talking, she stopped to haul out a seedling palm that had somehow managed to hide itself under a hibiscus bush. Tom had disdained tidy, formal gardens; this one was lush and thriving, its predominant greenness set off by brilliant blooms and exotic leaf forms.

She couldn't hear what Luc was saying, but the tone of his voice made it abundantly clear that he wasn't pleased. Not that he shouted; if anything his voice dropped, but the cold, unyielding menace in his tone raised bumps on her skin. He would, she thought with an inward shiver, make a very nasty enemy. So far he'd been reasonably polite to her; now she wondered why.

Silence from the house brought her upright. She picked up the limes, still warm from the sun, and walked inside, bracing herself for the discussion she knew they had to have.

Luc stood at the bar, his back to her as he poured drinks. Her steps faltering, she noted the strong lines of shoulders and back that tapered to lean hips above long, powerful legs. It didn't seem fair that one man should have so much—physical chemistry, a brilliant mind and that potent male charisma, as compelling as it was disturbing.

And extremely good hearing. Without turning, he said, 'I've finished. Come on in.'

She put the limes down on the table and stared at the

tall-stemmed glasses with the faint lines of bubbles rising through the pale liquid.

'Champagne?' she said uncertainly. 'What's the celebration?'

Eyes hooded, he handed her a chilled glass. 'I thought it appropriate,' he said with smooth arrogance. 'After all, you've just become a rich woman. Congratulations on a game skilfully played.'

Jo's fingers tightened around the slender stem so fiercely she thought she might snap it. OK, he was furious. She'd expected that, and she would not allow him to get to her.

Remembering her decision on the drive back, she thought *sensible, reasonable, practical...*

Trying to keep her voice steady, she said, 'I had no idea what Tom was going to do. I'm just as bewildered as you, and just as upset. I don't like being manipulated.'

His lip curled. 'Presumably he wanted to recompense you for your services. I only hope they were worth the money.'

Jo realised her teeth were clenched. If he was trying to goad her into losing her temper he was making an excellent job of it. Deliberately relaxing every taut muscle, she said, 'I don't blame you for being angry—Tom had no right to lumber you with my presence for the next six months. But if you think I'll be a whipping boy for your temper, think again. I'll walk out sooner than put up with insults.'

His face was unreadable, but his shrug conveyed much, and she had to stop herself from moving uncomfortably under his searching survey. 'I'm sure you won't,' he said, each word an exercise in contempt. 'Tom knew you'd stay.'

Goaded into indiscreet anger, she challenged, 'What

about you? How did he make sure you'd fall in with his wishes?'

His smile was a taunt. 'Blackmail.'

Jo felt a momentary flare of sympathy, one that died when she met a gaze as harsh as a winter storm. Forcing a brisk, practical tone, she asked, 'So what happens now?'

'We leave for New Zealand tomorrow morning.'

Her jaw dropped. Recovering, she expostulated, 'I can't do that.'

'Why?'

'Because I'm needed here. I have responsibilities on the island—'

'Your little business?' he said, his negligent tone more galling than contempt would have been. 'You can keep an eye on it from New Zealand while we're away. But as you don't need it to pique Tom's interest any more it would be better to sell it.'

'I am *not* going to sell it,' she snapped, fighting back a rising tide of anger.

'Whatever. But you're coming to New Zealand tomorrow with me.' He examined her light, floating dress and drawled, 'You'll need warmer clothes, I imagine. I'll organise that.'

Her brows shot up. 'You're accustomed to buying clothes for women?'

With a smoothness that somehow grated, he said, 'My PA has excellent taste, and an encyclopaedic knowledge of the best places to hunt down the biggest bargains.'

His comment reminded her of the pathetic state of her bank balance. The small wage she took from her business barely covered her expenses in Rotumea. In New Zealand it would go nowhere. A hint of panic slowed her thoughts. No way could she afford new clothes. Second-hand shops?

She stifled a quiver of nervous amusement at the thought of Luc's PA seeking bargains for her in opportunity shops. Fortunately she had the perfect excuse. 'I can't afford any new clothes,' she said baldly.

In a voice that made her stiffen, Luc demanded, 'Use the money Tom left you.'

'I don't want it.' When he went to speak she added crisply, 'Living in Rotumea is cheap. I can manage on what I make.'

'You'll be spending some time travelling with me.'

Jo unclenched her teeth far enough to retort frigidly, 'Why? Tom knows—knew—how much the business means to me. I can't believe that he'd stipulate that I abandon it to jaunt around with you.'

Luc laughed, a cold, almost mocking sound. 'Welcome to the world of big money, Joanna Forman.' He raised his glass. 'The part of the will that dealt with my inheritance stated that when I go to any place that might help you, I am to take you with me.'

'Help me—in what way?'

'With your business, of course.' He sounded almost amused. 'Tom enjoyed power, and he probably relished the thought of forcing both of us to do his bidding from beyond the grave. So here's to his memory.' Luc drank some champagne, then set the flute down on the table with a sharp click.

Stung at this injustice, she said, 'Tom wasn't like that.'

'Then why did he do it?' he demanded, his tone derisory.

The same question she'd been asking herself since

the solicitor had told her of the inheritance. The months ahead stretched out like a particularly testing purgatory.

Be reasonable, she told herself sternly, and forced herself to meet Luc's daunting gaze. 'I have no more idea than you do, but Tom would have had a reason. He wasn't an impulsive man. And we can't ask him, so it's useless speculating. I dislike the situation as much as you do, but the simplest way to deal with it is to take it one day at a time and try not to get in each other's way.'

'Indeed,' he said, a note of irony hardening the word. 'Unfortunately we have to share our lives for the next six months. That means there's no way of avoiding each other.' He paused, then added satirically, 'Unless you refuse the inheritance.'

And waited.

At that moment nothing—absolutely *nothing*— would have given Jo greater pleasure than to tell him fluently and with passion what he and that solicitor could do with Tom's bequest, and then turn and walk away.

Unfortunately she couldn't.

Before she was able to say anything Luc said with hateful sarcasm, 'But you're not going to do that, are you?'

She stiffened her spine and met his sardonic look with every bit of resolution she possessed. 'No,' she said shortly. 'I owe Tom's estate money and the only way I can be sure of paying it off is to obey the terms of his will.'

'Selling the business would probably clear the debt.'

Jo masked her rising panic with a fierce look. 'When I started, I promised the local people I'd never sell it to an outsider. It's their knowledge I'm using, and they have an emotional stake in the business.'

'That's very noble of you.'

'What about you?' Her tone changed from defiance to challenge. 'What have you done that Tom was able to blackmail you into agreeing to stay here?'

'That,' he returned, his tone warning her she'd over-stepped some invisible boundary, 'is none of your business.'

She shrugged. 'The reason I'm not walking away is none of your business either, but I told you anyway,' she said, then took a deep breath.

Remember—calm, reasonable, common sense, she reminded herself hastily.

Steadying her voice, she tried. 'Can't we just agree to disagree and leave it at that? I don't like quarrelling, and the prospect of spending the next six months at loggerheads is not a pleasant one.'

A thought of amazing simplicity flashed across her mind like lightning. Without giving herself time to think, she asked, 'Why don't you take over Tom's loan to the business? Then I could pay it back under the same terms as I was paying Tom, and we'd not be forced to live together for six months.'

He was silent for a few seconds, and when his answer came it was brief and completely decisive. 'No.'

'That way I don't get Tom's inheritance which is causing you so much angst, and we don't have to put up with each other,' she pressed.

His brows drew together. 'No,' he said again. 'Tom wanted you to have the money. I'm not going to take it from you.'

Startled, she asked, 'Then why not accept the situation and try to make it as painless as possible? Would that be so difficult?'

Her plea met with no answer. She surveyed his face,

lean and arrogant and unreadable, steely eyes half-shielded by his thick lashes. An uncomfortable silence stretched between them, taut and somehow expectant, thickening until Jo was desperate to break it.

She said, 'OK, I tried,' and turned away, only to stop abruptly when he spoke.

'Are you suggesting taking a different tack?' he asked without expression.

She looked over her shoulder. Something about his stance—alert, like that of a hunter—summoned a stealthy excitement that pulsed through her, fogging her brain.

'Exactly,' she flashed, feeling like prey.

'I must be losing my grip.' His voice was thoughtful, his gaze level. 'I'm not usually so obtuse.'

They seemed to be conducting two different conversations. She said uncertainly, 'I don't understand you.'

'I think you do. You should have couched your proposition in less obscure terms,' he said, reaching out to touch the nape of her neck.

Too late, Jo realised what he meant. She opened her mouth to tell him she'd made no proposition at all, but his touch sent shock scudding down her spine, a secret craving that smoked through her like some addictive drug.

'No!' she said, her voice dragging.

'Why not?'

He didn't sound angry. In fact, if she could only trigger her brain into rational thought she'd guess his main emotion was amusement. The tips of his fingers were stroking softly, unexpectedly gentle, sending voluptuous, agitated shivers through her.

'Why not, Joanna?' he repeated, his voice cool, his gaze speculative.

She wasn't going to tell him that her experience was as limited as his kindness. Forcing herself to meet the intense blue flames that had banished all the grey from his eyes, she said hoarsely, 'Because, regardless of what you think, I'm not into casual sex.'

'One thing I can promise you,' he said, his tone suddenly raw, 'is that there would be nothing casual about it.'

And he pulled her into his arms.

Nothing—*nothing*—Jo had experienced had affected her like Luc's mouth on hers, the wildfire thunder of her pulse as his arms tightened to hold her against his lean body.

Before she had a chance to resist, sensation raced through her, his kiss detonating an involuntary response hot as fire, sweet as honey, fierce as the pressure of Luc's mouth on hers. When her knees buckled his arms tightened around her and her heart rate surged; he too was aroused.

Within Jo a pulse leapt into life, primal and dangerous, summoning a swift, mind-sapping hunger. As though aware of her vulnerability, Luc deepened the kiss, causing her body to flame into a passionate need that built on her response to his first kiss.

And then he lifted his head, breathed something short and brutal and let his arms fall, stepping back. For a moment her only emotion was heated resentment at his abrupt transition from passion to control. Fortunately common sense stiffened her spine and cleared her brain. She grabbed the back of a chair and dragged air into her lungs, her eyes wide and defiant as she forced herself to meet his hooded gaze. Disconnected fragments of thought tumbled through her brain. His face was drawn and fierce—a warrior's face—and the sensuous line of his mouth had tightened into hardness.

'I'm sorry,' he said curtly.

Jo's heart beat so loudly in her ears she couldn't hear the dull roar of the waves on the reef. She shook her head, finding that somehow her hair had escaped from its confining ponytail.

Surely Luc hadn't run his fingers through it...? The thought fanned an insidious tremor of something far too close to pleasure, reawakening her nervous turmoil.

He broke into her thoughts with a harsh order. 'Say something.'

'For once,' she retorted thinly, 'I'm speechless.'

Anger rode her, fuelled by shame. Once again she'd been entirely under the spell of his kiss. She despised herself because the embers of that desperate sensuality still smouldered deep inside her.

But his kiss had been an arrogant act of power—one reinforced by her mindless response. He'd no right to assume she was proposing some sort of grubby liaison, then kiss her like that.

Why hadn't she remained quiescent—detached and unimpressed—instead of going up like dry tinder in his arms?

Because she'd had no defence against the hypnotic masculinity of it, the sheer male hunger that had summoned a similar sexual drive from some unawakened place in her.

'I find that difficult to believe,' he said ironically. 'And to refer to what I said before we kissed, there was nothing light or casual about it.'

He paused, and when she said nothing he added, 'But you knew there wouldn't be. We've been far too conscious of each other ever since your eyes clashed with mine at the resort. Are you going to deny that?'

Jo drew in another sharp breath and evaded the question. 'That has nothing to do with anything.'

His smile was tinged with cynicism. 'It has everything to do with it. I wanted you then.'

Another blazing pang of desire shot through her. She resisted it, obstinately folding her lips before any foolish remark could escape.

Luc's expression remained unreadable. 'And your kisses tell me that you want me. Like you, I dislike the idea of spending the next six months quarrelling, so I'm suggesting a much more pleasant way of passing the time.'

He almost made it sound reasonable.

In his world, it probably was. Luc had probably made love to any woman he wanted.

Humiliated, Jo fought a treacherous urge to give in to this potent desire and walk on the wild side, explore a world she'd never experienced.

Fortunately, another, much more protective instinct blared a warning. Allowing herself to be persuaded, surrendering to his terms and becoming Luc MacAllister's lover would be a risk too unnervingly dangerous to take.

She would never be the same again.

So, although she had to force the words through lips still throbbing from his kisses, she said stiffly, 'No. That's not what I want...'

His look—speculative and unsparing—shattered her already cracked composure, but she lifted her chin and continued, 'And when I suggested finding a way to spend the next six months other than quarrelling, I was *not* suggesting some sort of affair—if that's what you thought.'

Calmly he replied, 'In that case there's nothing more to be said. I apologise for misreading the situation. It won't happen again. Deal?' And he held out his hand.

Still dazed by her shocking need, she hesitated, then held out her own, shivering at the sensuous excitement that thrilled through her at his touch.

'Deal,' she said hoarsely, and forced herself not to snatch her hand away.

Six months…!

She winced, and broke into speech. 'Why do we have to leave tomorrow? It's going to make things difficult—not so much for me as for my manager.'

Luc frowned. 'I have to be in Auckland by tomorrow afternoon for a meeting.'

Something had obviously gone wrong, and Luc was going to deal with it.

But although he might be arrogantly accustomed to people accommodating themselves to his plans, she wasn't.

She said, 'That's impossible unless your meeting is very late in the afternoon. The next plane for New Zealand doesn't leave until two tomorrow afternoon.'

'A private jet will pick us up at eight tomorrow morning.' With an ironic smile he watched her eyes widen, and added, 'Also, I've just been informed that the following night Tom's favourite charity is holding a dinner in Auckland as a memorial to him.'

'So?'

'Apparently he wanted you to be there,' he said curtly. 'The charity is a children's hospital, and this is to raise funds for new equipment.'

Jo could think of nothing worse than going to such a

dinner with him. One day at a time, she reminded herself with grim resignation, and surrendered.

'All right, but I can't just leave everything. I need to organise things—my shop and the factory, as well as someone to look after the house.'

'You've still got time,' he told her crisply. 'Time you're wasting in argument. Anyway, it's only going to be for a few days.'

Her lush mouth—its contours slightly enhanced by his kiss—tightened. Luc's body alerted him in an involuntary and infuriating response, heat twisting his gut as raw hunger ricocheted through him.

She said coldly, 'You could have told me that at the beginning.'

'I don't remember getting a chance,' he said sardonically. But she had a point. He took another sip of champagne, and asked, 'Is it so impossible?'

She stared at him for a moment, her green eyes shadowed. 'No,' she admitted quietly. 'But it's not just me it's going to inconvenience. If this sort of thing happens again I'll need more time to organise.'

He said abruptly, 'It's extremely important for me to be there—I'd have told you before but it's just come up.'

'The phone call,' she said, recalling with a remembered chill the tone of his voice.

'Yes,' he said shortly.

Clearly he had a very good reason for getting back to New Zealand as quickly as he could. However, if they were to spend the next six months together—as flatmates, she thought with a shiver—he was going to have to understand she wasn't some kid to be ordered around...

He waited until eventually she said, 'Very well, I'll be ready.'

For some reason his frown deepened. 'I'll organise a set-up for you so you can video conference with your managers whenever you want to.'

'Thank you.' She tried not to be swayed by his unexpected thoughtfulness. After all, he'd probably just order some minion to see that she had video contact.

Later, safely alone in her room, Jo collapsed onto the bed and tried to whip up some remnant of common sense. So Luc had kissed her. And she—reluctantly she admitted she'd almost *exploded* with what had to be lust.

Nothing she'd ever experienced had come near the sheer primal intensity of his kisses. She wasn't a virgin; in fact, she'd hoped her one serious relationship would lead to marriage. She'd loved Kyle, and been hurt when he made it clear that he resented her preoccupation with her mother's health. Her discovery a few weeks later that he was being unfaithful had shattered her.

Their lovemaking had been good, but nothing—*nothing* like being kissed by Luc.

That was a miracle of sensation—unbidden, reckless and clamorous, a torrent of response that too easily had drowned every sensible thought in barbaric hunger.

And it felt so *right*…as though it was meant to be.

Stifling a shocked groan, she looked around the bedroom and fought a cowardly urge to hurl her clothes into a bag and flee from an intolerable temptation.

Think, she adjured herself fiercely. *Use your head.*

For some reason Tom had believed it was important she spend six months in close—make that *very* close—contact with his stepson. And he'd made it pretty near impossible for her to turn his legacy down.

So she'd just have to grit her teeth and cope—without

surrendering to this wild, irresponsible appetite she'd suddenly developed for Luc's body.

An ironic smile turned swiftly into a grimace. 'Oh, it should be so easy!' she muttered, pushing back the drift of netting that kept insects at bay.

Her sleep was restless, punctuated by dreams that faded as soon as she woke, leaving her aching and unsatisfied. In the morning she showered and dressed with care, then forced herself into the kitchen. One thing she was not going to do was walk out to the beach...

She was eating breakfast on the terrace when Luc appeared. 'Good morning,' she said sedately, refusing to respond to the sight of him in swimming trunks, drops of water polishing his sleek, tanned torso, his hair ruffled as though he'd merely run the towel over it.

His assessing look sent little ripples of excitement from nerve to nerve. 'Good morning. I won't be long— no, stay there. I can get my own breakfast when I've changed.'

And he disappeared into the bedroom.

Her heartbeat soared uncomfortably when he reappeared, dressed in a casual pair of trousers and a short-sleeved shirt. Chosen for him by whom? His mother? No, she'd died several years ago. A lover?

Someone who knew him very well, because the colour matched his eyes.

Without preamble, he said, 'We need to talk.'

Jo tried to match his pragmatic unemotional tone. 'When you've had your breakfast. Would you like some coffee?'

He gave her another of those straight looks. 'If you're having some yourself. You don't need to wait on me. I'm capable of making my own coffee. And my own meals.'

'It's habit,' she said calmly. 'I acted as Tom's hostess, so I do it automatically.'

Actually, she needed something bracing—a cold shower would be good—but coffee was supposed to make one more alert. Besides, it meant she could get herself out of his way without looking stupid.

It was all very well to spend half the night telling herself she could cope with the rush of sensual adrenalin that ambushed her every time she saw Luc, but when she actually laid eyes on him she had no defence against the hunger aching through her.

Getting to her feet, she said, 'Anyway, I need some and I might as well make some for you too.'

A false move, because he came with her into the kitchen and while she organised the coffee he assembled his breakfast.

She should have absented herself while he ate, she thought as she sat opposite him and drank her coffee. Sharing breakfast was altogether too intimate.

Mug in hand, she got to her feet and wandered across to the edge of the decking, keeping her gaze fixed on a bird with a yellow bandit's mask as it fossicked in the thick foliage of a hibiscus bush.

'What bird is that?' Luc's voice came from very close behind her.

She jumped, and whirled around. His hand shot out and gripped her shoulder for a moment, before releasing her.

Her breath locked in her throat as she stared mutely at him.

What could have been triumph gleamed for a moment in his hard eyes.

No! Gathering all her strength, Jo forced herself

to turn away, to fix her gaze on the bird, now warily checking them out from the fragile shelter of the leaves.

In a distant voice she said, 'It's a native starling.'

The bird shot out from behind its leafy screen, flying straight and true, its alarm call alerting every other bird to a threat. Previously Jo had always been a little amused at the starlings' propensity for drama and flight.

Now she knew exactly how they felt. Threatened.

Quickly she said, 'They're an endangered species. Tom and the chiefs were working on a way to save them. Unfortunately, that means killing off the doves that were introduced a century or so ago. They compete with the starlings for food and nesting sites. And the locals like the cooing of the doves. They call them the lullaby birds. Sadly for the starlings, they can only produce that harsh screech.'

She was babbling and it was almost a relief when Luc said from behind her, 'I'm sure Tom would have overcome that prejudice. He didn't like being beaten—and, as we both know, he had a ruthless streak a mile wide.'

Indeed. And it would be useless to keep asking herself what on earth Tom had intended to bring about with his condition.

Only one thing was certain; he'd have had a motive.

Actually there was another certainty—neither she nor the man with her would ever learn what that motive was. Unless Luc MacAllister already knew...

But he'd said he didn't, and she was inclined to believe him. Quickly, before she could change her mind, she turned and asked, 'Do you really have no idea why Tom would have done this?'

His already tough face hardened. 'No idea apart from the one I suggested yesterday—a determination to force both of us to his will.'

CHAPTER FIVE

Jo SHOOK HER head. 'I can't believe that,' she said decisively and with some heat.

Luc recalled her objection of the previous day. *Tom wasn't like that.*

Not with her, perhaps.

But he didn't say it aloud. For some reason it irritated the hell out of him to accept she'd been Tom's lover. More infuriating was the fact that she wanted him to believe she'd felt something more for his stepfather than the mercenary greed of her sort of woman.

But what really made him angry was the fact that her kisses had almost convinced him she'd been feeling genuine desire.

With hard-won cynicism—based on being a target too many times to recall—he'd been sure he could tell the real thing from the fake. Clearly she was good...

Well, Tom only went for the best.

Abruptly he asked, 'Have you packed?'

Her answer was even more curt. 'Yes.'

She sat silently on the way to the airfield, watching Luc talk to the taxi driver from the back of the car. The tropical sun warmed the cool olive of his skin, outlined the breadth of his shoulders and limned his arrogant profile with gold when he glanced sideways at the resort as they drove past.

So, he turned her on. *Get over it—and fast*, she ordered, and dragged her gaze away to stare blindly at the pink and yellow flowers of the frangipani bushes along the road.

Oh, face the truth! He did much more than turn her on; he set her alight, stirring her blood so she had to fight stupidly erotic thoughts. And the memory of his kiss sent hot, secret shudders right down to her toes.

She had to make some rules—unbreakable ones. The first was obvious. No more kissing—it was too dangerous. She'd liked it far too much.

Actually, she accepted reluctantly, *liked* didn't come near it. She couldn't come up with words that described what Luc's kisses did to her.

And she wasn't going to try. Dwelling on her weakness was not only stupid, it was reckless and forbidden.

The private jet was a revelation, and provided some distraction. She tried not to stare like some hick, but the opulent, ostentatious décor was blatantly designed to impress. Which surprised her; Luc didn't seem a man to indulge in such crass showmanship.

'You don't like it,' he said as she looked around.

She gave him a suspicious glance. 'I don't have to, do I?' she asked sweetly.

He smiled. 'It's not mine. I chartered it because it's fast and safe, not for the interior decoration. Buckle up; we're ready to go.'

She watched Rotumea fall away beneath them, a glowing green gem in a brilliant enamelled sea of darkest blue that faded swiftly to green. A mixture of emotions—part anticipation, part regret—ached through her heart.

Goodbye, Tom, she thought, before chiding herself for being overly dramatic.

'What's the matter?' Luc asked.

Startled, she looked up. 'Nothing,' she said quietly, wishing he weren't so perceptive.

After a disbelieving glance he handed her a magazine, a glossy filled with the latest in fashion. 'Is this all there is to read?' she enquired dulcetly.

'I believe it has excellent articles.' The amusement in his voice almost summoned a smile from her.

'Oh, that's all right, then.'

Whoever had told him that was right—it was both provocative and entertaining, as well as featuring the latest fashions.

Her incredulous gaze fell onto a photograph in the social pages. There stood Luc, elegantly dressed at some race meeting, and beside him a glamorous redhead.

His fiancée, according to the caption. Shocked into stillness, Jo blinked, forcing herself to keep her gaze on them, while something like cold rage squeezed her heart. How dare he kiss her when he was engaged?

A lean hand came over and flipped the magazine closed so she could see the publication date. A year and a half previously...

'Long out-of-date. Perhaps I could get a reduction in the charter fee,' Luc said. 'The week after that was taken she eloped with Tom's nephew. They're married now, with a baby on the way.'

'Oh,' Jo said inadequately, furious with herself because her first emotion was a violent relief, followed almost instantly by astonishment at the ironic amusement in his tone.

Clearly he hadn't grieved too long at the couple's betrayal.

She said, 'Tom's nephew? He didn't mention it.' Then wished she'd stayed silent.

'Possibly he didn't think you'd be interested,' he said negligently.

Or perhaps Tom hadn't considered it to be any of her business. He'd fleetingly referred once to a past relationship of Luc's with the daughter of an Italian billionaire, and she remembered a casual conversation about Luc's mother's hope he'd marry into the French aristocracy she'd come from.

Apart from that, nothing about Luc's personal life.

The seatbelt sign tinged off, and automatically she looked up. Luc met her gaze, his mouth curved into a satirical smile. 'I believe much the same thing happened to you,' he said coolly.

She went rigid. 'How did you know?'

'Don't look so startled.' He shrugged. 'When you moved in with Tom I had you checked out, of course.'

Outraged and a little afraid, she spluttered, 'You had a nerve!'

His gaze was keen and unreadable. 'As I said last night, welcome to the world of the rich and powerful. And your lover was a selfish pup to make you choose between your mother and him.'

'He didn't think—' She stopped again.

'Go on.'

It was her turn to shrug. Discovering that Kyle disliked her mother had been bad enough; what had shattered her was that he'd believed all the gossip about Ilona.

'He didn't like her,' she said stiffly.

'Why?'

Because he thought she'd been little better than a call girl. In their final argument before he'd left Jo he'd laughed in her face when she'd mentioned marriage, and told her brutally that no woman with a mother like Ilona Forman would be a suitable wife for him.

It still stung. Jo looked down at the magazine and turned the page, saying distantly, 'They just didn't get on.'

Luc nodded and bent to open a folder. After a few moments he realised that although he had a bitch of a meeting ahead of him, he couldn't concentrate.

Joanna's lover had probably realised her mother was being totally unreasonable to demand such devotion. She'd spent much of her daughter's childhood foisting her onto her sister while she flitted around the world on modelling shoots, walking the big catwalk events and being a muse to designers—whatever the hell a muse was.

At least she'd left her daughter enough money to start her business.

He had to admire Joanna for that. Even with Tom's help and advice, getting her skincare product out onto the marketplace, steering it into profit must have taken guts, creativity and hard work.

And loyalty to those who worked for her.

Not that he'd change his mind about her. And in six months' time she'd be amply recompensed for her services to Tom.

Warily Jo sent a surreptitious glance his way. He was frowning as he read his documents, black brows drawing together over that uncompromising blade of a nose. Jo looked quickly back at the magazine, glad she wasn't the person or persons waiting for him to arrive in Auckland.

Shortly afterwards the steward came into the cabin with an offer of morning tea. Luc drank his the same way he drank coffee—black and to the point. Jo liked hers with milk, and after finishing it and one of the small muffins that accompanied it, she sat back on a wide sofa while Luc went back to his folder.

In Auckland it was raining, a soft autumn shower that stopped before the steward slid the door open. Shivering a little in the cool air, Jo hurried inside to be processed by customs and immigration officers.

Luc said abruptly, 'I'll organise an immediate advance of the money Tom left you.'

'Were there any conditions?' she asked with a snap.

'Bruce Keller wouldn't tell me if there were,' he returned indifferently. 'If he didn't say anything to you, then no, there were no conditions.'

She sighed. 'Thanks. And I'm sorry I bit—I'm already tired of this situation.'

And tired of being forced down a road she'd not planned to take. It hurt to think that Tom had done this to her—hurt more that her image of him was slowly crumbling.

'Think of the end result.' It was impossible to discern Luc's emotions from his voice. 'Give Bruce Keller the data and he'll make sure the money is in your bank account.'

Jo bit her lip. 'You have his contact details?'

Luc's brows lifted. 'I do.'

Well, of course. Clearly he thought he was dealing with an idiot. Heat warmed her face. If he hadn't whisked her so unceremoniously off the island she'd have been better prepared.

But she didn't care a bit what Luc MacAllister thought of her.

'Where are we going?' she asked, looking around as they left the building.

'To Tom's place on the North Shore.'

The house on the North Shore was about as different as anything could be from Tom's home in Rotumea, although it nestled into a garden of palms and luxuriant foliage beside a beach on Auckland's magnificent harbour. Jo examined the double-storeyed building of classic, clean architectural lines and much glass as the car eased up the drive.

'Very tropical in feel,' she observed when the car drew up outside a double-height door.

Luc sent her a narrow glance, clearly recognising the jibe. 'Tom's natural environment,' he said calmly, switching off the engine in front of a huge double door. 'Auckland has a pretty good climate for outdoor living. I'm sure you made the most of it while you lived here.'

'Of course,' she said automatically, then stiffened. She couldn't recollect having told him she'd spent her childhood in Auckland.

Of course, he'd had her investigated—hired some sleazy private detective to poke around her life looking for dirt.

Distaste shivered through her, alleviated only by the cheering thought that it must have been a very boring investigation for whoever had done it.

Chin angled away from Luc, she got herself out of the car and went around to the boot where he'd stowed their cases. The soft sound of waves on the shore eased her tension a little, yet made her feel wrenchingly homesick for Rotumea.

One day at a time, she reiterated briskly, and reached in to get her pack from the boot.

Only to have Luc take it out. 'It's all right, I can manage,' she said stiffly.

'So can I.' After hauling his own suitcase free, he set off for the huge front door.

Baulked, she walked beside him, and was startled when the door was opened by a middle-aged man with an expressionless face.

He was Sanders, she was informed as Luc introduced them. Jo had never met a man with only one name before, and he seemed surprised when she held out her hand and said, 'How do you do.'

He shook it but dropped it as quickly as he could.

This was not at all like Rotumea, or the New Zealand she'd grown up in. Perhaps the two years she'd spent in the tropics had turned her into a yokel.

No, it was just that she'd become accustomed to the Rotumean way of doing things. In such an isolated society, everyone could find some blood relationship—however distant—so there was little social distinction. And Tom had fitted in really well—although, she conceded as she walked sedately into a high, light-filled entrance hall, he had been allotted the status of high rank in Rotumea...

As Luc would be. There was something about him that indicated strength—and not just of body. He moved with the lithe athleticism that spelt perfect health. One look at his hard countenance was all it took to appreciate the honed intellect and forceful personality behind his autocratic features.

'Is there something wrong with my face?'

His ironic voice brought her back to herself. Oh, hell, she'd been staring...!

'Not that I can see,' she said flippantly, hoping he wouldn't notice the heat burning across her skin. She looked around the high, spacious hall and breathed, 'This is lovely.'

'It was Tom's design.'

Surprised, she said, 'He didn't tell me he was an architect.'

'He wasn't, but he had definite ideas, and he worked closely with the architect, a chap called Philip Angove.'

'I've heard of him—I read an article not long ago that called him the only real successor to Frank Lloyd Wright.'

'I suspect he wouldn't exactly be pleased at the comparison, but he's brilliant.' Luc laughed. 'He and Tom had some magnificent differences of opinion, but Tom felt the result was worth the effort. I'll show you to your room while Sanders organises lunch.'

Her room was large, with its own wide balcony overlooking a pool—yet clearer evidence of Tom's profound love for the tropics. More palms and a wide terrace surrounded the pool, and the gardens featured the same hibiscuses that grew wild in Rotumea, but instead of the island's tropical abandon this garden had a lush, disciplined beauty.

'The en suite is through there,' Luc said, nodding at a door in the wall. He glanced at his watch. 'Lunch will be in half an hour—I'll collect you. If you like, Sanders can unpack for you.'

'No, thanks,' she said hurriedly. Sanders might be accustomed to doing such chores, but she wasn't accustomed to having them done for her.

Luc's smile was tinged with irony. 'There's nothing of that slapdash tropical informality in Sanders. He's British and has stern ideas about what is proper and what isn't. You'll get used to him,' he said. 'He, on the other hand, might find you bewildering.'

Childishly, she pulled a face at the door as it closed behind him, but quickly sobered, turning away to draw in a deep breath and set herself to unpacking. The wardrobe, she discovered, was a dressing room. She hung up the contents of her pack, smiling a little ruefully at the tiny amount of space her clothes took up.

But once showered and dressed in a shirt of clear blue over slender ivory trousers she walked across to the window and looked out beyond the pool. Beyond it, through the dark foliage of the pohutukawa trees that fringed all northern coastlines, she caught a glimpse of white sand and the sea.

Her main emotion, she realised with surprise, was a profound sense of homecoming.

Putting aside the fact that the man she was to share her life with for six months thought she was little better than a prostitute, it was good to be back.

So she'd just keep out of Luc's way.

A knock on the door set her pulses haywire, forcing her to admit that she'd grossly oversimplified her emotions. The kisses they'd shared, backed up by Luc's admission that he wanted her, meant she'd never feel completely at ease with him.

With a silent heartfelt vow that she wasn't going to lose her head over him, she squared her jaw and opened the door, only to feel her foolish heart sing at the sight of male temptation in a business suit that moulded itself lovingly to his powerful frame.

'Ready?' he asked.

'Yes.' OK, so she was going to have to work on controlling her body's disconcerting response. She'd do it. Familiarity had to breed contempt. As her mother used to say occasionally, very few men were worth a single tear. Absolutely.

Lunch was set out on the wide roofed terrace leading to the pool. Without thinking, Jo picked three frilly,

silken hibiscus flowers and arranged them in a scarlet
dazzle at one end of the table.

Looking up, she caught Luc's eyes on her and realised what she'd done. 'Sorry,' she said, ignoring an
odd quiver somewhere in the pit of her stomach. 'Habit
dies hard.'

'Feel free.' He clearly couldn't have been less interested.

It wasn't the first time she'd eaten with him, yet the
tension she always felt in his presence had become su-
percharged with a heady awareness that set her on edge.

Unlike Luc, who seemed fully in control. Trying to
match his cool reserve, she masked her inner turmoil,
and they ate the meal like polite strangers.

She was relieved when he left for his very important
meeting, but after a few irritating minutes spent wondering how he was dealing with whatever emergency
he was involved in, she opened her elderly laptop and
began to work on it.

The afternoon dragged. Sanders delivered her afternoon tea, followed by dinner without any sign of Luc.

Forget about him, she ordered, and applied herself
even more rigidly to work.

A knock on her door near ten that night brought her
head up from weary, frustrated contemplation of the
screen. Heart jumping, she forced herself to walk sedately across the room and open the door.

'What's the matter?' Luc demanded after one penetrating glance.

'My computer's died,' she told him baldly.

He looked a little tired, his olive skin drawn more
tightly over his autocratic features. Jo felt an odd impulse to tell him to go to bed and get a good night's
sleep.

Fortunately it was derailed when he demanded, 'How much have you lost?'

'Nothing—it's all backed up—but it won't work, no matter what I do to it.' She would have liked to know how the important meeting had gone, but she didn't have the right to ask.

'Let me see it.'

Reluctantly she stood back to let him in. One grey glance took in the laptop set up on the makeshift desk, and he said, 'How old is that?'

'I don't know.'

'No wonder it died. It looks like a relic from the eighties.'

'Possibly it is,' she retorted with some asperity, 'but it's worked fine up until now.'

His stepfather wouldn't have been able to resist trying to find out the problem, but Luc said, 'You need a new one.'

'I know.' Jo didn't try to hide her frustration. Why did the wretched thing have to break down at the most inconvenient moment?

Luc gave her another of his penetrating looks. 'I'll lend you one of mine until you organise a new one.'

Surprised, she said, 'Won't you be needing it?'

'Not this one.' His incisive reply cut short her instinctive response to refuse.

Abruptly abandoning the computer, he went on, 'I forgot to tell you to let Sanders know about any food you're allergic to or dislike hugely, and he'll make sure it doesn't appear on the menu.'

'He's already asked, thank you, before he cooked dinner. But Luc, I can make my own meals—'

He gave her a brief smile. 'Not in his kitchen you won't.'

'Oh. OK.'

Clearly she needed to know the boundaries of Sanders' sphere of influence, but before she could ask tactfully, Luc said, 'Is there anything you need or want now?'

'No, thanks.'

He nodded. 'The computer will be here tomorrow morning—probably after I leave for another meeting, one that might last all day.' Grey eyes scanned her face. 'Go to bed,' he commanded. 'You look exhausted.'

'Fury with an inanimate object can do that to you,' she said wearily. 'Goodnight.'

She slept heavily, so soundly she didn't wake until after nine. Sanders appeared as she came down the stairs, and said, 'Mr MacAllister has left. He thought you might like to eat breakfast on the terrace.'

'That would be lovely,' she said, and smiled at him. His response was a mere movement of his lips, but he seemed a little less stiff than previously. 'I'm sorry if I've interrupted your routine. I don't normally sleep in.'

He unbent enough to say, 'Travelling has that effect on some people.'

It seemed a shame to waste such a glorious, beckoning day indoors, but once she'd finished work she could spend time in the pool.

The computer arrived around ten, with a desk and an office chair as well as a set of shelves and a filing cabinet. Under Sanders' supervision they were carried into her room and a temporary office was set up.

It worked well; the computer had been cleared and once she'd had a little more practice at dealing with its foibles she'd be fully confident with it. She ate lunch out on the terrace, and was on her way back to her room when the telephone on a hall table rang. Automatically she picked it up and said, 'Hello.'

'Who is this?' a woman demanded. 'Have I the wrong number? Is this Luc MacAllister's house?'

'Yes.' Answering had not been such a good idea, especially when she looked up and saw Sanders—more poker-faced than normal—advancing towards her, intent on taking over.

'Are you a cleaner?' the woman asked. 'Where is Sanders?'

Chagrined, she said, 'Sorry. He's on his way,' handed over the receiver to him and escaped.

But not fast enough to avoid hearing Sanders say, 'Certainly, Ms Kidd. I'll make sure Mr MacAllister gets your message.'

Whoever she was, Ms Kidd had no manners. And Jo had to endure a mortifying moment when Sanders told her that answering the telephone was his duty.

'Yes, I realised that,' she said ruefully. 'I'm afraid it was an automatic reaction.'

He relaxed infinitesimally. 'Mr MacAllister has all his calls screened except on his personal phone. You'd be surprised the sort of people who try to get in touch with him—reporters and such.' His tone indicated that reporters and poisonous snakes had a lot in common.

'I won't do it again,' she told him.

He nodded and said, 'Mr MacAllister's personal assistant has just rung. She'll be here in half an hour to take you shopping.'

'What?' she said, bewildered, before remembering the conversation about clothes she'd had with Luc.

'For tonight's dinner, I understand,' Sanders elaborated.

She'd pushed any thought about the dinner out of her mind, but had to admit to a secret relief that Luc had remembered.

CHAPTER SIX

LUC'S PERSONAL ASSISTANT turned out to be a superbly dressed woman in the prime of her life. At first Jo guessed her to be in her forties, but after half an hour or so in her company, she changed her mind. Sarah Greirson was probably the best-preserved sixty-year-old she'd ever come across. With a mind like a steel trap, an infectious sense of humour and an encyclopaedic knowledge of Auckland's best bargains, she made shopping for the dinner gown an amusing and fascinating experience.

In turn, she was intrigued by Jo's fledgling business. So much so that when they returned to the house Jo raced up to her room and returned with a jar of rehydrating cream.

'Thanks for being so helpful,' she said, and gave it to her.

Sarah looked taken aback. 'Are you sure?' she asked.

'Sure of what?' Luc said, appearing unexpectedly in the huge sliding doors that led out onto the terrace.

Jo jumped, colour beating up through her skin. Very aware of the older woman's perceptive gaze on her, she said swiftly, 'Of course I'm sure. I'll be interested to see how you like it.'

'I'm *very* interested in trying it out,' Sarah said

cheerfully. 'Thanks so much.' She turned to Luc. 'And thank you for asking me to do this. Once I'd convinced her that hiring a dress would not be a good look we had a great time, and she'll be stunning.'

'Of course,' Luc said smoothly. 'She always is. I've got some papers for you before you leave, Sarah.'

Alone, Jo let out a ragged breath, and closed her eyes before walking out onto the terrace.

She always is... What was he up to? She waited until her heart rate levelled out, only for it to shoot up again when she turned to see Luc standing in the doorway, watching her with a quizzical amusement that brought another flush to her cheeks.

'Tired?' he asked, walking across to her.

'No—at least, yes, a bit.' She produced a smile. 'Sarah is a perfectionist in every sense of the word. Standing around has never been my thing, especially when people are inspecting me as though I'm a piece of meat, and discussing my measurements to the last centimetre.'

His brows lifted. 'You're pleased with the result?'

'It's a beautiful dress. And so are the shoes and the bag.'

Not to mention the new bra Sarah had insisted on, and the sheerest of tights.

She finished, 'Sarah has superb taste, and fortunately we agreed. I won't shame Tom. And I'll pay you for them when I get access to the money Tom left me.'

His expression didn't alter, yet a tenuous shiver snaked the length of her spine. 'You won't,' he said curtly.

She stopped herself from biting her lip, but ploughed on, 'That's why he left it, so I wouldn't be an expense on you. And, speaking of expenses—we need to talk about sharing them.'

Frowning, he said, 'We do not.'

Jo opened her mouth to expostulate, but the words died unsaid when he reached out and put a finger across her lips. Eyes widening, she froze, her heart thudding uncomfortably in her ears. Every nerve tightened; she could see a pulse beating in his throat.

He was too close—suffocatingly close. Her brain wouldn't work and she couldn't move.

Very quietly, in a tone that meant business, he said, 'I don't need any contributions to household expenses.'

'And I don't need charity—' she began, then stopped, stomach knotting because each word felt like a kiss against his finger. She could even taste him—a smoky male flavour that spun through her like a whirlwind.

He dropped his hand and stepped back. 'It's not charity. I want something from you.'

She'd just drawn a swift breath, but his final sentence drove it from her starving lungs. 'What?'

Her voice was too fast, too harsh, but she thought she knew what he wanted, and his proposition was going to hurt both her pride and her heart.

'Not what you think,' he said curtly, each word cutting like a whiplash. 'I don't need to buy or blackmail women into my bed.'

He paused. Jo waited, conscious of a vast feeling of relief alloyed by a sneaky and wholly treacherous regret.

When he resumed it was in that infuriatingly ironic tone. 'You're making heavy weather of this, Joanna. It's only for six months—in the grand scheme of your life barely long enough to consider.' He added on a cynical note, 'And think of the reward when it's over and you can thumb your nose at whoever you want to.'

Stung, she retorted, 'Thumbing my nose is not my

style.' Her smile showed too many teeth. 'In fact, I don't believe I've ever seen anyone do it. Have you?'

'What a deprived life you've led,' he remarked idly. 'Children do it all the time.'

'Not me. Did you?'

He grinned. 'Only once. My mother caught me and after her scolding I never did it again. She said it was vulgar, and although I was too young to understand what that meant I understood it was bad.'

Intrigued, she said, 'So you were a good kid and obeyed her.'

He raised his brows. 'Of course,' he said. 'Didn't you obey your mother?'

'Most of the time,' she said wryly. Her indulgent mother had made up for the times she'd been away with treats and much love. A little raw at the memories, she asked, 'So what do you want from me?'

'A truce.'

Her brows shot up. 'I believe I suggested that not so long ago.'

'You did, and I agree—the least disagreeable way of coping with the next six months is to ignore the fact that we're forced to obey Tom's whim, and get on with our respective lives without getting too much in each other's way.'

Of course he was right. She should be glad he'd seen reason—she *was* glad he'd seen reason and agreed with her. It was the sensible, practical, *safe* attitude.

Right now she needed safety very much.

So she nodded firmly. 'It's a deal,' she said and added rapidly, 'I've never been to a charity dinner. How do they run?'

'Drinks and mingling first, then excellent food, then

a comedienne.' His smile held wry humour. 'I suspect the entertainer was chosen more for her looks than her wit.'

Some hours later, her hair coiled sedately at the back of her neck, Jo examined herself in the mirror. Wearing the clothes Luc had paid for, her make-up as perfect as she could get it, she thought dryly that she had one thing to thank heaven for—he hadn't held out his hand to seal the deal. She recalled only too vividly the way her intransigent body had responded to his touch.

As though champagne instead of blood coursed through her veins...

She was going to have to overcome this fascination, the way one look from those hard grey eyes sent chills—delicious, sparkly, *sexy* chills through every cell in her body.

'And you are just one out of a million or so women who probably suffer the same silly reaction whenever he looks at them,' she told her reflection, and turned—carefully—to pick up the evening bag Luc had also paid for.

She'd spent some time practising walking in the strappy shoes, but was still cautious. Two years spent in the tropics, where footwear was either sandals or thongs, hadn't prepared her for heels. She crossed her fingers against any chance of tripping.

Luc watched her come down the stairs, noting that Sarah had done a magnificent job. Critically he decided he preferred that sensual mass of amber hair loose, but the bun at the back of her neck certainly gave her an elegant, sophisticated air.

The ankle-length dress—a slim thing a shade darker than her hair—skimmed Joanna's curves. Too closely, he thought, his body tightening. He chided himself for being a fool; possessiveness had never been a problem in his previous relationships. He'd expected fidelity—

Where the hell had that thought come from? They were not in a relationship, and weren't going to be.

He resumed his survey, noting the swift burn of colour along her cheekbones. A piece of jewellery set off her slender wrist, a metal cuff the same colour as the dress.

And she walked like a queen, head held high, straight-backed and slender.

She looked exactly the way he wanted—like his lover, dressed by him, ready for him.

However, the glance she gave him when she reached the bottom of the staircase was narrowed, her smoky green eyes direct and challenging. 'I hope you think this was worth it,' she said with a lift of her square chin.

'Every cent,' he said coolly, enjoying the sparring.

'Which I'll pay back as soon as I get Tom's money,' she reiterated firmly. 'And you should give Sarah a nice bonus. She deserves it.'

He took her arm, feeling her tense against him as he turned her towards the door. 'I don't discuss Sarah's salary.'

'I wasn't discussing her salary. I was subtly pointing out that I'm sure her job description doesn't include dressing your dinner partners.'

She smelt delicious, softly sensuous as a houri. To stop the swift clamorous surge from his body, he said, 'It includes whatever I want her to do. How are you getting on with the heels?'

'Warily. Ambling along the beach at Rotumea in bare feet is no training for heels this high.'

Her words summoned a vivid image—sleepy, golden

and sleek as she rose from the hammock in her bikini, and again his body reacted with a fierce, primitive hunger. Controlling it was surprisingly difficult. 'Do you want me to walk you like this, or is it easier if you step out on your own?'

She relaxed a fraction. 'I hate to admit it,' she confessed, 'but it will probably be better for my confidence to lean on your arm.'

'In that case, use me as a prop whenever you want to.'

On the drive across the bridge he started to tell her about the charity, then broke off. 'I suppose you've already heard of this from Tom.'

'No,' she said. 'I knew he supported charities but he never spoke of them.'

'Possibly he thought you wouldn't be interested.'

'I'd say he realised I can't yet afford to support anything,' she said crisply. 'He wasn't the sort of man to boast about his generosity.'

He looked down at her, his teeth flashing white in a humourless smile. 'I've never thought of Tom as being sensitive.'

'He did a lot of good for Rotumea and its people.'

'He could afford it, and he enjoyed his holidays there.'

Jo frowned at his dismissive tone. 'Didn't you like him?'

'He was a good stepfather,' he said evenly. 'Strict but very fair. He did his best for me, just as I'm sure he did his best for the islanders—for anyone who worked for him, in fact.'

He sounded as though he was discussing a schoolmaster, she thought and wondered again. Had the struggle for control after Tom's stroke soured their relationship too strongly for any repair?

At the venue they were ushered into a room filled with women in designer gowns and men in austere black and white. No one stared—or if they did, Jo thought, they made sure neither she nor Luc noticed. Yet she felt out of place and acutely self-conscious, especially when an exquisite woman swayed up to them, her smile a little set, her gaze softly shielded.

'Luc,' she breathed, and reached up to kiss him with all the aplomb of someone who knew she wouldn't be refused.

A fierce sense of denial ripped through Jo when Luc inclined his head so the woman's mouth grazed his cheek. She forced her stiff body to relax. Even that one syllable revealed who the woman was—the Ms Kidd of the phone call.

He straightened and said, 'Natasha, you haven't yet met Jo Forman, who's staying with me.'

He introduced them, adding, 'Natasha is the star of a very popular television show.' And with a smile at the other woman, he explained, 'Joanna has spent several years overseas, so she doesn't yet know anything about local television.'

What to say? Jo fell back on a platitude. 'Congratulations. I'll look forward to seeing it.'

In return, she got a practised smile and a look that was keenly suspicious. 'Thank you,' Natasha Kidd said sweetly. 'I hope you enjoy it.' She glanced up at Luc. 'I must go back to my friends, but I'd love to have a chance to chat later. So nice to meet you, Joanna.'

Her discomfort increased by a steely glance from Luc, Jo hoped her smile appeared genuine and unfeigned.

Everyone there seemed to know Luc; as waiters circulated with champagne and delicious nibbles a stream of people came up, and she was subjected to surveys that varied from veiled to avid. Like zookeepers viewing a rare animal for the first time, she thought, her sense of humour rescuing her.

Meticulously, Luc introduced them, mentioning that she owned her own skincare company.

Clever Luc. The topic interested everyone, and her feeling of dislocation began to ease.

Finally, some invisible signal indicated it was time to move. Luc took her arm, smiled down at her and said, 'Well done.'

'Thank you.' She hoped her smile showed no hint of challenge. 'What a lot of friends you have.'

His brows lifted. 'Not that many,' he told her. 'How many people do you call friends?'

And when she went to answer, he said coolly, 'Not acquaintances, or even people you like—but real friends? The sort you can ring at midnight and even if they're in bed with their latest lover they'll forgive you.'

Startled, Jo looked up, saw a glimmer of humour in the grey eyes and had to smile. 'None,' she said, dead-pan.

His smile set her heart singing. 'So what do you call a true friend?' he asked. 'Someone you can trust implicitly?'

'One who'll listen for an hour to me complaining when a new formula brings me out in a rash,' she said smartly.

His brows shot up. 'Has that happened?'

'Once. Turns out I'm allergic to one of the ingredients.' Jo totted up her friends, admitting, 'Actually, I can only think of three who'd listen for any more than twenty minutes. So I guess that gives me three good friends.'

'You're lucky,' he observed.

She stared at him. 'Yes, I suppose I am,' she said slowly. 'How about you?'

'One,' he said laconically.

Jo wasn't surprised. He didn't seem a man who'd give his trust easily, and a life spent in the cut-throat world of big business would have honed his formidable self-sufficiency.

Looking across the banqueting room, she caught Natasha Kidd's rapidly averted gaze and stifled an odd sense of foreboding. Was she Luc's lover?

Not yet, Jo thought, recollecting the hunger beneath the other woman's lashes as she'd looked up at him. But possibly she had hopes, and saw Jo as an obstacle.

Jo wished she could tell her that any relationship she had with Luc was safe. But it was none of her business, and she had no right to interfere.

The evening was well run, the food magnificent, and in spite of Luc's reservations the beautiful comedienne proved both extremely funny and very clever. Their table companions were interesting and kept their curiosity within bearable limits. Again Luc mentioned her business, and to her delight one woman extolled the worth of her products.

And the amount donated to the charity exceeded expectations enough to cause excitement and applause.

A very glamorous evening, Jo thought when it was over. So why was she glad to be leaving?

She thrust the thought from her mind to concentrate on smiling and nodding as they moved through the crowd. Luc moderated his long strides and exchanged the odd word with various acquaintances, but made sure he didn't stop.

Natasha Kidd was nowhere in evidence, thank heavens.

Outside it was raining, harbinger of a tropical depression that had the north of New Zealand in its sights. Staring straight ahead as they drove across the Harbour Bridge, Jo thought how alarmingly intimate it was to be cocooned in warmth and dryness with Luc when outside the lights dazzled and flared in the rain.

'Tired?'

She shook her head. 'Not at all.'

'Did you enjoy yourself?' A note in his voice made her cautious.

After a moment's thought, she said, 'It was very interesting.'

His laugh startled her. 'I've seldom heard less enthusiastic praise.'

She shrugged. 'I didn't know anyone there except you, but everyone was pleasant, the dresses were stunning and the food was delicious. Didn't you enjoy yourself?'

'Mostly,' he said, almost as though startled by his admission.

Jo couldn't help wondering why.

But that thought went out of her head completely when she checked her email after she'd showered and got ready for bed. One from Meru in Rotumea made her heart jolt.

I'll contact you at ten tomorrow morning on the video—it's important.

CHAPTER SEVEN

Jo STARED INTO the darkness, listening to rain that became heavier as the night wore on. Shards of confused dreams buzzed through her head—surely caused by Meru's ominous message, but somehow dominated by Luc's imposing presence. He'd just kissed her again…

No! She forced her wayward brain away from the memories. Worrying about Meru's message would play infinitely less havoc with her emotions than reliving those fevered moments. Even dreams of Luc's kisses had the power to set her pulse soaring.

Meru didn't flap easily, so whatever she had to discuss was not going to be good news.

The night seemed to drag on for ever, but eventually she fell asleep and dreamed again, waking to a dull light glimmering through the curtains. Rain beat against the windows, driven by a gale off the sea. Hastily she leapt out, but of course it was too early—Meru would still be in bed.

Still, there was work she could be doing. She opened the link on the computer, biting her lip as she waited for it to come through.

Nothing happened.

Angrily she stabbed at the keys, until a peal of thunder made her close down the computer and hastily switch off the power, grimacing in resignation. This tropical depression probably reached all the way from New Zealand to Rotumea, so it was more than likely there'd be no power on the island. So the communications system would be down.

Sighing, she accepted she'd have to possess her soul in patience, as her aunt would have said. Shower first, she decided, and then try again to see if Meru could get through.

But she'd only got halfway across the room when a noise erupted into the drumming of the rain—a violent crack that made Jo jump, and then a loud sighing crash.

'What—?' she gasped, swivelling towards the window.

She'd just pushed back the curtains when a knock on the door reminded her she was still in her nightgown, an elderly shift that finished at mid-thigh and was too transparent to be decent.

'Wait—I won't be a moment,' she called, and grabbed her dressing gown, also of faded cotton, though marginally less see-through than her gown.

She opened the door a fraction, her heart flipping when she saw Luc. 'What is it?' she asked.

Another bolt of lightning lit up Luc's unshaven face, followed by thunder rolling across the heavens.

'What happened?' she demanded.

'It sounds as though a tree's come down,' Luc said grimly, and strode into the room as the lights snapped off.

Together they peered out into the grey murk.

'Over there.' He pointed. 'On the beach front.'

Jo craned her head. Yesterday a large conifer had blocked the view of the outer harbour, but now she saw tossing, roiling waves as they pounded onto the shore.

'The Norfolk Island pine,' Luc said curtly. 'I'll collect Sanders and we'll make sure no one was walking past when it got struck.'

'I'll come with you.' She turned away, but Luc caught her arm.

As though on cue, lightning flashed again, and thunder rumbled like a distant cannon. Jo froze and for a moment the sound of the storm faded into nothingness against the reckless drumming of her heart.

Something kindled in Luc's hard eyes, but he dropped his hand and said harshly, 'You'd better get dressed.'

'All right.' Colour burned up from her breasts, and she took a step towards the wardrobe.

He went on, 'But stay inside. There's no need for you to get wet.' And you'd only be in the way, his tone implied.

Jo bristled, then managed to calm down. He knew this place; she didn't. More moderately she said, 'All right. But if I can help, let me know.'

'I will.'

He left then and she fled to the dressing room, closing the door behind her with a bang that echoed the drumming of her heart—only to have to open it again as she realised that without power she couldn't see.

How did Luc have that effect on her? Even with the door open the window provided hardly enough light to dress by, but she stripped off her night-clothes and dressing gown and hauled on a T-shirt and trousers, resenting that now familiar, wilful excitement that ached through her like an addictive drug.

The scream of a chainsaw cut through the keening of the storm, bringing her back to the window. Red lights were flashing from the road; someone had turned on a car's hazard lights as a warning.

They were soon joined by other lights as emergency services arrived, but the trees on the boundary prevented her from seeing what was happening, and the persistent, inexorable rain kept her inside, pacing restlessly around her room and trying hard to think of anything other than Meru's email.

Half an hour after the power had been restored she still couldn't contact Rotumea. She had to content herself with sending an email making another time for a video conference with her manager, before going downstairs.

Sanders appeared silently and sketched a small smile. 'Good morning. Breakfast is ready if you are. Mr MacAllister asked me to tell you not to wait for him.'

She was drinking coffee when Luc's voice brought her to her feet. After a moment's hesitation Jo went out of the room, stopping when she saw Sanders coming along the hall.

'I thought I heard Luc,' she said.

He allowed himself a small smile. 'Mr MacAllister is in the mudroom getting out of his wet-weather gear.' He indicated a hallway. 'Second door on the right.'

Mudroom? After a second's hesitation, Jo headed for the second door. Luc was shrugging out of a waterproof jacket, his hair darkened and glossy against his head, his features somehow made more pronounced by the shadow of his beard.

He looked up as she came in and his eyes narrowed. 'What's the matter?'

'Nothing,' she said automatically, wondering if her restlessness was painted in large letters on her face.

She held out her hand and took the wet coat from him.
'I can't get through to Rotumea. How is it outside?'

'Give me that.' He whipped the coat from her and
turned to hang it up, giving her an excellent view of
broad shoulders dampened by rain.

The room suddenly seemed far too small and she
wished she hadn't come. Why had she?

Because she wanted to make sure he was all right.

How stupid was that!

Hastily she said, 'I wondered if the tree had fallen
near any houses.'

'It missed the nearest place by a few feet, although
it gave everyone there a hell of a fright. They were
lucky. We've cleared enough off the road for traffic to
get through now.'

'That's good,' she said, hoping her expression was
as cool as his.

He frowned. 'You look a bit wan. Did the rain keep
you awake?'

'No,' she said too abruptly.

'Then what did?' He reached out to trace the skin
beneath her eyes with a fingertip. 'These dark circles
weren't caused by *nothing.*'

He hadn't moved any closer, but his touch set an
exquisite anticipation singing through her. Her breath
locked in her throat and she couldn't move, couldn't
think of anything other than Luc's dark face, intent and
purposeful as he scrutinised her.

She swallowed and managed to produce something
she hoped sounded like her usual voice. 'I just had a
restless night.'

'So did I,' he said, his voice suddenly harsh. 'I wonder if it's for the same reason.'

Jo squelched a nervous urge to lick her lips. 'Who

knows?' she said, and managed to summon enough motivation to move back a step. 'You'd better have a shower before you start to get cold.'

His mouth quirked upwards. 'See you later, then.'

Stiff-shouldered, Jo walked away, hoping he didn't realise just how strongly his male charisma affected her.

But how could he not? Luc was experienced; Tom had told her once that he'd been a target for women ever since he'd arrived at puberty.

Everything about him proclaimed a man who accepted the elemental power of his masculinity, just as he accepted his brilliant brain and formidable character. He deserved more than to be a target—a horrible term. It made her feel ashamed of being a woman. He deserved a wife who'd love him.

Where had that thought come from?

Jo shook her head impatiently. She was being idiotic. Luc MacAllister would do exactly what he wanted when it came to choosing a woman to marry. She had her own pressing concerns to deal with right now. Crossing her fingers, she took refuge in her room.

And heaved a huge sigh of relief when at last Meru's face appeared on the screen before her—a relief that rapidly dissolved after one look told her to brace herself.

'What's wrong?' she blurted.

Without preamble Meru said, 'I heard something from my cousin yesterday that is…a problem. You know my cousin Para'iki?'

'Yes, of course.' He was a chief. Jo's stomach tightened in anticipation of a blow.

'Jo, the Council have received an offer for the plant essence—with much more money than we are paying.'

'Did he say how much—and who was it from?'

Frowning, Meru said, 'I don't know how much, but

more—he said a lot more. As for who—' She gave the name of a worldwide cosmetic and skincare concern owned by a huge corporate entity.

'Why them?' Jo said shakily. 'They cater to the midstream market, not to ours. Why do they want the essence? It's scarce and it's expensive…'

'I don't know, but it seems to me that if they are now deciding to expand into the upper bracket of the market, this would be a good way to do it.'

'Yes, of course.' Jo let out a long breath. 'Does Para'iki have any idea how the other chiefs feel about this?'

Meru sighed. 'Nobody will know until they have finished discussing it, and that could—*will*—take weeks,' she said dolefully. 'It is not a thing to be decided without much thought and care—you know that.'

No, the decision wouldn't be made lightly. The chiefs had to take a lot more into consideration than their verbal agreement with her. They had to plan for the future of Rotumea and its people.

Meru said worriedly, 'My cousin said to tell only you and to ask that you tell no one else until the decision is made.'

Jo swallowed. 'Of course I won't.'

The older woman said, 'He also said that Tom signed a paper with them when you were setting up the business; do you know what that was?'

Startled, Jo asked, 'A paper? Do you mean a legal document?'

'I think it must have been, or perhaps not—they would need nothing legal from Tom, his word was enough. But my cousin thought it would do no harm to remind the Council what Tom had promised…'

Tom had spoken for her during the negotiation process, but as far as Jo knew that was all he'd done. Her bewilderment growing, she said, 'I don't know anything—haven't heard anything—about a document. Tom certainly didn't mention it.'

'But perhaps you should look for one.' Meru sounded troubled. 'He was very respected, Jo. It is probably not important, but it might be.'

'I will.' Although it was foolish to hope that somehow there might be something that would save the day. Tom's papers had gone to the solicitor, who'd surely have let her know if anything concerned her, but she'd check. Just in case...

She produced a smile. 'Meru, thanks so much for letting me know. Please thank your cousin for me too. And remember—whatever happens, you and everyone on Rotumea will be fine.'

'Yes, but what about you?'

'I'll manage,' Jo said as confidently as she could. 'Don't worry about me.'

But when she'd closed the link she sat with her eyes closed while thoughts tumbled through her brain, each one heavier with foreboding than the last.

Only for a moment, however. After a ragged breath she stood, exhaled and took in a painful breath, then straightened her shoulders. Worrying wasn't going to help. First she needed to concentrate on keeping the business going. And then she should make plans in case the chiefs decided against her.

And once she got back to Rotumea she'd look for that document, if it existed, even though she couldn't see how anything Tom had signed or written could possibly make a difference.

Logically, a huge corporation could offer a much better deal than she had, even if she used all of Tom's legacy when it was finally hers. He'd warned her that relying on a verbal agreement was dangerous, although he'd acknowledged that on Rotumea it was common practice. Had that mysterious piece of paper been some sort of safeguard?

As soon as she got back to Rotumea she'd look for this document—if it existed.

But oh, it would be heartbreaking to give up the business she'd created and worked so hard for.

A sharp knock snapped her head around. Pinning a smile to her lips, she walked across and opened her door.

Luc's intent gaze searched her face. With an authority that sparked instant resistance in Jo, he demanded, 'What's worrying you?'

She lifted her chin. 'It's got nothing to do with you.'

His brows climbed. 'I'm taking that as a refusal to discuss the matter.'

And not liking it, judging by his tone. Had no one ever refused him before?

Jo clamped her lips on the smart answer that sprang to mind. It would be stupid—downright foolhardy— to add to the mixture of emotions and sensations he aroused in her.

As calmly as she could, she told him, 'It's just something I have to deal with.'

'Does it concern the young cub who made an idiot of himself over you on Rotumea?' His voice didn't alter, but his eyes were hooded.

For a moment she didn't realise who he was talking about. Sean had receded into a distant past. Memory jolted into action, she said shortly, 'No, it has absolutely nothing to do with him. It's not personal.'

And parried another piercing scrutiny until, apparently satisfied, Luc nodded. 'Your business, then.' And before she could answer, he finished, 'All right. There's obviously a problem, so if you want to talk it over, I'm available.'

'Thank you.' Luc's disconcerting way of swinging from autocratic command to something approaching support unsettled her.

And warmed her dangerously.

Possibly after six months she'd be used to it. An odd pang of regret hit her. If only they'd met as strangers, without his preconceptions of her relationship to Tom affecting his attitude...

Stupid, stupid, *stupid*! If it weren't for Tom they'd never have met at all—in normal life they moved in circles so distant they might as well live in different galaxies.

But she wished Tom had told her more about his stepson. Understanding Luc would have helped her, given her some guidelines on how to deal with the situation, instead of groping blindly, fighting against an attraction that was doomed to frustration.

Luc said, 'What are you thinking?'

How was he able to read her mind? Shaken, she said hastily, 'This whole business—you, me, enforced togetherness—is weird. Even though I know it's useless, I can't help wondering why Tom insisted on it.'

Luc bit back a short answer and said more temperately, 'It's quite simple. All his life Tom succeeded at doing exactly what he wanted, and I expect he couldn't resist extending his influence after his death.'

And watched with a sardonic amusement as her head came up and that firm chin angled in challenge.

'Whenever we talk about him we seem to be speaking of two different people,' she said, her gaze steady.

The way she idolised his stepfather was beginning to rub some unsuspected sensitivity in him to the edge of rawness. Luc resisted the urge to tell her to grow up, to accept that men behaved differently to the women who shared their bed.

Especially if they were young and lovely...

Into his mind there danced the image of her that morning, with her magnificent mane of hair tousled around her face above shabby night-clothes. He'd like to see her in satin, or something silken that clung lovingly to her breasts and revealed her long, elegant legs. His breath quickened as he imagined running his hands through that hair, turning her face up to his...

Clamping down on a savagely primal response, he said, 'You're twenty-three, aren't you?'

She lifted startled eyes to meet his. 'Yes. What has that to do with anything?'

'It's old enough, I'd have thought, to realise that people present a different face to every person.'

Jo thought about that for a moment, before returning sweetly, 'That's a huge generalisation, and do you have the research to back it up?'

Taken by surprise, he laughed. 'Spoken like a true scientist. No, but if it's been done I'll find it. I'm giving you the benefit of my experience.'

'Very cynical experience,' she shot back, daring him with another swift tilt of her chin.

Luc could see why Tom had been intrigued by her—apart from the physical allure of young curves and burnished skin, of course. She'd have been a challenge, and Tom enjoyed challenges.

As did he.

'I don't consider myself a cynic,' he said coolly. 'I've

learnt to be careful in relationships, but that happens to most of us, I imagine.'

Shrugging away the memory of a previous lover, paid to rave to a magazine about his prowess in bed, he said, 'Once most people get past adolescence they guard against flinging themselves into relationships without first making sure both parties understand the implications and expectations.'

She pulled a face. 'You make love sound like a business deal.'

'Love, no. It's marriage that's the business deal,' he said cynically.

She gave him a long, assessing stare. 'I bet you'd insist any future wife sign a pre-nuptial agreement.'

'Of course.' Too many promising entrepreneurs—including several mentored by Tom—had been burned by reckless marriages that ended in acrimony, forced to sell up to provide a former spouse with unearned income for the rest of her life.

He awaited her answer with anticipation.

'Actually, I think I probably would too.' She smiled. 'Although I've never considered it before, it does seem a sensible precaution.'

In any other woman in her situation he'd appreciate and understand such pragmatism. For some reason, in Jo it irritated him. For a moment he surprised himself by wondering what she'd be like in the throes of a heartfelt love, prepared to offer herself without thought of profit.

Cold, hard reality told him it would never happen. He doubted that such unconditional love existed. Even if it did, any woman who'd taken a man forty years older as a lover, bartering her body for the prospect of gain, was far too cold-blooded to allow herself to fall wildly in love. Joanna had made a very good show of shock when she'd discovered how much she'd inherited, but her chagrin at the condition in Tom's will revealed her true emotions. She'd expected the money to be hers immediately, to spend as she wished.

He owed it to Tom to make sure she learned how to take care of her inheritance, but once the six months was up she'd be able to do what she liked with it.

Yet somehow he couldn't see her squandering it.

Of course, plenty of courtesans had been excellent businesswomen...

He said coolly, 'Anyone who doesn't insist on a pre-nup is an idiot.'

With a look from beneath her lashes—a look she probably practised in front of her mirror—she said, 'I'll keep that in mind.'

No doubt of that, Luc thought caustically. He said, 'I'll be out for the rest of the day. What are your plans?'

'If this rain eases I'm going to spend the afternoon with a friend in Devonport,' she told him. 'You've seen her—I was with Lindy and her husband the night we... ah...met.'

He nodded. 'Do you have a current New Zealand driver's license?'

'Yes. But Lindy's coming to pick me up.'

He nodded. 'OK, then. I'll see you tonight.'

The rain did ease, although it didn't stop while Jo spent the day catching up with her friend in the small flat Lindy and her new husband were renting.

'Until we can save the deposit on a house,' Lindy said cheerfully. She grinned at Jo. 'Not everyone has your luck! Fancy living with a tycoon in a huge, flash mansion on the prettiest and most private beach on the North Shore. What's he like?'

Jo didn't need to think. 'Formidable.'

'Full of himself? Arrogant? Intimidating?'

'Not arrogant, and I haven't seen any signs of conceit.' She allowed herself a small smile before adding wryly, 'But very, *very* intimidating.'

'And gorgeous,' her friend supplied with a grin. 'Are you going to try your luck with him?'

'Do I look like an idiot?' Jo demanded, hoping her tone hid the embarrassment that heated her skin.

'No, but you're blushing.' Lindy laughed. 'Go on, admit you fancy him something rotten.'

'He's not my type,' Jo told her, picking up her teacup and hiding behind it.

'What's that got to do with anything?' Lindy asked. 'I never thought Kyle was your type either—he was too selfish—but you fell for him.'

'And look where that got me,' Jo said grimly.

Lindy knew of Kyle's betrayal. 'He was a louse,' she agreed. 'Charming and witty and great fun, and selfish to the core. I bet he wanted you to put your mother in a home.'

Jo bit her lip. 'Yes,' she said tonelessly.

'And when you wouldn't he slept with Faith Holden to punish you. I know you were shattered when he walked out, but I'm sure you realise now you're well out of it.'

'Of course I do.' Jo set her cup down. 'But Luc MacAllister is nothing like Kyle—and we don't have that sort of relationship anyway.'

'He was watching you that night at the resort on Rotumea,' Lindy persisted. 'And you were very conscious of him too.'

'He knew who I was, of course. I suppose he was

checking me out.' She grinned. 'Though if he was watching anyone, it was you. You looked fantastic.'

'Honeymoons do that for you.' Lindy's infectious laugh rang out. 'You should try one some time. Seriously, you haven't let Kyle put you off men completely, have you?'

'Of course not,' Jo said firmly, ignoring the apprehension that contracted her stomach muscles. 'But right now I'm having too much fun with my business to spare the time for any sort of relationship, especially one as big as marriage.'

'Well, enjoy your stay with Mr Gorgeous Tycoon. And don't try to fool me into thinking you're not just the teeniest bit lusting after him, because I won't believe you.'

'I'm not into wasting my time,' Jo said a little shortly. 'He's had a couple of serious affairs—one with that stunningly beautiful model Annunciata Someone, and the other was with the almost as stunning Mary Heard, who writes those brilliant thrillers. Clearly he likes beauties in his bed, and I know my limitations.'

'You might not be model-beautiful, but you've got style,' Lindy said loyally. 'Anyway, I'm not suggesting you fall in love with the man—that would really be asking for trouble.'

Jo looked at her with affection. 'Exactly,' she said. 'Don't worry about me—I'm not planning to do anything at all for six months but cope with Luc MacAllister as best I can, and run my business.'

'OK, but you're selling yourself short. Even if you don't want to fall in love with the man, I bet he's fantastic in bed.' She fanned her cheek with one hand and laughed at Jo's startled face. 'Don't look so shocked—marriage hasn't stopped me appreciating an alpha male!'

What startled Jo was the jealousy that ripped through her—a fierce, quite unwarranted possessiveness she'd never experienced before.

Lindy sighed. 'Funny how a woman just knows, isn't it? Some men just kind of reek of sex appeal, and they don't even have to be handsome—although it helps if they look as good as your tycoon. I wonder what clues us into it?'

'I don't know, and I'm not going there,' Jo said cheerfully. She glanced at her watch and said, 'I'd better go, Lindy.'

'Oh, stay for dinner. We can run you home afterwards, and it would be so nice to have dinner with you.'

Jo hesitated. 'I don't have a key,' she said, 'so I'd have to be back at a reasonable hour.'

'That's not a problem. We're early birds. My beloved gets up at some ungodly hour in the morning to run umpteen kilometres before breakfast. Should you let someone know?'

Sanders took the news with his usual taciturnity, and they organised for her to be home by ten. Smiling, she told Lindy, 'He sounded just like my mother used to.'

Lindy said with awe, 'Your Luc has a *manservant*?'

'He's not mine! And it's Tom's house—*was* Tom's house—so I guess Sanders was Tom's employee.'

'Good heavens... Is he a kind of valet?'

'I don't think so—more a general factotum and cook, which he does extremely well. The whole set-up is way out of our league, Lindy.'

Just before ten that night Sanders opened the door to her and said, 'Good evening.'

Jo acknowledged him and turned to wave Lindy and her husband goodbye. 'Thank you, Sanders. I wonder when this rain is going to stop.'

'Not for another couple of days, according to the weather forecast.' Sanders ushered her inside. 'It's a very slow-moving tropical depression. They're forecasting floods in the upper North Island tomorrow.'

He paused, then said, 'Mr MacAllister isn't at home yet. He rang to say he'd be late. Is there anything I can get you?'

'No, thanks,' she said, stifling a suspicious regret.

Up in her room she showered and got into her nightclothes, then sat down at the computer. Nothing from Rotumea... Sighing with frustration, she closed the computer down.

Not that she expected any news so soon, but it irked her to be away at this delicate time. She had no doubt Meru and Savisi would be lobbying tactfully for her, but she really needed to be there herself.

Tom, you really made a mess of this, she thought dismally, getting up to wander across to the window. Of course he couldn't have foreseen this particular situation, but the offer to the chiefs had come at the very worst moment.

Conservative to a man, the members of the Council would be more likely to listen to their relatives who worked for her, but even so... She should be there, planning strategy.

The conversation with Meru echoed through her mind. Papers...

Some small door in her brain popped open. 'Of course!' she breathed, closing the curtains and turning back to the room.

If Tom had hidden papers she knew where they'd be—in the old Chinese chest where he kept his precious whisky.

He'd shown her the secret panel once, laughing when she'd expressed dismay that it was empty.

Perhaps there was now something in it...

She wasn't going to sleep tonight. The hours stretched ahead of her, filling her with tormenting fears that drove her downstairs to a bookcase in what Luc called the morning room.

It contained an eclectic selection of books ranging from bestsellers to local histories, one of which she chose. Clutching it, she tiptoed back up the stairs and had just opened her bedroom door when she heard a sound behind her.

Every sense springing into full alert, she stopped and swivelled around. Luc was a few paces behind her, saturnine in his black and white evening clothes. He looked...magnificent.

And vaguely menacing. Feeling oddly foolish, she swallowed and scanned his unreadable expression, heat flooding her skin. 'Oh. Hello. I went down for a book.'

'And have you found what you were looking for?' he enquired coolly.

CHAPTER EIGHT

LUC'S VOICE WAS deeper than normal, the words almost guttural. His gaze, narrowed and darkening in the semi-gloom of the hall, never left Jo's face. She saw heat in the depths of his eyes, and something else—a keenness her body reacted to with a sharp, frightening hunger.

Run! Every nerve and muscle tensed at the instinctive warning. Like a shield, she held up the book so that he could see it. 'Yes, thank you,' she said too rapidly, clumsily half-turning in an attempt to escape his penetrating scrutiny.

Her heart was hammering so loudly she was sure Luc could hear it, and a delicious, tempting weakness dazzled her mind.

Run—run while you can...

Yet her body resisted the command from her brain, refusing to obey even when Luc reached out to rest the tip of one long finger on the traitorous pulse at the base of her throat.

Eyes holding hers, he asked in that roughened voice, 'Are you afraid?'

Without volition, Jo shook her head. 'Of you?' Her voice was husky and low. 'No.'

'Good.'

If she'd heard nothing more than satisfaction in the

single word she might have found the self-possession to pull away. But it seemed torn from his throat, raw with desire, as though he too had fought this since their gazes had clashed in the sultry, scented warmth of a tropical night.

It's too soon, the nagging voice of caution insisted. For once, Jo wasn't listening—didn't want to hear. Her whole being was concentrated on the subtle caress of Luc's finger while it slid from the pulse in her throat down to the first button of her loose shift.

Her breath came faster, keeping time with her heart, with her racing blood, with the emotions and sensations that surged through her, catapulting her into a place she'd never been before.

She craved Luc with a hunger powerful enough to wash away everything but that blazing need. And this time she didn't try to fool herself, as she had with Kyle. This wasn't love. She expected nothing more from Luc than fulfilment of desire, the unchaining of the passion—intoxicating, compelling and intense—that had been smouldering inside her.

He was experienced enough to discern the need flashing through her. In a rigidly controlled voice he asked, 'Joanna, is this what you want?'

For a second, a heartbeat, she wavered.

Until he bent his head and kissed the smooth skin his hand had revealed, his mouth a brand against her sensitive flesh, his subtle, fresh male scent overwhelming her feeble defences.

'Joanna?'

His lips against her skin were exquisite, shocking. Her breasts lifted when she dragged in a breath and muttered, 'Yes.'

He gave a smothered groan and lifted his head and

kissed her mouth, and she surrendered. Luc kissed her as though he was dying for her, as though she had been lost to him and was now found again—as though he had longed for her during too many hopeless years...

And she kissed him back, glorying in his hunger, in the powerful force of his body, in the sensual magic they made together.

And then Luc lifted his head and demanded, 'Are you protected?'

Stunned, she stared at him, saw his eyes harden, and he said curtly, 'Tell me.'

Jo bit back a wild urge to lie. 'No. No, I'm not.'

He said something beneath his breath, something she heartily agreed with, and let her go.

'I don't have anything either,' he said.

Shivering, she stood still while the rain poured down outside, the sound of tears, of pain and loneliness. Her fierce physical frustration gave way to bleak humiliation.

It took every ounce of courage she possessed to mutter, 'I'll go, then,' and turn blindly towards the door.

'Joanna—'

She shook her head. 'No, leave it at that,' she said, fumbling for the handle. It wouldn't open and she flinched when his hand covered hers and twisted the opposite way.

For a few seconds his warmth enfolded her, his grip tightening as though he didn't want to release her, and then the door gave way and he stepped back.

Shaking inwardly, she shot through the door and turned to close it, forcing herself to look up as she searched for words to say that might break the tension. None came.

In the darkness he seemed even taller, looming like some image from a dream.

'It's all right,' he said, each word level and cold. 'I can control my baser urges, if that's what you're afraid of.'

Her chin came up. 'I'm not.' She refused to admit even to herself that she wished—oh, for just a second— that Luc MacAllister wasn't always in control.

With a sting in her voice, she said, 'And I thought calling desire a base urge had departed with the Victorians. Goodnight, Luc.'

The door closed firmly, its small click barely audible above the renewed thudding of the rain.

Luc turned and headed for his own room, cursing his unruly body.

And his stupidity in not making sure he'd been prepared. He knew why; he'd been confident of his immunity. The fact that Jo had been his stepfather's mistress should have quenched his dangerous, unwelcome hunger.

But when he'd held her, kissed her, all he'd thought of was taking her, of making slow, deliberate love to her until she forgot every man she'd ever had before him, until she was lost in her own need.

For him.

Had she been faking it? He strode into his bedroom and switched on the light, his expression set and hard. He didn't think so—and in his youth he'd gained enough experience of the wiles of women to judge whether their passion was real or assumed.

Desire could be faked, but that delicate shudder he'd felt beneath his hand, the heat of her exquisite skin on his palm, the rapid throbbing of the pulse in her throat, the widening of her eyes as she'd looked up at him—all spoke of real hunger.

So, she wanted him.

Making love to her would have rid him of this itch, because that was all it was—nothing personal, merely a primitive heat in the blood. Calling it anything else would be giving it an importance it didn't possess.

But they had to spend six months together. Making love to Joanna would be stupid for so many reasons...

He walked across to the windows and looked out at the rain. He'd like to be somewhere wild right now, watching waves crash against cliffs.

The memory of Joanna's face as she'd closed the door against him played across his mind. Seductive lips, made a little more sensuous by his kiss, the smoky depths of her eyes half-hidden by long lashes, the faint, elusive fragrance of her warm satin skin...

His body hardened, his hunger so powerful he had to lock every muscle to stop himself from swivelling and walking back to her room. His hands folded into fists at his sides.

Control of his life had been wrenched from him. The months ahead loomed like a term of imprisonment or a journey into forbidden territory.

Tom, you bastard, just why the hell did you set this up? What was going through your devious mind when you designed that will?

When Jo woke the rain had stopped. She blinked at the brilliance that glowed through the curtains, colour burning through her skin as memories swarmed back—of Luc holding her against his powerful, aroused body... and the erotic dreams her untrammelled mind had conjured during her sleep.

She wanted Luc with something like desperation. It was all very well to realise that going to bed with him would have been the most stupid, reckless, dangerous thing she could have done.

Her body didn't agree.

Driven by restlessness, she got up and pulled back the curtains, trying to be grateful for the iron control that had put an end to their lovemaking.

Respect wasn't something she'd expected from Luc, but it seemed he respected her decision that the game wasn't worth the candle.

And in turn she owed him respect for his instant acceptance.

With Kyle it had been different—he'd been eager for sex almost immediately, calling her an ice maiden when she'd refused. He'd insisted that he'd make sure nothing happened. She'd been steadfast, and later he'd laughed about it, telling her his words had been angry because he'd loved her so much, and her refusal had seemed cold and unfeeling...

Like an idiot she'd believed him. She should have guessed then that for Kyle his own needs came first.

She stared down at the glinting, dancing water in the big pool. Working with figures was her least favourite part of being a businesswoman, but she needed that discipline right now. Not only would it drive away the memories that fogged her brain with delicious thoughts of Luc's passion, it would force her to concentrate on what was really important.

But before she started on the accounts she'd ring Lindy, get the name of her doctor and see if she could wangle an appointment.

For a moment she wavered. Wouldn't getting protection make her more vulnerable to the hunger prowling through her?

What if somehow she found herself in Luc's arms again—surely it would be easier to keep her head if she was faced with the prospect of pregnancy?

Not going to happen, she thought stoutly as she pulled on her bikini and wrapped a sarong around her. Now that she knew how susceptible she was to Luc she'd be forewarned. Getting protection would simply be a sensible precaution—one both her mother and her aunt had insisted was the mark of a responsible woman.

Ignoring a treacherous flutter in the pit of her stomach, she picked up a towel and a change of clothes. Something told her that the silent Sanders would not approve of wet people wandering through the house, so there was bound to be a cabana or pool-room—whatever they called such an amenity.

There was. Sanders himself showed her how to get there. And very luxurious it was too—as immaculate as the rest of the house. Nothing like the house on Rotumea, she thought, aching with sudden grief. This place had been decorated by someone with exquisite taste. The house on Rotumea hadn't been decorated at all— Tom had just bought what he liked.

Dismay gripped her when she realised Luc had beaten her to the pool, tanned arms cutting incisively through the water, wet hair slicked into darkness. When he saw her he stood up.

Jo swallowed. He was too much—all sleek, burnished skin with the long, powerful muscles of an athlete. Hastily she said, 'Oh, hi. Great minds and all that...'

His expression was unreadable. 'I'll be out in a moment,' he said, almost as though conveying a favour.

'No need. I don't take up much room.'

He raised his brows but said nothing before diving back under.

Possibly exorcising the same demon she'd been wrestling with all night—a physical frustration so intense it burned. Jo dived in neatly and began to swim lengths too, determined to ignore the image of broad, water-slicked shoulders and chest—and the tormenting memories of how secure she'd felt in his arms...

She swam with steady strokes, forcing herself to focus on counting laps, hugely relieved when Luc hauled himself out.

The sun beat down with gathering heat, but she kept swimming until Luc called from the side, 'Breakfast.'

'Coming.' She finished the length before climbing out.

Even in a short-sleeved shirt and light trousers, he looked tall and powerful, very much in command.

Made uneasy by his unsmiling regard, she walked briskly towards him.

'It's all right,' he said curtly. 'I'm not going to leap on you.'

'I know that,' she retorted, embarrassed by a stupid blush.

'You're not acting as though you believe it.'

To which she had no answer. 'I'll get dressed and be out shortly,' she told him and forced herself to walk at a slightly slower pace past him.

Her shower was the swiftest on record, although her fingers were clumsy as she pulled on her pareu and combed her hair back from her face, wishing it didn't curl so obstinately. The pareu clung to her damp skin, revealing bare shoulders and every curve of her body. Under Luc's hooded scrutiny, clothes that were normal everyday wear on Rotumea—her bikini, the pareu—somehow seemed to constitute an overt attempt at seduction.

She bared her teeth at her reflection, braced herself and went out, her head held high. Luc was standing in the shade of the jasmine sprawling across the pergola, talking into a cellphone, his brows drawn together.

He looked up and something flashed into his eyes, a flaring recognition of what had passed between them the previous night. Her skin tightened.

This was not a good idea…

He said something sharp and conclusive into the phone, snapped it shut and strode towards her.

'You'll be cold,' he said. 'I keep forgetting you've spent years in the tropics.'

'Not that many. This is fine, but I'll sit in the sun instead of the shade.'

He nodded. 'I'll pull out the table.'

Before they sat down he asked, 'Are you wearing sunscreen?'

'Yes.' Skin like hers was very much at risk from New Zealand's unforgiving sunlight.

'So these freckles weren't caused by the sun?' He indicated her nose, where five pale gold dots lingered.

She stiffened, only relaxing when it was clear he wasn't going to touch her. 'They're relics from my childhood,' she told him. 'Even though my mother and aunt insisted I wear sunscreen all the time—and my aunt used to make me wear an island hat whenever I went outside in Rotumea—I still got freckles. These ones just don't want to go.'

'They're charming,' he said coolly. 'How do you manage to achieve that faint sheen, as though you're sprinkled with gold dust?'

Heat flamed in the pit of her stomach. Trying for a light rejoinder, she said, 'I've called my freckles lots of things, but never charming. As a kid I hated them. As for gold dust—it's a pretty allusion, but the colour's entirely natural.' Keeping her gaze steady with an effort of will, she returned his scrutiny. 'You're lucky. That built-in Mediterranean tan must be a huge help in resisting the sun.'

'It is,' he said casually. 'I don't rely on it entirely, however.'

All very civilised, she thought as she picked up a napkin, sedately unfolding it into her lap.

Watching them, hearing them no one would know that last night they'd kissed like famished lovers...

He said, 'I'm going to ask a favour of you.'

'What sort of favour?' she asked warily.

'An easy one for you to carry out, I hope. I'm asking for your discretion. I'd rather you didn't divulge anything of Tom's will or your relationship with him while we're staying together.'

Whatever she'd expected, it wasn't this. Frowning, she said, 'I'm not ashamed of anything I've done, if that's what you think. And I'm not going to lie about—'

'I'm not asking you to lie,' he interrupted austerely, 'but there's bound to be gossip.' He indicated the table with a sweep of his hand. 'Help yourself—or Sanders can cook breakfast for you if you want. And if you'd like coffee, I'll have some too.'

'No, thanks.' She helped herself to cereal and fruit and yoghurt, and poured the coffee.

Luc resumed, 'There's already been speculation about your place in his life. It will make things less stressful for everyone if you refuse to discuss your relationships with him or with me.'

He was clearly bent on damping down that speculation, but she felt obliged to point out, 'Usually a "No Comment" is taken as confirmation. If anyone is rude enough to ask, I'll tell them the truth—that my aunt was his housekeeper, and after she died I took over her position.'

His brows rose. Had he expected her to resist? She said, 'But how do we explain my presence with you?'

'We don't,' he said calmly. 'We fly back to Rotumea once I get this mess here cleaned up.' He looked at her narrowly. 'You did well the other night.'

'I'm not entirely sure in what way,' she said crisply, feeling sorry for whoever had created the mess he was dealing with.

He shrugged. 'It's called networking, and it's a necessary part of life when you're starting a business. Tom must have told you how important it can be.'

Sadly, she said, 'Yes. I wish he hadn't done this. It wasn't like him to leave things in such an ambiguous tangle.'

'He was always devious, but the stroke affected him.' Luc made no attempt to soften the blunt statement.

Reluctantly Jo nodded and drank a fortifying mouthful of coffee before saying, 'I need to be in Rotumea to run the business. It's very personal. Tom knows—knew—that. I'm sure he wouldn't have intended you to take me around like some…some extra piece of luggage!'

Luc leaned back in his chair and surveyed her. 'Tom was first and foremost an entrepreneur. He'd be thinking of the contacts you'd make.'

Exasperated, she demanded, 'And what contacts do you have in the world of skincare?'

'Very few, but I have a lot amongst those who use skincare. Witness those at the dinner that night.'

She looked up, and met a gaze that held cynical amusement. 'So that's why you mentioned my tiny business?'

'It's all part of the game,' Luc pointed out, not attempting to hide the cynical note in his voice. 'The demographic you're targeting has money. They frequent charity dinners, and by and large they're prepared to pay considerable sums for a good product.' His smile was brief, almost a taunt. 'I'm sure that anywhere I go you'll enjoy checking out spas and beauty shops and places like that.'

'If that was Tom's reasoning, he could have a point.' And because her voice shook a little, she asked, 'When do we go back to Rotumea?'

'I have probably three days' work here.'

Good—so she'd have a chance to get that prescription. 'Fine. I'll check out the day spa here that stocks and uses our product.'

'Will you be trying for more business?'

'Not in Auckland,' she said. 'In the demographic I'm targeting exclusivity is a big asset.'

'While you're here, do you have any relatives you want to contact?'

She shook her head. 'Not a one. How about you?'

His brows lifted. 'Several in France and Scotland—none here now Tom's gone. How did you manage to end up with so few?'

She shrugged. 'My mother and my aunt grew up in care. My father came from a very religious family—they didn't approve of Mum, and they certainly wouldn't have approved of her having his child out of wedlock. He was killed in a motorbike accident going to see her, and they blamed her. They never contacted her. I don't even know who they are.'

Brows knotted, he said in a hard voice, 'If that's the sort of people they are you're better off not knowing them.'

Jo was oddly touched by his sympathy. 'I don't miss them. And while we're here I'll put flowers on his grave.' With a challenging glance she finished, 'What about these Scottish and French relatives?'

And held her breath, wondering if he was going to tell her to mind her own business.

Instead he said evenly, 'My mother grew up in Provence in a half-ruined chateau. She had no siblings. She met and married my father—a Scottish gamekeeper—when she was visiting a school friend in the Highlands. It was a love match, but she couldn't cope with life there, and she returned to the chateau. I was born there. Five years later, after my father's death, she married Tom.'

He sounded like a policeman giving evidence, the colourless summary doing nothing to allay Jo's curiosity. What he left out was intriguing. Had his mother's family owned that half-ruined chateau?

For some reason she felt a pang of sympathy for him. Squelching it, she said, 'A half-ruined chateau—how very romantic.'

He reached for his coffee. 'It's not ruined any longer,' he said indifferently.

'Does it belong to your family?'

'It belongs to me.'

She recalled Tom's wry comment that Luc's mother had wanted her son to marry into the French aristocracy. Because she'd been an aristocrat herself? So what had her family thought of her marriage to a gamekeeper?

And of Luc himself, product of what they possibly felt was a misalliance?

Or not. After all, she knew very little about French aristocrats down on their luck, or tumbledown chateaux.

And nothing about Luc, except that he kissed like a demon lover, and that just looking at him set every cell in her body on fire...

'That's an interesting expression,' he said mockingly.

Flushing, and hoping she didn't sound defensive, she said, 'I'm picturing a half-ruined chateau in Provence.'

'Once you get your hands on Tom's legacy you'll be able to see as many as you like,' he told her. 'In fact, that amount of money will probably buy one for you. It might even be enough to turn the building into a live-able home instead of a wreck, but there wouldn't be any change.'

'I'll be quite content to view from a distance, like any other sightseer. And Tom's money will go to grow-ing the business.'

'How do you plan to conquer the cosmetics world if the base ingredient in your products is confined to only one small Pacific island?'

'As Pacific islands go, Rotumea is actually quite large,' she returned. 'And there are other, much more common ingredients we use too—coconut water from green coconuts, coconut oil, the essence from Rotu-mea's native gardenia.' She met his eyes squarely. 'I haven't yet worked out all the fine details of my plan to take over the world of skincare, but when I do, I won't be telling anyone about it.'

'Tom taught you well.' His smile was coolly ironic.

It always came back to Tom.

Deliberately Jo relaxed her stiff shoulders. What she and Tom had shared was precious to her. And she wasn't going to keep trying to convince Luc that his stepfather had never so much as touched her, beyond the occasional—very occasional and very brief—hug.

Just keep in mind how very judgemental Luc is, and you'll be safe, she told that weak inner part of her that melted whenever Luc's gunmetal gaze met hers.

She drank more coffee and said cheerfully, 'He had a lot to teach. I'll bet he was a help to you when you started.'

Luc gave a short, derisive laugh. 'Not Tom,' he said. 'He told me I'd learn far more if I made my own mistakes.'

Again she felt that strange sympathy. 'And did you?'

'I learnt enough to take his life's work away from him.'

Jo blinked and ventured, 'You had a reason.'

His wide shoulders lifted in an infinitesimal shrug. 'I did.' After a pause, he added, 'I told you he changed after the very minor stroke he had. Not vastly, not obviously, but there were…incidents. He made decisions that could have—in one case definitely would have— led to disaster. The man who built Henderson's from scratch would never have made such decisions, but Tom wouldn't admit or accept that he could make a mistake. He had the failings of his virtues, and his determination got in the way.'

Which put a different slant on events. She'd known Tom before that stroke, but only as a child and during the holidays. While she'd lived in Rotumea he'd had the occasional spurt of what she'd thought was slightly irrational behaviour, but as her aunt had taken the incidents without comment she'd assumed this was normal for him.

But as head of a huge organisation, with thousands

of people dependent on his health and managerial skills, one wrong decision could cause chaos. Perhaps Luc had been justified in ousting him.

Of course, Luc could be lying...

One glance at his strong features changed her mind. Lying didn't fit him. His behaviour last night had convinced her of his fundamental honesty as well as his formidable self-control.

Of course, he might have been trying her out, not really wanting her...

She had to stop second-guessing—something Tom had taught her to do, only he'd called it seeing situations clearly and from every conceivable angle. In business it worked well, but she was beginning to feel that in personal life it wasn't so efficient.

'You don't believe me,' Luc said without rancour.

Of course, he didn't care what she thought of him.

'Actually, I do,' she said, keeping her voice level. 'I can't see Tom ever admitting to a weakness. As you say, he had the faults of his virtues.'

'At least he didn't fail in the generosity stakes,' Luc observed.

That hurt, but she said calmly, 'No, he didn't. Although, being Tom, he still insisted on having the final word. You and I are caught in a trap of his making, with no way out.'

Luc laughed without humour. 'I'm sure that thought gave him great—and certainly as far as I'm concerned—rather malicious pleasure.'

'Whereas I think he meant some good for both of us by it.' Still smarting from his remark about Tom's generosity, she couldn't resist adding, 'Possibly you'd know him better if you'd seen more of him.'

And immediately wished she hadn't. Luc's expression didn't alter, but she received a strong impression of emotions reined back, of anger.

He finished his coffee, pushed his plate away and said calmly, 'We were estranged for the last years of his life. He wouldn't see me after I took over. When my mother sided with me—because she'd noticed and been worried by the change in him—he saw it as a betrayal, and although they kept up a pretence, they didn't live together as man and wife after that.'

Ashamed, she said, 'I'm sorry, I shouldn't have said that.'

'Especially as you were presumably the reason he settled in Rotumea and forbade either of us—or any of his friends—from visiting him.'

Stunned by his caustic tone, she said, 'I most certainly was not!'

He got to his feet and shrugged. 'You must have been. And I despise him for choosing to use such a weapon against my mother.'

The cold contempt in his voice shrivelled something vital inside Jo, made her feel sick and angry at the same time. 'I don't believe he thought of any such thing.'

And immediately cursed herself for saying anything at all. She tried to make it better. 'He always spoke of your mother with affection and respect. And we were *not* lovers.' Passion—a violent need to force him to believe her—made her voice harsh. She blurted, 'The very idea makes me feel sick.'

No emotion showed in his face, in those hard eyes, as he looked down at her. 'Your nausea obviously didn't worry Tom, or drive you away.' When she would have burst into speech again he held up his hand.

'Leave it, Joanna. Just leave it. He certainly wasn't the saint you seem to believe him to be.' His mouth twisted. 'And I can understand him. I've made it more than obvious I'm not immune to your not inconsiderable assets, so who am I to mock him? My mother was his age, and not well for the final years of her life. You must have been like a breath of fresh air to him, as well as a handy weapon.'

CHAPTER NINE

BACK IN ROTUMEA, Jo unpacked, then walked out onto the wide lanai. Sunlight streamed through the trees— so intense it looked like shimmering bars of gold in the salt-scented air. Her heart jolted when she realised Luc was gazing out to sea from the shade of a tangled thicket of palms.

It was all she could do to shield her hungry gaze. The past days in Auckland had been outwardly serene, but beneath it she'd been battling chaotic emotions. Luc's contempt hurt her more severely than Kyle's betrayal.

Facing that truth still terrified her.

Without preamble, she said, 'Would it be difficult for you to work with someone here? A housekeeper?'

Luc turned, brows drawing together. 'Not unless she talks.'

'She won't.' She expanded, 'The business is getting busy, and I'm going to be away most days.'

He nodded, although his gaze remained narrowed and keen. Colour warmed the skin over her cheekbones. Of course he knew why she was doing this.

He said, 'I'll pay her.' When she opened her mouth to protest he said curtly, 'At least you won't then feel obliged to offer me coffee or meals. And presumably you'll feel safer.'

Jo struggled to hide her chagrin. She'd hoped—use-lessly—he wouldn't realise just how dangerously vul-nerable she was. When Luc kissed her all self-control vanished, sweeping every vestige of common sense with it.

Heat burned up from her breasts, but before she could answer he went on, 'You obviously have someone in mind for the job.'

'My factory manager has a cousin who'll be per-fect,' she told him.

Luc nodded. 'Organise her hours any way you want,' he said indifferently. 'I'll be away for the rest of the af-ternoon.'

Jo turned, relieved to be summoned to the house by the shrill call of the telephone.

Five minutes later she hung up, her gaze falling on the Chinese chest. Now was the perfect time to see if Tom had hidden something in the secret panel. Frown-ing, she pressed the centre of one of the mother-of-pearl flowers, letting out a sharp hiss of breath as the panel slid back.

'Yes!' she breathed triumphantly. It did hold some-thing—not a thick wad, but definitely a couple of doc-uments. One fell onto the floor; frowning, she picked it up.

A strange feeling of dislocation made her pause. 'Oh, don't be silly,' she said out loud. Fingers shaking a lit-tle, she unfolded it.

It was a copy of her birth certificate. Astonishment froze her into place as her gaze traced her father's name—so young to die, unknown to her except from a few faded photographs and her mother's loving rec-ollections.

He'd been handsome, her mother had said, and kind.

And funny. He was a mechanic; they'd been planning to marry when he'd been killed. Ilona hadn't known she was pregnant, and she'd been forbidden to attend his funeral by his parents, yet although her heart had been shattered she'd been so glad she carried his baby, so glad she had someone else to love, someone to take care of…

Why had Tom wanted a copy of her birth certificate?

Just another thing she'd never know, Jo thought drearily, and slid it underneath the small pile.

Looking at papers clearly never meant for her seemed too much like an intrusion. She sat down at the table, her fingers pleating and unpleating, until in the end she opened up the first sheet of paper.

It was the document Meru had told her about. A quick check revealed it was of no use to her—merely a note saying Tom guaranteed that her business would be conducted in a suitable manner.

She firmed her trembling lips. It was too much—the unexpected reference to her parents, the inevitable loss of her business—all of those she could cope with, but the constant tension of living with Luc had left her raw and fragile, as though she'd lost a layer of skin.

'Get over it,' she muttered and started to fold up the papers, saying something beneath her breath when one slipped out of the pile. She glanced at the heading as she picked it up and frowned again. It was from a medical laboratory in Sydney, Australia, and to her astonishment her name leapt out from it.

Stunned, she read it. Then, her hand shaking so much she dropped it, she picked up the document it had been folded with. Tom's handwriting leapt out at her. *Dear Jo*, it began…

She dragged in a painful breath and closed her eyes a

moment before forcing them open and reading the letter he'd written to her some time before he'd been killed.

Three times she read it, before setting it back on the table and stumbling to her feet. She had to clutch the back of the chair to steady herself.

Luc walked in, took one look at her and crossed the room in long strides, demanding, 'What the hell's the matter?' as he grabbed her by the upper arms and supported her. 'It's all right,' he said roughly, pulling her stiff body into his arms. 'Whatever it is, we can deal with—'

'I know why Tom made it a condition that we live together,' Jo interrupted, her voice shaking.

Luc held her away from him, grey eyes searching her face. Struggling for control, she thrust out a hand towards the papers on the table. 'Look.'

His expression hardened. She waited for him to respond, but he said nothing until he'd put her back into the chair. Only then did he pick up the letter and began to read it.

Jo watched until he looked up, his narrowed eyes so dark they were almost black. 'He is—was—your *father.*'

'Yes.' Nausea and a great sorrow gripped her. 'My mother came to Rotumea twenty-three—no, twenty-four years ago. After my father—' she stopped abruptly, then resumed '—the man she thought was my father was killed.'

'How old was she?'

'Eighteen,' she said succinctly.

His frown deepened. 'Tom would have been thirty-five.' He paused, then said deliberately, 'It was just after my mother told him she could have no more children. I suppose it makes sense.'

Jo shivered. After another stark few moments he

asked, 'Why didn't she realise she was pregnant with his child?'

She swallowed. In a voice so muted he could hardly hear her, she said, 'I th-think it must have been because she believed she was already pregnant with my father's...with Joseph Thompson's baby.' She hesitated and swallowed, but clearly couldn't go on.

A surge of compassion and another unfamiliar emotion overtook Luc. Mentally consigning both Tom and Joanna's mother to some cold, dark region of outer space, he said, 'It must have been that. Otherwise—'

He stopped abruptly. He'd already made one huge mistake about Joanna; he wasn't going to compound his cynical mistake by saying that her mother would no doubt have asked for financial support if she'd realised the child she carried was Tom's.

In that steady, expressionless tone she said, 'She was engaged to him—to Joseph Thompson. They were going to get married, only he was killed in a road accident. Every Sunday we used to visit his grave and leave flowers on it. She loved him and missed him until the end of her life. I was named after him.'

Luc frowned. 'How could she have made such a mistake?'

'I don't know.' She shook her head, then said, 'But it's not possible to know the exact moment of conception.' Bright patches of colour flaked her high cheekbones. 'And there was only a week...'

Her voice trailed away as Luc nodded. Her mother's lover had died a week before she came to Rotumea; shortly after that, according to Tom, an attempt by him to comfort her had ended in his bed. If she already had cause to believe she might be pregnant it had probably never occurred to her that she carried Tom's child.

Tom's only child.

He asked, 'Are you all right?'

And thought disgustedly that of all the stupid things to ask, that was probably the most stupid. All right? How could she be *all right*? Everything she'd ever thought or believed about her family—the foundations of her life—had been turned upside down. No dead young father, her conception an accident known to no one, not even her mother.

'I'm OK,' she said automatically.

He scanned her white face. 'You don't look at all OK. In fact, you look as though you're going to faint.'

Her head came up and some fugitive colour stole through her white face. In a much stronger voice she said, 'I've never fainted in my life.'

'Nobody would blame you for starting now,' he said curtly, and turned away to get her a glass of water and put on the electric jug. She needed some stimulant— coffee would probably be best. He'd put some whisky in it and make her drink it.

Actually, he admitted grimly, he could do with a stiff whisky himself...

He looked across the room. 'Where did you find these papers?'

Limply she told him.

His eyes on the electric jug, he said, 'It appears that when you were a child Tom had no suspicion you might be his.'

'So he says...said.'

'But when you arrived here to look after your aunt he realised you not only *looked* like his mother—you sounded like her, have hair the same colour and texture.'

'Yes,' she said again numbly.

'Hence the DNA sample.' He waited, and when she

said nothing he elaborated, 'It would have been easy enough to get one with you living in the house.'

'I suppose so,' she said, still in that flat, stunned voice.

Luc paused. 'Did you notice any change in his attitude to you?'

'No.' She thought for a moment, then said slowly, 'Actually, yes. I suppose I did.'

'In what way?' Luc demanded.

She searched for words. 'He talked to me about his family, about how he'd got to be the man he was—all sorts of things. I just thought he was lonely.' She pressed a clenched fist to her heart, then forced it away, staring at her fingers with a look that summoned another unfamiliar emotion in Luc. 'He was really helpful when I thought of starting my business—made me do a proper business plan, discussed it with me. He invited friends of his who came to the resort to dinner—people he respected—introduced me to them...'

Her voice trailed away.

Recalling his own scathing refusal to believe anything she'd said about her relationship with Tom, Luc said bleakly, 'He did you few favours there—most of them are sure you were his mistress.'

She fired up. 'Then they must be totally lacking in any sort of empathy or understanding. He behaved like an uncle.' Again her voice thickened as she fought for composure. Taking a deep breath, she finished, 'Or a f-father.'

She dragged her gaze away from the letter to look back at him. 'But why keep it a secret? And why did Tom set up this whole situation?' She gestured wildly, encompassing the room and Luc.

'Tom trusted no one,' Luc told her uncompromisingly. 'Once he'd got this report, he wanted you to stay in Rotumea so he could find out what sort of person you are.'

She said numbly, 'It just seems…outrageous. Everything he's done. He was *testing* me?'

'Of course.' Luc paused, scanning her white face. That unusual compassion twisted his heart. She'd had enough.

But he owed her the truth—something Tom hadn't given her until too late.

He said, 'He was let down badly by his first wife. My mother married him because he was rich and was prepared to set up her family in the style they'd been accustomed to before they'd wasted their inheritance. After I was born she'd been told it was unlikely she'd have any more children, but she didn't tell Tom—she hoped the diagnosis was wrong. And I took Henderson's away from him. Why should he trust you?'

Jo was silent for a moment, then said quietly, 'I suppose I understand. At least we had that time together.'

Squaring her shoulders, she looked him in the eyes and said bluntly, 'I just thought he was lonely and bored. You'd taken over the enterprise he'd spent his life building, so it amused him to dabble in something as tiny as mine.' She paused, then decided to say it anyway. 'And it appeared you didn't care much about him.'

'I cared a lot,' he said curtly, adding in a level voice, 'but I also understood his desire to lick his wounds. Rotumea was his bolthole and his refuge. I'm sure he enjoyed helping you set up your business, and I'm equally sure he was pleased—and proud—to discover that his only child had something of his entrepreneurial spirit.'

'Just as he was proud of your ability,' she said, not quite knowing why.

Luc shrugged. 'I doubt that he ever thought of me as a son.'

Something about his tone caught her attention, although her swift glance found no regret in his expression. A sharp pang of probably unnecessary sympathy persuaded Jo into an impulsive reply. 'He always spoke of you with pride and affection.'

'You don't have to sugar-coat his attitude,' he said with crisp disbelief.

Her head came up. 'I'm not. I don't lie. He certainly didn't like being dumped, but he was quite proud at how efficiently it was done, without weakening the business or lowering its value in the marketplace.'

Luc gave an ironic smile. 'Yes, that would be Tom.'

She shivered. 'He knew for almost two years that he was my father. It seems such a waste. We could have been a…a family.'

It hurt that he hadn't wanted that. After all, families accepted each other as they were—without testing them.

Or was that a stupidly sentimental view?

Not without sympathy, Luc said, 'He wouldn't have been Tom if he hadn't checked you out thoroughly.'

'But he *knew* me,' she protested, trying to contain her pain. 'I used to come to Rotumea at least once a year for the holidays. Quite often he was here. In a way, he watched me grow up.'

'He knew you as a child.' He shrugged. 'A woman is an entirely different thing.'

'Why didn't he trust women?' she asked directly.

After a few taut moments Luc answered, a trace of reluctance colouring his voice. 'His first wife enjoyed the money he was making, but resented the time it took—time away from her. A few years into the marriage, when he'd overstretched himself and was skating very close to bankruptcy, she left him for his biggest competitor.'

Jo thought that over before saying, 'So he had one bad experience with a woman and that turned him sour on all our sex?'

Luc shrugged and poured water into the coffee pot before saying, 'There would have been other experiences, I imagine. Rich men are targets for a certain type of person. Which was possibly why he chose my mother—a practical, unsentimental Frenchwoman who married him for his money.'

This seemed to be Jo's day to ask questions. Why not an impertinent one? He could only give her that steely look and refuse to answer. 'And what did she bring to the marriage?'

Then immediately wished she'd kept quiet. It was too personal—something she had no right to know.

However, instead of the stinging riposte she expected, Luc said, 'This is guesswork—my mother wasn't one to talk about her emotions. She'd married once for love and that had been a disaster. I imagine she agreed with her family that her second marriage should be one of convenience. Tom was the ideal choice. And it was happy enough.' His mouth twisted. 'Much happier than many I've seen that began with high romance, only to disintegrate into chaos.'

Startled by this unexpected forthrightness, Jo realised she and Luc did have something in common, after all—mothers who'd used their beauty to secure a future for their children.

Luc went on, 'Their marriage was one of equals; as her husband, he was introduced into circles that boosted his career, and in return he supported her—and me—in the style she believed was her due. He practically rebuilt the chateau for her, and made sure she never wanted for anything again.'

And possibly she'd hoped Tom would be satisfied with Luc as a substitute son.

How had that affected Luc? A quick glance gleaned no information from his expression. From what he'd said, she suspected he had his mother's very practical attitude to marriage.

He said levelly, 'Tom would have been pleased when he found out you were his daughter. But even then, he'd have wanted to be sure he could trust you with that knowledge.'

At Jo's soft, angry sound, Luc shrugged. 'The prospect of acquiring large amounts of money often changes people, bringing out the worst in them.'

She nodded, accepting the coffee he handed her. She'd read enough to know that was true.

Luc went on, 'He'd have planned to tell you in his own good time, but that bloody coconut robbed him of the opportunity.'

Tears clogging her voice, she said, 'He was so fit, he looked after himself, he ate well—he thought he'd live for ever.'

'He was sure he had all bases covered,' Luc agreed. He was watching her, his brows drawn together. 'You really were fond of him, weren't you?'

'Yes.' She blinked ferociously and steadied her voice. 'It's odd, isn't it? He was a father to you, and a sort of father to me, but he never knew what it was like to be a real father.' She glanced up with a smile that trembled. 'I suppose that makes us sort of siblings.'

'Like hell it does!' Luc took a step towards her, then stopped.

Jo's breath blocked her throat, something dying inside her as she watched him reimpose control. He said between his teeth, 'We share an affection for a man, that's all. And now we have to work out what to do about this situation.'

His words killed the hope she'd kept locked in her heart—a weak and feeble hope she'd refused to face.

Because facing it meant she'd have to accept something else—that her feelings for Luc went far deeper than mere lust.

'I know,' she said huskily.

He looked down at his clenched fists as though he'd never seen them before. 'First,' he stated, his voice showing no emotion, 'we have to see out the six months Tom stipulated.'

She opened her mouth, then closed it again. He was right. They had to do that. But at what cost to her? Luc wanted her—he'd admitted that. But somehow, without realising it, she'd grown to crave more than the passionate sating of desire. And one glance at his stony expression told her that even without the barrier of his beliefs about her relationship with Tom, Luc was not going to surrender to what he probably saw as a temporary passion.

The months ahead stretched out like a prison sentence.

'I suppose so,' she said quietly.

Luc looked down at her. 'Drink your coffee. The next thing we need to do is contact Tom's solicitor and get some advice about his revelations.'

She gave him a blank look. 'Why? He left me enough to live on for the rest of my life.'

'As his daughter, you have a claim to his entire estate,' Luc said briefly.

The cup in her hand trembled so much she set it down on the saucer. 'I don't want it,' she said, snapping each word out. 'I do *not* want anything more than he left me. I don't need it. If I end up with a fortune it will be one of my own making, not his. I will not contest the will.'

Luc looked at her, his mouth curving in a smile that held no hint of humour. 'Oh, yes,' he said levelly. 'You're his daughter, all right.'

And felt a coldly searing shame. Tom's silence and his own cynicism had made him angry and suspicious, even as he'd reluctantly come to admire her. *Admire?* He watched her get up, his gut tightening. There was a lot to admire about Joanna Forman, but that was too simple a word. His emotions were complex, warring with each other.

But he had time to assess them…

During the following weeks Jo sensed a subtle easing of Luc's aloofness. Slowly, carefully, without discussion, they negotiated a system of living together. She relished his dry sense of humour, and found herself eagerly driving home each afternoon to match wits with him. His keen intelligence intrigued her too much. And she enjoyed the rare moments when his spoken English revealed his French heritage.

However the tension was still there—ignored, controlled, but never entirely repressed. Luc had told her he felt nothing but lust for her, and she was too proud to be used.

So she warned herself to be satisfied that they were tentatively approaching something like acceptance of the situation.

The social life she instituted for them helped. The island chiefs and their wives were eager to meet Luc and, a little to her surprise, he seemed to enjoy being introduced to them.

'For a man who knows little of Pacific customs, you're proving very adaptable,' she said one evening, waving their last guests goodbye.

Luc gave her an ironic look. 'Protocol exists everywhere,' he observed negligently. 'Anyone with any common sense finds out what the prevailing customs and usages are before they travel. And these people are forgiving.'

And he made her laugh with a story of his naivety when he'd made his first trip to China, finishing by saying, 'They were charmingly polite about every mistake I made, and after that I vowed I wasn't going to be so stupid again.'

Perhaps it was the pleasant evening they'd had, or perhaps the eternal beauty of the stars overhead, jewelling the velvet sky with their ancient patterns, that persuaded Jo to ask something she'd often wondered about.

She said, 'Did you manage to deal satisfactorily with the mess you were handling while we were in Auckland?'

A certain grimness in his expression made her add hastily, 'If you can't talk about it, forget about it.'

His shoulders lifted briefly. 'I trust your discretion.'

Which startled her as well as gave her a suspicious frisson of pleasure.

Deliberately, Luc said, 'One of the executives there embezzled over a hundred thousand dollars.'

Shocked, she said, 'What was it—gambling?'

'That would have been easy to deal with. Her child— her oldest son—developed a rare form of cancer. She found that a highly experimental treatment was on offer in America. She didn't have the money to pay for it, and couldn't get it anywhere, so she took it.'

Jo frowned. 'What happened to the boy?'

'He died,' he said shortly.

'Oh, that's so sad.'

'Yes. No happy endings.'

Glancing up at the autocratic profile etched against that radiant sky, Jo decided not to ask how he'd dealt with the situation.

However, he said, 'We came to a decision that satisfied everyone.'

Including the poor woman who'd lost her son?

He went on, 'She's still working for us—under stringent supervision—and will pay back the money.'

And that did surprise her. When she remained silent he gave a swift, sardonic smile. 'You thought I'd sack her? Prosecute her?'

'Well, actually, yes,' she admitted.

'I do have the occasional moment of compassion,' he said smoothly. 'She is an excellent executive, and she's paid a heavy enough price—her marriage broke up over her actions and the strain of their son's illness.'

If she hadn't known that nothing cracked that granite façade he presented to the world, she thought a little wistfully, she might have thought her comment had struck a nerve.

Quite often they dined at the resort, occasionally with friends or business associates of Luc's who'd flown in. To Jo's surprise, she liked his friends. His easy companionship with them led to some wistful moments. Slowly, guiltily, she realised she wanted more—much, much more—from Luc than friendship.

Each day his controlled courtesy grated more, pulling taut a set of nerves she hadn't known she possessed.

Adding to her stress was the slow progress of the Council of chiefs on making any decision. They had accepted Tom's document, but Meru's cousin remained infuriatingly silent about any deliberations.

Between fear for the future of her business and her growing feelings for Luc, Jo endured long nights when she turned restlessly in her bed and wondered whether he too was awake—so close and yet so distant from her.

Almost certainly not…

It was a relief when, after a telephone call, Luc informed her he had to go to China for a meeting. 'We'll leave tomorrow and be away for five days.'

'I can't come.'

'Why not? I think you'd enjoy Shanghai, and contacts there should be valuable.'

'I can't leave Rotumea because any day now—I hope—I'll learn whether I still have a business,' she told him.

'What?' He frowned and asked curtly, 'What's going on?'

When she'd explained what was happening, his frown deepened. 'All right, obviously you have to be here for that.' He paused. 'Shall I stay?'

'No,' she said, touched by his thoughtfulness. 'It may not be decided yet. They hoped to have a consensus by now, but a couple of expatriate chiefs arrived from New Zealand yesterday, and they'll probably bring the wishes of the Rotumean community there to be considered.'

But there was no decision for several days. 'Something has happened,' Meru told her. 'I don't know what it is, but it means they cannot come to a decision yet.' She paused, then said quietly, 'I think you are going to lose, Jo. They will be very sorry, but of course they

have to think of everyone, not just you. And this firm
is promising big things—they have a very good eco-
logical reputation, you know, and they are prepared to
work with the Council to make sure the island is not
changed in any way.'

'I know,' Jo said huskily. 'It's all right, don't worry.'

On the day Luc was due back, Jo woke late, slitting
her eyes against the bright morning light. He'd been
away less than a week, yet she'd missed him. How she'd
missed him! His absence was an aching gap in her life,
a silent emptiness that echoed through the days and
haunted her sleep at night.

For the past two months she'd been continually tense,
struggling to contain a need that grew ever stronger,
engraving itself on her heart so deeply she'd never be
able to erase it.

She gritted her teeth. She could cope; she had to
cope. In a few months they'd have fulfilled the conditions of Tom's will, and could pick up their lives again.
And she'd be spared the pain of seeing Luc ever again.

A gull called from outside, its shrill screech drowned
out by the alarm siren of the blackbird in the garden.
Taken by surprise, she hurled back the sheet and leapt
out. That bird was a drama queen, but something or
someone was out there, and today Luc was coming
home—no, she corrected, he was coming *back*. Rotumea wasn't his home, never would be. Just as it wasn't
hers. Yet excitement exploded through her, a starburst
of foolish anticipation doomed to be frustrated.

She grabbed the first thing to hand—a sarong slung
over the back of a chair—but had only wound it halfway
round her when she heard a car door slam. She snatched
up a hairbrush, dragging it through her tangled locks,

then took a deep breath and walked out onto the terrace, stopping after the first step. Her heart contracted.

Watching the blackbird as it peered nervously through the screen of hibiscus blossoms, Luc stood against a screen of bold magenta bougainvillea. A half-smile curled his mouth. Her heart began to beat rapidly. He was so...so *magnificent*, hair gleaming in the golden light, his natural tan deepened by the tropical sun.

And she loved him.

CHAPTER TEN

THE REALISATION HIT Jo with the force of a blow, shocking her into immobility. Panicking, she heard herself drag in a jagged breath. It wasn't possible. She didn't know Luc well enough to take that final step. He'd shown himself to be judgemental and inflexible and autocratic and intolerant and…her mind ran out of adjectives.

But not recently, she thought despairingly. And then Luc turned, his face hardening when he saw her. Suddenly aware of her scanty sarong, she shot backwards into the shade of the terrace.

In a voice that sounded as though he'd been goaded beyond bearing, he demanded harshly, 'Damn you, Joanna, why can't you be dressed and ready to go to work?'

The words whirling around her mind, she blinked.

He headed purposefully towards her, stopping only a few inches away. Eyes widening, she stared up into his face. He looked as though it had been a hard sojourn in Shanghai. His arrogant bone structure was more prominent, but the grey eyes were hot and urgent, and when he made an odd sound deep in his throat and pulled her into his arms she didn't resist, melting into him with a shaky sigh of relief.

'What happened with the Council of chiefs?' he demanded.

She tried to pull away, but his arms tightened. 'They're still talking.'

His face hardened. 'How long do they need?'

He was holding her so close she could feel the stirring of his body, the hard shifting and flexion of muscles as though he clamped some tight control on them.

'Luc,' she said fiercely into his chest, 'let *go*.'

'You want this—don't lie to me, Joanna, I see it in your eyes every time you look at me.' His voice was rough and harsh, and the pressure of his arms around her didn't slacken.

'I didn't mean let *me* go,' she said indignantly, jerking her head upwards to glare at him. '*You*—I meant let yourself go.'

He stared at her as though she were mad, then startled her by emitting a short, unamused laugh. 'Very well, then—but only if it's mutual.'

Jo's heart missed a beat. 'You've just said you know it is.'

His eyes narrowed. 'The passion is mutual—how about the surrender?'

For a moment she hesitated, but only for a moment. 'Of course it is,' she said fiercely.

He bent his head. But instead of the fierce hunger she expected, his kiss was soft and tantalising, a slow sweet pressure that sent her pulse soaring. Enraptured, she returned it, letting instinct take over to openly reveal the love that had flowered within her so unexpectedly.

He lifted his head and surveyed her with an intent, almost silver scrutiny. 'Enough?' he asked.

'No.' A sudden thought struck her. 'Unless you're

tired,' she added heroically, every cell in her body objecting to such restraint.

Something moved in his eyes. 'Not *too* tired,' he said in that thick, hard voice, and startled her by lifting her as though she were a child and shouldering through the doorway.

He carried her into her bedroom, standing for a few seconds to survey the tangled sheets on the bed before easing her onto her feet.

This time his kiss was different, much more carnal. Jo's blazing response shocked her—her reckless, overt need was both delicious and intoxicating, singing through her body like a siren's lure.

When he lifted his head and held her a half-step away her sarong fell to the floor, a puddle of coral and peach and blue-violet, leaving her only in her narrow bikini briefs.

Luc's hands tightened on her shoulders, then relaxed.

Eyes kindling, he said, 'You're beautiful. But you know that. And I want you—you've known that too, ever since we first set eyes on each other. And at the moment I don't give a damn for all the reasons we shouldn't be doing this.'

Jo had never felt so sensuous, so at home. The soft sea breeze caressed her skin, lifting the ends of her hair around her face, and Luc looked at her as though she was all he'd ever desired. She didn't know what to do, what to say.

So she let her expression tell him that a desperate need raced through her like some headstrong tide, carrying her further and further away from safety.

Nothing else but this moment, this sensation, made sense to her.

'Neither do I,' she said honestly, and reached out to

touch his shoulder, tracing the hard swell of a muscle with a light, sensuous finger.

He tensed as though she'd hit him, then gave a low, triumphant laugh and yanked his shirt over his head, before stripping off the rest of his clothes.

Her low, feral murmur took her by surprise. It surprised him too, but he smiled and lifted a hand that shook slightly, reaching for her again, easing her against him as though she was precious to him.

Sighing with voluptuous pleasure, Jo relaxed against him, shamelessly letting him support her.

When his lips met hers rational thought fled, banishing all foreboding as she surrendered to the magic of her stimulated senses, the pressure of Luc's mouth as he explored hers, the erotic slide of heated skin against skin...

He lifted her again and set her down on the bed, sprawled across the sheets she'd left only a few minutes previously. He didn't join her; instead he stood like some pagan conqueror gazing down at one of the spoils of war.

In his face she read a fierce appetite that matched hers, roused it further and took her higher than she'd ever been. Without thinking, she held out her arms to him.

He didn't move.

Surely he wasn't going to call a halt now...

Quickly, before she could think better of it, she blurted, 'I'm taking the Pill.'

Luc's smile was taut and fierce. 'And I've got protection.'

Her heart soared as he came down beside her in a movement that lacked a little of his usual litheness, and slid his arms around her as though he too had been craving this moment, dreaming of it night and day, desired it like a man lost in the desert longed for water.

He bent his head, but didn't take her hungry mouth. Disappointment ached through her, only to disappear when he dropped a sinuous line of kisses from the corner of her mouth to the pulse in her throat.

'You taste like honey and cream,' he said against its frantic throbbing. 'Sweet and rich, with a tang.'

Shudders of exquisite pleasure shivered along her nerves, as he found the lobe of her ear and bit it gently.

With the pathetic remains of her willpower, Jo held back a gasp, sighing languorously when he transferred to the juncture of her neck and shoulder, biting again so gently she could barely feel it. More pleasure shimmered through her.

'I didn't know—' she breathed into his throat, her voice dying when he bit again, applying slightly more pressure.

'What didn't you know?' His voice was low and raw, as though he was holding himself in rigid restraint.

'That it—that anything could feel so good,' she whispered.

'Here?' Another sensuous nip sent more excitement seething through her.

'Yes,' she croaked, and turned her head to do the same to him, her hand over his heart.

She felt it leap beneath her palm, felt the swift tension in his muscles. A sense of power, of communion, of a subtle forging of bonds, surged through her when he slid a hand down to cup her breast, the lean fingers gentle yet assured as they stroked the tip into a taut little peak.

A groan ripped from her throat and her body tightened, driven by an urgency that brooked no disappointment.

'Ah, yes, you like that,' he breathed, and bent his head to kiss the spot, then took it into his mouth.

'Luc...' His name emerged as a long, shuddering sigh.

He lifted his head and watched her tremble with something so close to rapture it made her need even more keen, piercing her with a demand she couldn't articulate.

His hand slid further down, traced the narrow curve of her waist, moved past her hip and found the slick, heated folds at the juncture of her thighs.

'Yes,' he said, and came over her, testing her gently until she seized him by the shoulders and pulled him down and into her, drugged by a sensuous craving that insisted on satisfaction.

Her boldness cracked his iron control. A rough, feral noise erupted from deep in his throat and he thrust, deep and ever deeper, until at last the mounting wave of ecstasy broke over her, carrying her so far beyond rapture she thought her heart would break its bounds.

Even as the wave crested and ebbed he flung his head back, muscles coiled and flowing while he took his fill of her, finally easing down with her into a sated serenity punctuated only by the heavy beating of her heart against his.

Jo had never felt such sweet sorrow at the end of exhilaration, yet with it came a powerful contentment and peace, as though the experience had gone beyond the physical and was transformed into something spiritual.

For her, her mind told her drowsily. Not for Luc...

Right then, she didn't care. It was enough to hold him while their pulses synchronised to a steady regular beat, to savour his weight on her, his long muscles lax, his head on the pillow beside her.

But too soon he said, 'I'm far too heavy for you,' and before she could tighten her arms around him he turned onto his side and pulled her against him with her head on his shoulder.

No, you're not...I think I might have been born for this. Another thing she didn't dare say aloud.

So she made an indeterminate noise, and they lay together until he said, 'If I don't move soon I might go to sleep.'

Love and concern for him forced her to remember he'd flown in from China.

'Didn't you sleep on the plane?' she asked.

He paused, then gave a short laugh. 'Not much.' He released her and swung himself off the bed. For a moment he looked down at her, grey eyes narrowed and unreadable, before turning away and beginning to pull on his clothes.

Jo lay for a few seconds, wondering what to say, where to go from here. Before she'd made up her mind, he picked up her sarong and tossed it to her.

'Too tempting,' he said harshly.

Fumbling, she draped the cloth around her, feeling oddly empty, only to have to stand up and arrange it.

Fully dressed, Luc asked dryly, 'What happened to the businesswoman who raced off to work at the crack of dawn every day?'

Her whole world had changed, yet nothing had; they were back to fencing with each other. Perhaps the foils had been blunted a little, but they were still sharp.

Steadying her voice, she said, 'She got waylaid,' and then blushed. 'I'll head off in half an hour or so,' she said quickly. 'You'll be able to sleep then if you want to.'

'Jo,' he said quietly.

Desperately clinging to the remnants of her dignity, she faced him. 'What?'

He paused, scrutinising her face before saying, 'I thought I had enough strength of mind to resist you. I was wrong. Are you all right?'

Pride provided the answer. She even managed a smile. 'Of course,' she told him brightly. 'You don't have to be told you're a magnificent lover, surely?'

And was bemused by the tinge of colour along his autocratic cheekbones when he said, 'I'm glad you think so. It was…special for me too. And we need to talk once you get home again.' He turned and left the room.

His tone had been courteous enough, but an undernote to his words stayed with her. It hadn't been contempt, yet it left her feeling oddly disassociated and uneasy, and she spent too much time that morning at work wondering about it when she should have been marshalling her argument for continuing her contract with the Council of chiefs.

It was a relief when Meru knocked on her door, even though the older woman looked worried. 'Jo, something's happened,' she said.

Jo's heart skipped a beat. She'd believed she was ready for what was probably going to be a refusal, but the worry that clawed at her was fierce and devastating. 'Do you think the decision will be made today? Has your cousin any idea which way the chiefs might be going?'

Meru sighed and sat down. 'Yes. But something unexpected has happened.'

'What?' The single word snapped out.

'There has been another offer.'

Whatever she'd expected, it wasn't this. 'From whom?' she asked blankly.

'I don't know, but it raises the first offer. I think we are going to lose, Jo.'

Jo reined in her shocked dismay. 'In that case, get your cousin to persuade the Council to sign a written contract—one made out by powerful lawyers who know the island. One that stipulates all of our employees' jobs will be safe.'

'Yes.' Meru looked anxiously at her. 'Jo, what will you do?'

Jo swallowed a lump in her throat. 'I'll set up another business—in New Zealand, probably.'

Meru's eyes filled with tears. 'We'll miss you,' she said, and came across and hugged her hard.

When she'd gone Jo sat for long moments, staring blindly at the computer screen.

Everything had been pushed off balance, all the foundations of her life revealed to be shaky. The knowledge that she was Tom's daughter had begun the process...

No, she thought, determined to face facts. Meeting Luc had started it. She'd started by disliking him as she fought that fierce physical attraction, then reluctantly learned to respect him. Falling in love had stolen up on her, ambushed her heart. *Making* love with him had set the seal on her change of emotions, and it had been—life-changing.

The end of all her dreams and plans for her business was life-changing too, she thought wearily, only in an entirely different way. Before she'd met Luc she'd have been completely devastated by the loss of her business, but that unexpected, newfound love had changed her.

What now?

Love battled with desire, fought caution, resisted everything that urged—begged, demanded, *insisted*—she yield to it.

She got to her feet and walked across to the window, staring out across the rustling feathery tops of the coconut palms. The faint evocative perfume of gardenia mingled with petrol fumes and the ever-present salty tang. Heat hit her like a blow. Closing her eyes, she wrestled her way to the hardest decision she'd ever made—much more difficult than choosing to care for her mother in the face of Kyle's threat to walk out on their relationship.

Did she have the courage to take the chance that Luc might learn to love her?

It didn't seem likely. All his lovers had been beautiful, yet the relationships had died. Did he even believe in love—the unconditional sort her mother had known, a love that lasted a lifetime? Because only that would satisfy her.

It didn't seem likely.

And she couldn't—wouldn't—cope with emotionless sex that meant nothing more than the satisfaction of carnal needs. Loving Luc as she did, such a surrender would kill something vital, something honest and basic in her.

So she'd tell Luc there would be no more rapturous moments in his arms…

Her hands clenched on the windowsill.

Glimpsing paradise only to be forced to repudiate it would be like enduring hell, but she had to do it.

At least Luc wasn't at home when she reached the house. Shaking inwardly, Jo went inside and showered, turning off the water to hear a car coming towards the house. Luc, she thought, her heart going suddenly into overdrive. She dragged on a long loose shift before forcing herself to walk sedately outside.

That foolish wild anticipation abruptly died when

she opened the door to Sean Harvey. He surveyed her with the insolent half-smile that had become his usual greeting for her.

'Hi, gorgeous,' he said, eyeing her up and down. 'How are things going?'

'Fine, thank you,' she said without warmth.

'I hear you've had some good luck.'

Uneasy under his stare, she asked, 'Really?'

Then remembered with relief that she'd been interviewed by the local newspaper a few days previously, and had mentioned that the latest range of skincare creams had been accepted into one of New York's most prestigious stores.

'Yep.' He never took his eyes off her. 'Word is that you're actually Tom Henderson's daughter.'

She felt the colour drain from her face. 'Really?' she said again, buying time. 'And where did you hear that?'

'Around,' he said casually. 'Is it true?'

She shrugged. 'My ancestry is no one's concern but mine.'

'So it is true,' he said, still watching her, his gaze as cold as a shark's. 'Why not admit it?'

'Why did you come here?'

He sneered, 'Could the secrecy have anything to do with your mother being a call girl? Was old Tom ashamed of you?'

'My mother was not a call girl,' she said sharply, despising him and so angry she had to stop and draw breath before she could say, 'Pity *your* mother didn't wash your mouth out with soap more often. I don't know why you're here, and you can leave right now.'

'What if I don't want to? After all, your lover's not here. You must be lonely, looking for a little warmth.'

She stepped back and slammed the door in his face,

knowing it was flimsy protection. The house had few external walls.

At least the sound of a car engine meant Sean wasn't hanging around. Relief almost swamped her until she realised the vehicle was coming down the drive, not going away. The engine died, followed by a second's silence before she heard Luc's voice. His icy, ominous tone sent a shiver scudding down her spine.

Fingers shaking, she opened the door to see Sean trying to maintain his insolence in the face of Luc's anger. As she stepped out, Sean's hand clenched into a fist and he took a step towards Luc, lowering his head like a charging bull.

Shock ricocheted through her.

In a silky voice loaded with menace, Luc ordered, 'Don't try it.'

Intensely relieved, she saw Sean hesitate then drop his hands and step back.

'Sean's just going,' she said crisply.

Without looking at her, Luc ordered, 'On your way, then.'

Sean waited until he was in his car before he wound down the window and sneered, 'Not even you can put a stop to this, you know. Everyone on Rotumea knows.'

Gravel spurted from the wheels as the car surged forward, missing Luc by a foot, then shot down the drive.

Luc came to the door in a swift, noiseless rush, his expression controlled. 'What the hell was he doing here?' he demanded.

'He came to tell me he knows I'm Tom's daughter,' she told him shakily, furious with him. 'Luc, he tried to run you over! Why didn't you get out of the way?'

'I've outbluffed better players than him,' he said contemptuously. 'How did he find out?'

'I don't know, and I don't care.' She expelled pent-up air and steadied her voice. 'I don't know why he's being so...so *stupid*! We've never been anything more than friends—and not even that after the night he bailed me up at the resort.'

The night she'd met Luc. It seemed so long ago, as though she'd never lived before she met him...

He said now, 'I did tell you once that money has the power to change most people. Get used to it.'

'But *I* haven't changed!' She combated her fear and anger by banging a fist on the balustrade. 'I'm just the same person I was before!' And stopped, because of course she wasn't. She'd changed, but it had been love that did that, not money.

Luc took her elbow and steered her through the door. 'What did you tell him when he said he knew?'

'That my ancestry was no one's business but mine.' She took in a deep breath of warm, flower-scented air and tried to compose herself.

'And you've not told anyone?'

'No.' But then she felt colour drain from her face.

'You did.' He sounded bored, as though it was only to be expected.

Realising she was clutching his sleeve, she dropped her hand and took a deep breath while she strode across to the kitchen. Defiantly she said, 'Yes. Lindy.' And shook her head. 'But Lindy wouldn't tell anyone—I asked her not to.'

'Not her husband?'

She hesitated. 'I don't think she'd tell him. I don't know.'

'Marriage changes people too. She might think you didn't mean him.'

His cynical intonation made her angry. 'Surely it

doesn't matter? I didn't tell her about the condition in Tom's will.'

'It matters,' Luc said curtly. 'Brace yourself, because the media is on the way. A gossip columnist got in touch with me an hour ago.' He demanded abruptly, 'Have you seen your lawyer yet?'

Hands shaking, she opened the fridge and got out the iced water. 'No. I told you, I don't need to.'

Luc said something under his breath, and she hurried on, 'It's nobody's business but mine who my parents were.'

'Agreed, except that as Tom's only child you have a moral claim to his estate.'

'I don't,' she said instantly, swinging around to fix him with a fierce glare. 'I don't want anything to do with it. I'll take what he left me, but no more. As for the press—well, they can say what they like. I'll stay here—they'll soon get bored in Rotumea.'

His gaze narrowed, then he shrugged. 'I'll get changed and then we'll talk.'

Ten minutes later, walking beside him along the beach, Jo tried to stifle a tenuous joy that could only be temporary.

Casually, Luc asked, 'Why don't you want anything more from Tom's estate?'

Jo stopped, watching a frigate bird soar and wheel in the sky. The sun dazzled her eyes and the familiar roar of the waves on the coral reef was no comfort.

She tried to organise her objection into words that made sense, finally saying, 'If he'd told me—if we'd been able to relate to each other, forge some sort of family feeling—I might feel differently.'

'I can understand that, but you told me that he treated you like an uncle—or a father.'

Surprised that he'd remembered, she said, 'He did, but…I never felt that we were family, the way it was with my mother and Aunt Luisa. If I'd known—if he'd told me—I might feel I have some further claim on his estate, even though he left me more than enough. But then, if he'd wanted me to have anything more than what he left me in his will he'd have seen to it. He didn't.'

He stopped and looked down at her, grey eyes hooded. 'He probably intended to before that damned hurricane.'

'In the Pacific they're called cyclones,' she said bleakly. 'And you don't know what he'd have done.'

She tried again to make him understand. 'Luc, I don't want anything more. I was shocked enough to get what I did. You deserve to head Henderson's. I think he knew that, even if he was angry with you for taking his place.'

Hoping she'd said enough to convince him, she met his piercing gaze staunchly. 'I don't know what lever Tom used to force you to obey his condition, but he had no right to do it.'

'His lever,' he told her deliberately, 'is that you have the power to make my life a hell of a lot harder.'

'What?' For a moment she thought her heart had stopped beating. She'd had too many shocks this morning. This was something she couldn't—didn't want to—deal with.

The cold, controlled anger hardening his expression cut her breath short. Pulse thundering in her ears, she waited.

He said, 'At the end of six months you'll be asked by the solicitor how you feel about me. Your opinion decides whether or not I take full control of Tom's estate.' His face more arrogant than she'd ever seen it, he went on, 'It won't be the end of the world if you say I'm the biggest bastard you've ever come across—I'll get what

I want eventually, but possibly not before considerable damage has been done to Henderson's. The shares will fall once shareholders hear you're his daughter.'

'Why?'

'They'll anticipate a legal battle for control.'

'So that's why...' Jo stopped, unable to continue. Now she knew why he'd relaxed his iron restraint enough to make love to her—because he wanted that power, that control over Tom's empire.

Sick to her soul with disillusion, she closed her eyes. Loving him was breaking her heart, but this—this was even worse.

'That's why I agreed to this farcical situation,' he said, each word clipped and cold and precise.

Whatever Tom had intended by his eccentric will, it couldn't be allowed to wreck Luc's career. But oh, how could he have used her with such calculated cynicism?

Pride forced her voice to remain steady. 'And after you'd vented your spleen for a few weeks by being as nasty as you could, did you decide that seducing me into some meaningless lovemaking would be the easiest route to my agreement?'

'Don't try to tell me that this morning meant nothing to you,' he said between his teeth. 'I was there, Joanna. I know how you look when we make love, and it wasn't *meaningless*.'

She stopped, and turned blindly back. *No*, she thought in anguish as his hand on her arm froze her into place. *No, don't try to persuade me with lies...*

He said, 'I made love to you because I couldn't stop myself. And because you wanted me as much as I wanted you. I wasn't capable of thinking beyond that—certainly not planning to seduce you.'

'Let me go,' she said thinly.

He paused, then let his hand fall. Jo set off towards the house, her thoughts in turmoil, her insides churning. He caught her up after a pace.

Dragging in a long silent breath, she said as calmly as she could, 'You don't need to worry. I'll stay. When the six months are up I'll tell Mr Keller that you're the ideal person to take over Henderson Holdings.'

Luc examined her silently. She was pale and her voice was shaky, but she met his gaze without wavering.

'Tom's played with our lives enough,' she said dispassionately. 'I don't want to live by his rules any longer. From now on, I suggest we don't mention his name. And I'll try not to get in your way.'

What the hell did she mean by that? Luc suspected he knew. She was closing the door firmly on any further lovemaking. After a silent, furious epithet, he tried to convince himself it was sensible.

Hell, you've made a total hash of this.

Surprising himself, he realised he believed she'd keep her word once this damned probation period was over. Probably because she'd fought so hard for her small business—not for herself so much as for the people who worked for her.

Yet every fibre of his body was taut and angry, as though something infinitely precious had been taken from him. Sensible or not, he wanted her in his bed. Their lovemaking had been a wondrous thing, satisfying a need he hadn't known existed in him.

If he believed in love, he might even think he was halfway there.

It was going to be sheer hell keeping his distance. But he'd misjudged her so badly he owed her that.

'Right, it's a deal,' he said, and held out his hand.

After a moment's hesitation she put hers in his. Her

grip was warm but soon loosened, and images of her almost shy caresses, of the heat of her body and her ecstasy in his arms flashed into his mind.

His treacherous body reacted immediately. He dropped her hand and took a pace backwards. 'That's settled, then,' he said, controlling a primitive urge to take her in his arms and comfort her. 'No more dancing to Tom's tune. But you do need to talk to a lawyer about this. Do you have one?'

Long lashes shielded those slumbrous green eyes, hiding her emotions from him. 'I use the local one,' she said. 'And I don't see any reason to consult a solicitor; if you can cope with the next few months, so can I, and then it will be over.'

And we can go our separate ways, her tone told him.

Luc set his jaw. 'Nevertheless, see the lawyer.' He glanced at his watch. 'Right now, I suggest we go to the resort and have lunch.'

The more people around them the better; at the resort he'd be able to subdue his fierce desire to pull her into him and kiss her into submission, before making love to her all afternoon.

The effort showing, she shrugged. 'I'll just snatch a sandwich here—I have to meet the chiefs this afternoon to hear the result of their interminable deliberations.'

He nodded. 'Good luck.'

In spite of everything, she thought almost bitterly as she turned away, it hurt that he didn't offer to accompany her. Moral support would have been welcome.

Joanna arrived back at the house well after the swift tropical twilight had darkened into a velvet night. Luc heard the sound of her car and half-turned in the shelter of one of the big trees by the beach. Immediately he forced himself to stay. He'd been trying to make sense of the decision he'd come to—and was failing.

Infuriatingly, his desire still warred with his intellect. Why had he been crazy enough to reveal the power she'd been given in Tom's will? It had been a huge, reckless gamble—yet it had been the right thing to do.

What he really wanted to know was the reason she'd given him her loyalty. Because that was what she'd done when she'd told him she'd stay on so that he could keep his position at Henderson's without the infighting that would be inevitable if he'd been deprived of it.

As though she knew where to find him, she walked swiftly down the path beneath the coconut palms. He waited until she was within a pace before asking, 'What was the decision?'

With a little cry she swivelled. 'Oh,' she said, exhaustion flattening her voice. 'I didn't see you.'

'I realised that.' His voice was dry.

Abruptly she told him, 'The Council decided not to take up the other offer.'

Silence stretched between them, tense with unspoken words, hidden emotions. Luc broke it. 'Good,' he said roughly. 'Jo, marry me.'

Stunned, Jo stared at him, her involuntary flash of incredulous joy evaporating as quickly as it had come. She drew a sharp breath and blurted, 'Don't be an idiot.'

But her voice broke. Desperately she hoped he hadn't caught that moment of sheer elation. What on earth was he doing now?

He shrugged, his expression unreadable in the darkness. 'This is the first proposal I've ever made, so I'm probably making a total hash of it, but I'd hoped that by now you'd have realised I'm no idiot.'

'Luc, this is ridiculous.' It took every ounce of self-possession to ignore the splintering of her heart. 'You don't have to marry me to make sure I'll keep our deal.'

'That's not why I asked you,' he said roughly.

'Then why did you?' A spark of humiliation persuaded her to ask, 'Because the sex was good? I'm sure you've had just as good before.'

'You have every right to be bitter, but I did not make love with you to win you onto my side.'

She drew in a deep breath. 'I'm not into expedient marriages, I'm afraid, like your—' and stopped precipitately because she'd just about been unforgivably rude.

Of course he guessed what she'd been going to say. 'Like my mother? Her first one wasn't expedient—it was all lust and parental defiance. The second was certainly financially practical.' He didn't wait for an answer. 'I'm not offering anything like the bargain she made with Tom.'

Jo had to boost her faltering courage to ask, 'So what *are* you offering?'

And *why*? Because there could only be one *good* reason—love.

He paused for at least three heartbeats. 'Ours would be a marriage of equals.'

Sorely torn, Jo hesitated, then took the biggest gamble of her life. 'I must be like *my* mother. She loved Joseph until she died—his name was the last word she said. I think that's possibly why she chose the life she did. She was no call girl,' she added, Sean's contempt vivid in her mind. 'She was a model and, in spite of the gossip, her relationships were long and faithful.'

'So *tell* me,' Luc said in a voice she'd never heard before. He stepped out of the shadows and looked down at her, starlight emphasising the strong bones of his face. 'Tell me what you want.'

'I've just told you.' She dragged in another jagged breath and met fierce grey eyes, narrowed and demanding. 'I want to marry someone I love—without limits, without fear, with total commitment and honesty.'

He said between his teeth, 'When we made love you gave me everything, without limits.'

'Desire isn't love,' she said sadly.

'I think that's what I've been trying to tell you.' He didn't move and his gaze never left her face. 'I've been attracted to women, lusted after some, made love to a few. Love is not a word I've ever used. Jo, do you feel anything more for me than passion?'

'I...I...' She struggled for words, then surrendered to the hard command of his expression. 'Of course I do. I love you. But that's not...'

When she stopped, he waited a few seconds before saying levelly, 'Go on.'

'That's not what you want to hear, is it?'

Incredulously, she saw his hands clench by his sides. 'I can't tell you I love you because I don't know what that is. I've had no experience of it. I *can* tell you that in spite of all I believed about you, I wanted you from the moment I saw you. It tore me apart. And as I got to know you I learned—with immense reluctance—to admire you. You're staunch and fearless and loyal, you work for what you believe in. You forced me to accept that you were not the woman I believed you to be.'

Eyes still holding hers, he shook his head. 'I'll admit I toyed with the idea of seducing you to make sure you gave me a good recommendation. I wanted to despise you for selling yourself to Tom, yet I couldn't reconcile my prejudice with the woman who spoke of him with such affection—a woman who'd cared for her sick mother and aunt, the woman whose main worry when her business was threatened was the welfare of her workers. Every day I saw some new instance of your spirit and your honesty, until I gave up looking for the wicked gold digger. If this is not love, trust me, it's a damned good substitute.'

'But will it last?' she asked quietly, unable to articulate the inchoate mass of doubts and fears that swirled through her.

'As long as I live.'

It sounded like a vow.

Jo looked at him and tried to speak but the words died in her throat and tears sprang to her eyes.

'Don't *do* that!' he ordered roughly. 'Joanna, marry me and I swear you'll never regret it.'

A wild response shuddered through her, insisting that she take this chance, and surrender without reservations.

But all she could say was, 'All right,' followed by a yelp of shock when he swooped and lifted her, and held her in a grip so tight she gasped for breath.

'Oh, *hell*,' he said remorsefully, and put her down and kissed her. After a while he looked around and said in a low, intense voice, 'Much as I'd like to make love to you here, there's a canoe with three fishermen in it not more than fifty metres out in the lagoon. Come back to the house with me.'

Laughing, tears still weirdly falling, she took the hand he held out and turned back to the house with him. 'It will be all over the island within two hours,' she gasped.

'Do you mind?'

'Not a bit.'

He lifted her hand and kissed the palm, then tucked it into the crook of his arm. 'There's nothing we can do about the media. And there will be innuendos—that I've married you only because you're Tom's daughter.'

She pulled a face. 'So, who cares?'

Luc grinned and hugged her. 'His will won't be accessible to the public until it's probated, which will give us some time to brace ourselves. Although, if I know Tom, that provision will never be available.'

'Do you think he had some idea of this? Of us?'

He looked down at her. 'I don't know, but I wouldn't be in the least surprised. Would you?'

Jo shook her head. 'No, not surprised at all,' she said slowly. 'Luc, do you mind if we get married here?'

'When?'

She laughed, feeling an enormous lightness and freedom and—yes, relief, as though everything had come together for her and Luc. He hadn't said he loved her—and she valued his honesty. One day, she thought with complete trust, one day he'd say it and she'd value the words even more because he'd wanted to be certain.

'In three weeks,' she said demurely. 'That's how long it takes here in paradise.'

They were married on the beach in front of the house, with friends around them. Jo wore a long floating sarong—cream silk appliquéd with pale gold hibiscus flowers made by the local grandmothers during their sewing meetings. Frangipani flowers the same colour were tucked into her hair, and her sandals were jewelled with the glittering beads that adorned her bolero jacket. She carried a spray of the precious gardenia from the island, its scent floating clear and sensuous in the sultry air.

The reception was a glorious mixture of Polynesian, European and French customs, as were the guests. Lindy was maid of honour, still mortified that a workmate had overheard her tell her husband that her best friend, Jo Forman, was Tom Henderson's—yes, *that* Tom Henderson—*daughter*...

It was a noisy, touching ceremony, the church choir adding their superb harmonies to the gentle hush of the waves on the beach. Jo blinked back tears several times, her hand firmly held by her new husband as they were congratulated by Luc's friends—some with faces seen often in the news—and hers, by her workers and several old school friends.

'Meru told me something today that made me realise how very lucky I am,' she told her husband, when the music and dancing had died away, and the guests had trooped off, leaving the beach empty once more. The sun had long set, and a golden lover's moon hung close to the tops of the coconut palms, casting its enchantment over the island and the sea.

Luc cocked a brow. 'What?'

'She told me that the reason the Council of chiefs didn't sell the rights to their plants was because they were made a better offer by someone else.'

He looked bored. 'Doesn't sound likely,' he said dismissively.

An upwelling of something close to pure delight tinged her smile with magic. 'It doesn't, does it? Would you like to know who made that offer?'

He shrugged. 'None of my business.'

'As it happens, I haven't been told,' she told him. 'Neither was Meru. It's a deep, dark secret, but she said she was pretty certain you know.'

He looked down at her, eyes silver in the moonlight,

and laughed. 'I suppose you want me to tell you who it is?'

His body tightened when she sent him a glance that was both demure and mischievous. 'I don't think you should make it too easy for me to find out.'

Luc's grin widened. 'How good are your powers of persuasion?'

'I've never extended them before, but I bet they'll do the trick.'

'I like your style,' he said, and turned her into his arms and looked down at her. 'In fact, I like everything about you.' He paused. 'No, that's wrong. Joanna, I love everything about you.'

He said it calmly, his voice steady, yet she saw his love in his eyes, heard it in his voice, felt it in the gentleness of his arms around her.

It resonated through his words. 'I love you more than I ever expected to be able to feel. I wouldn't face it because it scares me. I don't *want* to love anyone as your mother loved—it makes me feel totally out of control—but I can't help it. And each day it gets stronger.'

Coming like that, unexpectedly, after the happiest day of her life so far, his confession was infinitely precious. Her eyes filled with tears, and she stepped into his embrace, holding him fiercely. 'I love you too,' she said simply. 'I'll always love you.'

Much later, lying locked in his arms after coming totally apart in them, Jo heard him say, 'Happy now that you know it was me who made the chiefs the offer they couldn't refuse?'

'I knew the moment Meru told me,' she said simply.

'Did you, indeed?' He tilted her chin and subjected her to one of his unrelenting surveys. 'So when did you know you loved me?'

'When you came back from Shanghai.' Smiling, she turned her head and kissed his shoulder. 'You were watching the blackbird doing her usual operatic show of suspicion, and you were smiling and…well, I realised that what I was feeling had to be love.'

'So you agreed to marry me before you knew about my dealings with the Council of chiefs?' He moved a little restlessly. 'I'm not usually such a coward. I don't even know when I fell in love with you—it was a process, not a moment.'

She hugged him, replete with pleasure yet still able to thrill to the instant flexion of his muscles. 'I think that realisation is always part of a process, but I already knew before you told me,' she said demurely.

His chest rose and fell with silent laughter. 'How did you guess?'

'When we got married without any suggestion of signing a pre-nuptial agreement.'

'That's when I realised that you truly loved me too.' Luc laughed again before saying quietly, 'Thank you, Tom, wherever you are.'

'Amen,' Jo said.

And locked together, the soft sigh of the trade winds carrying the perfumes of the island to them, they slid into a sleep without cares or fears for the future.

* * * * *

MILLS & BOON®

Why shop at millsandboon.co.uk?

Each year, thousands of romance readers find their perfect read at millsandboon.co.uk. That's because we're passionate about bringing you the very best romantic fiction. Here are some of the advantages of shopping at www.millsandboon.co.uk:

* **Get new books first**—you'll be able to buy your favourite books one month before they hit the shops

* **Get exclusive discounts**—you'll also be able to buy our specially created monthly collections, with up to 50% off the RRP

* **Find your favourite authors**—latest news, interviews and new releases for all your favourite authors and series on our website, plus ideas for what to try next

* **Join in**—once you've bought your favourite books, don't forget to register with us to rate, review and join in the discussions

Visit **www.millsandboon.co.uk**
for all this and more today!